THE LIST

D1456533

THE LIST

A NOVEL

KELSEY MERCER GRANT

THE GRANT SERIES

The List is a work of fiction. References to real events, establishments, organizations, or locales are intended only to provide a sense of authenticity, and are used fictitiously. All characters, incidents, and dialogue are drawn from the author's imagination and are not to be construed as real. Any resemblance to actual persons, living or dead, is entirely coincidental.

Copyright © 2020 by The Grant Series, LLC
All rights reserved.
Published in the United States by
The Grant Series, LLC.

No part of this book may be reproduced in any form or by any electronic or mechanical means, including information storage and retrieval systems, without written permission from the author, except for the use of brief quotations embodied in critical articles and book reviews. The scanning, uploading, and distribution of this book without permission is a theft of the author's intellectual property. For permission, please contact The Grant Series, LLC. Thank you for supporting the author's rights.

Library of Congress cataloging data will be available.

Paperback ISBN: 978-1-7347677-0-4
eBook ISBN: 978-1-7347677-1-1
Hardback ISBN: 978-1-7347677-2-8

Printed in the United States of America.
www.thegrantseries.com

First Edition

To those of you who have been made to feel less than by someone else.

To everyone who helped make this book a reality. Your stories— whether real, urban legend or somewhere in-between—made this book so much better than we even could have imagined.

CONTENTS

THE LIST

ONE

CHANCES

I DON'T KNOW how much longer I can keep this pace. My heart feels like it's going to beat out of my chest and my lungs are burning. Sweat keeps dripping into my eyes, causing them to sting.

With the back of my hand, I wipe my brow so I can focus on the narrowing trail. The river has swallowed several feet of the path, making it difficult for anyone to pass on this part, giving me the advantage.

As he nips at my heels, I skirt by the gaping hole where a tree once stood, leap over the ankle-breaking roots, and onto the safer part of the trail. Now the only obstacles in the way are the hikers, but with how I'm flying, they're peeling off into the brush before I can even get close to them.

The density of the canopy changes as the trail widens, allowing sunlight to beat through the leaves, turning the soft mud into dust. I veer to the middle of the path to block anyone from passing, knowing he's close. He's waiting for his chance, but I'm not going to give it to him.

My thighs burn and the stitch on my left side feels like it's turning into a mass, making it almost impossible to breathe, but there's only a half mile left. I can do this. I can push through the pain. This is my year to beat him!

As I whip around the last bend and onto the steel bridge, my body begins to hum. Sweet endorphins course through my veins, giving me the power to kick it. I pitch forward on the balls of my feet and glide over the wood planks lightly coated in river sand. The vibration pulses through me as he pounds on the boards behind. I pump my arms and lengthen my stride, hoping to pull away, then bound onto the worn path toward the lone tree in the clearing.

I can't hear anything except for the voice in my head telling me to run faster. My body lunges for the tree as I feel him next to me. I throw my hand forward as far as I can, but it's no use. His hand smacks the tree first and I scream inside, knowing I lost again.

I tear out my AirPods and lean forward, trying to catch my breath. The palms of my hands rest firmly on my knees. Short gasps enter my thumping chest. I peer up at him through wispy, stray hairs and catch his broad smile—UGHH, he's enjoying this victory even more than last year.

Nick raises both arms in the air like he's Rocky, making it known to everyone that he won. Then he reaches for the water bottle hidden in the tree branches and gulps from it. As he flips his wavy, brown hair off his sweaty forehead and out of his eyes, he busts me staring at him. Embarrassed, I turn to watch a beat-up car swerve into the handicap spot, then back out of the packed parking lot. Over the crunching gravel, I hear him taunt, "You can always try again next year."

My fingertips push his sweat-streaked shoulder to let him know he needs to stop gloating but instead of moving backwards, he lunges toward me. I twist to get away but I'm not quick enough. His arms wrap around my waist and he lifts me high into the air, twirling me like I weigh nothing.

Even though I'm upset I lost again, I can't fight back the

laughter. My long, dark blonde hair whips back and forth as I try to wiggle free. "Aren't they cute?" I hear a lady say to her husband as they pass us on the way to the river. My body instantly tenses and so does Nick's. He lowers me down until both feet hit the compacted ground, and I quickly step away from him to smooth out my fitted, light pink tank top and black shorts.

Nick puts his hand to the back of his head and rubs at something, appearing a little uncomfortable. He doesn't look at me, only at the path leading to the water through the trees. Then he starts to walk in that direction without saying a word. I smooth back the thin hairs off of my face and adjust my ponytail higher, grab my water bottle, and follow closely behind him.

Nick Sullivan is well over 6 feet tall. His white t-shirt is plastered to his tan skin revealing a lean torso and defined yet still developing muscles. He's so different now. I never thought I would look at him as more than a friend. He was always the goofy guy who made me laugh, someone I could count on to include me in the games during recess.

I'm not the kind of girl to sit on the sidelines and watch the boys play. I'm not afraid of getting a little dirty. Unlike some of the other boys, Nick would include me in the games. He's big enough to handle losing to a girl. Well, sometimes.

I know he still has my back, but now I want him by my side. To be the one to hold my hand and not just to lift me up after I fall. I don't know when my feelings changed. There wasn't a moment when I knew that he was the guy I wanted to call more than a friend. It happened gradually.

When I saw him with other girls, I wanted to be near him. Then it started to bother me when he was into other girls. It seems to bother him when I talk to other guys, but he never says a word about it. Maybe I'm imagining it, or I'm just hoping. I don't know.

3

All I know is he's not that goofy kid anymore. He's really grown into himself. I like the way I feel around him. Safe. Comfortable. Myself.

He's more focused—definitely more confident. You can see it in the way he walks. He has this adorable shoulder swag. His arms move with him but never touch his sides, emphasizing the distinct lines of his biceps. His gaze is always up, forcing him to flip his hair out of his eyes, just like he does when he talks.

I continue following him down the stairs, still not speaking. Expecting him to stop, I rest on a smooth rock next to the railroad tie steps and slide off my grubby shoes, but he just continues to the beach area by the stream that cuts around a small island, then feeds back into the river. Dogs race through the shallow water, around boulders, and onto the pebbly sand, splashing people at the river's edge.

I take a sip of water, then chug it as my body screams for more. Nick circles around the beach, then he sits down next to me. The silence is deafening so I stand upright, stretch my tightening muscles and head to the water. The small rocks prick my bare feet as the grittiness changes closer to the shore. I search for sandy patches and awkwardly leap from one to another while trying to avoid the dogs shaking their wet fur at the most inopportune times.

My shoulders relax as soon as my aching feet slide into the chilly water. I tilt my head to the sky and close my eyes, feeling the warmth of the sun on my face and the cool breeze blowing off the river, enjoying the last day of summer.

There's a small splash and sigh next to me, causing me to jump and shift onto a sharp rock. "Ow, that hurts," escapes my lips, and I hear a stifled laugh beside me. After a few seconds, I peer over at Nick who seems content, lost in his own world. He's grinning, one that reaches his cheeks revealing a small dimple. I would love to know what he's thinking right now but don't dare ask. Instead, I fall back to small talk. "So how was your summer? I don't feel like I saw you at all after the Paris trip."

Nick continues to stare off in the distance, distracted. I glance over and spot a group of kayakers on the other side of the river that has his attention, in particular, the young woman in the skimpy red and white bikini climbing out of a yellow boat. He flips his hair to the side and answers my question, "It was a lot of fun. I loved Spain. What about you?"

Peering through the cold water at my tired feet, I shrug, not having much to add. The long days of training followed by empty nights tucked safely in my bed reading my favorite books are not worth sharing. "Same, except we didn't travel like you did. Paris was my big trip."

He doesn't answer the question that has been burning in my mind all summer—who was the drop-dead gorgeous girl plastered to him in so many photos? They looked like they were together the entire time.

Nick's lips twist into a smirk as he says, "The Paris trip was fun. Well, up until the very end."

I shift my weight side to side, feeling the need to lighten the mood. "Yeah, it was a lot of fun. Although, I thought Ivy and Chris were going to kill each other. They have such a love-hate relationship."

Nick lets out a chuckle before saying, "A lot more hate."

Then I blurt out without thinking, "I'm surprised no one else coupled up on that trip." *Damn it, Kels. That was way too obvious!* I immediately turn my head away from him, feeling the heat spreading from my chest to my cheeks, hoping the heat rash I get from running will hide the growing blush.

I muster the courage to look at him, needing to see his reaction, but he doesn't seem to notice. He bends over the murky water, then straightens with a flat rock in his hand. He shakes it off and skips it across the rippling surface, disappointed when it dives on the second bounce. He picks up another one to try again for his lucky three skips, murmuring, "Yeah, you'd have thought something would have happened after spending so much time together."

Trying to protect myself from being rejected, I deflect the conversation to another potential couple. "Yeah, I think Hope and Sam are cute together."

Nick gapes at me, completely surprised by this. "Really? I didn't notice the two of them together much. She's always so . . . quiet. He seems to go for the more athletic type—girls more like *you*."

Feeling his eyes study me after the word *you*, I turn a darker shade of bubblegum pink, a color I doubt the heat rash will hide this time. Yes, Sam may have liked me last year, but I never gave him a thought especially since Hope has been crazy about him since sixth grade. I exhale deeply and mention the possibility of the two of them together again, hoping it will come true for her sake. She deserves to be happy. "No, I think he likes Hope. She's so different one-on-one than in a crowd. Wickedly funny. I think she showed him that side of herself on the trip."

Nick leans over to get another brown rock out of the water. Instead of throwing it, he flips it through his fingers. With a sideways glance, he asks, "So what about you, Kels? Did you notice anyone on the school retreat last week? There are lots of new kids this year."

Here's my chance to let him know how I feel. I stare at him, waiting for him to look at me with his dreamy, green eyes, but he just studies the rock. He looks distracted and not particularly interested in my answer, so I lose my nerve. "No, I really didn't get to talk to many new people. My group was small, and Lucy was there. How about you?" I bite down on my lip, nervous I'll hear about the new girls all the guys were talking about on the retreat.

Nick throws the rock, cringes as it almost hits a black dog

swimming out to retrieve a stick, then turns his attention back to me. "No, some of the new girls are cute, but I didn't meet any of them. Chris met a girl named Bree. He didn't leave her side the entire time until we split on the buses. She seems nice. Surprisingly, she transferred from Chase. I remember her brother from church league basketball. He's good enough to make their varsity team—I wonder who she'll root for when we play them? You know how fired up everyone gets when we play each other. Did you meet her?"

I did notice Chris with a new girl. Nick seemed to be a third wheel with those two. Unfortunately, we weren't in the same group, and I only got to see them in passing or from afar. I respond with a coy smile, "We were introduced at the end of lunch. I'm sure I'll get to know her when school starts. Do you think Chris will bring her around Ivy? You know Ivy's parents always throw a party at the beginning of school. Her mom has to schmooze the new parents." Rolling my eyes, I add, "She's always networking."

Nick looks down. I know that look—he's not telling me something. With his hand to the back of his neck again, he spills, "Well, the Collinses threw the party last night at the St. Regis to get to know the Westovers and the Wells. I was surprised you weren't there—it was different this time. There were only four guys and four girls with their parents. On the car ride back, my parents complained about how Ivy's mom intentionally planned out the couples. Of course, there was Ivy and Chris. I still don't know which girl I was supposed to pair with, but Mare and I talked most of the night. . . ." His voice trails off when he sees me wince.

I silently stand there, allowing it all to sink in. I'm not surprised I wasn't invited, based on how Ivy acted after all the Paris stuff. She ignored my calls, but we've been friends forever, and it wasn't that big of a deal. I figured she would get over it. I rationalized that her ghosting me was due to something going on with her and not something with me—that maybe she needed space because she was embarrassed something was happening with her dad again.

The last time her dad cheated, she cried on my shoulder for hours, fearing her mother was going to leave. Mare was too popular to care before. Maybe she's there for her now? Why else would she not want my help?

Noticing I'm visibly upset, Nick moves closer and lightly punches my shoulder. "Kels, don't worry about it. You didn't miss anything. It felt like even more of a school fundraiser with Ivy's mom laying it on thick to the new families. Probably conspiring with the headmistress again."

I look up at the darkening sky as my question makes its way out. "Who all was invited?"

A shadow slides over his face as he rattles off the names. "Kim Westover. You know their family is royal somehow, so Ivy's mom was all over them. Kim talked with Brian Staples the whole night. And Mare Bradley, the new guy Robert Wells, Kylie Pruitt, Chris, and Ivy. Chris was miserable being next to Ivy."

I feel the knot in my stomach and taste bitterness in the back of my throat. The Collinses excluded us from that secret society group that does mother-daughter functions together and now this. It's like they're trying to punish us but why? Maybe they need something and my family has nothing to offer them. We're not political and don't play the game, nor do we have the money to be major players.

I pick up a jagged rock and throw it across the babbling water to release pent up frustration. I need to go run again and am about to challenge him to a sprint when I feel a cold nose at my thigh. I look down and there's my Gracie, wagging her white tail waiting for me to rub her drooping ears. I bend down to give her a good scratch. Nick joins as she circles around, wanting attention from both of us.

8

I hear her name called in the distance and Gracie spins toward the trees, whipping her fluffy tail in my face, but she doesn't leave our sides, enjoying the back rub too much. My mother is on the top step at the end of the path, looking refreshed after her hike. She stretches her arms high in the air, briefly showing her muscular stomach. She's in excellent shape for forty, still as limber as she was when she competed in those dance competitions in her twenties.

While waving the leash in the air, she whistles for Gracie to come back, not wanting her to play in the river. Every time the water's cloudy, Gracie gets an ear infection. As if she knows exactly what I'm thinking, Gracie breaks free of my hold and pounces around in the shallow water, then shakes her coat and sprays us in the face before racing back to my mom.

We both wipe the water and coarse sand off our faces as we stand up, a little too close to one another. My heart jumps to my throat as I realize I could lean forward and kiss him right now. I think he feels it too from the silly grin on his face. Neither of us moves. Instead, we stare into each other's eyes, almost like we're searching for something. Waiting for a sign. I try to read his thoughts but all I see are his enlarged pupils with various shades of dark moss and forest green swirling around them.

I'm about to move in closer but lose my footing as something slippery presses on my shins. Startled, I step backwards and away from the dog that is running in between our legs leaving a disgusting layer of wet grit and ending the moment. I run my hands over my slicked back hair, then turn away from him to tiptoe back toward the steps, wondering what would have happened if we were alone.

He follows closely behind. Our hands brush once on the steps, but I don't look over at him. We throw our dirty shoes in the trunk, wipe the dust off our bare feet, and climb in the back seat. I gaze out the window as we drive to Nick's house, feeling the last day of summer slipping away as well as another chance.

TWO
FIRST IMPRESSIONS

WE INCH along the main drag leading into Smith Academy campus behind a long line of cars, probably waiting on the kindergartners who take at least five minutes to climb out of the back seat. The first day is always the worst. I remember how my mother would make me pose in front of the columns and then by the front door with the head of the lower school. Parents have to get that photo to post on Facebook.

I don't miss those days of having to walk in a single file line, being told who you can sit with at lunch, and who you have to partner with on the many field trips. In some ways, it was easier always having to include everyone, but I think it made some people want to go in the opposite direction. Things are much more exclusive now.

I twist my wrist and tap the screen to see it's only 7:30. I still have plenty of time to haul it across the gardens and find my seat for the First Day of School assembly. You'd think I would be excited to go back and see my friends but things are—

"You're picking at your nails again," I hear my mom voice her concern from the driver's seat. It's my nervous tick that drives her crazy. I tent my fingers together, shrug like it's not a big deal, and then casually gaze at all the wilting maples roasting in the summer heat.

Why am I so nervous? I've been at this school for 10 years. I know most of the kids, and the new students seemed okay on the retreat. Well, most of them. I need to avoid the new ones who spent all their time kissing up to Mare and Ivy, and then everything should be the same as all the other years. Except—don't think about it. Block it out.

Knowing my mother is patiently waiting for me to explain why I'm peeling the polish off my newly manicured nails, I look at her and give the most obvious reason. "It's the first day of school. Everyone's a little nervous, Mom."

She gives me a quick glance and then places her hand on my knee to comfort me. "Yes honey, it's normal. I can't believe you're in high school now. Time is flying by so fast."

My mom discreetly wipes a tear from the side of her nose and switches the subject to my afternoon schedule. "Remember, you have your private session with Ned at 6 o'clock, so I'll pick you up at 5:15 right outside the track after cross country practice. Make sure you drink lots of water throughout the day. You know he's going to work you hard with that soccer tournament coming up in Raleigh?"

I roll my eyes, frustrated by the fact she never listens to me about changing coaches. "Yes Mom, I'll hear how worthless I am the entire session." She rolls her eyes back at me, not wanting to discuss this again. "I know, but he gets results."

I open my car door and am hit by the oppressive heat radiating off the asphalt. The humidity coats my lungs as I inhale sharply. I trudge toward the back of the car to grab my 15 pound backpack. It's almost ripping at the seams due to all my new textbooks. I heave it over my shoulder, push the button to automatically close the trunk, and then notice the motion in the car. My mother is waving my bright red water bottle in the air and passes it through her window. As soon as I take it, she hits the gas, still waving goodbye, and leaves me to fend for myself.

I turn toward the sea of students flowing into campus. The new football players bounce on the balls of their feet right by the stairs, pretending to throw or catch the pass of a lifetime. They're waiting for the annual parade where seniors ride down the main road onto campus while hanging out of their cars. The parents stand at the entrance with tears in their eyes as their child begins their final year.

When the music echoes across the gardens, we know to make our way to our seats to avoid being run over by the entire senior class and football team trailing behind them. Luckily, we have at least thirty more minutes before their grand entrance.

As I scoot by several middle schoolers eagerly jumping in the air for a high five, one of the guys looks me up and down with his mouth slightly ajar. Gross, I can feel him peeling my black Lululemon leggings off with his eyes. I quickly move to the left of a short middle schooler to block his view but can still feel his gaze. His beady eyes are ogling me in a creepy, lecherous way. I should have worn something longer to cover my butt or just worn a skirt that would have been more comfortable in this heat. I hate it when my mother is right!

I don't see the light gray backpack thrown on the bottom step. My foot catches and I jolt forward, but I'm able to grab the railing and quickly steady myself. *Stop being such a klutz! Get it together, Kels.*

I stand up, reach for the elastic waistband of my leggings to ensure they're not down too low, smooth out my top, and scan the crowd. It doesn't look like anyone noticed my graceful stunt, with the exception of the creep who is licking his upper lip. The middle schoolers are too busy admiring the new players who have arms the size of my legs. These new guys could snap me in half if they wanted.

When I'm out of sight, I survey the grounds for friends and

notice Hope up ahead near the fork in the sidewalk. "Hope, wait up!" I holler over the heads of some middle schoolers and watch her tentatively twist around to see who called her name. Seeing my face and waving hand, she steps into the grass to allow the gang of giggling girls to pass by.

Hope Blakely has been one of my best friends since we were six. She can make anyone laugh with her witty comments but she prefers to stay out of the spotlight. She's much more of an introvert, a little like me. I think she wants to stay in the shadows at school since she's on center stage at home. Her mother is always riding her about her weight, and they go on a cleanse about every month. No weight comes off and she ends up wearing clothes one size too big to hide her social insecurities, even though she's a perfect size 6. I think she would have let Sam know her feelings by now if she hadn't been constantly told she's not pretty enough for a guy to actually like her.

The one thing she is confident about is her intelligence. She's brilliant and everyone knows it. She will most likely be our class valedictorian. Everything is easy for her with her photographic memory. I wish I could do so well without studying five hours a night!

Once I'm close, I hear Hope's sigh of relief. She hates to walk into school alone. "Hey Kels, I texted you this morning to see if you wanted a ride to school."

I lift my backpack onto my shoulder from my upper arm and reply, "Sorry, I was running late and haven't looked at my phone yet."

Hope's eyes dart side to side as she leans in to whisper in my ear. "Have you seen Ivy yet? She still hasn't stopped slamming me on social media. You'd think she'd have let it go by now."

Hope crushed a new Porsche right before the retreat in front of our entire grade. Who knew you could total a car when pulling into a parking spot!?! At least her parents offered to buy the crazy dad a new one. Robert, a new kid and one of the guys invited to Ivy's back to school party, had to pull his father off of poor Hope after she stepped out of her car. I would be too mortified to come back to school if my father was that aggressive toward someone.

I give Hope a little squeeze to comfort her. "I know. She's acting like a bitch. Since all the girls keep talking about how cute Robert is, maybe Ivy will let it go, especially since he's not happy about all her posts with photos of his dad's wrecked car."

Hope grimaces while looking down at her black and white Golden Goose sneakers. She needs more convincing so I offer another reason it may blow over soon. "Now that school has started, she'll focus on all the new kids and forget about it . . . or even better, maybe she'll mellow out and not be *so* competitive now that Ka-Kate is gone."

I pause, feeling a dark cloud pass over me. I told myself I wouldn't talk about her, but it just slipped out. It's too late now. I need to get it out. "I still can't believe she's not here anymore."

Hope's face grows paler and she seems to fade away for a moment, lost in thought, staring up into the clouds. "Don't think about it, Kels."

As we enter the courtyard overlooking the verdant lawn in between the dark red brick and limestone academic buildings, I notice a girl hunched forward, nervously darting her chocolate brown eyes side to side, searching for someone. She pulls a gorgeous brown lock neatly behind her ear and tugs on her earlobe.

As she leans back on the wall and crosses her Stars sneakers, I notice she has on the blue jumper I tried on at Neiman's that my mom said was too expensive. Looking back, I'm glad I didn't get it; it looks better on someone shorter so the pant gathers around the ankle. Now I understand why my mom mumbled something about it being too short on me.

The girl must have noticed my staring because she is

looking directly at me now, and it finally hits me that this is the new girl, Bree Aster, who hung out with Chris most of the time on the retreat last week. Ivy snubbed her on the bus ride, and she ended up riding in the back with silent Sarah.

I pull Hope toward her to introduce ourselves again, thinking how difficult it would be to walk in as a new student, and she seems to relax a little as we approach. Slightly too enthusiastically I say, "Hey, you're Bree, right? I'm Kelsey, and this is Hope," tilting my head toward Hope. "We met at the retreat. Do you want to walk with us?"

Bree's smile brightens as she replies, "Yes, I remember you. You're friends with Chris and Nick, right?"

"Yep, we've known them forever. I'm sure they're around here somewhere. Maybe we'll see them on the lawn," I mention while scanning for them.

Bree grabs her stuff, and the three of us walk along the stone sidewalk lined with iron lanterns and mature oaks toward the assembly hall at the end of the lawn. Bree mentions that she left Chase to come to Smith but doesn't elaborate on the reason, and we don't push it either. She seems pretty nice and not stuck up at all, so she must not be one of "The Fifteen," a group of mean girls who have matching backpacks designating the select members. After practice one day, a girl found a red X spray-painted on her bag since it resembled The Fifteen's signature pack. She didn't go back to school for a week afterwards. They are vicious over there at Chase.

As we walk through the gardens, we point out the various buildings so she knows where to go after assembly. Smith's campus reminds me of an Ivy League college. It's one of the old, elite private schools located in the heart of an upscale neighborhood filled with rambling McMansions and charming older estates. Each year they have massive fundraisers to expand the sprawling campus. Of course, they always have to outdo the other schools around us.

Lots of kids hang out on the limestone steps leading to the buildings; none of them are in any hurry to start the school year. Hope points discreetly and mutters behind a covered mouth, "There's Ivy sitting on the stone wall."

Bree stops dead in her tracks, stares at Ivy, then incredulously asks Hope, "Are you friends with her?"

Hope pauses, looking a little puzzled by her response, then flippantly answers, "Depends on the day. We've known her forever, so we've gotten pretty good at reading her ever-changing moods."

Bree bites down on her lower lip, probably not wanting to say anything more and possibly alienating the "lifers." To make her feel better, I attempt to explain our love-hate relationship with Ivy. "Ivy is Ivy. She'll grow on you like a weed, whether you like it or not." Bree chuckles, and a smile crosses her face, looking more comfortable with us again.

Ivy Collins is a tall blonde with tan skin. She cheerleads year round but doesn't have much muscle tone to show for it since she doesn't eat and stays superthin. As we stand under a massive oak, I study her to determine if it's safe to approach. She's sitting on the opposite stone wall, posing for a photo in her tight V-neck top and short shorts with Mare, Lucy, and Kim. Ivy pushes something on her phone, puts it down on the wall, and focuses on the boys in front of her. She seems to be in a good mood this morning.

I follow Ivy's gaze and see Nick with Chris and Brian, as well as a couple new boys, playing football on the lawn. I instinctively head that direction with Hope and Bree in tow. Behind me, Hope questions, "Kels, why are we going this way? —Ohhh!"

I keep thinking about Nick yesterday, throwing rocks into the river, looking like he wanted to say something, but he never got it out. Maybe it was only about that stupid dinner party I wasn't invited to, and he didn't want to upset me any more than I have been with all of Ivy's drama. I don't know.

Robert says, "Hello," as I pass him, bringing me back to the present. I turn around and say, "Hello," loud enough for him to hear and wave so he doesn't think I just ignored him. Then I continue on toward the lawn. Hope and Bree have caught up with me now.

Standing next to the other guys, it looks like Nick grew another couple inches in the last two months. Nick jumps into the air, stretches his long muscular arms to catch the ball, arches backwards losing his balance, and falls on the grass, taking a couple boys out with him, staining his collared shirt and crisply ironed khaki shorts.

Ivy mocks last year's JV quarterback, "Chris, you still can't throw the football."

Chris snorts, completely ignores Ivy's comment, and says, "Let's throw one more before assembly." Chris wipes his hand on his tailored blue board shorts and pulls down his wrinkled collared shirt covering his ripped stomach. He looks like he just came back from California with his bronzed tan and surfer look.

Nick chucks the ball back, and they set up for another play. Chris slaps the ball, looks up and notices us, more likely Bree, walking toward him. He then dodges a kid coming at him and throws a sloppy spiral too high for Nick to catch but, he tips it, making the ball flip end on end over his head.

Ivy bends over to grab her iced Starbucks, not seeing the football rotating through the air in slow motion toward them. I yell, "Ivy! Watch out!" She looks up at me, frowning just before the ball hits her square in the face. The blow knocks her backwards, causing her to lose her balance on the granite wall. She drops her coffee and screams as bright red blood starts to pour out of her nose.

Kim Westover, a younger version of the gorgeous Kerry

Washington, tries to catch Ivy but moves too slowly since her legs are crossed. Ivy flips over and lands flat on her back with her toothpick legs and Toms wedges sticking straight up in the air. She lets out another scream and quickly swings her body to the side. Ivy pushes off the stone wall with her frail looking legs and slides her butt across the ground to sit upright. She covers her nose with both hands to stop the bleeding.

Nick bounds over the stone wall like a cheetah. "Ivy, are you okay? Oh my God. It looks like a watermelon exploded. Someone grab a towel or something!"

Ivy screams hysterically, "I think you broke my nose! Look at all this blood. God, my outfit is ruined. Someone do something!"

Hope and I are almost there to help. Bree stands back from the gathering crowd with her arms crossed, nose wrinkled, and a smirk on her face. Ivy's white top and shorts are now red with bloodstains. Tears are streaming down her face, smearing her black mascara.

I lean over and grab Ivy's upper arm. "Let me help you up."

Ivy swats my hand away, raking her ring across the tendons below my knuckles. The sharp throb spreads through my hand, pulsing as it moves from my index finger to my pinky. Ivy doesn't notice the pained expression on my face or seem to care. "Kelsey, I'm fine. Go get me some tissues to stop the bleeding! Just look at my new shirt!"

I rise from my crouched position and move a safe distance away from Ivy, inspecting the red streak on my hand. Nick stands up to check on my hand and says, "Shake it," when he sees she didn't break the skin even though it feels like she did.

Ivy sneers as she notices Bree in the crowd. A slow hiss reverberates deep within her lungs for all to hear. "Linger much?"

Bree squares her shoulders and doesn't hide the satisfied look on her face seeing Ivy vulnerable on the ground. "No Ivy, you made it pretty clear you didn't want me around on the retreat. I was just coming over to say hi to Chris."

Then Bree struts over and stands beside Chris to emphasize that Ivy is not her concern. The muscles in Ivy's clenched jaw become more pronounced as she looks at the two of them together. Chris grins then whispers something in Bree's ear. Not wanting his attention off of her, Ivy hollers, "Chris, what the hell was that?"

Chris raises his shoulders and gives her an I-don't-know look, then simply states, "My fingers slipped. You just told me I can't throw, so you shouldn't be that surprised."

Chris and Bree distance themselves from Ivy, moving behind everyone else leaning over the wall, dying to get a glimpse of her lying on the ground pouting. Annoyed, Ivy turns her focus back on me. "Get the tissues now, Kels! Why are you just standing there like an idiot?"

Nick nudges me to move, and I back away from the crowd, stammering, "I—I'm going."

I run to the nearest bathroom, grab a wad of toilet paper and an extra roll laying on the counter, trying to get out of the room quickly. They must have just finished cleaning the bathroom since the disinfectant fumes are burning my eyes.

I push my way back through the crowd and accidentally knock someone's phone out of their hands. I scoop the phone off the ground and flip it over to make sure it didn't crack. All good. Then I stand up and hand it back to the person I bumped into while saying, "Sorry." It's Robert again. His family must either have bad luck, or they're always in the wrong place at the wrong time.

Nick is still by Ivy's side trying to calm her down. Ivy snatches the toilet paper out of my hand and places a wad under her nose. Seeing she's still bleeding, she slides over to the wall and pulls herself up. The crowd parts, giving Ivy a direct view of Chris; she glares at him with disgust and then walks away toward the nurse's office.

No one follows her. She has a mud stain down the middle of her shorts and pine straw all over her back. I stifle a laugh but the middle schoolers don't hold back. Most bust out laughing while others point and snicker as she walks by them.

Kim has a quizzical expression as she watches Ivy storm off. "Mare, what was that about?"

Mare enthusiastically spills, "Chris is Ivy's ex. Nick is his best friend, and he dated lucky Lucy here." She playfully nudges Lucy in the shoulder. "I still don't know why you broke up with him? He's hot."

Nick steps toward me, pretending not to hear Mare's "hot" comment. She always lets a guy know when she is interested. Unlike me.

Lucy snorts then turns her back to Mare, dismissing the jab. She bitterly asks, "Where are the new guys? I am so sick of all these *boys*."

When no one responds to her slam, Lucy rolls her eyes in frustration and stomps off toward the assembly. Kim's eyes dart from side to side, debating if she should chase after her or wait for Mare, who is trying her best to get Nick's attention. Her bedroom eyes linger over him, willing him to come her way, but he doesn't move from my side.

Mare sighs, signaling to Kim it's time to go by quickly circling two fingers up in the air, and the two of them join the crowd of upperclassmen hustling to their seats. The Pink Floyd song "Another Brick in the Wall" is playing in the distance.

Bree grabs Chris's hand, and they fall in line behind Kim and Mare. Nick peers over at me, tilts his head toward the lovebirds, then snorts. I shrug my shoulders and half smile with tight lips, wishing I was bold enough to grab Nick's hand.

"Kels, we need to get going. The music is getting louder." Hope pipes in.

"Yes, let's go. . . . Nick, ready?" I turn back to look at him but he's already walking toward the tree to grab his backpack. Hope and I catch up with him within seconds, and all three of us lumber in silence toward assembly, feeling the full weight of the first day of school.

Even Hope doesn't make one of her fabulously snarky comments. I think she actually feels sorry for Ivy. If it had been me, I'd be on my way back home already, mortified.

THREE

MANEUVERS

As EXPECTED, not many of my friends are in my morning classes. Hope is in all honors. Nick is on a more mathematical track, so there's very little overlap, especially since we don't take the same foreign language. I heard Chris may be in my history class this afternoon but haven't confirmed with him yet. I did notice Bree in math, but I didn't get to talk to her since she ran in late, completely out of breath. It's hard enough to get from one class to another, even if you know where you're going.

I was hoping to be able to catch up with them at lunch, but my Spanish teacher got so caught up in the syllabus that she let us out late. Most likely everyone else will be finishing up as soon as I sit down. Surprisingly, I see the cafeteria is still packed as I enter.

I drop my backpack by the glass windows along with the other bulging bags and head to the short lunch line for a panini, craving something Italian after smelling all the spices. One table is teeming with kids who have pulled up extra chairs, craning their necks, and listening to Ivy. She's probably retelling an overly embellished version of the football episode from this morning. One similar to the whispers in the halls.

Somehow, I'm the one at fault for Ivy's bloody nose now. *So much for keeping a low profile this year!*

Ivy is sitting at the middle of the table in a new outfit. Her mother must have brought her something new to change into this morning. Now she's in a stylish black top with a delicate, silver bead detail down the shoulders similar to the one I admired when shopping with my mother. But there's no way Ivy's mother bought one of those tops for her. It's well over a thousand dollars! My mother couldn't justify paying that much for a top even to wear for her photoshoot. I still can't believe she's going to be on the cover of a magazine, recognized as the best interior designer in the city.

As I maneuver by the athletes and away from the center table, Ivy raises her pompous voice so I can hear her, "If Kelsey had NOT yelled my name, I would have seen the ball coming and caught it." I feel her eyes on me trying to see if I'm listening, but I pretend not to hear. I'm too focused on the panini options of fresh mozzarella, prosciutto, honey glazed turkey, pesto, and sun-dried tomatoes.

Then Kim sweetly adds, "You're so lucky it's not broken. It's not even bruised! I would have—"

Mare interjects so all the attention is back on her. "The beauty of makeup. It took me at least 15 minutes just to cover the circles under her eyes. . . . You know, Nick was there so quickly to help you, Ivy. Where is he anyway?"

I peer over at the table when Nick's name is mentioned, and Mare is looking in my direction with her eyes narrowed to slits, frowning. I follow her gaze and see why she's not pleased. Nick is walking toward me with an adorable lopsided grin on his face. It looks like he missed the whole conversation—so oblivious like all the other boys.

Kim looks over, seeing the same thing and innocently inquires, "Are Kelsey and Nick a couple? They should be if they aren't. I dated a guy at my last school who looked at me like that."

I choke on the piece of cheese I just popped in my mouth, but manage to swallow it and peer over again just in time to witness Lucy spew, "SEE! He's all about her. Even Kim sees how he looks at her."

Kim stiffens during Lucy's outburst, but it doesn't seem to faze Mare. She simply stands, looks at the scared boys who were sitting next to her, and commands, "You two, move over to make a space and save my seat." They nod in unison, almost like they're obedient dogs following the wishes of their master.

I stand there dumbfounded by her grip on people. As I turn away in disgust, I feel someone's breath on my neck and almost jump out of my skin. I whip my head to the side, thinking Ivy may be coming for me, and narrowly miss Nick's nose as he jolts back. "Jumpy Kels?" Not waiting for a response, he wraps his arm around me, tilts his head toward Ivy, and whispers in my ear, "Why is she making up rumors about you? I thought you were friends?"

I lean in close so only Nick can hear me. "Apparently not. She only hangs with the cheerleaders now. Her mom probably told her to avoid me after the incident."

Nick seems to shrug it off as he weighs the different food options. He grabs a plate and mumbles, "It figures. Her mom tries to control everything. Ivy is still bitter about Chris, and seeing him with Bree on the retreat really pissed her off. They're probably trying to come up with some way to get back at him."

I muffle my laugh with a loose fist, then add, "Everything seems to piss her off now. Remember when Ivy wanted Chris to wait in that long line outside Patrick Roger to get her chocolates and he refused? She acted like a spoiled brat for the rest of the day!"

"Yeah, she made the day miserable for everyone else. Even

the teachers were annoyed with her." Nick smiles broadly as he pops a strawberry in his mouth.

I'm about to add another Ivy story but stop—Mare is standing right behind Nick with pursed lips and fists tightly balled with long red nails digging into her palms. *How much did she just hear?* Nick removes his arm from my tense shoulder, twisting around to see who spooked me.

Mare removes the cold glare from her horse face and goes right in to give Nick a hug. She purrs, "Nick, I saw how you helped poor Ivy out today. So sweet of you!"

Mare Bradley is the most flirtatious girl in school, probably to make up for her average, mousy looks, and straight figure. She releases him from the bear hug, places her arm tightly around his waist, and cleverly blocks the view of her face as she deals with me. Mare cocks her head toward Nick, raises one cheek in a smirk, and glares with so much contempt. When I don't move, she mouths the words, "LEAVE US." Stunned, I take off without my panini still crisping on the hot press.

While retreating backwards, I stumble over one of the chairs surrounding Ivy's table but quickly catch myself before tripping. Seeing another chance to cut me down, Ivy launches into an exaggerated full-body eye roll. For even more dramatics, she slowly claps and proudly declares, "If you're not careful, Kels, you will be the one with a broken nose." Everyone at the table laughs. Lucy cackles the loudest.

I feel my nose wrinkle at her jab but don't say anything back. *What can I say to that? I so wish I had Hope's quick wit right now. Or Kate's. . . .*

I yank my shirt down so it covers more of my butt and hurry toward the iron windows hoping to disappear—wishing I could go back to an isolated summer break without so much animosity. Instead of heaving my backpack onto my shoulder and leaving the scene, I grab hold of a chair to steady myself. I stare through the glass at the peaceful gardens outside, willing the palpitations in my chest to slow. I can see Nick's reflection holding my panini with Mare glued to his side, looking over at me.

I slowly turn back toward the crowd and mouth, "YOU EAT IT," as Nick waves the panini in the air with a puzzled look, then I sink down against the cold, glass window with my hands over my face. *Why didn't I just stand there and continue talking?* Nick came over to me, not her. I told myself this would be the year I would hold my ground just like I do on the soccer field. Why can't I be the one who goes after what she wants? Mare is going to step in just like Lucy if I don't say something.

The memory of the eighth-grade dance pops vividly in my mind. I remember the butterflies fluttering in my stomach while I sat next to Nick on the bleachers waiting for him to ask me to dance. Then Ivy and Mare ran over to tell Nick how much Lucy likes him and how he should ask her out. I did nothing to stop him, even after he glanced at me with an unsure look on his face. Instead, I encouraged him to go over to Lucy to test him. And then, the punch in the gut came when he walked away from me and over to Lucy, put his arm around her, and asked her to be his girlfriend.

I stare at my hands, thinking I can't let him walk away from me again. I need to speak up. This will be the year I tell Nick how I feel and ask him to the Sadie Hawkins dance in the spring. It'll be fine.

Hope approaches excitedly and interrupts my moment of self-loathing. "Kels, what are you doing on the floor—have you eaten yet? Please sit with me! Sam and I spent the entire free period studying together. I was so nervous, but I followed your advice."

I slowly rise from the cold tile floor, sneak another look over at Ivy's table, and deflate as Nick places his tray in the empty spot next to Mare and slides in beside her. I can't help but think, *It's never going to work out for us*, then redirect my focus to

Hope. She deserves the encouragement more than me right now. "That's awesome! Maybe one of us will get out of the friend zone this year."

I listen to Hope tell me everything, and she's doing exactly what I should be doing with Nick. My older friends told me guys will not do anything unless they know *for sure* the girl will say yes. They won't put themselves out there to be rejected. The girls that are all over the guys are the ones who get the attention, even though they may not be the girl the guy actually wants to be with. I glance over at Mare and that seems to be true. Mare is all over Nick, and he isn't stopping it.

I just can't do it—it never feels like the right time. Maybe it's the right time for Hope, or is she just making it happen? She has pined after Sam forever and never mentioned anyone else, unlike Mare, who will be on to the next guy in a week. There's no way she will commit to Nick. It's not in her, and there's little chance he will be into her. They just don't fit. But why is he sitting with her? Why didn't he come find me?

I tune out all the thoughts and listen to Hope. Seeing her this happy makes everything so much more bearable.

FOUR

THE LIST

THE SMELL of freshly baked cookies fills my nose as I enter the Student Activity Center, reminding me that I didn't eat lunch. I pass girls chatting on the stairs, talking about the new boys and the older ones they noticed now that we're in high school. I wave at them on my way to the snack bar for a quick bite before practice.

As I wait in line, I peer over at the boys in my grade perched along the metal railing watching something below. The music starts and I hear the cheerleaders practicing their routines on the basketball court. The guys attempt to mock their moves in an exaggerated fashion, thinking they're hilarious. I stifle a laugh since the real comedy is the guys' lack of coordination while attempting to dance.

Taylor Swift's "Blank Space" plays again but much louder, making it hard to hear anything else. The music reverberates off of the concrete walls. I repeat my order again, "An oatmeal cookie and a smoothie, please." I know I really shouldn't eat a cookie before I run because it always sits like a rock in my stomach, but they smell too good to resist.

I find an open picnic table, drop all my stuff, and try to relax for a minute. I take a bite of the cookie and revel in the warm gooeyness as well as the fact that the first day of school is almost over. I only have cross country practice and then soccer before I can go home, sink into bed, and finish my book before tackling the three-plus hours of homework.

Taking a sip of my strawberry banana smoothie, I see Hope out of the corner of my eye, looking like her day has been worse than mine. Her face is twisted in fury, almost a crimson color. Ivy must have done something again. I wave my cookie in the air, offering to share with her, knowing oatmeal is her favorite and it always helps calm her down. Without saying a word, Hope shoves her phone in my open hand, almost knocking my cookie out of the other.

Somewhat taken aback by her attitude, my eyes dart to her phone to see what has her so riled up. I take another quick bite, place the cookie on a napkin, and scroll down to see Mare's name besides Nick's. Then I see my name next to Hope's long-time crush, Sam. *What is this?* I continue to scroll and freeze, understanding why Hope is so angry. This is the list claiming dates for the Sadie Hawkins dance, and Mare has Nick, and I'm supposedly taking Sam. *What!?!*

I gasp and choke as the crumbs go down the wrong pipe. Coughing does nothing to remove the bits stuck in the back of my throat, so I take a swig of the smoothie, and the spasms slowly stop.

Through gritted teeth, Hope growls, "How could you? You saw how excited I was at lunch!"

Still processing, I croak through a raw throat, "I—I—I don't know why Sam is next to my name."

Hope slams both hands on the table with such force that my cookie bounces in the air and onto the floor. My smoothie teeters, then tips over, dripping over the table and through the metal diamond shapes. I jerk back to avoid the thick clumps from landing on my shoes and turn the bottle upright with my free hand. Hope does nothing to help. Instead, she stands back with a smug look on her face as if she's happy she made such a mess.

"Hope, really? Aren't you going to help?"

She spats back with so much venom, "Help? Like I will help you. I can't believe you're doing this to me after everything I've told you!"

"What are you talking about? Do you think I had something to do with this list?"

Hope's body stiffens as she notices the gathering crowd, intently watching this interaction. Even the mothers at the snack bar are staring. Before I can say anything else, she rips her phone out of my hand, turns on a dime, and storms off toward the door. Before she reaches the stairs, she whips around and yells, "BACK STABBER," for everyone to hear and stomps up the steps.

"Hope, WAIT! I didn't put his name down." I drop all the napkins and my smoothie to rush after her. As I reach the door, Nick strides through, blocking me from running out. He puts both hands on my arms and asks, "Kels, are you all right?"

I mumble, "Yeah," as I peer around him, searching for Hope and spot her halfway across the lawn, moving at a full sprint. There's no way I will catch her now. I let out a long sigh and turn back to Nick, who's looking at me like I'm crazy.

Not wanting to know the answer to this, I force myself to ask, "Did you know about the list?"

"Uh, no, what are you talking about?" He rubs my arms, trying to calm me down, but I feel like I may lose it after everything that's happened today.

I take a deep breath and, as calmly as possible, ask again, "Nick, I'm talking about the list for the Sadie."

His eyebrows furrow and he tilts his head back in surprise. "The Sadie? That's next spring. There's no way they're talking about that now."

"So Mare didn't ask you to go at lunch?" I softly question while praying in my head that he says no.

"No, nothing was mentioned about the dance at lunch. Everyone was talking about Ivy's nose."

This makes me chuckle and lightens my mood. "Well, someone put together the list, and your name is next to Mare's."

Nick scratches the back of his head. "There's no way girls are already asking dates. So much can change in the next six or seven months," he states and then lets out a nervous laugh.

I nod like I agree, but I know the rules, and this feels very real.

When I don't answer, he cautiously steps closer, looking like he might wrap his arms around me but he doesn't. "Kels, why are you so upset about this?"

I bite down on my lower lip. Should I tell him I plan to take him? No, I can't . . . not yet. I pull my usual and deflect. "Hope—Hope thinks I'm trying to steal Sam from her. I've never seen her so angry."

Nick flinches. "Sam? Why would she think you want to take Sam?"

"Because his name is next to mine."

He takes a step back, runs his fingers through his hair, then clears his throat. "Did you tell someone to put his name down?"

"No, Hope showed it to me a couple minutes ago, and that was the first time I've seen it."

Still studying me, he continues to press on about Sam. "But someone must have thought you wanted to take Sam."

"Oh, come on, then that would mean Mare told someone that she wanted to take you, and this list is real!" I counter.

He scratches at the back of his neck again and smirks, "Well, I didn't know she liked me."

"Really, you couldn't tell at lunch? She made it pretty obvious to me." I can't help but roll my eyes at him.

He shifts to the side, trying to hide the pale pink in his cheeks and doesn't reply.

As I open my mouth to ask him what he thinks about her, I spy Ivy and Mare bouncing our way in their cheerleading uniforms, giggling like middle schoolers and instead say, "Speak of the devil."

Nick turns to stand next to me and silently watches them approach. Mare takes hold of his hand while purring, "Nick, I need to show you something," and pulls him away with little resistance. He follows her all the way to the railing and waits for her to show him something on her phone. Ivy crosses her arms and lifts her chin high in the air. "What's up, Kels? How was your first day of school? No broken noses, I see." Then she cackles and continues on in a shrill voice, "Aren't they cute! Do you know what they're talking about?"

"I can guess."

When I see the mischievous glint in her eye, I know she's a part of this. I take another deep breath, roll my shoulders back to elongate my spine, and stare down into Ivy's snake eyes, which appear even more green with the purple bruising showing through all the makeup. Then flatly ask, "Ivy, are you a part of the list?"

While examining her bright, red nails sharpened to look more like talons, she casually answers, "Yeah, I started the list. Bree needs to realize Chris is not available."

While fighting the urge to scratch her eyes out, I calmly ask, "Do you have the list?"

Ivy flippantly responds, looking over at Mare and Nick getting cozy at the railing, "Yeah, you want me to send it to you?"

She tosses her phone in between her hands just to tease me. I eye the rose gold thinking I should not give her the satisfaction but give in and say, "Yes."

Ivy slowly types in her passcode while avoiding her long

nails, opens Google docs, and shares the link with me. My phone buzzes and I pick it up with both hands to prevent them from trembling. All the ninth grade girls are in alphabetical order on the list. Only a handful of guys have been claimed.

Kylie Pruitt is taking Robert Wells. He already has a date—boy that was fast! Kim Westover is taking Brian Staples. Interesting . . . they must have hit it off at Ivy's thing. Ivy has Chris. Hope Blakely and Bree Aster, along with many other girls, have a blank space next to their name.

Ivy slithers back to the cheerleaders and types something with all of them peering down at the screen. Then my phone, as well as many others, beep around me with a notification for a Google document titled THE LIST for the Sadie. I almost scream when I read the words, "Here's the official list for the SADIE! Sign up before your guy is claimed!" You have to be kidding—she's acting like she's doing everyone a favor!

Girls frantically pull up the list. Jane throws her drink in Kylie's face and storms off. Nick leaves Mare's side to walk over to the boys horsing around near the snack bar and tells Sam and Chris they have been claimed. The other boys jerk their phones out of their back pocket to see who else is on the list. Their shoulders slump forward when they don't see their names.

Girls anxiously discuss with their friends who they should take. It's apparent nobody is ready for this. The only ones who appear calm and happy are the cheerleaders who have a guy next to their name.

Nick tries to hold Chris back, but he squirms free and marches over to Ivy, pointing at his phone. Ivy calmly folds her arms over her chest while matter-of-factly stating, "I'm just planning ahead. You know we will be back together by then. You always come back to me."

Chris walks away with his hands above his head, chest rising and falling like he just ran a marathon. His facial expression shifts from anger to concern when he sees Bree walking down the stairs toward him. It's safe to assume Bree doesn't know anything about this list for the Sadie, and it wouldn't be good for Ivy to be the first one to throw this in her face.

During history class, I teased Chris about holding hands with Bree. He usually doesn't show his feelings like that, and I expected him to fire back. Instead, he asked for me to get to know her and introduce her to some girls, hoping she'll make friends fast. He opened up about how much he likes her and that she's the first girl he really wants to date. He is not the same guy as last year—he's much more ready for something serious, and this is not a good way for them to start a relationship.

I look around for Nick again, and he is still talking with the guys, gazing at the cheerleaders. Since he can't stop watching Mare, he must like her. *I can't believe this is happening.* Not able to hold it together any longer, I quickly move toward the bathroom, slap open the door, and beeline into a stall to cry.

Before I can get more than a tear out, I hear a girl sobbing next to me. Looking under the partition, I recognize the Star shoes and blue pants. I take a deep breath, then exhale slowly to steady my voice before I ask, "Bree, are you okay?"

Bree slams open the stall door and yells, "What the hell is this list?"

I walk out into the main area of the bathroom and stare at her, taken aback by her rage. Then try to explain the history of this stupid list to calm her down. "It's a tradition, but all the girls are supposed to get together to decide who is taking who. I think some boy mom created this list years ago to ensure all the boys get asked. They said it would lessen the drama. This is not how it usually works—this has to be a joke. The dance is not until next year."

Bree is so much more upset than I expected. I'm glad Ivy didn't get to her first. There may have been a catfight.

She clenches her jaw. "Chris does *not* think this is a joke. He said he is going to say NO when she asks him, but then he won't be allowed to go with anyone else since he said no. What kind of rule is that?"

"Yep, the guys can't say no if they want to go. It's another rule to make sure none of the girls get rejected. Just another way to shelter us from reality—I'm so sorry. This really sucks for you. . . . I can tell the two of you really like each other."

Bree's shoulders slump forward and begin to shake as she sobs again. "I know we only met seven days ago . . . but I feel like I've known him forever. . . . I can't believe this is happening. . . . I thought the girls here were supposed to be so much nicer than at Chase. That's the whole reason I changed schools!"

I don't know what else to say to calm her down. Ivy seems to be ruling the school, and things can only get worse if this continues. No one is here to stop her now. "Yeah, this has not been the best first day," I mumble, then give her a hug and let her cry on my shoulder until there are no more tears left. She took all of mine too.

FIVE
HOPE DISAPPEARS

To AVOID all the kids at the student center, I sneak out the back, cut through a patch of trees, and wind around a path that leads to the far side of the stadium. The football team is already practicing from the sounds of it. Whistles blow, hands clap together, and the coach yells, "DO IT AGAIN." I drop my bag and backpack in the shade, reach for my hairbrush and rubber band, and pull my hair into a high ponytail. It's too hot to have it low on my neck.

I watch as one guy gets popped and rolls around on the ground. Another player runs over with his hand out, but the guy stays curled in a ball, clutching his stomach. I jump as the coach's voice booms across the field, "GET UP! OR YOU'LL BE FETCHING WATER WITH THE GIRLS!"

The guy slowly stands, looking a little dazed, and I can see it's one of the new guys in my grade. He's in my math class, but I can't remember his name. His face is beet red, and he's dripping in sweat. We make eye contact, and I give him a smile, pretending like I missed the whole thing, then stare off to the left of the field.

My cross county team is hanging out behind the football

36

goal. Hope is stretching by the long jump pit. Several girls are on the sidelines watching the quarterback run suicides in full pads. He obviously knows he has their attention with how he's strutting between the runs.

I step out of the shade and hustle over to join them. The catcalls start as I walk by the bench, but I study my phone and ignore the stupid remarks. *No, I'm not here to cheer you guys on. No, I'm not going out with one of you after the game on Friday. Do they really think that kind of stuff works on us?*

As I get close to the girls "stretching" their quads, I hear the not-so-subtle whispers about me and Hope. I'm not up for this discussion, at least not until I make things right with Hope, so I veer away from the gossip and toward the long jump.

She's facing the other direction and doesn't seem to notice me approach. I clear my throat then begin, "Hope, can we talk? I know you're upset, but I didn't put Sam's name down. I would never do something like that to you."

Hope sits up and torques her body in an awkward way. She studies me with her scorching, brown eyes, then shrugs like she doesn't care. "That's not what I heard."

Even though she appears to be calm, the spite in her voice indicates she's even more fired up than before. Someone must have said something to her. With my hands out in front of me, I plead, "Hope, I promise! You've gotta believe me."

Hope slowly shakes her head then bitterly snaps, "I DON'T. . . . Besides, you saw Nick was going with Mare so you decided to take someone who would make Nick jealous. Sam did like you in middle school but he has moved on. . . . You're acting like Ivy."

Completely stunned by the fact that she thinks I'm as conniving as Ivy, I step back. Someone—no, Ivy—must have told her I'm behind this list. Before I think about how to respond, the words slip through my lips, "Did Ivy tell you this

—how can you believe her over me? After everything she has done to you!"

Hope arrogantly snorts twice, then twists back around, signaling this conversation is over, but I'm not done. Now I'm the one who's mad. I take three steps around Hope so we're facing each other again. With one hand on my hip, I fire back, "What happened to the winsome advice you always give me? You always look for the best in people."

Hope rolls her eyes and retorts, "And look where that has gotten me, Kels!"

"What has gotten into you? How can you believe I did this to you? You were mad at Ivy this morning about all her posts. I don't understand how you can believe her over me now? We've been friends forever—"

Then she belts out for everyone to hear, "WE WERE FRIENDS! I saw you talking to Ivy. She put down Chris thinking they would get back together. At least she is being honest about it. But you keep saying you had nothing to do with this. . . . Think about it. Who would have put Sam's name next to yours without you asking them to do it?"

She pauses like she's waiting for me to answer, but as soon as I open my mouth, she continues on, "You know the boys think you're full of yourself—you and your permanent bitch face. You know Sam would never say no since he's so nice, and you *really* need a date for this dance. Don't deny it, you might as well own up to the person you REALLY are."

As the tears well in my eyes, I quickly wipe them away before they roll down my cheeks. I can't let her see me upset like this. She knows just where to stick in the knife and twist it for the most damage. The fact that she's siding with Ivy over me cuts the most—she doesn't even like Ivy!

I was going to tell her to add Sam's name next to hers, and that I would let everyone know he is not my date. But there's no way I'm doing that now! I stare right back at her, feeling the heat rise deep within me and snidely comment, "Well, it looks like I will be taking Sam. Have fun finding another date!" As soon as the words leave my lips, I regret it, but it's done.

Hope fires back. "Have fun with the target on your back! I'm off the hook now!"

I want to turn back around and ask what she meant by that but know if I do, I will lose it. I continue walking toward the other girls, then change direction. I need to get away from all this—I need to clear my head.

My legs move underneath me toward the trail. My walk turns into a run and then into a sprint. I race right past all the football players, set my watch, and turn on my music. "Out of the Woods" starts to play. Nope. I listened to that yesterday running with Nick.

I hit skip and "This Feeling" comes on. My body begins to move in sync with the beat. I cross the wooden bridge with the lyrics running through my brain. *How do I think with my head and not the thing beating madly in my chest? How do I let Nick know I feel this way? How do I make Hope understand this is just another stunt to give Ivy control? Ivy doesn't care about anyone but herself. None of this makes any sense. How did this day go so wrong?*

I look over at the abandoned campgrounds across the creek and remember the fun times at summer camp. It was so much easier then. . . .

I turn my focus back on the rocky trail and speed past several adult walkers. What are they doing here? They shouldn't be out here at this time of day.

"Paris" comes on and I feel like I'm going to lose it again. I remember laughing with Nick outside Cafe de Flore, sharing Ladurée macarons as we waited in line at the Musée D'Orsay, Kate whispering that we are soul mates. *Why doesn't he see it? Maybe he just doesn't feel the same way towards me? Maybe Kate was wishing it will happen for me just like I wished it would for Hope?*

I feel my body slow so I switch it to "If Today Was Your Last Day"—a song that pushes my body to the edge. My pulse quickens and my muscles ease into the stride as the endorphins release. It's never too late. I can fix this. I will not let anything stand in my way this time.

I wipe the sweat off my brow as I cross the asphalt road. Usually, I dread this part of the trail with the steep hills, but now I welcome the challenge. I raise my knees high up in the air and pounce on the larger rocks, launching myself upwards. "Raise Your Glass" blares in my ears.

As I reach the summit, I shorten my stride to prepare for the loose rocks on the decline. My heart skips a beat as Hannah appears from the other side of the hill. I quickly dart further to my side as she moves to the other. I lose my footing and slide on the gravel but am able to stay upright and regain my balance after almost hitting one of the massive pines framing the trail.

Oh my God. . . . That was a close one—too close! The last thing I need right now is to twist an ankle or break a wrist.

The rest of the JV team thunders by on my left with enough room for me to whiz by them. These trails are too narrow to run in the middle. What was Hannah thinking coming up the hill like that?

I run past the maintenance area and down another hill into the trees. "Call Me Maybe" mixes into my playlist. I picture the Harvard baseball team pounding their fists on the van ceiling and smile. This is only high school—I shouldn't get so worked up about this. It's not like I'm going to meet the *one* at Smith.

As soon as the path meets the babbling creek, I feel the temperature drop 10 degrees. I love running through this part of the course. My feet pound on top of the wood planks as I cross under the road. "New Romantics" plays, and it's the perfect song to finish on. One that is fun and playful. Not so serious. I mouth the words as I run onto the track.

As soon as I reach the finish line, I look at my time. 18:03. Nice! And I didn't even stretch!

My coach is across the field looking at me in her typical judgmental way. For once, her scowl doesn't bother me. I know she will forgive me once I tell her my time. It's 53 seconds faster than last year.

As expected, her expression changes to one full of hope. She's determined to win State this year after our unexpected loss last fall. I stretch as I listen to her preach about the importance of running as a team. Luckily, it doesn't last long. I head over to the bleachers and grab my stuff, quickly towel off and escape out the back to avoid the other girls.

My mom is parked at the far end of the lot. I can tell she's deep in thought by her furrowed brow and the way her fingernails are rubbing across her lower jaw. I slowly open the car door so she doesn't jump and hit her head on the sunroof. She hates it when I surprise her.

The serious look on her face relaxes into a wry smile. "Honey, your track shirt is on inside out." I look down and see the seams around my collar and sides. Oh well, I really wasn't paying much attention when I threw on my clothes. I quietly chuckle and pull it over my head so it's on the right way for soccer.

She lightly pats me on the shoulder and asks about my day. I respond with little emotion, "Fine. Same old, same old." That seemed to appease her since she doesn't drill me with more questions. Instead, she goes on and on about how her client cannot decide between modern or transitional in style and emphasized the fact that they want things to feel warm and comfortable, which really insulted her. She always makes her designs feel extraordinarily cozy, even if they are modern. But I'm relieved I don't have to talk. I bob my head up and down feigning interest.

We arrive at my session early since traffic is not that bad. I hop out of the car as my mom yells, "I will be back at seven and tell him I will bring a check this time. . . . Wait!" She leans across the console and asks, "Any requests for dinner tonight? Your dad had a bad day at work, and Chinese always makes him feel better."

I take two steps back toward the car so the girls walking by don't hear the conversation. "That works. Just order me my usual fried rice." As my stomach growls, reminding me that I didn't get to finish my snack, I add, "And some spring rolls and dumplings, please."

My mom is about to say something about my appetite but refrains and only nods. I quickly move away from the car to avoid the dust kicking up in my face as she pulls out of the lot.

I stretch again to loosen my legs. The last thing I need is a torn muscle. Shortly after 6 o'clock, my coach calls me over. He doesn't start slow. Instead, he boots the ball for me to settle with my chest and shoot into the goal. I'm glad my legs are warm for this.

After several more drills, we break. I enjoy the fact he hasn't yelled at me once today. Instead, he compliments me on how fast I'm moving toward the ball and the fact my touch has drastically improved over the summer. He even comments that if I keep playing like this, I may get a verbal offer to a Division 1 school like some of the older girls I scrimmage against. Well, I worked hard enough this summer. At least something worked out for me today.

SIX

BLAME

I WAKE from my nightmare dripping in sweat and completely tangled in my sheets. I wrestle my hands free to press them against my damp face and try to recall the fading dream. I was running along the river. . . . There were several footsteps behind me. . . . I skirt by a hole with exposed roots . . . and then I'm pushed from the side. Instead of falling the five or six feet to the bottom, the hole turns into a wide, never-ending pit. I desperately grasp for roots as I tumble but cannot hold on. Some rip out of the ground. I twist my body and reach upward toward a large mass but miss. I continue to plummet into the darkness, staring up at a circle of sunlight, which gets smaller and smaller the farther I fall.

I throw my hands to my sides and lay there, breathing very deeply, trying to calm myself down. The image of me tumbling in the darkness slips away, but the unsettling feeling of dread and helplessness remains. I bear hug my pillow and feel my damp tank top and shorts press against my clammy skin.

I look at the clock. It's only 6:06. I still have thirty more minutes before I have to get ready for school, and I hear myself moan. I really don't want to go back. The list, the fights, the calls I received last night—it's just too much to bear.

I can't believe people think I orchestrated the entire list to steal one of my best friend's boyfriend. Hope and Sam aren't even dating! Kate couldn't believe it either. She was the only one who could calm me down. Nick didn't call, even with all the rumors. Instead, I received a text saying *the list is real*. *Mare told me she wanted to make sure she could take me*.

REALLY!!! I throw off the covers and debate what I should do. I don't have enough time to run, and yoga does nothing for me. After about 15 minutes of pacing and unsuccessfully pushing everything from my brain, I collapse back on the bed and stare at the ceiling. I consider calling Kate again, but it's too early. I need to figure this one out on my own anyways.

Okay, this is simple. Tell Hope to take Sam. Tell Nick you want to take him. . . . Or should I let things work themselves out on their own—UGHHHH.

Shower—I need to shower. I need to hold my head up high as I walk through campus. Everyone will be judging me . . . and everyone will be looking.

———

I make it across campus unscathed but know I won't be for long. I'm about to walk right into a hornet's nest. I take a long, deep breath and step through the glass doors.

Students buzz all around me. The tension is high. Many look ready to attack at a moment's notice.

Hope doesn't hide her feelings toward me. Her usually gentle hazelnut eyes are filled with hatred. Kylie and Jane are yelling at each other in the far corner with Robert overhearing the argument, looking really annoyed. A new girl whirs by me with tears in her eyes, probably heading toward the bathroom.

Someone must not have told her the guy she claimed already has a girlfriend.

Bree stands with her back to the wall. Her arms are crossed with Chris shielding her from the rest of the crowd. Nick is right beside the two of them but isn't paying them any attention. He is watching Mare gossip with Ivy.

I step toward Nick, feeling the need to apologize for yesterday, even though he was the one who walked away, and to let him know I didn't put Sam's name next to mine. Hopefully, this will open the door for him to admit he doesn't want to go with Mare.

When I'm halfway across the room, the obnoxious bell rings signaling we have to take our seats. For once, I resist the urge to follow the rules and keep moving toward Nick. I step out of the crowd so he can see me approach. He hasn't moved either. His gaze is still fixed ahead almost like he's tracking something. His nose is high in the air following a scent. At any second, he should notice me, feel my gaze as people normally do when someone is watching them intensely, but he doesn't look my way. He's too locked in on Mare.

Nick suddenly pushes off the wall and closes the distance between them. She turns toward him and flutters her thick eyelashes, acting all surprised he's coming at her. Then she stares right at him, like he is the only one in the room, and twirls her hair around her little finger. From the grin on his face, I know he's loving every minute of it. Her older sisters taught her how to play the game well.

My heart stops and a drowning heaviness falls over me as Nick wraps his arm around Mare's shoulder. I shield myself in the crowd and abruptly stop moving forward. My feet feel like lead. I just can't follow behind them. I stare at the dingy ceiling, fighting back the hot tears with one hand limp by my side and the other pressed to my chest. All these years of waiting for him to make his move were for nothing!

I pitch forward as I'm hit from behind. Then I'm rammed again by a pack of guys who force me to move along with them. I helplessly blend back into the crowd and miraculously make it down the long staircase toward the front of the auditorium and into my seat without losing my breakfast.

As soon as I sit down, Chris notices something isn't right. Before he can ask, I pretend to reach for something under my seat and keep my face hidden under a mass of hair. He nudges me, but I don't respond. I need to pull myself back together first.

Our pretentious headmistress Dana Williams clears her throat demanding our attention, and I pop back up, not looking at anyone but her. "Good morning. I hope everyone had a great first day of school. We look forward to another fabulous year here at Smith. The football team plays Chase this weekend. Please come out and support your team. They worked very hard all summer getting ready for the season."

Her eyes brighten as she continues to gloat about our school's greatness. "I predict we triumph once again in the state championships with the addition of our new star players, in particular Raymond and Marcus. That school down the road wanted them to play for their team but lost again. It is hard to resist joining our family." She beams at the two of them sitting in the middle row toward the top.

"With their top players getting into a little trouble over the summer, they don't stand a chance against us. It's too bad since their headmaster is such a stand-up guy." She snorts, thinking her humor is well received, but it's not. We all sit there in silence, embarrassed by our leader. She reminds me of a slimy toad croaking out speeches, similar to the ones Mr. Collins gave in *Pride and Prejudice*. Maybe Jane Austen used that last name for a reason, and Ivy is related to him!

My phone buzzes and I look down, along with everyone else around me. The most recent list has been sent. Now most of the girls have claimed a guy. Bree, Hope and a few other girls still have blank spaces next to their names.

I steal a glance over at Nick and see he looks pleased, more confident than ever, and it's not a good look on him. I prefer the self-assured type, but he's moving it to a new level. How quickly he has changed!

I feel my stomach lurch; the gurgling sounds seem to reverberate in my throat. Chris looks over at me again with a concerned expression. Or is it a disgusted one? I can't tell right now.

I focus my attention forward at our conniving headmistress trying to tell another joke to engage the students. No one's paying attention with the new list in their hands.

In the shower, I decided I wasn't not going to participate in this stupid list. The best thing would be for me to sit this one out. There isn't anyone else I want to take, unless I put myself out there and ask an upperclassman. Surely one of the cross country guys would say yes if I asked them, then I shrink even further in my seat, unsure they would actually say yes. I don't talk to them much.

I feel eyes on me from above and look over. Hope is glaring at me like I killed her cat. Ivy has a smirk on her face. It's obvious she is enjoying this. I'm her new target now that Kate's gone.

It's only been a week, and the friend groups have splintered, partly due to the stupid list, and partly due to the new kids in the grade. Now there are different tables designating who goes with who. The popular kids reserved the center table, and the wannabe girls and boys have claimed the tables around them, pulling up random chairs to cluster around Mare, Ivy, Kim, Nick, Brian, Kylie, Robert, and Lucy.

The drama kids are on the far left with plenty of room on the side to act out if needed. The football athletes commandeered the table closest to the food to ensure their plates are always piled high. And then several other outliers scatter around the perimeter. I'm not sure where I fit just yet.

I look over toward the side and see Bree sitting alone at one of the tables next to the floor-to-ceiling iron windows, engrossed in some book. I head toward Bree to keep her company since I promised Chris I would look out for her. Ivy has made it clear to all the girls they are not to talk to Bree. She must feel like a leper, kinda like me.

I stand across the table from her and ask, "Do you mind if I sit down?" In somewhat of an aloof manner, Bree nods but doesn't look up from her book. I lower my tray and slide out the red plastic chair that makes a screeching sound as it sticks to one spot.

Bree still doesn't say a word; she seems pretty focused. I look out into the courtyard and spy some middle schoolers chasing each other around the gardens. Back then, I didn't realize how good I had it. The high school teachers have already loaded us with so much work that we don't have any free time to socialize, especially if you play a sport.

The only time you can meet with your teachers to ask questions is during a free period. Practice starts shortly after school ends leaving very little time to sneak in a snack, change clothes, and get on the field. There isn't any way you can fit in fifteen minutes with a teacher.

I pick up my panini, take a bite and the pesto and cheese ooze out the back onto the plastic tray. Luckily, no one saw it because my back is turned toward the rest of the lunch room.

As Bree continues to study, I check my phone and see there is a text from Kate.

Any better?

I text back, *Nope*

I set my phone down on the table but it beeps immediately. I read, *It will get better. Ignore Ivy. Others will follow your lead.*

I type, *Hope so. I wish you were here.*

Dots. . . *Wish I was there to take down Ivy with you. Miss you. Gotta go. Talk tonight.*

Not feeling much better, I lean over the table to see what Bree is so focused on—French. She probably has her entry exam to determine which class she should be in since she's new. I know some kids studied abroad or hired a tutor over the summer so they can take a tenth grade course instead of ninth grade honors. Most likely she followed suit or took more advanced French at Chase from the book she is studying.

Once Bree puts her pencil down to take a bite of something green, I break the silence. "I can't wait for this day to be over. Hope still doesn't believe me that I had nothing to do with this list." This gets Bree's attention. She lowers her fork and says, "Wait. . . what? Since you were one of the first on the list, I figured you helped make it."

Falling back into the hard chair, I blurt back, "What? No! I would never do that. I just can't figure out why someone would put Sam's name down for me."

Bree has a curious look on her face as she relays, "You know, I overheard two other girls fighting in the bathroom. Kylie was saying the same thing to Jane."

I put down my sandwich and wipe my fingers on the flimsy napkin. I have not heard anyone else actually say they have an issue with this list besides Bree and Hope. No one wants to challenge Ivy on this so everyone is just going along with it. I imagine there are more people upset about this too if Bree overheard them in the bathroom. Thinking out loud, I say, "I wonder who else feels this way? At this point the list is just causing more problems and should be deleted."

Bree's eye flash, then she nods and comments, "I agree.

Chris is still so angry at Ivy for putting down his name. I can't believe he ever liked her."

I have thought about this a lot. It doesn't make any sense why a nice guy like Nick would date Lucy or Mare, or why Chris would ever date Ivy. Ivy used to be nice all through lower school and most of middle but something changed in her in eighth grade. She started spreading rumors about her best friends—saying some of us were talking badly about another friend group so she could get them to talk to her. She so badly wanted to be one of the popular girls. One of the girls the boys talked to and talked about.

Bree seems to be waiting for a response so I explain, "In middle school, people paired up just so they could say they had a boyfriend or girlfriend. I don't think many people took it seriously, and I'm surprised Ivy is still hung up on Chris. Maybe she is too insecure to see that he has moved on?"

Bree's face lights up as she grabs for her phone beside her tray and opens Snap. "You know what, you're right!" She types *B.S. I'm not going to follow it and neither should you* across a screenshot of the list and then hits send.

As the phones buzz behind me, I look at the reflection in the window and see a bunch of kids around the lunch table looking at their phones pointing at the Snap. Ivy rises, and I hear what sounds like a stampede in those chunky wedges behind me.

Ivy's face is full of venom as she sneers, "B.S., really? Bree, you lost. Chris is my date."

Within seconds, Bree's chair flies against the window, she leans over the table toward Ivy, and fires back, "Chris is going to say NO! He's not your date and never will be again!"

Ivy steps back, stunned that someone actually challenged her since Kate is gone. I see different emotions cross her face until she settles on one—amusement. She crosses her arms, slightly turns her chest, and scoffs. "Chris will be done with you shortly. You don't have any friends here," then she looks at me like I'm nothing and continues, "at least any friends who matter. Chris would never date a reject. He will move on. You'll regret changing schools."

As Ivy sashays back to her seat, Bree yells, "Whatever!" But Ivy doesn't acknowledge her. Instead, she high fives Mare and tells everyone at the table to ignore the Snap. She assures them that the list is real, but the boys around the table look nervous. They're wondering if they really do have dates for the dance.

Well, not all of them. Nick looks perfectly secure with Mare draped over him.

SEVEN

POWERFUL INFLUENCES

As SHE WALKS through the front door of the administration building, Headmistress Dana Williams discreetly brushes the crumbs out of her wavy, blond hair and off of her white blouse, attempting to remove any evidence of the extravagant gift she received from a prospective family this morning. It's frowned upon to accept donations or presents from anyone applying to the school, but Dana could not resist this one. She and her daughter Taylor devoured the almond croissants and apple danishes within minutes of opening the perfectly wrapped box. It took all her willpower to save the pistachio croissants for later.

Dana makes a mental note to mention this family to the head of admissions. They spared no expense to have those decadent pastries overnighted from Paris—they deserve a private tour of the school and a special welcome for when their daughter comes to shadow a student. What student would really impress them? HMMM—Mare Bradley knows how to put on a good show. Yes, that will work perfectly.

As Dana enters her drafty office, she smells her piping hot cup of coffee and the stale pastry from the communal kitchen that her receptionist always leaves on her desk. Dana tosses the crunchy pastry in the trash then reaches for her dark roast with a little cream and cinnamon on top. She kicks off her shoes, places her bare feet on the massive desk and savors the ten minutes before assembly preparations.

Her bay window overlooks the gardens, allowing her to observe the students as they start their morning. Every day she intently observes the children from prominent families establish their hierarchy through various means. It's the same social dominance that will persist through adulthood. The newbies don't have a shot here—connections are the only thing that matter.

She peers into the mirror leaning against the wall, admiring her reflection. Too often she is asked if she's related to "that woman in the tornado movie" and then she has to act like she doesn't know what they're talking about. If she says yes, they will ask for an autograph, which she cannot offer. That bridge has been burned. After Dana revealed a private, personal matter at a cocktail party and was overheard by someone in the media, her cousin refuses to return any of her calls.

To prevent any more mishaps with the family, Dana learned how to disguise her manipulative side through sophomoric hyperbole. She didn't even need acting classes like her cousin. She's a real natural.

Dana's assistant Ursula buzzes, "Mrs. Williams, Karen Collins is on the phone." Dana puts down her coffee and says, "Oh, what now? Put her through in a minute."

Dana looks into the mirror again, adjusts her collar, and smiles. She was taught by her mentor to always speak with a smile. People can hear it in your voice, and they can never tell what you are thinking. She bares her teeth, picks up the phone, and sweetly says, "Hello, Karen."

In an overly chipper voice, Karen keenly addresses her partner in crime. "Hello Dana! I hope you had a great break.

How is your older daughter, Samantha, enjoying Georgetown? Didn't that incredible soccer player, Ellie Sims, sign with the Hoyas? They should have a fabulous team with Ellie and Samantha playing for them."

Dana refrains from sharing her latest scheme to ensure Taylor an acceptance into Georgetown but can't resist gloating in some fashion about her win. "Yes, Ellie was so lucky to have gotten a scholarship at Georgetown. I pulled some strings to get her in there. You know she was not the best student."

Karen prudently plays along. "That's *awfully* sweet of you. We are so fortunate to have you as the head of our school. I hope you help my little Ivy out when the time comes. You certainly know how to take care of things, just like the incident over the summer."

Dana pauses, thinking Karen's idea to get them more money for the school did not go as planned, but she decides to stay quiet. She wants to hear what Karen is really calling about.

Karen senses the tension and changes the subject. "Things are going well with the PTA. It looks like we will raise more money this year than in the past. You'll be able to use them toward the Student Life Center. It was a good idea for you to take over the finances for the club."

Dana relaxes her smile a little. *Yes, I am always doing things to better the school and my family. Some of the money will find its way into my daughter's college fund.* She revels in her success boasting, "Well, that is nice to hear someone else agrees I made the right decision on that. I do know how to manage money like a CFO. We are still roughly 10 million short. It looks like I need to get the rest through corporate funding."

Karen jumps at the opening. "Kim Westover's parents have agreed to host the ninth grade party at their home this year. Another friend of theirs may be moving up from West Palm Beach. They're sick of being inconvenienced by all the hurricanes. Anyway, they are one of the Waltons, the founding family of one of the big-box chains. I planned the party around when they would be in town so they can come and listen to the plans for the new building. Since they may be wanting to move this winter and will need a school for their sixth and ninth grade girls, I thought it would be a good idea for you to meet them at the party. I will introduce them to you after your presentation on the building. You may be closer to getting that 10 million after the event. I hear they are quite generous."

Finally Dana has a real reason to smile and compliments her conspirator, "You always know how to come through in the end."

Karen seamlessly transitions to the matter at hand. "Well, thank you. Now I would love your help with something. Our daughter, Ivy, is quite upset about this list that was started by some girls who have been at Smith for a while. It seems another girl wants to take her boyfriend to the party and is trying to get the list abandoned so she can step in. Could you take care of this for us? It seems silly to have a list, but it's a Smith tradition. It would be a shame to have some girls create more unnecessary drama and make the Sadie even more of a problem for you."

Dana groans, thinking, *not this stupid dance again*. Every year there's something. She finally responds, "I will take care of it."

The bell tolls and all the kids rush to their seats, trying to avoid getting a tardy. Headmistress Williams goes over the morning events, droning on about how great the football team did last Friday. They beat Chase in overtime. Every Monday we hear the same thing. Blah, blah, blah.

As my elbow slides off the plastic armrest, my head jerks up, realizing I dozed off during the monotony. Chris looks over at me, startled, then settles back into his chair. He may have been asleep as well, judging by the glazed look in his eyes.

I hang my head forward, allowing my long hair to cascade around my face and discreetly wipe my mouth with the back of my sleeve. As I scan for drool, I realize I have on my navy blue leggings instead of my black ones that go with my loose black Lululemon top. I look like a bruise and feel like one too.

Please, please can I crawl back in bed and go to sleep? I was up until 2 a.m. working on my history paper about Henry VIII's many wives. The assignment was to write about which one I can relate to the most. I'm sure my classmates will write about the famous Anne Boleyn, the vixen whose actions resulted in the English Reformation just to win over a man. I prefer Catherine Parr, who avoided execution and was very sympathetic to the bastard children of the women before her, restoring their good names. She also earned the trust of the king, who left her in charge when he was off fighting the French, which is no small feat. She even published several books, not worrying about the controversial subject matter.

When the bell buzzes, I grab hold of both armrests to help myself up and make it halfway before I hear the tap over the microphone. "Ninth grade, please stay after assembly."

Chris leans over and whispers in my ear, "It must be about that football player who was caught in the locked file room looking over the math exam. I figured they would give him a pass like they always do for the star players, but silent Sarah saw it, and reported it to the honor council. I can't believe she spoke up about this since she never talks. I would hate to be her right now. Do you see the looks she's getting from the players?"

I glance around and several of the cocky football players are blatantly staring at her. She appears to be in a trance, clenching her hands together as if trying to repel the glares. However, no one else seems to have any clue about it. The word must not be out as much as Chris thinks. I will walk out with Sarah to ensure no one approaches her since there's no way she can stand her ground on her own.

I turn my focus back to Mrs. Williams, who is patiently waiting for the rest of the upperclassman to leave before starting in on our class. Mrs. Williams says in a mocking tone, "It has come to my attention that several of the girls have started the list for the Sadie. We understand this is the first big dance with dates and all of you are undoubtedly very eager to plan the evening, but this bickering has to stop. Since all the boys have dates, the list is set and there is no need to discuss this dance any further until invitations arrive. The girls who have not selected a date have plenty of time to decide. There are many sophomore boys at Smith who would love to go to the Sadie. Until the invitations arrive in January, there will NOT be any more discussions about this list. Girls are not permitted to ask the boys until they have received their invitation. UNDERSTOOD?"

In unison, we all respond as instructed, "Yes, Mrs. Williams, we understand."

She smiles down at all of us satisfied this matter is handled and announces, "Very good. You are dismissed."

There's an unintelligible grumbling mixed with a rustling of clothes as people stand to leave. Behind me someone mutters, "How can the school tell us we have to take a certain person?" I couldn't agree more—I didn't even write Sam's name down!

I slowly get up, head toward Sarah, who has not moved yet, and wait to cross the stairs into the row she is sitting, then feel eyes on me. Hope speeds by me and doesn't say a word. Sam is right behind her and gives me a small smile as he passes trying to catch her.

Mare is up ahead with her arm around Nick even though it's hard to maneuver up the stairs walking side by side with the center handrail. I look back at Sarah, but she has disappeared up the other stairs. Bree stands to my left, letting everyone else scoot by her, waiting for me to proceed. I look one more time for Sarah, and when I confirm she is out of sight, I ascend the stairs.

As soon as most of the kids are out of earshot, Bree whispers, "So do you think Ivy's Mom called the headmistress?" I tilt my head back and consider it. She's right, it has to be Ivy after the B.S. comment. I chuckle under my breath, "Bree, you must have really gotten under her skin for her mother to call!"

Bree beams at my comment. "Well, someone needs to stand up to her. She's as nasty as some of those girls at Chase."

EIGHT

HOMECOMING

I SUCCESSFULLY BLOCKED out the debates on who will be the Homecoming King and Queen. I ignored the whispering about the various picture parties before the dance since freshman are not allowed to have dates . . . another school rule. I convinced Bree and Chris I couldn't make it due to soccer and was looking forward to spending a quiet night at home without Mare or Ivy.

But when we scored 10 goals in the first half and the refs called the game due to the Mercy Rule, this gave me enough time to make it to the second half of the dance. Ignoring my protests, my mother drove like a maniac to get home and harped on how important it is to attend these types of school functions. The words "you will thank me later" actually came out of her mouth.

Like she can understand since she was so popular in high school. When I was rifling through her closet for a new outfit, I found several love letters guys wrote to her back then. She had her pick, and they put her up on a pedestal. How nice!

She has figured out things at school are not going well and is always asking me who I hang out with at lunch. She's desperately trying to get me to open up, trying to understand why I don't fit in anymore. It's simple, really—Kate is at boarding school, Hope is not speaking to me, Nick ignores me, and I don't have any good friends, with the exception of Bree and Chris, who are always together. And I won't follow Ivy and Mare and listen to their gossip. But for now, I do have to listen to my mother. So I'm walking into this dance—alone as usual.

I take a deep breath, flip my hair over my shoulder, and step into the gym. The strobe lights flash right into my face. I shield my eyes and dart over to the corner behind a plant. As the spots start to fade out of my vision, I see silhouettes on the dance floor and lanky figures on the sidelines and near the punch bowl but no one that resembles Bree and Chris.

From out of nowhere, Ivy strolls over, looks me up and down and snickers, "Didn't you wear that black silk Alice and Olivia dress last year? It looks a little tight on you now. Have you gained some weight?"

Channeling Bree, I snap back, "Yep, I wasn't sure I was going to make it so I didn't buy a new one. It makes sense you would remember it since you asked to borrow it. You said it was one of your favorites, but I guess you're going to cut down everything I wear."

Ivy's nostrils flare as she takes a step back, angered and shocked by my response, but she quickly recovers. She dismisses me with a flick of her wrist and motions to Kim that it's time to leave me behind. Kim gives me a quick smile and mouths, "Hello," then follows Ivy like a devoted puppy dog.

I look past them and notice Hope dragging Sam on the dance floor with a little resistance. He is the only guy out there right now. Bree, Chris, Nick, and Mare are standing by the bathroom covering their ears as a new song booms across the speakers.

I slowly maneuver through the crowd toward the bathroom. Bree sees me coming and prances over to give me a hug. She excitedly exclaims, "You made it. You look beautiful." She takes a step back to admire my outfit and pays me a much needed compliment, "Kels, I love your dress. Is that Prada?"

Her excitement is contagious and makes me glad I did come to the dance. "Thank you! No, it isn't Prada, it's Alice and Olivia. . . . I love your dress too. It looks so good on you!" Bree looks down and gives her best Marilyn Monroe impression in the red silk flare dress. She moves her shiny, chestnut brown curls out of her face and gives me another hug. Then we pose for a photo of the two of us.

"Lip Gloss" blasts over the speakers and we squeal. I knock off my suede heels and run onto the dance floor looking behind me to see if Nick is going to follow us. He doesn't move, instead he continues to shout at Mare over the music, but he's looking right at me.

Bree and I stomp to the song and mouth the words. Nick struts out on the floor and moves to the beat like a rapper, emphasizing the word "Popping." I can't stop watching him. He's hilarious.

One of my favorite songs, "Don't Start Now" plays. More girls stream onto the floor. I twirl around making those flipping motions with my hands like they do in the music video, trying to avoid Nick but can't help glance over at him when she sings about walking away and knowing how.

The song ends and a slow one starts. Oh, no . . . "Stairway to Heaven." Who picked this song? I try to make a quick exit as Mare prances onto the floor and flings her body into Nick. Then she turns her beady eyes on me to make sure I know Nick is hers.

I look past her and spot Hope outside searching for something in her purse. Knowing I need to get this over with, I grab my heels and beeline for her. Her face turns sour as I approach. With her eyes darting to the side looking for an exit, I reach for her arm and quickly ask, "Hope, can we talk?" She jerks her arm away but doesn't move. So I begin again, "Did you come with Sam?"

Hope juts out her chin, purses her pale pink lips and shouts, "YES!"

I ignore her immature outburst and say as sweetly as possible, "Well, I'm so happy for you. You're really cute together. When invitations arrive, ask him to the Sadie. You're the one who should take him. I will keep his name next to mine to ensure no one else claims him for the dance."

Hope stands there for a moment, speechless. Skepticism crosses her face and then she speaks so loudly that the group next to us can hear. "There's no one else you would want to take. The majority of the boys, if not all of them, are claimed for the Sadie. Why would you do that?"

The group of girls moves closer to catch my response, looking very intrigued. I turn my back toward them to block them from overhearing. "I'll figure it out. Have fun with Sam tonight. Again, I'm so happy for you."

Sam apprehensively approaches us with two drinks in his hands. He looks charming in his light blue dress shirt and silver tie. He must have grown since his slacks are about two inches too short, showing his charcoal socks and black loafers.

I politely smile at him and nod but don't dare to say hello. I peer over at Hope, smile at her once more, then quickly walk away so Hope doesn't think I'm trying to talk to her boyfriend. Instead of leaving the scene, I discreetly plant myself behind the column, hoping to hear what she says to him.

Sam seems to tread lightly while he inquires, "So what did she want?"

I hear a pause and then Hope says with disbelief, "She told me to ask you to the Sadie."

Sam exhales, and I can hear the smile in his voice. "I never thought she wrote down my name. She likes Nick. Always has. He is just too blind to see it."

I press my body against the column for support. WOW, so everyone knows I like Nick, except him. Or does he know?

I look to my side, and Ivy is giving me the evil eye. I roll off the column and head back into the gym to avoid another confrontation.

The slow song is finally over and "YMCA" comes on. Kim motions to Ivy they should go dance, but Ivy points at Chris and makes her way toward him. Kim just stands there for a second all by herself, then skips onto the dance floor, bopping her head all the way there.

Ivy slides next to Bree and yells so she can be heard over the music. "Bree, who are you taking to the Sadie? I know you don't belong to a club so this might be your only opportunity to see one." I stand close enough so I can hear everything.

Chris puts his arm around Bree and yells back, "Bree and I played tennis last weekend and then ate in the Park Room. She has plenty of friends who will take her to the various clubs. She doesn't need to go to the Sadie to get in." It seems Ivy forgot he is a member of the Driving Club.

Bree puts her hand up in front of Chris's chest to let him know she will handle Ivy. She squares her shoulders, flips her hair, then begins, "I don't normally advertise this, but my parents are members of The Town Club, The Driving Club, and The Golf Club." She points at Chris then continues, "Our parents may even play on the same tennis team this fall. I can see the inside of *the clubs* whenever I want."

Ivy puts her hand to her ear trying to act like she can't hear Bree, but I know she heard every word from the jealous look on her face.

Seeing Ivy feign ignorance, Bree wraps her arms around Chris, gives him a kiss on the lips with her leg kicked up in the air for effect, then grabs his hand and pulls him away. Chris chuckles as they push right by Ivy.

Ivy's face turns the color of a cherry as she watches them

walk away from her. Then she turns her sights on me. Damn it, I should have left when I had the chance.

I brace myself for the snide remark but Ivy switches gears and puts on her best *I care* voice. "I'm just trying to help. Why are you all excluding me? I hate it that we never talk anymore."

REALLY? I should not be surprised she is putting this on me. I place one hand on my hip and defend myself, "You're the one ignoring me."

Ivy pouts. "I'm sorry you feel this way. Let me make it up to you. . . . Why don't you come with me and some friends to the Halloween party? We are dressing as disco girls. I'm sure Kim has plenty of extra dresses you can choose from. You should see her closet!"

I know I shouldn't even be considering this, but she has just invited me to the Halloween party of the year. It's a huge deal to go to this as a freshman. I'm sure Nick will be there since he's on the basketball team with the host.

Ivy senses my hesitation and steps closer with her hands pressed together pleading dramatically, "Please come. It will be like old times going to the dances together."

I concede. "Sure, sounds like fun."

"Great. Meet us at her house around 6:30."

Thinking about my overly scheduled weekend, I respond, "I'll be there around 7 after soccer. Thanks so much for inviting me, Ivy."

For a second I forget about all the stuff she has done and am about to give her a hug, but then I come to my senses. I've been told I am too quick to forgive and forget, and they're right.

"Kels, let's go dance!" Ivy points at the girls in the middle of the dance floor and glides toward them emphatically swaying her hips back and forth to the music, and I follow behind her.

Ivy notices something and suddenly moves to the left. Kim is shimmying down so low her butt is almost touching the floor. I attempt to get Ivy's attention by grabbing her hand and yell over the music. "I think we need to save Kim," but Ivy waves me off and continues on toward Lance, a good looking junior all the girls talk about.

I veer toward Kim, watching her grab Brian and pull him close, so close he is plastered to her body. Then she arches backwards splitting her dress up the side seam revealing she's not wearing a bra or underwear. As Kim desperately tries to hold her dress together, Brian just stands there with a shocked look on his face, doing nothing to help.

I run as fast as I can to shield her from the crowd while Bree goes to the other side to do the same. Bree motions to Chris to do something, so he grabs the closest jacket to him, runs out with it, and quickly wraps it around Kim.

Appalled, Bree asks, "Chris, whose jacket is it? She's swimming in it!"

Unsuccessfully hiding his frustration, Chris replies, "Bree, what do you want from me. . . . I grabbed the closest one on the floor."

Bree softens her tone a bit. "You're right. Thanks, Chris. This hides the entire dress and rip that's almost down to the hem."

Chris seems to relax and moves behind the swaying Kim who looks like she may pass out at any moment. As she hunches forward, I steady her with my left hand and lean in to ask, "Are you okay?" Her face is hidden so I can't see if she heard me but a weak voice emerges. "Yes, but I'm feeling a little sick. . . . Can we go? I need to go."

I wrap my right arm around her shoulder and curl her into me in an attempt to hide her from the crowd. They are starting to notice something is going on. She rests her head on my chest and we slowly start moving toward the door. Her right hand is almost white since she is griping the coat lapels so tightly. Bree puts her arm around her and laughs so we look like three girls having a great time at a party.

The teachers are on the right side, obliviously amused about something else. I lean over and whisper to Chris, "Block us. We need to get her out of here before the teachers see," and he moves forward.

Kim, Bree, and I slowly make our way down the stairs. Chris is close to Bree in case we need some help. Nick and Mare are behind us. The people we pass are too busy talking to their friends to notice anything is awry.

Once we're safely hidden under the trees in the back parking lot, we all seem to relax. "Bree, hold her for a second," and I let go of Kim once she has a firm grip. I blow on my hands and order an Uber. Then we wait, shivering in the cold, hidden so the teachers don't yell for us to come back inside.

Nick has his arms around Mare's waist, nuzzling his head in the crook of her neck, and Chris is warming up Bree by rubbing her arms. I turn away from Nick. It's too painful to see him like that with Mare. I stand there holding a very embarrassed Kim, wishing I was Mare for once.

Gas lanterns light the long, pea gravel driveway leading to Kim's old stone farmhouse tucked back on at least 10 acres along the Chattahoochee River. The Uber driver pulls up to the massive facade and leans his head out in awe. Bree, Mare, Kim, Chris, and Nick climb out saying thanks to the driver, totally unfazed by their surroundings. I walk behind them admiring the cobblestone lined path leading to a koi pond with a bronze sculpture of a girl running across the water.

Kim fumbles around in her purse trying to find her keys. When Mare hits the doorbell after a minute, Kim looks up and says, "My parents are at a charity function and won't be home for hours. . . . My key is in here somewhere. Aw—here it is." Her fingers shake as she removes a single key and inserts it into the lock. Impatient this is taking so long, Mare pushes the door open and marches into the stone mudroom lined with rows of cubbies.

I let Kim walk in ahead of me and follow her into a vast kitchen. She waves one hand in the air while clutching the coat with the other and says, "Help yourself to whatever you want," then disappears down a long hall.

The guys immediately plop down on the bar stools at the enormous island. Mare pulls out sparkling waters from the under counter beverage cooler. She walks into the butler's pantry and appears with several bags, then hollers, "Catch," and throws a bag of Lesser Evil Popcorn and Grain-Free Sea Salt Tortilla Chips at Nick. She finds a plastic tub of guacamole in a refrigerator hidden behind a long wall of shiplap painted the same soft cream color as the cabinets on the back serving area. It's obvious she has been in Kim's house a couple times.

I'm mesmerized by the kitchen. The tumbled limestone floor resembles something in an old French Monastery and perfectly compliments the light brown wood island covered in the most gorgeous slab of Calacatta marble I have ever seen. I run my fingers over the smooth counter as I move about the room. My mother would freak out seeing this!

"Earth to Kelsey." Nick snaps his fingers in my face, and I flinch. I scan the room, and everyone is staring at me. Standing in front of the extra large farm sink and nickel faucet washing off a platter, Mare sneers, "Kels, you're drooling." She takes every opportunity to cut me down.

I ignore her jab, turn back to Nick and comment, "This is the most amazing kitchen I have ever been in. It reminds me of that 12th-century monastery right outside of Paris that they turned into a hotel." I snap my fingers trying to recall the name. Nick's face lights up and finishes my train of thought. "The Fontevraud Hotel." I lightly touch his arm and excitedly agree, "Yep, that's it! I wish we could go back to Paris!"

Mare slams her plate down in the sink and everyone jumps. Casually she says, "Whoops, it slipped," but it's obvious it was intentional, and I cautiously step away from Nick. No one says anything for a couple minutes until Kim walks into the room rubbing her head mumbling, "I'm still a little woozy . . . and so embarrassed."

Mare rolls her eyes at Kim. She has no sympathy for her and announces with much displeasure, "Kim, everyone is already at the restaurant ordering desserts and drinks. Let's go." Kim looks at her in disbelief. "Mare, are you crazy? I'm not going out."

Mare stomps her foot like a child. "Oh, come on, put on another dress! No one will notice."

Kim shakes her head side to side as she sits down at the empty stool. She sighs loudly, then informs us, "It's already on Snap."

Everyone pulls out their phones and hits the app. She's right, the side of her breast and naked hip is out there for all to see.

Kim picks up a chip but then flicks it back in the bowl. She moans, "The lovely Lucy just posted it."

Bree has no filter and bitterly says, "Wow! What a bitch."

Kim splays her fingers on the island and lays her head in between her hands. "Ughh, you guys go, I'm staying here."

I look around at everyone, and it's obvious the others want to go, but Kim shouldn't be alone after such a mortifying event so I offer to stay. "Kim, let's watch *Crazy Rich Asians*. I really don't want to go to the party."

Kim looks up relieved and gives me a big smile. She mouths, "Thank you," and then cradles her head in her hands.

Mare argues, "No, Kelsey. You have to go. Kim, you need to get out. Go get dressed."

Kim mouths, "Please stay," to me and ignores Mare.

I stand my ground and respond, "No, Mare, I'm good here. You guys go."

I peer over at Nick and can tell he doesn't want to go either. He looks tired. Seeing we're not going anywhere, he grabs Mare's hand and moves her back toward the stools, then gestures for her to sit down. "We can all stay. Let's pick a movie everyone wants to watch. Not some chick flick."

Mare puts her arm around him blocking his view of me and Kim, then whines in a really annoying voice, "Nicky, come on, everyone is expecting us. We have to go. The Uber is here!" Nick hesitates for a second, and she jumps at the opportunity. Mare grabs his hand and drags him toward the front door. Nick looks back disappointed, hoping someone will persuade Mare to stay, but nobody says a thing.

I look down not wanting to watch him leave with her. He does everything she wants. What happened to him? How is he dating such a narcissist?

Bree walks over to Kim and gives her a hug from behind. "Kim, I would stay with you if my brother wasn't picking me up at the restaurant. My mother would freak if she found out I left early and went to someone's house with Chris, and I don't want to share the dress incident as the reason we left. You understand, right?"

Kim nods in agreement. "Don't worry about it. Have fun for me." Bree squeezes her shoulder and says to the both of us, "I'll fill you in on everything." Chris says his goodbyes, and then they rush out to catch the Uber, knowing Mare is impatient and might leave them behind to make sure Nick doesn't change his mind.

As soon as I hear the door slam, I turn to Kim and look down at my dress. "Do you mind if I borrow some PJs or some leggings and a shirt?"

Kim slowly gets up and gives me a hug. She murmurs in my hair, "Thanks for staying. I really did not want to go out. . . .

Let's find you something to change into. We can watch the movie in my room."

I follow her down a long hallway that opens into a two-story family room with mirror image limestone mantels on each side. The fireplaces anchor two sitting areas with a different but complementary personality. Something is missing . . . aww—there are no lamps.

Kim lumbers up the curved stone treads to a landing overlooking the family room and down another hallway. Her bedroom looks like a master suite with Tiffany blue walls. Kim walks over to her mirrored dresser and throws some PJs at me.

I catch them and inquire, "Where's the bathroom?" Kim points behind me. "Past the sitting room on the right."

My jaw drops as I enter a gray Carrera marble bathroom that could easily be on the cover of a magazine. I lean against the smooth countertop enjoying the warm, heated floor under my chilled feet and text Kate. *Hope ur "date" is going well. Got lots to tell you. Call tmrw.*

Then I quickly text my mom to let her know where I am so she doesn't freak out. As I'm waiting for a response, I slip out of my dress and climb into the super soft white cotton PJs with a fun, pink trim. I look into the full size mirror and see they're cropped on me since I'm so much taller than Kim. I smooth my frizzy hair and examine the red bump on my forehead. The concealer has worn off already. It doesn't matter, nobody will be coming back here.

As I walk out, my phone buzzes to let me know my Dad will get me. Kim already has the movie cued up to play and an open bag of popcorn for us to munch on. Kim throws a faux animal blanket at me when I reach the gray velvet sofa in front of her king poster iron bed, and I curl up in the plush throw. Too bad she didn't start a fire in that carved limestone fireplace. I can feel the draft even under the blanket due to all the windows in her room.

As Kim sits there staring at the remote with slightly shaking hands, looking like she may cry, I reach for her hand and ask, "Are you okay?"

Kim murmurs something so low it's hard for me to hear, so I move next to her on the bed and ask for her to repeat it. She admits, "No one spiked my drink. I had one of those canned margarita drinks from my parents' bar before we went to the dance. Luckily, I read how much alcohol is in one of those mini cans after I downed it, or I would have had two. They are so good. Anyways, it hit me when I was on the dance floor—I'm so embarrassed."

I look around and wonder why she would need to drink by herself, but who am I to judge? So I act like it's no big deal. "Don't be. It's fine."

Kim continues on saying, "I was so stressed out about this dance. My parents have been on me about not having a date. My mom told me that if I lose 10 pounds, then maybe a boy would like me. She's always on me about how I look."

I can't believe she feels this way. All the boys look at her. She could easily be a model with her beautiful, heart-shaped face, flawless skin, bright black eyes, perfectly shaped eyebrows, full lips, and gorgeous figure.

She's staring at me, waiting for me to say something so I tell her what I truly think. "What are you talking about? Brian likes you. All the boys look at you. You're so pretty. You have perfect skin! Not a single blemish. . . . Your mom is crazy. Anyways, we were not supposed to have dates. Another stupid school rule."

Kim studies my face to see if I'm being sincere, then lets out a sigh of relief. A smile emerges, and she throws her over-stuffed pillow at me. "You're not wrong about my mom. She doesn't get it that girls want to have curves. Her generation is all skin and bones with a tuck here, and a tuck there, or a jab here to fill in their face. She doesn't get all the Kardashian hype. She always asks why anyone would want to have a butt like that? She saw the Spanx advertising an instant butt lift and was appalled!"

I cannot stop laughing. She's so right. My mother says the same thing.

Kim looks at me with one eyebrow raised and states, "You are lucky to have your curves. Women pay for that!"

Incredulously I respond, "What?"

Kim continues to give me a hard time. "You know it. You wouldn't wear those tight leggings all the time if you weren't okay with it? The only reason the boys haven't grabbed your ass in the halls is they would be expelled."

I hear I need to wear longer tops from my mother but am shocked to hear this from Kim. All the girls wear tight leggings and most do not have long tops. Why would I be different? "Kim, it looks like we need to go shopping. I definitely don't want any of those guys at school grabbing me!"

Kim bursts out laughing. "Nope, they all act like idiots. I can't believe Brian didn't help out. He just stood there staring at my open dress."

I forgot about that. He totally did freeze. Even after we left, he didn't move to come with us. Maybe he doesn't like her after all. I throw a pillow at her trying to distract her. "Let's watch the movie. Maybe we will meet a guy as amazing as Nick?"

Kim raises an eyebrow and I clarify, "Nick in the movie, not Mare's Nick." This appeases her but my stomach has flipped, and I want to throw up. I can't believe the words "Mare's Nick" just crossed my lips.

NINE

THE AFTER PARTY

Trying to appear more sophisticated than her peers, Ivy balances her mojito mocktail with a pineapple and mint skewer on one hand while pinching the stem with her other. She dramatically moans, "I feel *so* bad for Kim. Her friends should have told her that dress was too tight." Then, she pops a chunk of pineapple in her mouth and chews with her mouth open.

Several lanky boys gather around to listen to Ivy speak. One leans in too close, and Ivy lightly shoves him back. "You're in my personal space," she quips, and the others shuffle a safe distance away.

Ivy spots Mare and Nick in the archway with another crowd and hollers, "Mare, Nick over here!"

Mare slips through the boys, pushing them back to make room for her and Nick, then complains, "I have been at Kim's trying to calm her down. She's a mess!"

Ivy rolls her eyes at Mare's attempt to show some compassion then plays along. "She isn't going to make it tonight? I was *so* looking forward to seeing her." When really, she was just looking forward to mocking the wardrobe malfunction.

Not even trying to hide the jubilance, Mare responds,

"Nope, she's staying in with *poor* Kelsey. They're going to watch a movie instead. What fun!"

Nick grunts at the comment, then walks away to hang out with Brian, Robert, and some other guys in the corner. As he approaches, Robert gives him a high five and asks about Kim. Brian stares at his shuffling feet while Nick answers, "She's fine. Staying in with Kelsey to watch a movie. So Brian, why didn't you come with us tonight? You were right there when Kim's dress . . . ummm malfunctioned."

Brian shamefaced, continues to look down, and mutters, "I figured she was really embarrassed and didn't want to see me after that. I was trying to give her some space."

Nick shakes his tilted head side to side, letting him know he is an idiot. "You should text her so she doesn't think you skipped out on her. She's pretty upset about tonight."

Brian shifts his weight back and forth, looking uncomfortable, almost pained. "Nick, you're right. I'll text her. Speaking about being upset, Mike raged after someone took his jacket. You guys need to get that back to him soon. I've never seen him that upset, it's too bad he can't channel that rage on the football field. Maybe he would actually do something worthy of his scholarship."

Nick chuckles at the thought of Mike getting upset. He is the most mellow guy on and off the field. He heard one girl describe him as a 300-pound teddy bear. "Yeah, he really can't jump more than a foot off the ground."

As all the boys in the group snicker, the manager yells, "All kids on the patio or you will be escorted out of the restaurant," making everyone jump.

Even with the announcement, several adult patrons walk out the door since they have had enough of the noisy freshman running in between the tables and bar. One boy knocked into a lady spilling her martini all over the front of her sequined top, and he didn't apologize.

Chris and Bree are sitting at a corner table sharing a Nutella marble cheesecake and tiramisu. Nick snags the empty seat next to them before all the other kids overtake the drafty patio and sinks into the chair. Bree swallows her bite and asks, "Nick, where's Mare? Picking on the other girls with Ivy?"

Nick snorts and ignores the comment. He's too tired to defend her right now. Besides, Mare and Ivy are already making their way across the room towards their table.

Bree picks up her phone and ignores the mean girls approaching. She gasps when she sees a text from her brother asking, *Where are you? I'm outside!* That was 20 minutes ago.

Then she reads the other scathing texts afterwards. *where the hell r u ... if I have to park you will pay for this....*

Bree looks up and notices Dave and his friend Charlie fighting their way through the crowd. As they pass through, girls stop mid-conversation and gawk at the eye candy.

Dave is clearly not happy. Bree jumps from her seat, meets him about five feet from the table, and immediately apologizes so he doesn't yell at her in front of her friends. "I'm so sorry. I didn't see your text until just now. We can go. Just let me say goodbye to Chris first."

Bree looks over at Dave's friend and says, "Hi Charlie," then blushes a pale pink.

"Hey Bree, how's it going?" Charlie casually responds back.

"Good, s—s—sorry if I messed up any of your plans." She lowers her head, hoping no one noticed her stutter.

Charlie waves it off, saying, "Nope, the party was lame. I wanted to get out of there."

Dave chuckles. "Yep, you can't avoid her much longer."

Charlie gives Dave a sideways glance, then grunts and looks back down at his phone.

Dave gives him a forceful pat on the back then scans the room and nonchalantly asks, "So Bree, where's the girl in that photo?"

Bree tilts her head to the side and replies, "What photo?"

Dave quickly responds, "The one from tonight. The girl in the black dress at the dance."

Bree thinks for a second—too slowly for Dave, who whips out his phone and points. "This girl."

Bree peers over and skeptically asks, "You mean Kelsey?"

Charlie looks over at the photo and then moves in closer with his eyebrows raised. Intrigued and somewhat shocked, he asks, "Wait, she's a freshman?"

Bree tucks her hair behind her ear, feeling really uneasy and confused. They never ask about any of her friends. She questions Dave again, "You're talking about Kelsey, right?"

Dave anxiously says, "Yes! The girl in that photo!" Then he bumps Charlie's shoulder to move him away from his phone and playfully taunts, "Charlie, I saw her first—you have enough girl problems right now."

Charlie rolls his eyes and looks down at his phone again.

Bree is about to ask why but is knocked forward as someone hits her on the shoulder. She stumbles into Dave but quickly straightens up and notices the curious stares. Everyone is waiting to see if there will be a catfight.

Ivy takes her place next to Charlie and coos, "Bree, sorry I tapped your shoulder. It's a little tight in here. So, who are your friends?"

Bree does a full-body eye roll and snorts derisively at Ivy. "This is my brother and his friend. They're *my* ride."

Ivy lightly brushes her fingertips down Charlie's arm, hoping he will look up from his phone. When he doesn't acknowledge her, she purrs like a cat in his ear, "I need a ride. How about you take me home?"

Charlie steps to the side, creating enough space for her hand to drop and looks at her like she has two heads. Dave's temper rises as he's dismissed once again.

Bree takes the opportunity to step in between her and Charlie and indignantly announces, "Sorry, the car's full."

Dave impatiently looks at Bree, waiting for an answer to his question, then blurts out, "Bree, I had to pay to park and walk several blocks to get you since you didn't answer my texts. Now that we are here, we might as well meet your friend."

Bree responds in a huff, "Dave, get over yourself. Kelsey's not here. She stayed with Kim to help her—"

Ivy cuts in trying to use a soft, seductive tone, "Yes, our friend's dress ripped wide open at the dance."

Charlie chokes like he swallowed a fly and croaks while pointing at Dave's phone, "That girl's dress ripped?"

Bree shakes her head and corrects him. "No, Kelsey's dress didn't rip. *Kim's* did, and Kelsey stayed with her to calm her down, being a good friend, unlike someone else standing *here*. Kim was pretty upset about it, Ivy. You should be more *sympathetic* towards your friends!"

Ivy gives Bree a death stare as Dave's face droops. "Well then, Bree, let's go. I don't want to hear anything from dad about you being late for curfew."

"Fine!" Bree fires back and then quickly turns around. She says goodbye to Chris and Nick while Ivy lingers by Charlie, hoping he will pay her some attention but is disappointed yet again. All the other girls stand around wishing they were next to him.

Bree returns the knock on Ivy's shoulder as she passes by. Over her shoulder, she hollers, "Dave, let's go." Then she dodges her way through the crowd, embarrassed about the scene they made. She wanted to keep her life and her brother's separate, but now she's going to field a lot of questions about them at school. Ivy is not going to let this go.

Bree is not paying attention and walks right into an entourage entering through the enclosed waiting area. Dave and

Charlie freeze as several of the women face them. Bree steps back and apologizes profusely to the lady who is pulling her short skirt down after being knocked backwards with such force.

One of the sisters in a popular reality show steps forward and coyly smiles at Charlie, tilting her head slightly so her blonde hair partially covers her eye. After a moment, she glides in front of him, slightly narrows her eyes, and takes in his scent.

Then she turns toward the group, absolutely exuberant. "This is what I'm talking about. The cologne needs to have a citrusy, cinnamon smell. Masculine yet irresistibly yummy," she beams with her hands clasped in front of her plunging neckline, revealing the tops of her pushed up breasts.

Charlie stands there puzzled by the comment then takes a step backward to let the posse pass. The other sister brushes against him with her nose toward him and grins. While moistening her lips, she announces, "Yep, that's it. Now let's relax and stop talking business."

Dave and Charlie watch them skim by them, then they follow Bree outside, leaving a group of girls trailing the celebrities.

Even after two days, everyone's still talking about the after party. Ivy sent the photo of her with several stars to the entire world. Now even the middle schoolers are surrounding her and hanging on her every word. I wouldn't be surprised if they ask for her autograph.

Kim and I hide in the corner to get away from the chatter and try to knock out some of our English vocab words. She still feels awful she kept me from the party. Honestly, I'm not that disappointed. I have never understood the fascination with celebrities.

Bree skirts by the giggling girls and bounces over, looking really happy. "Everyone can't stop talking about the sisters. They completely forgot about my brother and his friend crashing the party to pick me up. I could not have asked for anything better to happen that night!" She announces as she climbs into the chair across from me.

Kim's face drops then starts in again, "Kels, I'm *so* sorry. I feel awful I kept you at my house."

I pat Kim on the hand and let her know for the fifth time that it's fine. "Really, I had a great time. My feet hurt after the dance, and I wanted to lay down and relax." In truth, I wanted to see Nick, but he would have ignored me anyway, and seeing him with Mare is torture, so it's best I didn't go.

Finally, Kim leans back into her chair and smiles as if this time it actually sinks in, but then I follow her gaze and see Brian entering the lunchroom. That cheered her up pretty fast! Bree peers over her shoulder and back at Kim's smitten grin, then asks while pointing over her shoulder, "What's up with him?"

Kim leans forward and recounts her conversation with Brian. "He came over yesterday with a single rose and apologized for not helping with my dress. He said he was embarrassed and thought he would make me feel worse by coming back with us. He asked me to go to the football game with him this Friday. It was adorable." She beams the entire time.

"Well, I'm impressed Brian finally stepped up. It's nice to hear some of these guys can admit when they're wrong and go after what they want," I spout without thinking first.

Bree narrows her eyes, trying to catch on to the meaning behind that but then shrugs when it luckily doesn't register.

I steal a glance at Nick, who is right next to Mare, eating a panini, appearing to be really bored. It looks like Mare is showing all the girls how to properly apply mascara. I can't imagine how enthralling that must be for Nick. I watch him shift his weight and turn toward Robert to tune out the girl talk.

He could just come over and sit in the empty seat right next to me. I will pay attention to him, but it's probably not the kind of attention he wants. I won't fawn all over him.

TEN

THE HALLOWEEN PARTY

MY MOM CANNOT STOP TALKING about the perfectly manicured grounds and the outside facade of the Westover's plantation as we drive down the long driveway. "Oh my, oh my, I never knew this was back here. This is truly spectacular, Kels. What do the parents do again?"

"Mom, Kim's mom was a model in Brussels, but really her family is royal in some way, and her dad played for the NBA. Remember James Westover? That's him."

"Oh, okay, that makes sense then." I know she is dying to see the inside, and I would introduce her to Mrs. Westover so she can get a quick tour, but I'm so late and need to get ready. "Mom, I will try and sneak in a couple photos of the inside for you. I'll see if I can bring you over another time to see the house, okay?"

"Yes, please take a couple photos. I think this is just what my new client would love, and it may get them to actually make a decision on what direction I need to go."

She pulls up to the front door and peers through the car window, hoping for a quick peek inside, as I rush out yelling, "Thanks for bringing me."

I sprint to the front door and jump up and down, trying to stay warm, thinking I should have put on my long-sleeved sweatshirt over my soccer jersey. After a minute or so, Kim's mom opens the door slightly to let me in while attempting to block the music from bleeding out of the house. She waves to my mom, then closes the door quickly.

Mrs. Westover places a hand to her ear, trying to muffle the noise of "Stayin' Alive" pulsing off of the limestone walls in the grand foyer, and fakes a smile welcoming me inside. She looks absolutely stunning in her fitted black dress that shows off her petite frame and long legs. As expected from Kim's comments about her mother, she is really very thin and looks like she needs to eat something. Seeing the faint wrinkles around her eyes and above her upper lip reminds me of what I heard our French tour guide repeatedly say to our teacher. "Eat the croissant. You will thank me later. French women know it's better to choose your face rather than your fanny. You will look younger at the age of 40 if you do."

Mrs. Westover looks me up and down, with her eyes stopping at my muddy cleats. Then she points at my shoes and back at the door, implying I need to remove them before entering any further. I mouth, "SORRY," then quickly slip them off and place them outside the front door so they don't mess up the house. Oh, I can't believe I forgot that! I'm such an idiot sometimes. When I step back inside, she's already on her way down the hall but stops to point up the staircase, and I bolt up, shouting, "THANK YOU," over the music on my way.

I really just want to get out of these sweaty clothes. My soccer game was rough. One girl blew out her ACL, and another was taken off the field on a stretcher. These refs suck. They wait until it's too late to call the fouls, and the game gets out of hand. These young guys don't think girls can play rough, and by the time they figure it out, someone is on the ground injured.

Last week someone popped my finger out of joint when I was blocking her from getting the ball. It's still black and blue and puffed up like a blowfish.

As I make my way down the hall after getting a couple photos of the living room and foyer from above, the music gets louder and louder. Strobe lights flash through the doorway of Kim's bedroom. A free-standing speaker-looking thing with a disco ball on top is shooting beams of light to the beat. Kim's room is a mess; clothes are thrown all over the place, indicating she couldn't decide which dress to wear to the party.

Kim spots me in the doorway and struts toward me in very high heel boots like she is on a catwalk. She wraps her arms around me, screaming over the music, "I'm so glad you made it!" I thank her for having me, then pull back so I don't get dirt all over her dress.

Kim looks the part of a glamorous '70s actress in a gold and black sequin dress that clings to her body. She even has on glittery eyelashes to match the dress. Instead of her usual perfectly straight hair, the hair salon teased it to have many tight curls spraying from her pretty head.

She bops along to the music as she heads over to her dresser and puts on huge gold earrings. I follow her, then move toward the bench, zeroing in on the pizza box. I flip open the lid and sigh once I see it's empty. I'm starving and need to eat now. The potato chips on the ottoman will have to do, so I grab a handful and munch on them while Kim finishes getting ready.

Ivy wobbles by in her metallic Go-Go boots, and I know her feet are going to be in rough shape by the end of the night. She has weak ankles and has never been able to walk in heels.

On the bright side, she looks almost as good as Kim in her A-line, white leather dress with a black metal zipper that extends all the way from the bottom to the top. She has it unzipped so far down her chest that it's revealing her red lace bra. If it were a little higher, she would look the part of a sexy '60s nurse rather than a stripper. Some shameless guy may unzip the entire thing off of her, but she would be fine with it—we all know she loves the attention.

Mare walks out of the bathroom and flat-out ignores me. In contrast to Kim and Ivy, Mare looks like she is going to a rodeo instead of a disco party in that skin-tight red dress with a plunging neckline and cowboy boots. Her hair is stick-straight instead of flowing like how all the girls sported in the '60s and '70s. The best thing about the outfit is it shows off her some-what muscular legs, but they're mostly covered by the silver-tipped boots.

I really shouldn't be so judgmental; I might not look much better than her since I haven't even started getting ready yet. Forcing myself to move, I grab the sparkly silver dress laying on the bed and walk across the hall into the guest bathroom to take a quick shower. I scrub the grim off me, dry my hair, then squeeze into the tube top style dress that feels two sizes too small for me.

Turning side to side looking in the mirror, I notice it barely covers my butt. Oh well, it doesn't matter—no one will be looking at me anyway, but Kim is definitely going to have a good time teasing me about this.

I throw all my stuff back in my bag and join the girls nervously talking about the party. It's such a huge deal to get an invite as a freshman. While Ivy brags about how she got us all an invitation and elaborates on all the things she's done at the parties over the past month, I somehow manage to keep a poker face. She's really getting around—no wonder the guys whisper about getting mono from her!

When she finally finishes patting herself on the back, I take the opportunity to change the subject. "I'm surprised they are having the party after last year."

Kim, who is already on edge after Homecoming, twirls around and asks me, "Why? What happened last year?"

I bite down on my lower lip, wondering if I should share everything I heard, especially since it's so hard to believe, then decide it can't do any harm and will let Kim know where not to go. And, people may mention it tonight anyways. "Kim, I heard everyone knows the master bedroom is off limits but a new girl either did not know or was too drunk to notice. Meghan said Lily was at a table with a bunch of boys drinking and then disappeared with Mason. When someone in the master bedroom screamed 'WHORE!' at the top of her lungs, Lily ran out of the party while trying to get dressed at the same time."

Kim's mouth is wide open and Ivy pipes in. "Well, there were other people in the master bathroom shower, who will not be named," and Ivy smirks, making sure everyone knows that she knows something we don't. Then she continues, "He gave me the details. Mason's mom walked into the room and saw Mason and Lily on her bed. She screamed 'Whore,' Lily popped up, grabbed her skirt and underwear, and raced out of the room. Well, she was essentially pushed out." Ivy smirks again, enjoying relaying someone else's humiliation.

"Mason's mom told him he was an idiot, and he should know better than to use her bedroom. He joked about how his room was already occupied. He mentioned something about cameras recording too. I'm not sure what he meant by that, but his mom wasn't happy about the camera remark. She quickly moved on to who the girl was since she didn't recognize her. Mason said it was Lily. Then Mason's mom asked if she was on scholarship. Mason nodded and made some snide remark about being an awesome tennis player who knew how to handle a racquet."

Ivy makes a gesture with her hand and laughs, thinking she's so hilarious. Mare is the only one who laughs, which really irritates Ivy, and she turns on me. "So Kels, you still haven't kissed anyone yet, have you?"

I feel my face turn beet red, since I'm still unable to control my blushing, but I don't break eye contact, letting her know she's not going to intimidate me anymore.

Ivy flips her hair over her shoulder and glares at me, waiting for me to answer, but I don't. Pouting, she adds, "I see, you're saving yourself for someone in particular," and as she says this, she looks at Mare, hoping for a response from one of us. I still don't give her one, but Mare does by throwing a pillow in Ivy's face.

Ivy snickers as she pulls a feather from her lip then continues on with her story as if nothing happened. "Anyways, his mom lectured him on being more careful and not wanting the family to be sued for his actions. He blew it off, saying their attorneys locked everything down, and there's nothing to worry about. That's when his mom yelled him, saying he could be accused of rape, get kicked out of school, and it would be the end of his career. She emphasized the fact that she would not be able to help him get out of a rape allegation, and that would haunt him for the rest of his life, especially with social media these days. She threatened to not let him have another Halloween party, but he promised nothing like this would happen again and calmed her down. She then asked for Lily's full name and said she would take care of it. My friend slipped out of the bathroom as soon as the mom left to avoid being humiliated too. Lily got such a bad rap, she didn't come back this year."

Wow, I haven't heard any of this from my soccer friends. "Ivy, where did she go?"

Flippantly, Ivy responds, "Some boarding school. Probably got a scholarship there too since she won State for Smith." Then she claps her hands together and pops up from her seat to disappear into the bathroom. The rest of us stay seated processing the story.

Kim seems even more nervous than before with her knees bouncing against her velvet bench. Trying to comfort her, I rest my hand on her leg and she places hers over mine and sighs, then glances up with a slight smile looking a lot more composed.

Ivy appears with several different shot glasses. *What? No, she has to be crazy.* I have never had a drink before and have no intention of starting right before this party.

Holding up all the shot glasses for us to see, she proudly advertises, "Tonight everyone is going to be drinking. Let's have one shot of vodka here so we can tell everyone we've already been drinking. They'll believe us when they smell it on our breath. This way we won't make fools of ourselves at our first big party."

Ivy glances over at Kim and she blushes. Why does she put up with that?

Remembering what some girls told me about these parties, I relay the warning. "Yeah, I was told not to accept a drink from anyone. One of my friends picked up a drink that was left on the counter along with several others and started to drink it. Her guy friends rushed over and told her to spit it out. There were drugs in it."

I look back at Ivy, feeling very uneasy. "I'm not sure about this, Ivy. We can stick together and be fine. Plus, I haven't had anything to eat yet."

Kim doesn't hesitate and takes the shot from Ivy's hand. "I'm in. I'm not going to embarrass myself again. This will be my only drink." Kim downs it without flinching.

Mare reaches for her shot. "Me too. Nick doesn't want me to drink at all at the party."

Ivy hands me a shot. Exhausted and feeling a little pressured, I give in. "Fine." I swallow the clear liquid, cringing as it burns my throat, but once it's down, the warmth in my stomach actually feels good.

Ivy reaches behind the bed and pulls out two bottles. "I brought some Powerades for us as chasers." She throws Kim and Mare one. Ivy leans over again and hands me an open one and starts drinking her own.

I want to get the taste out of my mouth so I down it, but the biting taste still lingers.

Ivy claps her hands together and announces it's time to go. We wobble out the front door, yelling, "BYE," to Kim's mom, and hop into the Uber. The guy immediately turns up the music to tone out all our nervous giggling on the way to the party.

The black Lincoln town car pulls up to the recently restored white clapboard home across from the Governor's Mansion. I pass by this house every day and can't wait to see the inside.

We enter through the massive wood door into a vast foyer that spans all the way to the back of the house. About forty kids are hanging in the foyer, mostly juniors. Some are nibbling on a tray of Jello eyeballs and brownie bites with eight pieces of licorice coming out of the sides to resemble a spider.

The general theme is the '60s and '70s so I don't feel out of place. Lots of the older girls have the bodysuits with flared bell bottoms, keeping them warm. One has a neon psychedelic swirl pattern in all the wrong places; the boys seem to love it, though.

I move away from the crowd of juniors and toward the back of the foyer, admiring the two straight staircases hugging the back side walls leading to a wide landing where some kids are staring out the windows overlooking the backyard. The landing connects the two staircases to a central staircase leading to the second floor. I'm definitely not going up there.

I run my fingers over the cold, gold button on the top of the turned wood newel post and try to pry my fingertips under it to see if it will pop off revealing the deed for the home, but it doesn't budge. It must be there for appearance instead of the original purpose. I run my fingers along the paneled wall toward the wide open door leading to the backyard under the landing, feeling a little wobbly in these high-heeled boots.

In the distance, there's a DJ mixing in the pool house with tons of kids dancing on top of a glass dance floor covering the pool. The nebulous pink and purple clouds appear to swirl around the white pool house. I follow the music outside. Bree is on the dance floor dressed like Daphne from Scooby Doo. Her partner in crime is watching on the side with Nick and some other basketball guys. With his California surfer dude looks, Chris can pull it off being Fred wearing the red necktie, blue pants, and white shirt.

Nick went the easy route looking good as Shaggy Rogers. I do love him in green. Brian is dressed like a dog, and it's not the best look for him. Is he supposed to be Scooby Doo?

I zip off my boots and join Bree on the dance floor. We bounce around, mesmerized by the acrylic dance floor floating over the crystal clear water.

Ivy struts over and yells over the music, "Bree, are your brother and hot friend coming?"

A surprising frown appears for a second, but then Bree puts on an unusual poker face and turns her back toward her, ignoring the comment. Ivy sneers and knocks her shoulder as she walks away. I have no idea what Ivy is talking about, but I'm not about to ask with how irritated Bree looks right now. Her whole body has tightened up as she stomps to the beat.

"Dancing Queen" winds down and "Lip Gloss" starts to play. I notice some guy, who seems familiar, walk on the dance floor looking me up and down. Dylan maybe? He's dressed like a vampire with slicked back, black hair, piercing black eyes, and fake blood dripping down his chin. It's too bad he doesn't look more like Damon from *The Vampire Diaries*.

He stands in between Bree and me and starts to move his shoulders side to side, motioning for me to dance with him. Then he leans in and I hear an arrogant, unctuous voice that matches his greasy hair, "I noticed you dancing to this song at Homecoming and asked the DJ to play it as soon as you walked in. I'm Dylan." This guy is a close talker—maybe it's because the music is so loud, but I don't like it. His beady eyes are really creepy.

I nod and introduce myself. "I'm Kelsey, nice to meet you," but I'm not happy to meet him at all. I just need to play nice since I'm pretty sure he is a good friend of the host. The last thing I need is to get us kicked out of the party within the first hour. *Just keep on popping, Kels.*

I sway my hips and shoulders with Dylan mirroring my moves. The DJ plays the same songs from Homecoming, and I twirl around and around, feeling really good, especially when I ignore Nick and Mare on the side of the pool with his friends. I do so well until "Don't Start Now" comes on, and then I can't fight the urge to look over at Nick and mouth the words about dancing with someone else, even if it's only with a creepy guy named Dylan.

Expecting him not to notice me at all, I see him staring back at me with this sick look on his face—a little green like his shirt. Or is it disgust? His lips are pursed together almost in a snarl, his nose is wrinkled, and his cheeks are raised.

I turn away from him, thinking he has no right to judge me. I can dance with another guy. It isn't like he wants to be the one dancing with me.

A slower song comes on, and Dylan moves closer, too close. How did he get so close? I move back but am pulled into his chest, and I feel the warmth, but it's not comforting. I don't want this.

My body feels loose, kinda like jello. Maybe I can wiggle out of this? I bend my knees, but he pulls me back up. I kick my leg backwards for balance and stumble again. I need to stand up straight but can't—the vodka must have kicked in. Of course, one shot and I feel it. . . . It figures. I'm such a lightweight.

Then I feel Dylan's breath on my neck. Did he just lightly kiss me right below my ear? I push him back and see the lecherous smile across his face—I don't like it. I don't like it at all.

I get out the words, "Heyyyy, I don't feel so good. The vodka is not sitting well in my stomach. I'm going to go sit down." I step toward the house, but he pulls me back to him and holds me much tighter than before. So tight our noses almost touch.

Smelling the smoky whiskey on his breath, my stomach flips, and I need to get away from him—from the disgusting smell. I bend my neck back, trying to create space between us and weakly say, "I really don't feel so well. I'm going to the bathroom."

Dylan ignores my pleading and plasters me to his chest again. "Hey, you're fine. I got you." His eyes bore into me, and I know I'm in trouble. I need help—I need help now. Nick is not by the pool anymore, but Ivy is. I'm about to call her name but notice what she's doing, and it hits me, she will not be any help. She's taking photos of the entire thing and giggling, loving every minute of it. I should've known she wouldn't be here for me.

Then I see movement to my right, and Nick is standing here with his hands in fists. As I hear, "Kelsey, I really need to talk to you," I relax but Dylan's body tenses.

Dylan pushes Nick with his pointer finger. "What do you want?" Nick looks Dylan straight in the eye and doesn't back down. "I need to talk to Kelsey." Dylan relaxes his grip while he puffs up his chest, and I take the opportunity to push away from him. Dylan lets go of my shoulders—well, maybe it was more of a push—and mumbles, "Take her. She isn't that much fun."

I lose my balance and almost fall backwards. Nick sees me

stagger and grabs my upper arm, then puts his arm around my shoulder and guides me to the stone patio. I watch him grab my boots, and he slowly carries me inside to the main powder room off the foyer.

I look at my tall boots dangling in front of Nick wondering how he knew where my boots were. He closes the powder room door behind us and refuses to make eye contact. I don't want to look at him either so I try to focus on the room covered in a silver blue wallpaper with some kind of green vines floating to the sky. Are those birds nesting in the trees all around? It's so busy that it's making my head spin.

I press against the floating marble sink to stabilize myself. Being drawn to the shiny gooseneck faucet, I lean forward to run my fingers over curves but lose my balance. Nick grabs my arm to steady me just before my forehead hits the metal. I hear a thud and lean back into his warm body, enjoying being so close to him and the smell of his musky scent, then peer down. Nick dropped my boots when he reached out to catch me.

I lean over to grab them off the floor and try to put them on. Why did I agree to such high heels? As I struggle to get my left boot zipped, Nick leans over to hold the two pieces of the boot together so I can zip them all the way up, and then he stands back up. I put my head on the cold marble to keep the room from spinning again.

Why am I so dizzy? I mumble, "Nick, I think I need to eat something."

Nick continues to hold onto my waist as he says, "Yeah, you had *a little* too much to drink."

My head shoots up from the soothing marble, and I almost hit Nick in the chin. "What? Noooo. I only had a shot." I hold up one finger and see Nick's reprimanding scowl in the mirror.

He notices me looking at him, and he seems to soften. He reaches around and pulls my hair off my forehead and behind my ear. Then so sweetly says, "Kels, I can smell the liquor on you. You had a little more than one shot."

I turn to face him and stumble again, but he steadies me with both arms. He shakes his head and opens his mouth about to say something but stays silent. I try to focus on him, loving being so close to him like this. My fingers run along his smooth jaw while my other hand rests on his chest, and he doesn't move away from me. He doesn't even flinch as I touch him.

For several seconds, we just look at one another. His skin tone is not as sallow, and his cheeks have relaxed. His stormy eyes have cleared, and they're now a bright green color.

I so love his eyes. It's amazing how they change depending on what he is wearing. They look gemlike in that baggy, bright green shirt that ironically shows off his lean physique. In a year or two, he may have the same awesome bod as Chris Helmsworth.

Nick moves the stray, blondish hairs out of my face again and kindly asks, "Who did you come with? I'll text them and let them know we are leaving."

I look at my fingers and slowly tick off the names raising one finger after each name. "Ivy, Mare, and Kim."

As Nick pushes his hard body against mine to sandwich me in between him and the cold marble counter, I rest my head on his shoulder and smell the smoke on his shirt, reminding me of our camping trip together when we were ten. He must have been standing next to the fire in the pool house close to the DJ.

Nick pulls out his phone to type but hesitates for some reason, then puts his phone back in his pocket. Why didn't he text them?

After exhaling sharply, he wraps his arm around me and opens the powder room door. I put one foot in front of the other following his lead. Nick moves to the right and whispers in my ear, "Let's go out the side door so no one sees us."

Good idea. We turn the corner and there is Dylan with Lucy making out in the doorway to the study. He aggressively grabs her around the waist and pushes her waif-like body toward the room.

Lucy's emerald eyes flash yellow as she leers at us and says, "See what you're missing!" Then she topples over the arm of the sofa onto her back and Dylan climbs on top of her, kicking the door closed with his white sneaker. I'm not sure who she was talking to and judging by the look on Nick's face, he isn't either.

As he pulls me away, he mumbles, "Boy, he doesn't waste any time."

We don't see anyone else on the way out. After walking a couple houses away, my stomach starts to churn, and I think I'm going to be sick. I pull away from Nick and lunge behind a tree with my mouth slightly ajar. Yep, here it comes. The acid and potato chip chunks purge from my stomach, and the smell is vile. My throat and mouth feel like they are on fire as I throw up again.

As I balance myself against the tree, I try to pull my hair out of my face but miss several strands. Nick reaches around me, grabs the rest of my hair, and pulls it into a mass behind my head, then he rubs my shoulders as I vomit. I just want to cry right now! This is so embarrassing!

I stand up and wipe my mouth with the back of my hand, needing to get away from the stench. Seeing a patch of grass a few feet away, I let my body fall into it and hug my legs tight to my chest.

I rest my forehead on top of my knees and let my hair cascade all around me in an attempt to hide my face. Through my messy mop, I peer over at Nick and say, "Thank you for getting me out of there. Dylan was not letting go, and I don't know what would have happened if you weren't there."

Nick sits down next to me and continues to rub my back. "Any time. Why were you with him, anyway?"

I rub both eyes with my palms trying to block those images out of my mind. "I don't know. I was dancing, and then he was there with me."

Nick removes his arm from my back and plucks some grass from next to my thigh. I pull my dress down as much as I can without pulling it down at my chest. God, this is too small on me. I'm sure I'm flashing the neighbor across the street right now.

Nick deeply sighs. "Yeah, you would have been in that study with him making out."

Repulsed, I snap back my head. "My first kiss with Dylan. No way. I would never have done that."

Nick looks at me, unconvinced. "You're pretty drunk."

He's right. I'm wasted, and I only had one shot. One shot should not have made me sick like this.

I rip a chunk of clover from the patch near my ankle and throw it in front of me in frustration. "I don't understand. I was so careful. I didn't eat anything and didn't drink anything at the party. I don't know why all these things keep happening. Hope is still not talking to me. She doesn't believe me that I didn't write Sam's name on that list. I know this is crazy, but I feel like someone is out to get me. . . . I don't feel like I have any good friends anymore. Things have changed so much. I want Kate to come back." I sound like a 5-year-old.

Nick listens, occasionally nodding about how things have changed. He and I used to be so close, and now he's with Mare and never pays any attention to me. Well, until now.

I hear him sigh again, lean back and sink onto his elbows. "Okay, this weekend, you're coming out with me and a couple friends. You need to stay away from Ivy. She is not your friend. . . . Who gave you the shot?"

I mutter almost unintelligibly, "Ivy."

Nick looks up at the sky. "I figured. She had something to do with Kate getting kicked out, but I just don't know how."

I wipe my mouth and turn my head to get a better view of his face and see he is upset about things too, which is surprising since he hasn't said anything about her being gone. For months, it felt like he didn't care if Kate or I were at school.

Nick throws a stick into the street, hops up on his feet, and turns to me with both hands reaching out. He lifts me off the cold ground and says, "Let's go get some food in you. Hopefully, you can keep it down this time."

Food sounds good. Maybe it will absorb this vodka even though I doubt anything is still in my stomach after throwing up so much. "Okay, some greasy hash browns do sound good."

Nick holds my hands until he knows I can stand without falling. I don't want him to let me go, but he pulls away to grab his phone. "Let me send this text first so your friends aren't looking for you."

I just stare at him, loving how his wavy hair covers his eyes as he types. How he puts one leg forward and rocks back and forth when he texts. I miss him—I miss his kindness. Mare is so lucky.

ELEVEN
ENOUGH

I PULL the sides of my pillow tight against my ears, trying to block out the leaf blowers right outside my window. UGGGH— This seems to be my new Monday wake-up call.

I throw off the covers in a huff and climb out of bed to ask them to stop, but as I peer through the window, I see my mother is already out there in her pink silk bathrobe waving her thin arms in the air. Her blonde hair is still not brushed, and there's a flat part on the back of her head, marking how she slept.

One of the buff maintenance crew guys turns off his blower, takes off his headphones, and pretends to listen to her for a minute. She points at her watch, and it looks like she says the word, "Comprende?" and he smiles back at her, nodding yes. But as she turns her back to him, he nods to all the other guys, and they continue blowing off the yard.

My mother whips around utterly exhausted, throws her hands into the air, and slams the door as she walks back inside. I quickly put on some clothes, expecting her to be in my room within a minute to ask me to go outside and tell them to wait until 8 o'clock in Spanish. Instead of hearing footsteps on the stairs, the Vitamix kicks on and whines at a high pitch. She must be grinding up some sort of frozen concoction.

I crawl back in bed and pull the covers over me, still not feeling well from Saturday, and the manic humming sound is not helping my splitting headache. As I lay there, bundled under my warm feather bed and silk sheets, I replay the whole weekend in my head.

The morning after the awful Halloween party, Ned yelled at me for the entire first half of my soccer game and then sat me out for the second. My parents just shook their heads on the sidelines as I just stood there flat-footed, terrified I would throw up again if I moved too quickly. I blew my chance to prove to my coach and parents I deserved to travel to California for the next tournament, even after how well I played the day before.

When Virginia twisted her ankle, Ned put me back in, and I tried to move faster, but I just couldn't do it, which cost us the win. The look on my teammates' faces as I let the striker dribble around me and score is permanently seared in my brain. I pull the pillow over my face and scream into it.

Sensing someone above me, I throw the covers off my head and my mother is standing over me, looking really concerned. "Are you okay? I heard the scream down in the kitchen. I'm surprised your father didn't come running up here too. Maybe he finally got in the shower?"

"Yes, Mom. Just reliving my amazing performance this weekend."

Her face scrunches up as she remembers but doesn't say a word. Instead, she kisses my forehead and puts the smoothie next to my head.

"Next time you'll play better. . . . Anyway, how could you sleep through those blowers? I'm going to find another land-scaper! They ignore everything I say. . . . Oh well. Breakfast is by your bed. Hurry up or you'll be late."

As she bolts out the door to get ready, I swing my legs to the side and sit up slowly, careful not to move my head too quickly. I take a bite of the crispy bacon and wash it down with some of the green smoothie, hoping the grease will sit well in my stomach like the hash browns did.

Nick took really good care of me and managed to distract my parents, so they had no idea I had been drinking. I need to come up with some way to thank him, especially after what Bree told me. I so wish I had been there to see it!

Mare went ballistic when she couldn't find Nick. Everyone kept saying that he was last seen with me so she tore through all the bedrooms searching for us.

When Lucy reappeared, she let Mare continue on frantically searching the house until she was exhausted. Then she informed her that we had left out the side door. Mare screamed, 'What!?!' Then checked her phone and saw something that really upset her.

She threw it on the floor, shattering the screen, and crushed the Solo Cup in her other hand as she ranted about him texting he was with me and not coming back to the party. She didn't even notice the liquid running down her legs until she saw Lucy pointing at her, cackling like a witch.

At that point, Mare didn't utter a word. Instead, her nostrils flared like a hippo ready to snap its prey in half, and everyone shut up except for Lucy. She continued to needle her saying, 'He is always there for her. I can't count how many times we fought about her. He insisted they were just friends and even stopped talking to her to make me feel better, but it drove me crazy seeing the way he looked at her. He is still into her. Sorry! I thought you were cute together.'

But Bree said she wasn't sorry. It was obvious to everyone that she had no sympathy for Mare. None. Mare didn't know what to do about having a friend treat her with such disregard.

Even Bree was shocked by her apathy. Bree said Mare

looked like she was about to cry and ran off to find Ivy, who was somewhere with another guy by then, and she didn't come back the rest of the evening.

Apparently, Lucy shrugged it off and turned her attention back to Dylan, who definitely was not into her anymore. He had his sights on another girl, but Lucy tried to win back his affection. Bree said it was classic as well as really hard to watch, even with it being Lucy.

After Bree finished the story, I didn't know what to say, and she didn't know what to make of Lucy's comment either, especially since she has always been a bit delusional. We both agreed she must be wrong about him and that he doesn't like me. He is all into Mare or why else would he be dating her?

I cup both hands around my face trying to relax the muscles in my cheeks that are burning from grinning so much. The picture of Mare with punch dripping down her legs is beyond humorous.

Nick must have received a lashing from her even though nothing happened. He was just trying to help out a friend. She really needs to get over this and move on. He's with her, not me.

We ride to school in silence since my mom has some important meeting with a new client. I can tell she's running the entire meeting through her head by the way her lips move as she drives. As soon as I slide out of the car and say, "Bye," my mom has hit the gas to bolt off campus.

My head is still pounding as I tote my backpack across the lawn looking for Nick, but he's nowhere to be found. Maybe they had an early practice this morning? Dylan is over in the courtyard with Lucy clinging to his right side even though his body is completely turned away from her. He's talking to another girl in a short skirt that barely covers her butt.

I stifle a laugh and am about to change directions to continue on with my search but stop as soon as I feel a tap on my shoulder. I turn and Ivy is standing there, twirling her hair around her finger with a smug look on her face. Why does she always lurk in the shadows and come up from behind? I guess she likes the element of surprise....

Ivy is all decked out in a tight red sweater and black leather skirt, and she seems to be in a good mood today with how she is bouncing on the balls of her feet in excitement. Maybe she met someone at the party?

I play along and ask the question I know she wants to answer. "Ivy, did you have fun at the party?"

Ivy maniacally grins as she responds, "Of course. But you? What happened to YOU at the party? How many of those eyeball shots did you eat to grind with Dylan? If you wanted to get everyone's attention, you certainly got your wish."

Ivy puts her phone in my face and scrolls through the many photos of me on the dance floor with Dylan. There is one of me falling backwards with the caption LUSH written over my body, and I want to die right here.

I reach for the phone, but she pulls it away and sighs. "I told people not to post these photos, but too many kids from other schools were there and thought you were hilarious. It's all over Snap. Maybe you should go back to hanging with Hope until you can hold your liquor," and then slaps me on the back as she moves past me, making my stomach churn again.

As she saunters away with her hips swaying side to side, she looks back over her shoulder to make sure I'm still watching and flashes a grin, one so full of pride. Dramatically, she flings her long hair over her left shoulder with her nose so high in the air as if I can never be as good as her. She continues on with her signature power walk—the one she does every time she strikes and takes down her prey. Then it finally sinks in—her invitation was not an olive branch; it was her way to spew poison all over me. She set me up!

I sink into the shade of the old oak tree and close my eyes, seeing only different shades of red. My heart beats a mile a minute as my brain seems to freeze. Emotions churn through me, but the tears never come. Instead, I cry internally with each salty drop dissolving the mounting pressure in my chest.

A gust of wind blows across campus, and I pull my knees tight to my body. The swaying branches above me noisily creak as they rub one another. Then I hear a crack and a branch falls about twenty feet to my right, barely missing the students walking on the sidewalk, and I fight the urge to snap too—to challenge Ivy right here in front of everyone.

No one is here to stop me; no one has even come over to check on me. Bree and Chris are over on the wall and should have noticed me curled up under this tree by now. Nick is nowhere to be seen, most likely in a screaming match with Mare and won't be able to talk to me the rest of the day, maybe even for the week, and Hope still wants nothing to do with me. My only real friend is at boarding school and—that's it. I can get away from here and all this. I can go visit her. She's always there for me just like I am always there for her.

I grab my phone and text Kate without thinking what my parents will say.

Kate are u up for a visitor this weekend-miss you!

Kate responds quickly. *YESSSS!*

I respond just as fast. *Booking now*

I type in flights to Hartford. Really how expensive can these tickets be? Oh my God! $423. Oh well, there goes the little money I made babysitting over the summer. I type in all my information and hit confirm. Done! I will have to deal with my parents later.

I text Kate. *Booked . . . How do I get on campus?*

Kate responds. *Email shortly. CANNOT WAIT!!!*

I exhale and look up at the sky. I can make it through the week knowing I will be out of here this weekend and finally with my best friend again.

TWELVE

BOARDING SCHOOL

THIS CAMPUS IS EVEN NICER than Smith's. There are massive Georgian-style red brick buildings with white archways, multiple fireplaces, and massive cupolas casting shadows over the lush lawns. It feels a lot like William & Mary College in Williamsburg, at least in the original sections of campus.

As we pull up to the dorms, I see Kate through the grimy window of the shuttle. She's sitting on the top step laughing with three girls sitting below her. Her hair is blonder and much longer than last summer. She used to wear it stick straight, but these new beach waves suit her more carefree attitude.

The shuttle screeches to a halt, and I jerk forward, almost hitting my nose. It's a miracle I made it here in one piece—this guy doesn't know how to drive.

I grab my carry-on suitcase from above my seat and walk down the aisle as Kate runs across the lawn to greet me. She has always been the most athletic girl in the class, and it looks like she's moving more effortlessly than ever. Even with my faster speed, I doubt I will be able to keep up with her tomorrow during the campus fun run.

Once I reach the front of the shuttle, I find my wallet and

drop a five dollar bill into the tip jar. As he lifts his beanie cap in gratitude, I peer into his eyes and they are some of the saddest I have ever seen. I pull out another five and a smile crosses his face. Not one that warms his eyes, but at least it's something, and hopefully the extra money will help him out during the holidays.

As I'm about to turn around, someone wraps their arms around me from behind. Startled, I whip around and see it's Kate and give her a big hug back. It feels like it's been forever since we've been together.

When she pulls away, she notices something isn't right with me and holds onto both shoulders as she asks, "What's wrong? Are you okay?" She looks genuinely concerned, unlike so many people back home.

I bite down on my lower lip to fight back the tears and fake a smile. "Yes, just a little tired. I will rally once I get settled in."

She tilts her head like she always does when she is analyzing what someone really means but doesn't say anything back. She lets it go, at least for now.

Kate lifts my bag like it only weighs five pounds, bounds down the metal shuttle steps, and lands on the smooth granite curb. I smell the wood burning in the distance, the dry leaves, and moisture in the air. Even though the sky is a vibrant blue, I can tell snow is coming. *Please snow! Maybe I can stay here and miss an entire week of school!*

Kate drags me across the lawn toward her friends then pulls me into her shoulder. "Kels, you've met them already on Face-Time, but this is Lauren, Clara, and Sophia. Everyone, this is Kelsey."

Each one gives me a hug—a real hug—not some fake one for appearances. Immediately, I feel like I belong, so much more than I have in many months. I enthusiastically say, "Hi, it's so nice to finally meet you in person!"

Kate can't stop bouncing as she goes over our plans for

tonight. "Let's drop your bags inside. I want to give you a tour before it gets too dark. We have to go down to the water and watch the boys practice crew. Then there's this off-campus party. It's gonna be the best weekend ever!"

Her dorm looks more like a presidential suite. There's the main living area with a creamy linen sofa and two petite armchairs facing a flat-screen television on the long wall. Doors in each corner lead to the bedrooms. Kate's is in the far left corner looking like a Pinterest ad with pale blue walls, a down comforter covered in pearl-colored linens and matching curtains, and a coral red lamp for a pop of color. I drop my bag on the blue and cream Marrakesh wool rug, quickly pull on a pair of dark blue jeans, a chunky cream sweater, brown riding boots, and my gold necklace.

Then we all head out and explore the campus. As expected, the indoor track is unbelievable. The library with the different areas for different needs is, let's just say ... interesting.

The lake is my favorite part so far. Geese fly in a V formation above the guys carrying crew boats, strutting up and down the dock in their blue and yellow fitted tank tops and navy spandex shorts. As the wind whips off the water, my teeth chatter, reminding me I should have brought my coat for these frigid temps.

We walk off campus to a deep-dish pizza place with tons of boarding school kids and some college boys hanging out, playing darts, and shooting pool. Kate and I maneuver through the crowd to find a quiet booth in the back while the other girls join the college boys at the bar. As we're chatting about her classes, a girl who looks very familiar walks in the double doors, and Kate waves her over. "Do you know Lily? She was at Smith last year too."

That's how I know her! She looks a little different—she's actually smiling. I slowly nod in acknowledgment as she settles into the bright red booth. I respond, "Yes, we played tennis together at the fundraiser tournament. It's great to see you again, Lily!"

Lily's muffled voice comes through the thick, wool scarf as she unravels it, letting loose her gorgeous brown curls. "Nice to see you too. How do you like it here so far? Thinking of coming here?" Her nose is bright red and the pinkness in her cheeks makes her skin glow.

Instead of letting me answer, Kate interjects for some reason. "It has been nice to have someone around here from home. Everyone else is from New York or Connecticut and knew each other before school started."

Surprised to hear that Kate felt like an outsider for once, I comment, "It looks like it didn't take you too long to meet other people."

Kate rests her elbows on the dented wood table and leans in toward me. "People up here are nicer than the ones back home so it was easier. Plus, having roommates forces you to get to know one another pretty fast, and I lucked out being with Lily."

Lily smiles at the comment, blows on the warm hot chocolate she brought in from the shop next door, then casually asks, "So Kels, how are things at Smith?"

I sigh, knowing I have to get this off my chest at some point, and it might as well be now. "It's not been the best. Everything got messed up after the list for the Sadie."

Lily wrinkles her nose and squishes her cheeks with both hands, trying to transfer the warmth from the cocoa to her face as she says with some disgust, "I hated that dance. You should just skip it. Come up here instead that weekend. You'll have more fun."

As the seat cushion in the booth squeaks underneath me, I turn to my left and see a guy sliding in, looking straight at me, saying, "So who's the gorgeous new girl?"

Kate rolls her eyes and then introduces us in an annoyed, monotonous tone, "Kelsey, this is Jackson Remington. He's from New York and lives on the Upper East Side near my grandmother. Jackson, meet Kelsey. She's my best friend from home."

I'm able to get a quick read during her long winded intro. He is definitely charming in a rugged boy-next-door kinda way, but I can tell he's trouble. The thing that strikes me the most is his eyes. They are the most unique shade of grayish-green similar to the mist in the lush forests of the Pacific Northwest. They seem to penetrate your soul like cold rain that seeps into your bones.

Jackson scoots over closer. "My friends call me Jack."

I quickly respond back, "My friends call me Kels."

For some reason, this response seems to intrigue him, and he studies me intensely. I return his stare with the same vigor. I really don't know what has gotten into me. Maybe I'm just fed up with being bullied, or I have been around Bree too much lately. She always has the wittiest comebacks.

His eyes shift away when Kate clears her throat. Then Kate comes in with the ringer and teases, "Do you guys want some alone time?"

To send the message she needs to stop, I smack Kate's hand resting on the table. She whimpers, "Ow, that hurt." Then pouts as she pulls her hand back into the sleeve of her sweater. Jack, completely unfazed by Kate's jest, smirks while Lily nervously chuckles and takes another sip of her hot chocolate.

Jack motions to the waitress, and she comes running. From her enthusiasm, he must be a big tipper. He turns to me and asks if I want something other than water. I shake my head, and he orders another round of waters, a large white pizza loaded with meat and a Greek salad for the table.

For once, I'm not nervous. Jack is good looking and knows it, but he's not snobby about it. He has the gift of putting people at ease. Kate's parents are friends with his, so my guess is they're in politics too.

Jack focuses on me, asking personal questions about things back home, seeing if there's someone I left behind this weekend. He's trying to be sly but isn't succeeding. I was right about the penetrating personality, but I don't mind. He actually listens to what I have to say.

We sit for hours at the pizza place and miss the party. Kate plays pool with the guy she likes. He obviously likes her too by the way he mirrors everything she does and stands behind her every time she shoots the cue ball. He really does have the best dimples.

Lily raves about her teammates and coaches. She plays the number one singles spot and thinks she may have a shot to play for Harvard since the scout has already approached her. She doesn't mention anything about missing home. After getting to know her over the past couple hours, I can't see how she got herself into that mess. She doesn't seem like the type to get so wasted and end up in the master bedroom at a party.

The night flies by so quickly that we lose track of time, forcing us to rush back to the campus to make curfew. Kate and Lily dash through the door, but Jack grabs my arm and pulls me back, not seeming too bothered about breaking the rules.

I move out of the way of the other girls passing by and answer a couple random questions. When it gets awkward, I tell him to meet us at the race tomorrow to get him to feel better about ending the night. It's obvious he's trying to muster up the courage to kiss me, but I'm not interested in him like that. He can figure that out tomorrow instead of tonight.

As I stride through the doors, Lily and Kate make smooching sounds and giggle hysterically. They continue to taunt me as we race up the stairs. We quietly enter the dorm, trying not to wake any of the other suitemates.

Lily walks into the bedroom on the right, and I follow Kate into her room. I throw on my comfy plaid PJ bottoms and

Smith sweatshirt, then curl up on the sofa in the shared living room while Kate texts the pool guy.

Usually, I would scan my social media accounts to find out what's happening back home, but I don't want to know. It's so nice to get away from it all. Lily plops down with a thud next to me and turns on the television, searching Netflix for a movie. Scrolling through she asks, "How about *The Kissing Booth*?"

Kate enters the room silently mouthing the word, "NO," so I comment, "Noah is nice to look at, but I've seen it too many times. Besides, did they have to sleep together so soon after their first kiss?"

Lily and Kate look at each other with eyebrows raised so high they look like the golden arches, then Kate chuckles. "You still haven't kissed anyone. It happens more than you think."

I feel my cheeks flush and quickly move on to another subject so I don't get teased any more about my lack of experience. "Let's watch something else. How about *The Notebook* or *Sweet Home Alabama*?

Kate lights up. "*Sweet Home Alabama* is my favorite, but I watched it last Sunday. How about *The Notebook*?"

Lily enthusiastically says, "*The Notebook* it is! I love that movie."

As Kate throws me a blanket to curl up in, I mention what I have been thinking about all night, "You guys seem so happy here."

Kate plops down in between the two of us and gives Lily a side hug as she says, "Yeah, we love it here."

Lily smiles back with the same sentiment.

Then Kate pulls me close to her and happily continues on, "Yeah, you always know where you stand with everyone here. I don't feel like someone is out to get me."

I shift my weight back toward the arm of the sofa to look at Kate's face, surprised since nothing seemed to bother her at home. "You felt like that last year?"

Kate and Lily look at each other, completely shell-shocked by my question, then both stare at me as Kate goes right to the point. "Uh yeah, everyone's so fake. Ivy seems like your friend, but I swear she's always trying to find ways to make people look bad. Like that night."

Finally, she brings it up. I have asked her so many times about that night, but she has never wanted to get into it. She always blows it off, saying it's in the past, and we need to move on. Taking the opening, I eagerly ask, "What did happen that night?"

Kate sighs and leans back against the sofa, looking less like her carefree self. "Do you really want to hear it?"

"Of course, I want to hear it. I have been asking you since the summer!"

Kate bites her nails then tucks her hands under the fleece blanket in her lap. "Okay, fine. I've been trying to forget about this because it makes me so angry, but I will do it for you," she teases as she nudges my shoulder. I nudge her back and then pull my knees tight against my chest, excited to finally hear what all went down that night.

Calmly she starts the story, "So, Ivy and I were in that tight hotel room with those ancient wooden beams—remember the peeling plaster walls? Well, Ivy pulled out a bottle of champagne from her bag and said, 'Let's celebrate our last night in Paris.' When Ivy saw my hesitation, she teased, 'Oh, come on, go get changed into your PJs. I'll pour us a glass.'"

"So I changed, and when I returned, there were two glasses on the nightstand, and she handed me one. To encourage me to drink, she gave a toast with her glass high in the air, 'To new beginnings. I can't believe we're in high school.' I remember making a face as I took a sip and Ivy laughing before she advised me to, 'Drink it faster. You'll get used to it.'"

Kate self-consciously chuckles before saying, "I was such an idiot to believe her . . . but I did and downed the entire glass in one big gulp while she did the same. Then she poured me another and another. . . . Later, I remember commenting on how relieved I was that she didn't get that upset about me kissing Chris on the stupid dare, and how surprised I was that Nick did that to us. Then Ivy snorts—you know how she snorts more like an elephant than a pig—and says, 'I'm going to make Nick pay for it. I should have embarrassed him with Kelsey sitting there.'"

Kate looks over at me, seeing if I want her to continue, and I motion with my hands for her to keep going. I want to hear all of this!

"I told Ivy I was so glad she didn't. That *you* would have been mortified. And sorry about this . . . " Kate looks at me like I may get upset. "I may have said to Ivy that you will never admit how you feel about him."

I gasp, covering my mouth with both hands, then bashfully ask, "Really! Is it *that* obvious?"

Kate laughs at me. "Uh, YEAH."

"Well, he has been dating Mare now for about four months," and as the words come out, my shoulders sag, realizing that even if I had thrown myself at him like Mare, he would have chosen her. He has to know I like him if it's that obvious to everyone else.

Kate touches my shoulder, trying to reassure me. "He'll get tired of her soon. She's just a big flirt."

"Maybe. It doesn't matter. . . . I need to move on. Anyways, how did the teachers figure out you were in the hallway?"

Kate tilts her head like she always does when she is thinking about something. "I don't know, there are still a lot of holes that night. I thought Ivy was with me since we were drinking in the hotel room together."

Hoping my little bit of info will help her put the pieces together, I relay, "I was in Chris's room when the teachers knocked on the door and ordered us to get out. You were passed out on the floor in the hall when we were escorted out of the room. I tried to help you, but the teachers yelled at us to keep moving. She yanked me up and told me not to touch you."

Kate winces as if she were in pain. "Really?"

"Yes, I have never seen them so upset. All of us had to meet with Dean Johnson and write apology notes for sneaking out. I saw the list of kids who needed to report to the Dean, and Ivy was not on the list. So they must have taken you straight into their room and did not go check on Ivy."

Kate sighs and looks down with shame smeared across her face. The last time I saw her look like this was when she was eleven. That day her dad fell on their front sidewalk (we had sprayed it with water in hopes of skating on it the next morning) and broke his elbow while going out to get the paper.

After a minute, I hear Kate's soft voice say, "They did check on Ivy. They said she was sober, so they didn't believe my story. They said I must have been drinking alone and that I should talk to someone about my drinking problem."

"What?" I ask incredulously then add, "That's ridiculous! They can't believe Ivy over you!"

Until that night, Kate had never had anything to drink. I would know. We spent every minute together up until that trip, and then we didn't get to see each other until today. It felt like I lost my sister.

Pulling at the frayed edge on the blanket, she continues, "Yep. My parents said they believed me, but I'm not sure if they did with how they acted. I have never seen my mother lose it like that. . . . When I got off the plane, they informed me I was going to boarding school and days later sent me to my grandparent's house in New York for the rest of the summer. They controlled who I could see and took my phone away to ensure nothing was posted that could embarrass them again."

As she finishes, she throws her head back against the pillow and closes her eyes. I have never seen her take a moment before. She is usually so composed.

Lily and I sit there in silence, waiting for Kate to give us some indication on if she wants to continue or change the subject. Kate lets out a frustrated sigh and then adds, "They think the school wanted them to make a huge donation for the new Student Life Center. Smith assumed I wouldn't have anywhere else to go since all the other private schools have long waiting lists and public's not an option. There's no way my parents would let me go to North with all the metal detectors and elevator incidents. You know—"

Kate abruptly stops as a bedroom door opens, and Lauren emerges looking a little flush. As Kate says, "Hello," she nods and quickly closes the door behind her. Lauren sheepishly walks behind us to the pantry closet, pulls out two drinks and a bag of popcorn, and disappears back into her room.

We hear a giggle behind the door and music starts to play. Kate and Lily share a look, then Kate fills me in. "Lauren must have taken her ex-boyfriend back once again and doesn't want to hear the lecture from us. Next week she will be locked in her room listening to Selena Gomez after he finds a new girl to occupy his time."

Lily grunts then states, "I really don't understand what she sees in him. He's such a loser. . . . Okay, enough about this. Kate, continue."

Kate looks once more at the closed door, sighs with disappointment, and begins again. "Luckily, my mom knows the dean here and they needed a runner. Honestly, I'm so happy I'm here. I didn't realize how miserable I was until I came here."

I recoil after she says this, feeling stung. Noticing my response, Kate leans forward and puts her hand on my leg. "Awww Kels, I didn't mean it that way. I miss you and a couple other people but not a thing about Smith, the Collins family, and pretty much everyone else."

I'm about to tell her I miss her too, but Lily speaks up. "Are you talking about Ivy Collins, Hunt's sister?"

Kate turns her head in Lily's direction and quizzically asks, "Yeah? Do you know her?"

Lily clenches her fists and answers through her snarl, "Not her—her rotten brother. Hunt's the one who got me so drunk that Halloween night. I was playing beer pong but with mixed drinks—such a bad idea. Somehow I always had to chug and Hunt kept making me new drinks. . . . They must have been straight vodka with how wasted I was. I don't remember how I ended up in the bedroom and was out of it until Mason's mom started yelling at me and calling me a whore. I grabbed my clothes off the floor and managed to get my shirt on before I was shoved out into the hall. It was . . . humiliating."

Tears well in her eyes as she chokes out, "The next day my parents got a call from Smith saying they received a report that I was drunk last night. They said I could finish out the year but was not welcome back my sophomore year. If I was caught drinking again, I would be expelled. My parents were furious with me and the school. No one else got in trouble, and so many other kids were drinking. My parents were thinking of suing, but then we got a call from my new coach and here I am." She looks down at her hands, ashamed.

Kate hands her a tissue and gives her another hug. "I'm so sorry that happened, but it all worked out. We're here together and so much happier."

In a somewhat strangled voice, Lily says, "You're right, but last year was awful and a time I hope to forget."

Just then, I remember something and ask, "Didn't your mom go to school with Mason's Mom?"

Kate lights up. "You're right! I forgot about that. They both graduated together and still talk some."

Lily rips apart the tissue as she lets out a derisive snort. "That figures."

This is so much to take in. I have been oblivious to all the things happening behind the scenes. "Wow, I need to watch my back—more than I thought. I have been more focused on getting through school. You know, several kids have already had a mental breakdown and disappeared for a couple days. About half of the class has a psych eval test saying they have ADHD or anxiety and need extra time for the tests to help them cope. Even though I probably should get tested, my parents decided it was best for me to learn how to adjust and figure out how to take the tests like everyone else, but after they found out the psychologists are prescribing extra time even if it's not needed, they're second-guessing their decision. I have to rush to finish my tests in fifty minutes, while others can get as much time as they need. Some even get to come back to finish and most likely are looking up the answers before they return."

Kate shakes her head, chastising the absurdity, then mutters, "That's ridiculous. Then everyone should get extra time if that many people say they need it. Or just make the tests shorter so everyone can finish."

Lily stares down at her hands, hiding the pink in her cheeks. Maybe she needs the extra time as well so I change the subject. "Everyone seems so stressed out. Maybe that's why so many people are getting wasted at these parties. I haven't told you about last weekend. I was so drunk—"

"You were drunk? I wish I had seen that!" Kate leans in closer. "Tell me more . . . wait, did you hook up with Nick?"

I stop her before she can ask any more questions. "No, I didn't. He saved me from some ass who wouldn't let me go. It wasn't pretty. Someone must have slipped me something. The only thing I had was the shot at Kim's house and a Powerade that Ivy gave me before we headed to the party. I think Ivy—"

In unison, Kate and Lily say, "Ivy did it."

Instead of feeling relief that I'm not crazy, the hurt creeps in. The little hope I had that Ivy wasn't the one who did this to me is gone—all gone. But why? How could she do this to a friend or her enemy—no one deserves to be tricked like that. The pain is evident in my voice as I ask, "Why would she do that? Ivy can be a bitch, but spiking my drink is taking it to another level. Anything could have happened to me that night."

Kate sighs. "I don't think this is the first time Ivy has done something malicious. I'm almost positive she set me up that night. There's no other explanation for her being sober and our room being cleared for alcohol. I just can't prove it yet."

"But why?"

Kate looks at Lily and then at me. "Jealousy. Revenge. Maybe both. You saw how she looked after Chris kissed me. She should have blown up right there, but she didn't. I think she planned how to get even instead."

"You really think she wanted to get you kicked out of the school all because of a dare? That seems crazy, even for her."

Kate is trying to remain calm, but I can hear the anger in her voice. "I thought that too at first, but think about how she has changed. Each year in middle school, she seemed to get worse. More manipulative. When she couldn't have something, she would make sure no one else would want it. She made the brands that she could afford—like the 'soft and sexy' American Eagle brand—the 'safer' option to wear by cutting down girls who wore labels, calling them elitist wannabes. Remember when Sarah accused her of stealing her Lululemon tights after a sleepover?"

I nod.

"Well, I remember Ivy being upset about her mother refusing to buy a pair for her, and then miraculously, she had one exactly like Sarah's."

I remember that too. Sarah definitely took a lashing from Ivy after she accused her of stealing her leggings.

Kate continues at a faster clip. "Ivy has never felt like she's good enough—not at home or at school. She used to mock her mom for all her social engineering schemes, but now she has come up with her own to get what she wants—to be number one. The girl that can control it all."

I already know the answer but ask anyway, "So she started the list to control everyone on the first day of school?"

Kate presses her lips together and quickly shakes her head side to side. "Not exactly. She convinced the girls at school to start the list so no one would challenge her or her motives. She planned it perfectly."

I'm still not following her logic and question, "But why put my name next to Sam? Mare already claimed Nick. I didn't have a shot."

"Look at the list. Everyone on the Paris trip was affected by that list."

Crap, she's right. Jane and Kylie fought over Robert, Hope and I stopped talking over Sam, Chris couldn't go with Bree, and Nick . . . well, he didn't suffer at all unless you count him dating Mare as punishment.

Exasperated, I ask, "So how do I stop Ivy from controlling everything? You're at boarding school, Hope won't talk to me, and Nick is with good old Mare."

Kate leans over and grabs her phone on the coffee table. "The Mare thing will play itself out. I wouldn't worry about that. But for Hope. Maybe she will listen to me. She has never been a fan of Ivy, either."

I doubt it will work, but it's worth a try. Kate dials and I hear a click when Hope picks up. "Hope, hey, it's Kate. How are you? What are you doing right now?"

Hope clears her throat. "I'm at home studying."

Kate smiles at me, trying to reassure me she knows what she is doing. "Fun Friday night! Why aren't you out with Sam?"

"He's out of town with his parents looking at colleges with his older brother."

"Isn't there something else you can do?"

"No, I have a lot of reading to do for history. And—"

"And I know you don't want to talk about Kelsey, but are you still mad at her?"

Hope grunts. "Yeah, she tried to make things right, but I don't know if I will ever be able to trust her again. And I don't have to deal—"

"Why not? Deal with what?"

Silence.

Kate tries again, "Hope, I completely understand why you would be upset. But Kelsey wouldn't hurt a fly. You know that. Ivy, on the other hand, would not hesitate. She is the one who set me up in Paris, so you should listen to Kelsey and not Ivy about the list."

There's a thud on the other end and some rustling. Then Hope speaks again, "Wait! What? That was Ivy? Why would she do that to you?"

Kate repeats the same from earlier.

There's a pause, then Hope comes back. "WOW, maybe Kelsey is telling the truth."

Kate emphatically says, "YES! You should talk to her."

Hope's voice cracks. "I'll think about it. Listen, I need to finish this up. Sam is supposed to call soon. Can I call you tomorrow?"

"Sure."

"Okay, miss you."

"Miss you too."

Then they hang up. Kate shrugs. "I tried. . . . Maybe she will come around."

I shrug, not feeling very hopeful. "Maybe. Thanks for trying."

THIRTEEN
A PIECE OF CAKE

KATE DUMPS the contents from her backpack onto her once pristine desk, desperately searching for our Cake Race numbers. One folder opens up, and papers scatter everywhere in the room. "Damn it," Kate mutters as she dives under the bed to see if the numbers happen to be down there. As I tie my shoelace, I hurriedly say, "Kate, finish getting ready. I will look for them," and then get on all fours to gather all the spilled papers into a pile, hoping to find the numbers stuck to the back of a report.

I peer up as the door creaks open, and Lily inches her way through, careful not to hit me as she enters. "Come on guys. . . . We're going to need to sprint across campus just to get there in time for the start," Lily says while lifting her coffee mug to her lips.

Kate slides on one sock, grabs the other, and looks up, saying, "I need to find the numbers first. How are you drinking that before the race?" Then falls to the floor after putting on her second sock to search under her bed once more. One shoe is thrown out but no number. Then the other shoe is heaved out too.

Lily steps over some textbooks, leans over the desk, and removes the two numbers from the corkboard that have been staring at us in the face the whole time and taunts, "You mean these?" She waves them in the air as Kate peeks her head out.

"Thank God!" Kate says through a sigh, then leaps to her feet. Kate slides into her shoes, bending the backs at first then ties them in rabbit ears and calls out as she is running out the door, "Let's go!"

Kate is the first one out of the dorms and already in a full sprint when I hear her yell, "No time to talk. We're going to be late!" As I dash down the stairs to catch her, I see Jack waiting at the bottom, with a massive smile on his face. He didn't even bother to get rid of his bed head, but the stray hairs sticking up are cute somehow.

"Morning, Kels. Are you ready for a little competition," he teases as I tear by him with Lily at my heels.

From his tone, he's not expecting me to be that much of a challenge. I stifle a laugh and simply holler back, "Bring it on."

Lily strides next to me and mutters between breaths, "Am I going to listen to you guys flirt the entire race? If so, I'm going back to bed."

I whisper so Jack doesn't hear me, "I'm pretty sure that's how he talks to all the girls. He's harmless. You should know that by now." This makes Lily chuckle, and she keeps on running effortlessly by my side instead of turning back around. Jack catches up to us just in time for us to slow down to join the rest of the runners who are lining up on the lawn.

Kate gently pushes through the crowd to find her teammates and coach at the very front of the long line of students while I stay behind with Jack and Lily.

As I bend over to stretch my quads, the gunshot echoes, and dew is thrown in my face as the runners take off on the slick lawn. I wipe the dampness off my cheeks and file right into the moving crowd. Jack is right by my side, but Lily slides back to avoid the mass of kids fighting to get to the front of the line before the path narrows into the trees. She just needs to participate as an athlete; it's not crucial for her to do well. The pressure is on Kate and the other cross country runners to lead the way and win the prize—a whole cake.

Kate's up in front with her teammates but not that much farther ahead than me. I push my legs to move since this should be the faster part of the course, and I need momentum for the hilly section Kate told me about on the second mile.

I begin to pass several runners on the right side, more interested in talking about the night before than running for time. Jack stays firmly next to my side as we hike up the hills, past many dragging students who look more like swimmers and lanky volleyball players.

We whip through the trees and onto an open field, where I see Kate's hair blowing as the wind picks up. I bear down on the balls of my feet to catch her, hearing Jack start to pant as we dash by some of Kate's teammates. I pass another girl, and now I'm even with Kate, but she doesn't seem to notice since she is so focused on the slippery leaves scattered all over the wooden footpath.

The wind rushes through the trees with such force it lifts and swirls the wet leaves, making it look like golden rapids on a Colorado river. I leap off the wood planks and onto the solid ground. Kate is still next to me and Jack is several paces behind us. The slope changes to where I perform the best—the downhill.

This last part of the race is a straight shot to the finish, and I kick it in, so Jack has no chance of beating me at the end. I don't want to see another guy gloat about winning at the last minute. Kate speeds up as well and pulls ahead of me, laughing like she does when we race back home. I bound down the hill and catch her so we're neck and neck.

Tons of kids cheer us on as we pass the blurred faces and

colonnade of trees. Kate seems to get another boost of energy and glides like I've never seen her before. My legs scream in protest as I stretch to mirror her stride. But she isn't focused on me, she's trying to catch the trio of cross country guys only a couple feet ahead of us, laboring for their cake.

I can hear my heartbeat in my ears but keep moving, trying to get one more leg ahead to finish alongside Kate. A guy yells out, "YES!" as he crosses the finish line and two guys roll in right behind him. Kate pulls ahead at the last minute, and we finish a second apart.

I veer off to the side to let the cramp right under my rib cage ease, while Kate heads over to her coach on the sidelines. I raise my left arm to get more air into that lung and then head back to the crowd toward the water station. Jack comes up from behind and nudges my shoulder saying through heavy breaths, "Well, I owe you a congratulations . . . Second overall for the girls . . . You were flying . . . And it looks like the coach wants to talk to you too."

I turn around just in time to see Kate and her coach approaching. With a broad smile, Kate says, "Kelsey, this is my coach." She then turns to her coach and introduces me with a hopeful grin, "Coach, this is my best friend from home. She's a great soccer player as well as a cross country runner."

Her coach, who has the kindest face, sticks out his hand and firmly shakes mine. "Kelsey, it's very nice to meet you. I thought you were going to beat this firecracker here at the end," he teases as he nudges Kate's shoulder.

Quickly I respond, "Oh no, she's always been the better runner. I miss having her around to push me during the races."

Kate pats herself on the shoulder in a mocking way, enjoying the praise while her coach adds, "She certainly needs some pushing up here at school so if you have any interest in joining our team, please feel free to reach out. I would love to see you running with her again. We need to beat Deerfield next year. That was such an unfortunate loss." Kate's frame droops a little with this comment, but he quickly pats her on the back to straighten her up again.

Her coach puts out his hand again, and I gladly accept it, feeling my cheeks frozen in a grin, thinking this may be the answer to all my problems. "Yes, thank you. I will certainly think about it. I've only been here for a day and already love it."

He places his other hand over mine and holds it tight. He looks me straight in the eye and says earnestly, "Great, I hope to hear from you. Enjoy your stay with Kate. Please keep her out of trouble." As he says this, he winks at Kate in a grandfatherly kind of way. Aww—he seems like such a great coach.

Then he turns his attention to some other girls on her team. Several of them are peering over Kate's shoulder, hoping for a piece of the multi-layer cake with white icing and blue letters saying "Cake Race." Jack swipes the blue C off the cake and quickly sticks it in his mouth with the most adorable smirk. Kate feigns disgust then immediately closes the box to ensure no one else follows his lead. She playfully snaps, "Back off, Jack! I worked hard for it. . . . Anyway, I thought Kels told you to bring it, but it doesn't look like you were able to keep up with her."

His eyes narrow at the jest, but he quickly recovers, saying, "Ladies are always first. Kels is your guest, and we need to be nice to her to get her to come here."

Kate laughs. "Nice try. She smoked you and you know it."

Lily follows up on the comment. "Yeah, don't try to play the gentleman card here."

It seems Jack is used to being teased by them, but this last comment seems to really tick him off. Instead of firing back, he simply stomps off toward the guys on the sidelines, taunting the last few stragglers puffing down the hill.

"Don't worry, Kels. He just needs some time to pull his ego

off the lawn, and then he'll be back to try and impress you again. Lily, what's your bet on how long he can stay away?"

Lily taps her lips then answers, "Fifteen minutes, and then he'll be asking us for breakfast."

Kate peers over at him, then counters. "I give him five minutes with how he's shuffling back and forth."

Well, neither of them were right. He stayed with some guys I noticed on the crew team and didn't join us until we were on the football field, playing a game of touch. Kate's dimple guy, Will, is the quarterback as well as the captain. He put Kate and me on the outside as his wide receivers. This way, we can outrun the thick guys in the middle who would flatten us with one arm. Jack volunteers to play for the other team and is on me like white on rice.

Will fakes a pass to Kate, then throws a bullet that thuds off my chest, probably leaving lace marks on my skin, but I'm able to hold onto it and dash toward the end zone. I stiff-arm Jack to keep him away from me as I run, but he's able to duck under my hand and gently throws me to the ground, pinning my shoulders on the lawn as I roll to a stop. His eyes bore into mine, and I think he's going to lean in for the kiss but ends up on his side as Lily throws him off of me, taunting, "Come on, Jack. You'll scare her off!"

Then she marches off, looking really pissed off. Kate throws me a hand and lifts me off the ground, then leans in close and whispers, "I think you should sit the next one out, or you may get pinned again."

She nudges Jack with her foot. "Come on, Jack. Let's run one more play and see if you can guard Lily. Kels and I are going to watch, and then let's go grab some grub. I'm starving."

After breakfast, Kate, Lily and I go back to the dorms to shower and change into something warm for the rowing competition Jack talked us into doing with them. Kate and I get to be the coxswains, barking orders at the guys, which is something Kate loves to do. She has the confidence to give orders.

By the time we make it to the dock, the guys already have the boats in the water. I move to the left, and Kate takes the skinny boat on the right. A ripped guy with long sun-kissed blond layers and brown roots, puts out his hand to help me get in the front of the boat and introduces himself as I lower myself down. "I'm Luke. You must be Kelsey. I heard them announce your name for the second place this morning."

As he stares down at me with a lopsided grin that reaches his gorgeous ocean blue eyes, I try to pretend he's Chris back home to ease the butterflies and calmly answer, "Yes, but my friends call me Kels. Thanks, Luke." With that cut face and body of his, he makes most girls melt, and he knows it.

Out of the corner of my eye, I notice Jack moving to slide into the seat I will be facing, but Luke beats him to it in one swift motion, looking more comfortable on the water than on the dock. Lily guides a disgruntled Jack back to the other boat, telling him she needs his advice since this will be the first time she's ever rowed in a race.

As the other guys climb in and get situated, Luke leans in close with his hand on my knee, "Repeat everything I say to the rest of the team, and yell as loud as you can. Everyone needs to move together as a single unit. I can't wait to see Jack's face when we beat him by a boat length. He was bragging on how he plans to crush us before you guys showed up. I think he was expecting *you* to be on his team though, and I've thrown him off his game." His smile turns utterly mischievous as he goes on about beating his teammate.

Ignoring whatever this rivalry is between them, I remark, "I've *never* done this before or even seen a race, so you may need to repeat the commands a couple times." Once I finish expressing my trepidation, he leans in a couple inches from my face, bringing on some catcalls and whispers, "Then you are in for a treat."

Kate hollers across the starting blocks, "Luke, don't you start hitting on my friend. You and Jack may end up in a fight after this and not because one of you lost the race." Then, she laughs along with everyone else in her boat except for Jack, who's getting used to wearing a scowl today. They love to pick on him.

Luke doesn't let that comment go. He fires back, "Kate, you know you want to be the one I'm paying attention to." And the roars get louder as Kate's eyes narrow.

Without warning, Kate blows the whistle and Luke frantically yells, "Guys GO, ROW, ROW," and we awkwardly jerk across the water as the guys struggle to get a firm grip on the oars and attempt to find a rhythm. The other team seems to be in the same shape, not prepared to start so quickly.

Slowly the guys get into sync with their paddles dipping into the water and rising up high above the wake. The wind whips and we tilt ever so slightly toward Kate's boat so I bellow what Luke says, "PORT TO HOLD. STARBOARD ROW!"

Within seconds, we straighten up in our lane and glide through the water. As the guys look like goldfish gasping for air, I yell, "ROW, ROW!" even though it may not have any value except for me to feel a part of the race.

Everything seems to move in a perfect symphony of swooshes, grunts, exhales, and repeats. I lean back in the confined boat wanting the rush of flying across the empty lake to last as long as possible. Maybe it was for too long, though.

Kate's boat gains on us so Luke yells at me, "Power 20 in two, ONE! TWO!" I straighten up and roar the words. Instantly, we lurch forward, taking the lead. He barks so many other orders, and I have no idea what they mean. Puzzled, I yell, "FEATHER!" but then understand as all the blades flip upside down and skim the water and slice through the air to eliminate the wind friction. Kate's boat follows suit after seeing us do it.

I yell, "Row FASTER, POWER on 10," trying to encourage them to dig in deeper on the last bit of the race and push through the pain that's evident on their faces. As their bodies roll back with force, I hear the groans. A vein pops out of Luke's neck as he pushes through the water, willing the boat to move faster.

Inch by inch, we start to pull away from Kate and her team near the end. Water sprays my face as one guy turns his oar at the wrong angle, but it makes me feel even more alive. I understand why they put in so much time training to race for a mere couple minutes.

We pass the white flag in the water and Luke yells, "LET IT GLIDE." Then he leans back almost in the lap of the rower behind him, grinning contagiously. Looking up at me, he teases, "You did well. You seemed to enjoy ordering us around." I hear the rest of the guys chuckle at the jab as we cut through the placid water.

Smiling, I defend myself. "Well, I'm just a little competitive and felt like I needed to do something rather than just sit back and watch you guys row."

As I say this, he smirks and turns his head to say something to the guy behind him, and I take the opportunity to check out Luke's gorgeous body. He has to be at least a junior or senior with that much muscle. His arms and quads have separated into defined masses that are so taunt, he could easily compete in a bodybuilding competition. He even has the sheen of sweat, making his cut limbs glisten in the late morning sunlight.

From behind, I hear Kate taunt, "You guys started before the whistle so you're disqualified!" Luke shoots up to protest but relaxes when he sees she's only joking. Jack, on the other hand, is not happy about the loss, his second for today. Lily seems to be trying to calm him down or take the blame since she's not a rower.

We take our time getting back to the dock, enjoying the peacefulness on the lake and the warming air around us. Jack busies himself, getting the boats back in the house and all the gear neatly stored before finding us on the side of the lake with our legs stretched out. As soon as he sits down next to me, I offer an olive branch. "Next time, I'll be on your team and we'll win since I have much better pipes than Kate. I couldn't hear a word she said."

It doesn't seem to help much, though. He mumbles, "Thanks, see you guys tonight," and takes off to wallow without us around.

Laughing hard as we enter the dorm, the other girls stop and look up, waiting to hear what's so funny. Kate sums it up with one sentence. "We just barked orders at the crew guys at the helm in a race. So what's up with you guys?"

Lauren pipes up, looking like she didn't get much sleep last night and needs to take a nap. "We just got back from a party that has been going all day and should last all night. Some day-student's parents are gone and we have the house. Are you all going to come with us? Veronica is there barking orders at everyone, but you all can handle her like usual."

Kate gives me a sideways glance and asks, "Do you want to go to this since we missed last night?" Then teases, "Your boyfriends should be there too."

Not wanting her to know I'm enjoying the attention (since the guys back home treat me like a leper), I nonchalantly answer, "Whatever you want to do."

Kate rolls her eyes, knowing exactly what I'm doing and responds, "Yeah, we're in. When are you all heading back there?"

Lauren finishes drinking her tea and answers, "Around

seven tonight. We need to get some food in us first. There's a beer pong competition."

The rest of the afternoon, Kate and I wander around campus and through the charming town. It's nice to not be told what to do. We can do whatever we want, whenever we want—total freedom.

By the time we return to the dorm after seven, the place is empty. Pizza boxes are piled on the coffee table. I grab a slice and devour it like I haven't eaten in days. The run took a lot out of me this morning. We quickly change clothes, check our severely windblown hair in desperate need of brushing, and reapply our makeup. Then both of us grab another slice of pizza and follow the GPS to the party, which is only about a 15-minute walk.

By the time we arrive, the house is packed with boarding school students and locals. Lily is on the stairs in the front hall with some other girls, waiting for us to arrive. "Kate, you're late! Will has been asking about you. He's in the back playing beer pong." As she speaks, she hands us each a red Solo cup. I expect to see white foam on the top, but the liquid is surprisingly clear. Lily leans in close and whispers, "It's Spindrift instead of White Claw. I wasn't sure if you were wanting to partake tonight."

Relieved I'm not going to be pressured to drink, I whisper back, "Thanks, this is perfect."

The three of us, along with the other girls on the stairs, push our way back to the kitchen and find Will at one end of the breakfast table about to throw the ball. A petite girl with lots of blond curls down to her mid-back and quarter-sized blue eyes is clinging to his side, purring, "I know you can do it. You've got the best aim on the team."

Kate snorts, then moves into the room further to take her place at the middle of the table, with her arms crossed. She's waiting to see how long it takes for Will to acknowledge her and see how he handles the other girl coming onto him. So far, he hasn't looked up to notice, being so focused on his aim. It's obvious he has been drinking for a while with how he's swaying.

The white ball launches into the air and hits the front cup in the diamond pattern. "Shit," slowly escapes the mouth of a squatty boy with a square jaw and glazed over silver eyes. He chugs the cup, wipes his mouth with the back of his hand, then moves the back cup forward so it's in a small pyramid pattern.

It's his turn to throw, and he looks like he is going to arc it but instead bounces it at the last minute, and Will blocks it, causing the ball to fire at Kate, who puts her hand up and catches it like she knew it was coming.

Will's head slowly moves in our direction, and then his eyes open wide. "AHHH, there you are, Kate. Where've you been?" He motions for her to stand next to him and announces, "You're my partner next round."

Kate eyes the girl next to him, who quickly disappears from the table, making room for Kate to stand next to her guy. His arm is around her waist, pulling her tight to his side partially for balance as well as to be close to her. "Watch this," he slurs and becomes laser-focused on his throw. He bounces the ball and it skims into the cup on the far right without giving the other guy a shot of blocking it.

Within five minutes, the game is over and Will is setting up a new game for us to play. I take a couple practice shots and miss them all. Arching the ball is much harder than it seems, but if I bounce it, they will knock it out before it comes close to the cup.

Luke steps up, saying, "I'll play with her to even out the game. She looks like she's much better with her legs than her hands," and guffaws at his joke, making me more focused to prove him wrong.

Before we start, Kate lays down the rules, "The guys drink

the beer in the cups, we don't want that cheap stuff. We have our own drinks." Neither guy argues with her. They seem happy that we're playing and have probably already had too much to drink to even notice if we take a sip or not.

Kate throws first and hits the backline, but Luke yells, "Elbow! Shoot again!" Kate attempts to argue, but Will says, "Sorry babe, he's right." *Babe, really?* But with how she is fluttering her eyes at him, she's fine with it.

I scoop the ball out of the glass, wipe it with the towel on the back of the chair and pass it back. She hits the same cup again and banters, "Drink up, Luke! You too, Kels." He downs the cup in one swallow. I nurse mine so I don't get stuck drinking the disgusting beer.

I fake an air shot then go with a bounce pass and it reflects off the middle cup and ends up in the front one. Not bad for my first throw. Kate downs her cup and motions for Lily to get her a refill. *So this is how we are going to hide the fact we are not drinking?*

Will goes next with a bounce pass, and Luke slams the ball against the wall to prevent it from hitting its target.

"Man, you busted up the ball," I hear from a spectator, but Luke shrugs like it's all part of the game.

Another ball is produced from the pack on the kitchen counter and thrown over. Luke catches it and launches another one that swings around the rim, and Kate pushes it out with her finger before it hits the beer. Will makes some joke about being good with her hands and gets a smack in the arm for it. All the guys find it hilarious, though, and say something I'm not going to repeat.

Kate misses on the next throw, still pissed off about the comment. It's my turn next, and I sink it in the center cup, splashing beer onto a wasted Will, but he doesn't seem to notice and gladly downs the rest.

When it's my turn to chug, Luke notices I'm empty and

hands me the cup with the ball floating in it. I smell it and my stomach flips, remembering what happened to me last weekend.

Luke taunts, "Just drink the cheap stuff, princess."

Kate notices my hesitation and passes over her cup. She plays it off, saying, "I've had enough. She can have mine."

As I accept it, Luke protests, "It's not that bad. Look, everyone else is drinking it here." Then he turns toward Kate and says, "Besides, it looks like you're just fine and can keep drinking."

Will looks like he may join in so Kate gives him a firm kiss on the cheek and says all the right words, "You want me to be able to throw, right? You can drink mine. I know you can handle it."

Will eats up the attention and defends his girl. "Leave her alone. You just want to be the one to win."

Luke scoffs but doesn't respond. Instead, he focuses on his shot and sinks his ball with a bounce pass. Now there's only one glass on the table, and we are tied. Will misses his shot and I miss mine leaving it up to Kate. She wipes the ball, asks Will to kiss it for luck and sinks it without a bounce.

Immediately Luke yells, "Rebuttal," and tells me to sink it. Apparently, we can go for a tie.

Kate eggs me on, saying, "Kels cracks under pressure. She isn't going to nail this one." I ignore the comment and focus only on the cup to block out Kate's squished up face right behind it. She's desperately trying to distract me. I let it fly, and the ball hits the side of the cup. It looks like Kate is going to swipe it out, but it hits the tawny liquid first.

The crowd explodes in laughter as Luke throws his arms around me and points at Kate. "It looks like she proved you wrong. Overtime, baby!" I can't hide the wide smile of relief on my face as he squeezes the air out of my lungs.

Miraculously, we sink three in a row and win the game. Will

downs the remaining beers without saying a word about the loss and helps set up the game for the next group. Kate graciously says with a huge smirk, "Good game, guys! Kels, it seems you have better hands than Luke expected."

Luke nudges my shoulder and praises, "Yep, you held your own partner. Nice game." Then he heads to the keg for a refill.

Lily eagerly announces, "My turn to crush these guys," and we watch her play with some of the crew guys from this morning. Jack is nowhere in sight. Hopefully, he's not sitting in his room licking his wounds.

After another lively game with Lily winning in a record ten minutes' time, we decide to check out the rest of the house. As soon as I walk into the family room, I can feel the looming presence. Mean girls are the same—they suck all the air out and save it for themselves, like no one else matters.

Kate whispers, "That's Veronica and she could rival Ivy and Mare for their queen bee title."

Veronica is perched on the arm of a tall wing chair in front of a stone fireplace. I watch her flip her highlighted beach waves off of her heart-shaped face and survey her surroundings. In a shrill voice, she commands a meek, lemony-blonde hair girl to spin the bottle.

Everyone leans in and holds their breath, waiting for it to stop. It spins twice and points to a bespectacled guy whose thigh is shaking. Several of them lean back looking so relieved that it's not their turn and then taunt the two "victors." It's safe to assume many of them are there for the experience and not because of a certain person.

Jack is standing behind the sofa, mocking the guy who is following behind the hunched over girl, hiding her face from the staring crowd. Amusingly, they angle their bodies so they do not touch each other as they shuffle into the dark closet jampacked with coats and winter gear. What exactly do they plan to do in the confined space if they won't even brush shoulders going in?

Kate chuckles pretty loudly, almost like she wants to be noticed, making Jack aware of our presence, and he beelines for us. As he grabs my hand, then hollers to Veronica, "Our turn."

I immediately pull back, and Kate pries his fingers from my arm. "No, Jack. We don't play childish games like that. If you want to kiss a girl, you need to go for it the right way. Not because a bottle is pointed in her direction."

It's clear Veronica's feathers are ruffled as Kate mocks the game. She sneers back, "Well Kate, what other fun ideas do you have?" Then she flips her hair and places one hand firmly on her tilted hip.

Kate's eyes fire up. "Well *Ronni*, there's a more natural and fun way to spend your time. It's called hanging out with your friends. Maybe you should try it, but it may be a challenge since there aren't many people who would choose to be with you." Then she directs her attention to the cowering kids on the sofa. "Any of you are welcome to join us in the other room. We won't force you to do anything you don't want to do. Unlike this one here." She points at Veronica as she says it.

Veronica snaps back, "Don't call me that!" Then falls silent when several girls rise to join us.

Kate waves them over and then maneuvers her way into the other room and makes herself comfortable on the sectional sofa. Will stumbles in and sprawls out next to her. Kate places her hand on his thigh and keeps it there while he takes a little nap.

Jack takes the seat next to me before Luke can steal it. Lily climbs into the corner and curls up in a ball leaning on Kate's shoulder. She seems like she needs a nap too.

Luke sits across from us and the new girls pull up random chairs. After some small talk, Kate suggests, "How about a couple rounds of Truth or Dare. No Dares to tell people to make out." She looks at Jack when she says this, and his face drops in disappointment. "And the questions need to be pretty harmless. Nothing really personal. No questions about if you're a virgin or not. And there is no shame in passing on something. Okay?" Scanning the group, everyone seems to agree with their nods.

The first question is asked by Kate. "So Lily, name one hot guy on campus."

Lily acts like she has to really think about this one and then answers while looking straight at him, "Luke."

Luke steps over the coffee table and kisses her on the cheek. Before he pulls away, he whispers something in her ear and she blushes a bright pink in her already rosy cheeks. It looks like they have some history together.

Jack is next and, of course, asks me, "Truth or Dare?" I go with truth and brace myself for a question that will reveal my inexperience to this group when I see his mischievous grin. Fortunately, he asks something pretty trivial.

"So Kels, are you a play-the-field or commitment type?"

Without even thinking, I respond, "Definitely committed," and his eyebrows furrow since the way I say it implies I have a guy back home. I know what he will be asking on the next round.

Lily asks Kate her preference and she chooses dare, making Lily really think on what she should ask her to do. "I dare you to go hit on Veronica's boyfriend."

This gets a lot of sharp inhales and shakes of disagreement, and luckily, Kate's head is one of them. "No, pass on that. We don't need to get her even more angry."

Lily bursts out laughing, and I have no idea why. No one else seems to either with the blank look on their faces. "Kate, you can relax. I was just kidding. No, my dare is for you to do something even more stupid. Go get a glass of water and dunk Will's hand in it. Let's see if it really does make people pee."

Kate immediately hops up and prances out of the room. Jack leans over and whispers, "That is such an urban legend. It won't work, but if it does, Kate will end up single tonight."

I chuckle softly. He really does know how to make me laugh.

Kate squeezes through the chairs, careful not to spill water on anyone and gently lifts Will's limp hand into the glass so his fingers are fully immersed as well as part of his hand. Then everyone's gaze shifts to his pants and nothing happens for a couple minutes. It feels like time is slowly ticking by as we watch in silence. Kate calls it by slowly lifting his hand out of the water and says, "Nada, it didn't work . . . thankfully."

Luke adds, "Well, his head doesn't function all the time so that may have something to do with it."

As everyone laughs, Kate flicks water in Luke's face. "Stop, you're just jealous he gets all the girls, and you have to watch on the sidelines."

Luke leaps up and tackles her, spilling the water all over her. Kate squirms, hysterically laughing through the tickles, causing Will's eyes to open and then shut. Luke abruptly stops moving and says, "Really, I'm not the one who has to watch on the sidelines."

Then Lily says out of the blue, "You know, you guys really should go out and get it over with. This tension is exhausting to watch."

Kate pushes him off and attempts to wipe her soaked jeans and sweater with a blanket but then gives up since it's acrylic and can't absorb anything. She throws it on the back of the sofa and notices Luke is still standing over her, waiting for a response to Lily's comment. She glances around the circle, then peers around Luke's legs and clearly says, "Lily, I don't know what you're talking about. Luke is like a brother to me."

The guys that have gathered to watch behind the chairs, erupt in laughter and yell, "Burn," as Luke backs away and sits down in his seat, sulking ever so slightly. To divert the attention from him, he asks a girl I have not met, "Truth or Dare?"

She answers, "Truth," and Luke asks the same hot guy question, thinking she will say his name and make Kate jealous. Instead, she blushes profusely and answers, "Jack."

Luke's jaw drops but quickly pops back into place, looking a little more defined due to the clenching. I feel like an idiot. It's now obvious that she was playing the spin the bottle game since Jack was there and hoped he would join in.

When Jack doesn't acknowledge that she just put herself out there, the awful look of rejection crosses her face and then she peers down at her hands, totally embarrassed. She doesn't realize that he was whispering in my ear and missed the whole thing.

With all the eyes on us now, I interrupt him and softly say so everyone else can't hear, "Jack, she said you. Say something back."

He pulls away, appearing somewhat shocked and then remarks, "Thanks, Julia. You're pretty hot as well." This causes her to turn a beet red color, and she buries her head in her hands.

It's my turn again and the question I expected to be asked is the one given, and Jack seems to relax again after hearing my answer even though there's no hope we will hook up. He's adorable but not the least bit my type.

The game ends pretty quickly when Will wakes up and is ready to do something other than play a sitting quiz game. It took little encouragement from the group since the game was getting a little boring without the prying questions and embarrassing dares.

While we debate on what to do next, Kate finds the host to get the Sonos password and finds some rapper station. We spend the rest of the night twirling around the room to songs that I have never heard before. I dance with Jack, Luke, Kate's roommates and many others, not caring about anything. I have never had this much fun at a party! I so wish things were like this back home.

The next day comes, and I don't want to get out of bed, knowing I will have to leave shortly. Kate finally convinces me to throw on some clothes by telling me she will ask her mom to make some phone calls to get me in next year if things don't get better at Smith and reminds me of how excited her coach was when he saw me run. That's something to give me hope.

The suite is quiet then we leave to grab breakfast and hardly anyone is in the dining hall. My guess is many people snuck back out of their rooms and spent the night at the party house. As she eats her oatmeal, Kate asks how I feel about Jack and I shrug.

"Kels, I know he isn't Nick, but he's a good guy and he tried everything he could to get your attention. He asked if he could stay with me over the holidays so he could see you. He even mentioned New Year's. Why don't you give him a shot? It's not like anything serious will come of it with him here and you back home."

I stick my spoon in the thick mush and grunt. All I say back is, "Maybe. Let me think about it. . . . So what's up with Luke?"

Kate waves it off. "Nothing. He and Lily are on and off again. I'm not going anywhere near him until she's done with him for good."

Surprised she doesn't mention anything about her dimple guy, I ask, "So you are not that into Will?"

She scans the room to ensure no one is listening, then quietly responds, "No, Will is great and I do like him but he's not the kind of guy to date for long. He gets too *distracted* by all the attention. So many girls want him so I'm not about to get too attached. It's just fun."

I lean in and whisper, "So you would rather date Luke than Will?"

She hesitates before answering so I know how she truly feels. "No, I like Will. Luke is a player too. He's the kind of guy you want to date later, not now."

"So he's not like a brother to you?" I tease.

"No, but did you see the look on his face when I said it? I can't give any indication I have any interest or it could mess things up with Lily. She's worth more to me than him."

"Well, I think she has already picked up on it that Luke has a thing for you or she never would have made that comment."

"Yep, hence the brother comment to shut it down," she says with a glint in her eye.

I pick up my spoon and mutter, "I hope I don't meet the one and end up feeling like I'm the consolation prize."

"Kels, what are you talking about? You know that will never happen. You'll never be someone's second choice."

I shrug my shoulders and look over at the buffet. "You're wrong on that. Remember Nick?"

Kate kicks my foot and says, "Snap out of it. Nick has blinders on about you. I don't think he knows you like him. Anyways, do you really want to be with him with how you feel right now? It's time to move on to someone better. Someone who has made you feel good from the beginning. Someone like Jack—" Then she nudges my foot.

In a gloomy voice, I respond, "You're right. I'll think about it, but right now I'm dreading going back home. I'm tempted to miss my flight so I can stay another day, but I know that will only prevent me from coming back again, and I'll get a lecture on how I need to be more responsible and aware of my time."

This makes Kate laugh. "Yep, I can hear your mother now!"

FOURTEEN
REACTIONS

ON THE PLANE RIDE BACK, I replay the breakfast conversation in my head instead of watching the movie streaming three feet in front of me. Should I give Jack a chance since he offered to fly down over the holidays? Even though my heart didn't skip a beat when I was with him, he did everything right to make me feel like I was the only one in the room. Does't that count for something?

I can't keep waiting on Nick. Why do I keep focusing on him? I don't want to be someone's second choice, and that's how he makes me feel.

I want to be happy—truly happy. I want to feel like I did at boarding school.

All these thoughts run through my head until they're interrupted by a sudden shift in the air. I turn off the movie and flip to the flight path to see where we are, and notice we're only about thirty minutes from home. So, we should be staying at the same altitude or drifting down, but it feels like we are going up? I scan the open windows and see gray cloud-like wisps float by and then darkness. It's only around 4 o'clock—it shouldn't be dark!

I feel a bump. Then another and another. Each one seems to be getting a little rougher, but no one else seems to notice. They're too engrossed in their movie or various devices.

Then something booms through the plane, and we plummet several feet, making it hard not to panic. People frantically fasten their seat belts and grip their armrests with white knuckles.

Things begin to flash through my mind, and they're not pretty. I don't want to be remembered this way. I'm not the shy girl who everyone can walk on. I want to be more than that. I want to be happy like I was this weekend.

How can I be this happy at home? I have to change. I have to be better than this. I can be better than this.

All I need to do is put myself out there and go after what I want. I can defend myself just like I do for others. I will do all of these things if we don't crash. Please, give me the chance!

Things continue to get more intense. Even the pilot, who is supposed to be the calm one, has a nervous crack in his voice as he reminds us for the third time to take our seats and remain calm. Really!?!

Before he sounds off, the plane drops again, and we pitch forward as if we're going into a nosedive. The overhead bin opens up and a metal suitcase falls out, hitting a man who's reaching for a phone in the middle of the aisle. The blow knocks him out cold. His limp body slumps over the armrest, giving me a clear view of the deep gash on his scalp and forehead.

I bolt out of my seat to close the bin so nothing else flies out and am thrown forward. After clinging to the tops of the seats on both sides of the aisle, I'm able to climb back into my row, strap in, and help lift the man back into his seat.

As the plane stabilizes for a moment, the lady next to him shakes him to see if he will wake up, but he doesn't move. She places a hand on his chest to prevent him from leaning forward and hitting something else, but she's struggling. The stupid armrest blocks me as I lean over to help. Instead of trying to lift it up, I use it as leverage—big mistake.

The plane jumps again, causing my ribs to crack against the metal. Mother—that's going to leave a massive bruise!

With my right arm, I throw over my blanket for her to press on the gushing wound and hold him as still as possible with my left. People behind me start to scream as they notice a little blood in the aisle. Then, the putrid smell of vomit fills my nose, and the cabin seems to pulse with terror.

The guy to my right prays with his hands high in the air, then grips the back of the seat for dear life as another flash of light cracks outside the window and the plane rattles in the boom.

One lady screams, "GOD, NO. I'M NOT READY!" She's a couple rows in front of me, clutching her blanket to her chest.

After several minutes of total panic, the plane stops rocking, and we can see if the guy is breathing. The lady next to him checks his wrist, then moves to his neck, and sighs when she finds a pulse. From the expression on her face, I know she's as relieved as I am. I thought he was dead since he looks more like a wax mannequin in one of those creepy museums than a living person.

As I rub his cold hand and try to console him, saying, "You'll be fine," I notice the blood is slowly starting to flow under his skin, bringing a much more natural color to his lips and cheeks. I lean in closer as he mumbles a couple words that I cannot understand.

He slowly blinks his eye as if he is trying to get used to the spotlight on his face. Once he realizes his other eye is blocked by the soaked fleece, he jerks his head toward me and in a weak voice asks, "What's going on? Why am I so thirsty?"

I lean over even closer and pat his arm to comfort him. "You hit your head, but you're fine now. The lady is holding the blanket to your head just in case it starts bleeding again. We should land soon, and then we can get you something to drink."

He fumbles with his seat belt like he wants to get up, so I place my hand on his chest again and plead, "Sir, NO. Don't get up. We all need to stay in our seats. The storm has caused the plane to bounce all over the place, and you may hurt yourself again. The flight attendants aren't even getting up from the back of the cabin."

He groans and tries to look down the aisle and then turns back to me. "What happened again?"

I say as calmly as I can, "The plane was hit by lightning, but we're fine. The pilot said we will be landing soon."

I hear a faint, "Okay," and then he seems to melt back into the chair. The lady next to him quickly places a fresh white pillow against the wound and drops the soaked blanket on the floor.

After about thirty minutes of deafening silence, we land, and the paramedics rush onto the plane to check on the man. Even though he answers their questions, they insist on taking him off on a gurney after seeing the amount of blood he lost and the four-inch cut on his head.

As they strap him down, I notice the small Yale logo on his shirt, a Y with a bulldog in the middle of it, and I think of Nick since that's where he wants to go to school. The man reaches for my hand and asks for my name. I tell him, but they rush him off the plane before I'm able to catch his.

My mother has no idea any of this happened until one of the passengers stops us at the baggage claim raving about how well I did on the plane. I try to blow it off, fearful my mother will never let me travel alone again if she knew what I just went through. Still, the lady will not stop going on and on about how she thought she was going to die and that she couldn't handle seeing the blood, and it was good I was there to help out.

Then in mid-sentence, she snaps at the lady beside us who's acting like she's some kind of hero. I recognize the lady immediately. She was right in front of me. Heroes usually don't yell out that they are not ready to die and refuse to part with their *blankie*.

Once we get to the car, my mother grills me for more information, and I relay the entire scene as best as I can, making it sound better than it was so she doesn't feel like it isn't safe for me to fly by myself again. It's going to be hard enough to broach the subject of me going to boarding school next year anyway.

Instead, she surprises me by saying, "Kels, you really should be a doctor since these kinds of things always seem to happen to you."

Still a little shocked, I add, "Thanks for the vote of confidence, but I don't see that happening."

She continues on in that nurturing voice of hers. "Well, think about it. I'm sure we can get you a summer internship shadowing a doctor to see if you like it. I think you may be surprised and should really consider medicine."

And as soon as I say it, I regret it. "Well Mom, things like this only happen to me here. Everything was great up at boarding school, but as soon as we were close to home, the dark cloud appeared and welcomed me back here. Probably giving me a taste of what is to come once I get back to school."

My mother gasps and chokes out, "I didn't realize you felt this way."

I notice a tear rolling down the side of her nose and reach for her hand. "Sorry, I didn't mean for that to sound so harsh, but that is how I feel. Things are not good for me here. Getting away for the weekend allowed me to see how miserable I am here, and I want a change."

My mother squeezes my hand and simply says, "I want you

to be happy and will help you. You just need to let me in and not wait to tell me when things get this bad."

I nod and fight back the tears. She's right. How did I let it get this bad?

As soon as I walk in the door and drop my luggage, my phone rings, and it's Kate. Without even saying hello, she tells me to check my email. What else can go wrong now?

I sit down and open my mail. Since she's still not talking, this must be pretty bad. I click on the attachment and a video starts to play.

There is a black and white image of a hallway. It looks familiar. A door opens and Ivy steps out of the room dragging Kate into the hall. Ivy props Kate against the wall. She goes back into the room and appears with two bottles—it looks like one champagne and another sparkling apple juice. Ivy walks down the hall and around the corner. About a minute later, she sprints back down the hall without any bottles in her hands, runs right past Kate, and closes the door.

Professor Johnson turns the corner and sees Kate lying in the hall spread eagle. She sprints toward Kate, looking terrified. Prof frantically leans down to check on her, then pulls back quickly with a frustrated look on her face. She knows Kate's drunk.

Our professor walks a few doors down and knocks on a door. Chris answers and she yells something. Hope, Kylie, Jane, Sam, Nick, and I walk out of the room. I stop to check on Kate but am pulled back up. I say something, but the prof yells again and points toward the door. I look back down at Kate and then move on to my room. Everyone else goes into their own room as well. Prof knocks on Ivy's door. Ivy answers, rubbing her eyes like she's been asleep. Then the prof picks up Kate and carries her into the room.

My hands are over my mouth and I exclaim, "OH MY GOD! How did you get this?"

Kate's tone is eerily calm and collected. "I called the hotel saying I was the family attorney and asked if they still had the footage from that night. I guess they were afraid of a lawsuit and sent it to me right away! And get this, Smith has a copy of this too."

"The school has a copy of this too? How did Ivy get away with this if they have seen it?"

Kate is silent, but I know she's still there. There is an intense tapping sound on the other end like someone can't stay still or is frantically typing away on her laptop. Kate exhales deeply, then replies, "I know. I'm so angry right now. I'm going for a run. Call you later!" She hangs up before I can say anything. She's like me, we need to run to be able to think clearly.

I just stand there frozen—maybe I should go for a run to handle everything that has happened. Instead, I drop my bag at the door, run up the stairs, and climb into my warm bed.

FIFTEEN
SCHOLARSHIP

FOR HOURS, I have been staring up at my ceiling fan, hoping that the steady beat will lull me to sleep, but my mind will not stop racing. I just can't wrap my head around what I saw in that video. Ivy completely set Kate up. I never thought she could be that vicious.

Going to boarding school has been the best thing for Kate. She got away from Ivy and everything else. Kate said her mom would be happy to pull some strings for me to get in, but is that what I want? I lean over and grab a piece of paper and pen out of my nightstand and start writing: Pros and Cons.

The pluses for going to boarding school are simple. I would be with Kate and Lily. I would be at an incredible school that would help me get into a college in the Northeast. I would be able to run on that track, play soccer in their college-like stadium, and be on my own. But I would be away from home, and even though it's hard to admit, I would miss my crazy heli-copter parents.

As for staying at Smith, it would be more of the same. There aren't any surprises. I know what's expected, and I can handle the work. Boarding school seems to be even more grueling academically. I would miss hanging out with Bree and Chris and would obviously miss Nick, but who knows how I will feel by the summer. I would definitely not miss Ivy, Mare, or Lucy and all their comments.

So what's the best option? If I'm leaving to get away from Ivy, then I'll have to contend with another version of her—Veronica. Every school has mean girls—there's no getting away from that. Bree certainly didn't when she switched schools, but she's much better at handling herself since she dealt with it for so long.

Knowing I can stand my ground against them now, I will see if things get better and can make a decision later. The applications aren't due until January, so I have plenty of time to decide.

I roll over and peer at the alarm. With only three hours of sleep, I'm ready to try out the new me and pop out of bed. While I'm brushing my teeth, I turn on my phone and scan my texts, stopping at one from the school. School is cancelled due to the snow threat! Excellent! I can put this off for another day. I spit out my toothpaste and climb back in bed to catch up on all the missed hours of sleep.

The warnings of another Snowmageddon arriving around noon was just another false alarm. We only got a couple flurries and some ice, but I'm not complaining in the least. I got to spend the entire day in front of a fire reading another one of my romance novels. I wanted to finish the last thirty or so pages but was already running late for dinner and had to put it down.

Due to the ice on the roads, Bree was able to get us a reservation at the hot new restaurant, Le Colonial, that serves Vietnamese food with a Beverly Hills twist. Being dressed in bulky snow boots doesn't fit with the glamorous decor, but I'm not about to slip on these icy sidewalks. I've seen too much blood lately and don't want to end up like my neighbor during the last ice storm—twenty stitches and a scar above her lip. No, thank you.

Nick, Mare, Bree, Chris, Kim, and Brian are already seated on the shuttered veranda under several heat lamps. They left the lone chair at the end of the dark mahogany table open for me. At least I'm not sitting next to a depressing, empty eighth seat. Dumplings and spring rolls are already on the table.

I slide under the palm tree into the cold, hard chair. Bree finishes chewing her bite, wipes the sauce from her bottom lip with a white linen napkin, and inquires with a hint of annoyance, "Kels, what did you do this weekend? I didn't see you at the party, and you didn't answer any of my calls."

"I went to see Kate." I flatly answer, knowing this is going to surprise the group.

Nick bolts upright in his chair and chokes on his spring roll. Mare slaps him on the back with a little too much force, and it looks like he may spit it out, but luckily, the food stays inside his swollen cheeks. He quickly chews and swallows, then incredulously asks, "You saw Kate? I thought her parents banned her from seeing all of us? . . . Are you thinking of going there?"

Mare glares at him on the last part, then looks at me with disapproval. I ignore her like I said I would. I pour myself some steaming hot tea, warm my hands around the porcelain cup, and calmly respond, "Well, she's at boarding school so they didn't know."

Bree looks at Chris since everyone else is quiet. He tilts his head away from her and gazes at the lounge area. Bree rolls her eyes at him and then turns back toward me, asking with much curiosity, "Who's Kate?"

I scan the table while blowing on my tea, and it appears that no one is going to talk about this. Brian, Chris, and Nick have buried their heads in their Coke glasses, and Mare is pouting. Judging from the puzzled look on her face Kim has no idea what's going on but she has enough sense to stay out of it.

Trying to lighten the mood, I respond, "Kate's one of my best friends. She was kicked out of school last summer. It's not a big deal anymore."

Bree and Kim perk up as everyone else slumps in their seats. Brian shakes his head at Kim so she stays quiet, but Bree doesn't get the memo. She leans in, hoping for more dirt and enthusiastically asks the table, "Why did she get kicked out?"

Simultaneously, Nick and Chris grab another spring roll off the center plate and stuff them in their mouths so they can't answer, making me speak up again. I roll my eyes then reply, "She was caught drinking on a school trip. We all got in trouble that night."

Bree glances over at Chris, who is looking in every direction but hers, shifting in the hard seat as if the motion is going to soften it all of a sudden. Bree scoffs and then scans the rest of the table. Nick's arms are crossed over his chest, and he seems to be enjoying watching his friend squirm. From the glint in his eye, I know he's about to stir up even more trouble.

Nick swallows the rest of his spring roll and adds, "We were playing Truth or Dare, and I dared Chris to kiss Kate." Then he leans back in his seat, unsuccessfully wiping the smirk off his face as he watches the tension build in between them.

Bree's head whips back toward Chris with a piercing what-the-hell-are-you-not-telling-me kinda look, and he cowers in his seat, hoping the moment will pass. Still, Nick continues to make the situation worse for him. Exuberantly he taunts, "I didn't expect that kiss to last *soooo* long! It looked like Ivy was going to attack Kate at first, but instead, she shot daggers into the back of your head."

Nick bursts out laughing and then awkwardly stops,

wincing in pain. Muttering, "Ouch," he leans under the table to rub his walloped shin.

Chris fidgets in his chair and curses under his breath then finally justifies his actions, "Well, I wanted to get through to Ivy that we had broken up, and that did it."

Bree rests her elbow on the table, places her long fingers over her left cheek, and blocks Chris from looking at anyone else—well, except for me, all by my lonesome on the end. In an eerily calm voice, she asks, "Chris, *why* didn't I hear about this before now?"

Chris's mouth opens and shuts as if he doesn't know what to say, and then he turns toward me, pleading for help. I lean back in my chair and say, "Sorry, you need to answer this one."

His shoulders drop, and he exhales sharply, then turns back to his girlfriend and explains, "Because it doesn't matter. I don't like Kate. I have known her forever and we're just friends."

Bree asks in a shrill voice, "Friends with benefits?" Bree can be quite feisty when she's angry.

Chris gasps then exclaims, "NO!" He puts his hand over hers, but it's quickly pushed away. He was not expecting his comment to backfire.

Everyone is slowly shifting away from this side of the table. Nick poked the bear and should be regretting it now. The only one who seems to be enjoying this is Mare. It's like her favorite tv show is on, and she's hanging on to every word.

Bree's face is the same deep red color as that *Inside Out* character with the flat top. It looks like she may blow at any time. Chris keeps opening and closing his mouth as if he's tongue-tied. He's probably afraid to say anything else that may be taken the wrong way. But he should know not to call a girl a friend after he has kissed her—especially in front of his girlfriend.

To avoid another bathroom scene like the one on the first day of school, I assure Bree that Kate is not a threat to her, and nothing is going on behind her back. "Kate LOVES boarding school. I had to beg her to come home over the break. She wanted her parents to go to New York so she can spend Christmas with her boyfriend."

Bree's eyes open wide and then she asks,

"So . . . Kate doesn't like Chris. There's nothing going on? It was just a stupid dare?"

I place my hand on top of hers in another attempt to calm her. "Yes, it was just a dare—nothing else. Chris wanted to get through to Ivy that they were not getting back together, and it worked. Ivy left him alone the rest of the summer. Ivy started focusing on Chris again after seeing him with you. Chris never looked at Ivy the way he looks at you, and you had only just met. It drove her crazy."

Chris exhales slowly, knowing this should be sufficient to ease her concerns. He opens his mouth like he's about to add something, but to ensure he doesn't say anything stupid and have this conversation derail, I add, "Bree, you will like her. She is so much fun. I'll introduce you over winter break. We all can get together, well minus Ivy."

Nick's weight shifts back toward me, surprised by my comment since I have never excluded someone before. Mare moves with him, noticing his attention is no longer on her. She puts her hand high up on his thigh and squeezes, making him jerk up in his seat, and smiles as she sees my eyes on her hand.

Beet red in the face, Nick pushes her hand off and leans back. Once Nick's attention is away from me, she changes the subject to one she feels she can control. "Kelsey, you missed a lot last weekend."

I doubt Mare has anything of substance to report, but I play along. "Really Mare, what?"

Mare clears her throat to ensure she has everyone's attention, then grins as if she has life-altering news to share. "We were at a bonfire down by the lake. Some upperclassmen were there and several kids were vaping, as usual. The guys convinced Brandon to try it. He was having a good time joking about the quarterback, you know the one whose pants were pulled down during the game? Then, Brandon's eyes rolled back in his head, and he fell off the log. Foam came out of his mouth and his whole body convulsed. Most of the kids ran off since we were on private property, and they didn't want to get busted, but Nick stayed behind and waved the paramedics into the woods. Isn't that so sweet of him?" Mare pats his hand on the table. Nick looks down and shifts his weight away from her.

Mare is sickeningly smug about how she and Nick responded and is completely ignoring the fact that someone was hurt. Her small, beady eyes glimmer under the heat lamps expecting praise.

Nick looks too upset to talk so I turn back to his conceited girlfriend and inquire, "Mare, is he okay?"

She shrugs as if it doesn't matter.

Nick answers for her, "Kels, we haven't heard anything."

Mare places her hand on Nick's chest to stop him from leaning toward me and flippantly announces, "The video is all over social media. He's going to lose his college scholarship."

My head shoots back. "What? Instead of helping, they recorded him having a seizure? That is horrific! Who did it?"

Mare snorts, not caring at all about this and somewhat enjoying my reaction to the awful news. "The guy from Chase who also wanted that football scholarship, of course. It looks like he's going to get it now. No college wants someone who may be epileptic."

"Oh. My. God. What an ass! How could someone do that to someone else? The colleges have to see through this. He made one mistake. It's all over the news that the e-cigarettes are tainted with something. They need to know it's *not* his fault. They can't take this opportunity from him." Luckily the restaurant is empty or the entire patio would have been looking at me after that loud tirade.

Mare scoffs then responds callously, "It doesn't matter. His football scholarship is gone."

I look down. He does NOT deserve this. One stupid mistake and he can't go to college. Mare is being a total bitch about this.

I sink into my chair, so upset this happened to such a good guy. The words just flow out of me as if I had planned out what to say in advance. "Wow, Mare you could have a little more compassion. He is a seriously nice guy and has worked so hard for this. He's always the first one on the field before practice. We would stretch together sometimes. I remember him being so nervous about the scout coming to see him. It was his chance to be the first one in his family to go to college. Your parents can afford to send you to college; his parents can't. This is *not* right."

Mare's eyes narrow to slits as Bree nods in agreement. Kim tears up and curls into Brian's shoulder as he soothes her. Nick reaches out his hand and places it on mine, seeing I'm visibly upset, but he quickly removes it as Mare nudges him. She irritably asks, "Why are you comforting her? She's the one who just called me an unsympathetic bitch."

Expecting Nick to sit there silently as always, he responds, "That's not what she said. She said you need to have a little more compassion, and we all know she's right. Empathy is not your thing."

Stunned, Mare's whole body freezes, then something passes through that demented brain of hers, making her face twitch into a snarl. Through clenched teeth, she coldly says, "Really Nick? I think Kelsey is the one without the empathy or any morals. She's always hitting on other girls' boyfriends."

I feel my face twist into a smile as a good comeback crosses my mind. I begin, "Mare, I do not—"

Mare peels her eyes off Nick and interrupts. "I wasn't

talking to you. What are you smiling at? You think this is funny, do you?"

My smile broadens as I answer, "You were talking about me, and I want to make it clear that I have *never* hit on someone else's boyfriend. You and Lucy are both delusional about that. Maybe you need to learn how to have a friend who's a guy . . . a real friend and not someone who you have to throw yourself at to get them to pay attention to you."

Then I throw my napkin onto the table and abruptly make my way toward the bathroom to clear my head.

I roll my eyes as I hear Bree's voice in the background echo, "Boom!"

I should have stayed home in front of the inviting fire—or just stayed at boarding school.

SIXTEEN
APPEARANCES

I ALMOST BAILED on Kim when she told me Mare was going to join us dress shopping, but decided to suck it up and be there for her. She needs someone to help her find a good dress—not one that's so tight that it may malfunction again. After all, Mare was the one who went shopping with her for Homecoming. Knowing her, she would rip apart a dress that looks really good on Kim and try to persuade her to buy something that would make her look average—if that's even possible.

It's in Mare's DNA to cut everything down to make herself look good because she can't do it on her own. Wow, I'm certainly on a roll with this new me.

Mare prances out and twirls in a forest green, flare dress expecting a compliment. When I don't say a word, she stomps her foot like a child then finally asks, "Well, how does this one look?"

Trying to be the bigger person, I respond, "Awesome. Your eyes look amazing in it. Besides, you know how Nick loves green."

Mare stares at herself in the floor to ceiling mirror, waiting for more praise but doesn't get it from me. She flounces back toward the dressing room and announces over her shoulder, "Well, I think both look good on me, but the other one fits me better."

Kim passes her as she steps out of the dressing room and gets a quick look before Mare shuts the door. "Wait, Mare, I think Kelsey is right. That one does look awesome on you. . . ." but Mare doesn't come back out or acknowledge her.

Kim shrugs her shoulders, blowing off her attitude like normal, and turns back to me, asking, "What do you think about this one on me?"

She poses in a reddish-pink dress with a plunging halter top that perfectly skims her hourglass figure. She does a half turn, showing me what makes this dress really pop. The back scoops all the way down to a couple inches above her butt in a U shape with a single fold over the edge for more drama.

For a second, I don't say anything. Kim smiles when she sees my mouth in a full circle, showing my absolute approval of this one. As I'm about to say it's perfect, Mare maliciously taunts, "I think it's too tight. You may have a repeat of Homecoming."

Kim runs her hands down the dress, attempting to smooth out the nonexistent wrinkles, looking unsure of herself for once. She heads back into the dressing room, mumbling, "I'll see if they have a bigger size."

Mare waves her hand in the air like whatever, then stalks off back to her dressing room and shouts over the door. "Fine, don't look at what I tried on. . . . I'm buying the first one."

Good for you, Mare! You are so predictable. I lower myself into the chair outside the Akris section and flip through a magazine thinking, *What am I doing here? I'm just torturing myself sitting here watching them try on dresses for a dance I'm not even going to be at, and neither of them has noticed I haven't tried on a single one for the last two hours!*

I'm about to text my mom to ask her to pick me up when Kim comes out in another dress. She's pulling at the fabric under the arms as if a wire is sticking her. I lower my phone and state the obvious, "You don't look like you will want to be in that one for more than fifteen minutes. . . . Plus, I like the other one so much better. It was not too tight. I think it fits you perfectly, and it will make Brian and all the boys drool—I'll tell him he can't act like Scooby-Doo again."

Kim stops mid-step and bends over giggling. I laugh too, imagining Brian's look when he sees her in that sexy dress. A stern lady by Gucci shushes us, and we rush back into the changing area.

Behind a covered mouth, Kim gets out the words, "Yes, he was an awful Scooby. I don't know what he was thinking on that one." Then Kim looks over her shoulder toward Mare's dressing room and states, "I totally agree. I'm getting the red one. Thanks—wait, why are you not trying anything on?"

Finally, she notices! To hide my disappointment, I turn my focus onto her red dress and run my fingers over the soft material. Casually I respond, "Oh, I'm not going. I told Hope to take Sam." Then I hand her the dress and abruptly ask, "Try this on again. I'll get some photos of you in it so you can see how amazing you look."

As I turn away, I hear a gasp, and her emphatically state, "What? You have to go!"

I continue walking back to my magazine with my head straight forward and explain, "No, everyone is claimed. Hope and Sam are dating. They should go together. I will sit this one out."

I collapse in the chair and pretend not to care. Mare exits the dressing room, acting like she didn't hear a word. Kim turns toward her with both hands covering her cheeks, looking much more distraught than I expected, and anxiously says, "Did you hear that? Kelsey's not going to the Sadie. She has to go!"

Mare narrows her eyes and purses her lips—one of her cues that she may be getting ready to bite. She poses with a hand on her hip and tilts her head before asking the pressing question. "Really, why?"

I flip through the magazine with my hair covering my face so she can't see how upset I am that she is going with the guy I'm supposed to take to this dance. I simply reply, "Hope is asking Sam. There isn't anyone else I want to take."

Mare dismisses the subject with a half-laugh, then mumbles, "Oh well, that makes sense," and she briskly walks away.

As Mare pays at the register, Kim looks beside herself. I really didn't think she would care if I went or not, especially since she would be with Brian the whole time.

Kim grabs my arms and pulls me up out of the chair, rambling, "Kels, I will help you find a date. There are tons of sophomores who want to go with you. I think Henry may like you. Let's go find you a dress. I saw a couple that will make you look like a supermodel!"

I shake my head and inform her, "No, I'm good. I don't want to go with some guy I don't know," and then sit back down.

Kim stands over me looking really upset, maybe even a little guilty, and emphatically states, "I'm going to grab a couple of those dresses. You *are* going!" And she scurries off to all the racks near the glass railing. She whips through the dresses like she's on some kind of reality show and needs to find an outfit in five minutes.

The next thing I know, I'm trying on this gorgeous silver sequin dress that fits me like a glove. Mare's mouth drops when I walk out into the main dressing area.

Kim bounces over, exclaiming how beautiful I am so everyone in the near vicinity can hear her, "I told you this one would make you look like you are on the cover of a magazine."

I can't stop smiling. It's stunning and I feel absolutely beautiful in it. I turn side to side, admiring the delicate beading shimmering in the three-way mirror.

My excitement is interrupted when Mare cackles. "You're not going to the dance, so it would be a waste of money."

Growing impatient with Mare's indifference, Kim snaps at her, "She *is* going to the dance. We will find her a date! She has to buy this dress."

Kim's right! I need to buy this, but when will I get a chance to wear it? Maybe next year? My mother is going to kill me for spending this much on a dress, especially since I don't have anywhere to wear it.

I stare down at the dangling price tag contemplating if I should pull the trigger when I hear Kim pronounce, "If you don't buy it, I will buy it for you! That dress was made for you."

Aww, she really does care! I can see it in her pleading eyes and give in. "Okay, I will get it. But it doesn't mean I'm going to the Sadie this year. I can save it for next year."

As Kim bounces up and down, she enthusiastically replies, "We will see about that!"

All three of us pile into my mom's Range Rover and turn on the heated seats. My mom glances at the dress bag over my arm and sweetly asks, "Did you find something, honey?"

Kim leans in between the two front seats and jubilantly exclaims, "Mrs. Grant, just wait until you see her in this dress! She looks absolutely AMAZING in it!"

As Kim raves about the dress, I peer around Kim to see Mare's response, and it's as expected. Her lips are pressed into a firm line so tight it looks like she swallowed her bottom lip. She can't stand someone else getting attention. If this is how she acts all the time, I can't see why anyone would want to hang out with her.

My mom peers into the rearview mirror and smiles at Kim,

enjoying seeing someone excited about me for once and says over the music, "Kels, you have to try it on for me when we get home."

I give a half-smile knowing it will be going back when she sees the price tag.

The conversation switches to our holiday plans, and before we know it, we are at Mare's cold, gray modern home that fits her personality. Not hiding her feelings, she gets out of the car, and half-heartedly says, "Mrs. Grant, thank you for the ride. Kim . . . Kels, see you at school."

As we wait for her to walk up to the front door and enter, Kim whispers, "Kelsey, you have to go to the Sadie."

I turn away from the window and quickly say, "We can talk about it later," so my mother doesn't hear about this and lay into me about not going.

Kim doesn't take the hint and replies, "No, really, you need to go."

My mother is pretending like she isn't listening, fiddling with the music, but I know she's paying attention to everything going on in the car. I fake a smile, trying to hide how upset I am about how everything has played out and lie, "I'm fine. It's not a big deal for me to go. We can get dressed up another night and go out just with the girls. This is the perfect New Year's dress."

Kim inhales deeply and then whispers, "Kels, look . . . I'm so sorry, but I have to tell you this . . . I was one of the girls who started the list. I wanted to ask Brian, and Ivy said this was the only way I would be able to take him. You know Lucy liked him then too."

I move away from Kim instantly, but she leans over further sandwiching me between her and the door. She lowers her voice so my mother can't hear what she's saying, but from the stiffness in the front seat, I can tell my mother is listening to it all.

Kim rambles like this has been on her chest for a while, and she really needs to get it off. "Mare wanted to make sure she could take Nick, so we all filled in our dates. I found out later that Ivy filled in the names of several boys next to other girls' names. I didn't have any part in that, but since I was new, I was too afraid to stand up to her. . . . I didn't realize this would cause so many issues and prevent you from being able to go. You have been such a good friend to me, and if you still want to go after this, I promise I will help you find someone else. . . . I really am sorry."

I look out the window at the passing houses, completely dumbfounded. How could Kim keep this a secret, especially after she saw how much pain it caused? I crane my neck to see if anyone is at the Willy's or Starbucks as we pass by, trying to gather my thoughts. I need to act like I don't mind and respond as if I'm in a daze, "Oh, you didn't know. I wish you had said something sooner, though. Maybe then Hope wouldn't have been so mad about it."

Kim places her hand on my knee and I turn back to see the tears in her eyes. Then Kim says softly, "I know. I have been a horrible friend. I was afraid to say anything. Ivy was so mad at Bree when she typed B.S on Snap. You know how she is!"

That I understand. I've been keeping a low profile to avoid Ivy's wrath, so I can agree with Kim on that one, but still. She should have said something.

But instead of laying into her, I let it go because Ivy played Kim too. Lucy didn't like Brian. She has never liked Brian. I manage to vaguely respond to her plea, "Yeah, I know."

Kim sits there waiting for me to say something more. To say I forgive her, but I can't give her that, at least not yet. So I deflect by asking, "Are you ready for our math test tomorrow?"

She leans back in her seat and quietly answers, "Not yet. I still need to review some things."

There's a lull as I try to think of all the math homework. I need to focus on something else to stop the tears from falling.

We pull up to Kim's house. Instead of gawking at the surroundings, my mother is focused on me. Kim places her hand on my shoulder as she reiterates her apology, "I'm so sorry. You have to go. I will help you find a date."

I look at her mother waving in the front door and respond a little too coldly, "I'll think about it. Here's your house."

Kim gives a huge sigh of defeat, then turns to my mom. "Mrs. Grant, thank you for the ride."

My mom firmly responds without looking at her. "You're welcome." Then waves at her mom like nothing is wrong and rolls down the passenger side window to say hello.

Kim slowly climbs out of the car and lumbers over to her mother, who unzips the bag to look at the dress. My mom yells, "Bye," then turns around on the driveway a little too quickly, kicking up some gravel as she heads down the long road with Christmas lights framing each tree as we pass.

Then it hits me. I really don't have many friends at school. This week I tried to make some new ones, but they're more focused on the boys. They will do whatever it takes to get the guy. So much for girls sticking together. . . . And Kate was right —Ivy set it all up. She told Kim and Mare what they needed to hear so they would willingly go along with the list so early in the year.

The salty tears stream down my cheeks as I quietly whine, "Ivy set all this up. Why does she hate me so much?"

My mother pulls over and reaches behind the seat for me. I feel a warm hand on my shoulder. "Oh honey, it's not you. It's her. She's just like her mother. You can't let her control your happiness. You should go to this dance if you want to go. There are plenty of nice boys. You can go with a friend."

I nod like she's right but don't say a word. It's so much easier for her to say this. She had plenty of guy friends back then. All my guy friends have girlfriends, so I don't have that option.

I feel her place her hand on my knee and squeeze. Hesitantly, she tries again, saying, "I know you hate for me to give advice, but there's always that nice boy, Charlie from Chase. We know his family well. I grew up with his mom, and grandma is friends with his grandmother. You knew him when you were much younger. You actually have a lot in common. He's playing in the basketball game against Smith this weekend. It's perfect timing for you to reconnect."

I hide my face and shrug again, unsure if I really want to go to this stupid dance now. Who will I hang out with? Whose table do I want to sit at? No one's.

Then I hear my mother say in a firm voice, "Kels, look at me."

Frustrated, I raise my head toward the ceiling then look at her.

In a very serious tone, she says, "Are you going to let one night define you? One dance break you? I hope not. You're worth more than that."

I bite my lower lip to fight the tears from coming again. She's right. Ivy is not going to win this. I love to dance and have been looking forward to going to my first big dance in high school. Even though it will not be with Nick, there are plenty of nice guys I can take. My soccer friends know a ton of guys if it doesn't work out with Charlie.

I take the tissue from my mom to wipe my nose, then I straighten my back, and text Bree.

Bree ur brother goes to Chase right? Wanna go with me to the game on Friday?

Sure! He's been injured but may play in this game.

Excellent. I have someone to sit with and won't feel like a stalker. *Great! Let's meet there after the JV game?*

Bree responds pretty quickly. *That works. Something up?*

I bite down hard on my lip, almost drawing blood, debating if I should say something about Kim, but knowing Bree, she will overreact and say something harsh. Kim seemed pretty upset about it already, and I don't want or need any more drama. It's not worth it.

My fingers whip across the screen, and I hit send. *Nope all good. See you tomorrow!*

SEVENTEEN
RIVALS

I HEARD the Chase Hamilton Center, nicknamed the Ham, cost more than sixty million to build. Now I understand why. There's one main arena with a gorgeous basketball court surrounded by stadium seating. Easily two hundred fans can comfortably watch a game. The four additional practice courts are behind the arena.

With this much space, all the various Smith teams could practice at the same time right after school. No more 5 a.m. practices. I bet there will be another capital campaign after seeing this piece of work. The schools all seem to be vying for the city's elite. And if that's not reason enough, the smell of stale, dirty socks in our old gym should convince them to raise money for a new sports complex.

I follow the signs for the guest seating and find myself behind a large crowd gathered in the upper lobby, eagerly waiting for the junior varsity parents to move so they can fill in the stands for the varsity game. I ease my way to the railing and see Nick, Chris, and some other basketball players watching the varsity guys warm up. Smith is on one side in red, and Chase is on the other in a sea of yellow.

The metal slats rattle as I make my way down the stairs. I slide by several parents to stand in between Nick and a rotund man, who's camped out next to the railing, hollering at his son to meet him at the concessions. For no apparent reason, the guy sticks his butt out and launches me right into Nick. Sweat transfers from his arm onto mine. So gross . . .

I peel my arm off and roll to the side but can only move a couple inches away. I'm sandwiched in like a sardine. Nick stiffens and turns to see who is smashed against him and being used as a towel. He smiles as soon as he sees it's me but doesn't move over.

The man hears my grunt and shifts his weight forward. I'm about to wipe my arm on the back of my navy wool top and jeans but abruptly stop as I remember I need to look presentable tonight. Sweat stains will not make the best first impression.

I spot Nick's towel on the seat and pick it up by the corner, hoping it's dry. Nick scoots back a little, looking amused as I frantically scrub the film off my arm.

Nick taunts, "Kels, I don't have cooties."

"I know, but your sweat is slimy," I say without looking up. When my arm turns a little pink, I hand it back to him and remark, "It's all yours," then shuffle by him to take the open seat next to Chris.

Chris greets me while still staring at the guys practicing. "Hey, Kels."

"Hey Chris, where's Bree?"

He peels his eyes from the court, then scans the crowd above before responding. "She should be here any minute. She went to get us drinks."

"So, how was the game?" I ask casually, trying to ease my rising nerves.

Still pumped with adrenaline, Nick brags, "We won in overtime. Chris sank a three-pointer for the win."

"Congrats. Sorry I missed it."

Nick stops wiping the sweat off of his forehead and asks in a voice that almost sounds a little hurt, "You only came to watch the varsity team?"

"Yeah, I couldn't get here in time for your game. Sorry. . . . Are you all going to stay and watch too?"

Nick glances around to make sure no one is listening, then mumbles, "Yep, I want to see how good this Charlie guy is that Clayton keeps talking about. He's worried Charlie may be a higher pick for Duke."

Nick can't be talking about the Charlie I'm supposed to meet tonight. My mother must be crazy to think the star of their varsity team would go out with a freshman. I change the subject, so I don't break into a sweat. "Is Mare meeting you here?"

Nick points over to the back stands and exhales sharply. "Yeah, she watched my game and now wants to go get some pizza. I'm sure she will be over here shortly asking to leave, but I want to watch this game. She can go without me. I don't need to be with her twenty-four hours a day!"

Nick looks at me, expecting a response, but all I offer is a shrug. What am I supposed to say to that? I can't win either way.

Bree appears with four water bottles balancing in between her hands. I move closer to Nick to make room for her, and she gets settled just in time to hear them announce the starting players. The Chase guys run onto the court one by one. Her brother, Dave, is called first, followed by Charlie, who is number seventeen—my lucky number.

I don't hear any other names after that. I watch Charlie high five all the other players as they run onto the court, and my heart stops for a moment. He has this confident swagger that's adorable. And he's the best looking guy I've ever seen—by far. No wonder all the girls are calling his name across the court.

Bree nudges me and says, "I know," then tilts her head toward Charlie, and I realize I've been busted staring.

Clayton, our best player, and another guy get into a lunge position. The whistle blows and they spring over seven feet into the air. The ball is tipped toward Charlie. His long muscular arms snag the ball and he drives toward the goal. Charlie's chiseled physique glides across the court. Limber and quick. He stops short of the basket and sinks it in for two points. The only thing that would have been better is if he had dunked the ball.

Smith throws it in, Austin dribbles the ball slowly down the court and yells at the guys to set up for the play. He passes the ball to Sam, but Charlie intercepts the pass and charges down the court to lay the ball up on the glass for another two points.

Nick boos. "Come on guys!"

The girls on the Chase side continue to cheer for their team captain. "Go Charlie!"

I think I'm going to be sick. What was my mother thinking? There is no way he's even going to look at me. But then he does. I catch him looking over when the ball is right in front of me and about to be thrown in.

Bree notices it too and bumps my knee. I ignore her. She cannot know I'm supposed to meet him. She will laugh, and I don't need to hear it right now.

Clayton picks up on Charlie's pattern to drive down the middle and moves more toward the top of the key to block him. But Charlie adjusts and is able to continue scoring. Smith gets into a rhythm and is able to keep up.

After half time, the game gets more intense. There's lots of trash talk on the sidelines. Nick can't sit still. Bree is biting her nails.

It's tied with one minute left. Charlie dribbles the ball down, passes to Bree's brother, then Charlie flies under the goal. Dave passes him the ball back, Charlie jumps up, drops the ball into the hoop and comes crashing back down, knocking a boy backwards. No foul is called.

Smith goes down and scores a three-pointer, for a one-point lead. Charlie slowly takes the ball down, drives in the middle, but is shoved over before he can shoot. He takes two free throws, which he swooshes. Chase is up by one.

The Chase girls cheer. Smith is yelling for Clayton to dunk the ball.

Smith slows the game down to take some time off the clock. Eighteen seconds left. Austin bounce passes to Sam. Clayton moves to the key but is blocked. Charlie keeps up with the guy he's guarding, preventing Sam from throwing him the ball.

Sam is forced to dribble down the lane but is double teamed in the corner. We scream, "Shoot the ball!" Five, four, three seconds to go. Sam bounce passes through a Chase defender's legs to Clayton, then Clayton heaves the ball into the air for a Hail Mary. It goes around the rim and out. The buzzer blows, Chase wins 52 to 51. The yellow crowd rushes onto the court, screaming.

Bree is silent. She doesn't want to say a word against Smith, but her look shows she is proud of her brother. He shut Clayton down several times. I pat her on the shoulder and whisper, "Bree, Dave played well."

She lifts her chin and nods appreciatively.

Nick slaps his sweaty towel against the metal handrail and snickers, "Damn. Charlie is as good as they say he is."

Then Bree eggs Nick on by saying, "Yeah, he's really good at everything I hear."

Nick rolls his eyes in disgust. He is such a sore loser. He grabs his water bottle and throws on his Smith sweatshirt in a huff. He puts two fingers to his forehead and motions like he is giving a salute, then says, "Well, see you all later. I'm heading out."

Thank God he's leaving. I don't want to hear the comments

from him or get drilled with questions. I follow Nick up the stairs and say a quick goodbye. Mare is waiting in the lobby after getting some pizza with Ivy. She doesn't even see Nick approach; she's too engrossed in her conversation with Henry and Sam, who are both sophomores. Ivy is twirling her hair around her finger, hanging on their every word, and the guys seem to love it.

EIGHTEEN
THE SETUP

MY MOTHER IS WAITING at the top of the stands to walk over to the other side. Parents around us are complaining about the awful call resulting in the free throws. Saying they're disappointed is an understatement. Clayton was supposed to be our ringer, but he did not look too impressive out there, especially compared to Charlie.

We make it over to the other side after chatting with several parents along the way. I spot Charlie's mother, Mrs. Brooks, in the corner talking to another absolutely stunning mom. She's decked out in a gorgeous, camel hair midi skirt, cut on the bias, and a black sweater with animal print cuffs that are pushed up to her elbows.

A simple but elegant gold interlocking chain falls in between her surgically enhanced chest. Her diamond stud earrings are large enough for me to notice 15 feet away.

She can't seem to stay still. It looks like she's freezing since she keeps shuffling back and forth in her Christian Dior, lambskin boots. The lady points down at Mrs. Brooks' shoes. "Now I should have worn some boots like yours. My feet are killing me. Where did you get them?"

Why do women love to brag about being uncomfortable?

Mrs. Brooks looks down at her chunky low heel, black suede boots. "Oh, these are old Stuart Weitzman. They're one of my favorites. I can walk around in them all day. There's a newer version at the Weitzman store if you want to buy a pair."

The lady nods since she was just being polite. Most likely, she only wanted Mrs. Brooks to notice her new shoes, which are to die for.

Mrs. Brooks notices my mom and me standing there. Mrs. Brooks exclaims, "Oh, where are my manners? . . . Ali, this is a dear friend of mine from my youth, Jennifer and her daughter Kelsey." She motions to us and continues on with the introductions. "Jennifer, Kelsey, this is Ali Aster. Her son Dave plays with Charlie."

The striking lady narrows her eyes as she looks at me; she appears to recognize me but can't connect my name with my face. I, on the other hand, know exactly who she is. I put my hand out and give her the compliment she is yearning for. "Hello, it's nice to meet you. I was just admiring your outfit."

As she daintily shakes my hand, she turns her right leg out, kicks her heel into the air, and giggles like a schoolgirl. She loves the attention. Now I know why Bree is always dripping in labels.

I continue saying, "You must be Bree's mother. I'm a friend of hers from Smith."

Her face lights up like a light bulb went off in her head. Before I know it, she grabs both of my wrists and acts like we have known each other forever. "Of course, I knew I recognized you from all the pictures Bree shows me of her friends. How are you?"

I enthusiastically answer, "Fine. Thank you. I'm so glad Bree came to Smith. She—" But Mrs. Aster isn't listening. She has moved on to meet my mother.

"Jennifer, it's so nice to meet you. I saw you in the *Homes &*

Lifestyles Magazine. Congrats on being named the city's top designer."

My mother demurely smiles. She knows what's coming next.

"I would love for you to come over and tell me what I need to do with my house. We hired another designer a couple years ago, and I think we may be due for a refresh."

My mother nods. "Of course, I'm happy to come by. I have enjoyed getting to know your daughter. Bree is such a delightful young lady. She always looks so put together."

Mrs. Aster wrinkles her nose and suddenly looks away. No one says anything for a moment. My mother is completely caught off guard by her response.

To get rid of the awkward silence, I compliment her son. "Dave played very well, even through the pain. I only noticed him limp once or twice, probably because I was looking for it. Bree told me he twisted his ankle."

She smiles as I go on about Dave but is still distracted; she keeps peering over my shoulder. "Thanks. He is such a good player. Speak of the devil . . . there he is. I need to grab him before he invites all those girls over. Jennifer, I will call you about looking at our house. Bye-bye." Then she whisks off.

Mrs. Brooks and my mother are not bothered in the least that she left so quickly. But I am. What is up with her response after Bree was called a delightful young lady? Why didn't she want to hear more about her daughter? Maybe this is why Bree hasn't asked me to come over? She always wants to hang at my house.

My mom and Mrs. Brooks continue to reminisce about the old days. The longer I stand here, the more nervous I feel. I look around the gym, and it's pretty empty except for the girls waiting by the locker room doors.

Mrs. Brooks clears her throat and asks, "How is school going?"

I shrug and politely answer her question, "Fine. I'm adjusting to all the homework and what's expected of us at school. . . . How are you? Charlie played great tonight. He really won the game for them."

Her eyes twinkle and she giggles under a covered mouth. "I wouldn't say that, but he played well. He suspected scouts were out tonight to look at Clayton so he played extra hard."

She is the exact opposite of Mrs. Aster. Kind. Modest. Not flashy at all. She's dressed for a basketball game rather than a fashion show in her tailored, slim black corduroy slacks, a faded black sweater, and camel colored puffer vest.

My mother pats Mrs. Brooks on the arm and is back discussing the old times with fondness. "Charlie reminds me of John. I still remember his teammates carrying him off the court after he sank those two free throws for the win at the State championship. . . . That was such a fun night. So is Charlie following in his footsteps and playing baseball too?"

Mrs. Brooks beams with pride as she answers, "Oh, yes. Charlie has been playing since he was six. John coached him for many years, and then someone who played in the majors stepped in to coach their team. It was a good thing—you know how competitive John can be. He would keep Charlie out on the field for an hour after practice if he missed one fly ball. I don't think Charlie would still be playing if that other coach didn't volunteer to take over the team."

That sounds so familiar. My father would keep me on the field for hours after my practice. We would not leave until the sun went down. *Maybe all fathers are like this?*

My thoughts about being pushed by parents are interrupted by the hollow echo of the gym doors opening. Charlie exits and high fives some of his teammates as they separate. Within minutes, girls crowd around Charlie, desperately trying to get his attention. They madly giggle as they tell him how great he is, acting like he's some kind of celebrity.

He smiles and nods as he continues to walk by them, except when he sees one petite girl with auburn hair. She grabs his arm, but he pulls free and keeps on walking with a stern look on his face. God, he even looks good with a grimace.

Mrs. Brooks gives him a bear hug and congratulates him. "Good game. You played well."

Charlie blushes slightly from the motherly attention, mumbling, "Thanks Mom," then eagerly asks, "Where's Dad?"

She quickly dismisses the question. "Oh, he had to leave right before the game ended. Some work thing. He commented on how well you played before he left. You should be proud of yourself."

Charlie's lower lip disappears for a second, then he replies with less enthusiasm, "Thanks. The game could have gone either way in the end though."

Seeming to want to change the subject, Mrs. Brooks turns her attention to us. With a swift swoop of her hand across her chest, she presents us as if we are royalty. "Do you remember my friend from childhood, Jennifer Grant?"

Charlie gives my mom a firm, confident handshake and stares her directly in the eyes as he greets her, "Hello, Mrs. Grant. It's nice to see you."

Then Charlie looks at me apprehensively. It's obvious he knows this is a set up. I tilt my head downward, shift my gaze to the left, and then back at him. Feeling the butterflies flutter, I nervously touch my neck and then move a strand of hair behind my ear as I listen to his mom. "Charlie, this is Kelsey Grant. She goes to Smith. When you were much younger, you all played at the beach together the week your grandmother rented that house for the entire family to celebrate her big birthday."

Charlie lifts an eyebrow over his dreamy, bright blue eyes, and with the most adorable lopsided grin, he says, "Oh yeah, I remember now. How are you, Kelsey?"

I really can't look at him. He's the type of guy every girl stares at in the hall. In fact, several girls are looking at him right now. I try to smile with confidence but know it's more of a simper and manage to respond, "I'm good. You played well. You—" Then nervously giggle, not able to come up with anything else to add.

I look past Charlie, toward Bree's brother and that auburn hair girl, who has not taken her eyes off of him, and then divert my eyes back to Charlie with enough time to see his reaction.

Charlie looks over his shoulder, then back at me, and politely says, "Thanks." Then he angles his body away from me and toward the door. He's lost interest. I'm completely blowing it.

Very casually, he says, "Mom, I'm heading to Dave's house. See you around midnight."

I hear my mother sigh in disappointment as I feel a dull, sinking sensation in my stomach. I knew he would not be interested in a freshman.

But Mrs. Brooks doesn't let him off that easily. She pipes up, asking, "Oh, can you take Kelsey home first? I'm going to grab a drink with Jennifer."

Charlie purses his lips and straightens his posture, almost like an enlisted soldier who receives an order from his commanding officer. Then curtly responds, "Sure, happy to drive her."

As he pulls his keys out of his pocket, Mrs. Brooks looks at his bare legs and mothers him. "Umm . . . Charlie, it's freezing outside. Please go put on some sweat pants and your sweatshirt."

He rolls his eyes about being treated like a little kid but doesn't argue. He mumbles, "Sure, Mom," then strides over to the bleachers, away from the crowd of girls, and drops his navy backpack to pull out his clothes. I can't stop staring. He could rival the sculpture of David, cut at every edge. He looks more like a man than the scrawny boys in my class. As he leans over, I can see the side indentions on each cheek.

He kicks off his basketball shoes and pulls on his sweatpants. His basketball shorts rise up as he pulls on the pants, briefly flashing the distinct line of his upper quad.

As several girls rush to his side and ask him questions about what he's doing tonight, I turn my head so I can hear his answers. "No, I can't go tonight—No, I have to take someone home and won't make it." And I cringe hearing the annoyance in his voice.

They continue to bombard him with questions as he pulls his Chase basketball sweatshirt over his broad shoulders. I watch him move his neck side to side, then in a circular motion to ease the tension. As he softly says, "Goodbye," to the swarming girls, he grabs his backpack by the top handle. Within seconds he is by my side, muttering, "Ready to go?"

I nod slowly and force out a smile, but he doesn't see it since he has already turned back to my mom, saying, "It was so nice to see you again. I'll get your daughter home safely."

My mother puts her hand on his shoulder like they have known each other forever, and in her sugary sweet voice, she says, "Thank you, Charlie. Hopefully, you and Kels can catch up in the car."

I fight the urge to roll my eyes. Does she have to be so obvious? This is embarrassing enough.

Charlie nods like he's in agreement but doesn't say anything back to her. Instead, he moves on to address his mom in an equally sweet voice that just rolls off his tongue, "Mom, you know that unless you extend my curfew, I won't have enough time to go to Dave's and celebrate the win. This is a big night for us. I would really appreciate it if I can have another hour to be with my friends."

I want to die when my mom interjects and invites me along.

"Well, you can always take Kelsey with you. I'm sure she would love to meet your friends."

Seeing Charlie's shocked face, I throw him a lifeline. "Mom, I'm sure he wants to celebrate with *his* friends and not have some girl he barely knows tag along." But deep down, I'm hoping for another shot at making a better impression.

Charlie quickly adds, "Of course, she's welcome to come. We can talk about it in the car."

Then he looks at his mother to see if she is going to give in and from the amused look on her face, I think she may agree, but then she says, "Nice try. It's not even 10 o'clock yet, so you have plenty of time to take Kelsey to that party and introduce her to your friends. See you at midnight."

He quickly wipes the disappointment from his face and forces a smile. He extends his arm toward the door, showing me the way out, as he says in a resigned voice, "Okay after you, Kelsey."

I move quickly, knowing he's being forced to do this. He doesn't want to be here with me. I knew this would be a waste of time—and a let down. He follows me until we reach the doors, where he insists on opening them for me, acting like the perfect gentleman even though he's being punished.

The cold bites at my face and fingers, but I ignore it, trying to figure out how to stop this downward spiral. Even though he's right next to me, I feel like he's a mile away.

As we walk in silence, I will myself to feel bold, just like I did at boarding school. I talked to so many guys and had so much fun up there. Granted, none of them look quite like Charlie. Honestly, I've never met a guy like him. He has this presence that's intoxicating. I breathe in his scent—a citrusy blend of orange, sweet cinnamon, and ginger mixed with a little sweat. Not overwhelming but still intense.

To break the ice, I say, "Charlie, listen, I'm sorry about this.

We don't have to go to the party. You can drop me off if you want to hang with your friends."

With his head low and his hands tucked into his sweatshirt pockets, he peers up at me with a mischievous grin, then says, "So you *do* want to talk to me?"

I stare at him, surprised by his jest and as calmly as possible reply, "Yes . . . sorry, but it was a little awkward back there."

As he holds the door open for me, he agrees, "Yep, it seems like our moms have been scheming."

"Just a little," I tease back and climb in.

As Charlie walks around the hood of the car, I watch him and wonder if he will take me to the party or not. I feel like it may be a possibility after seeing how he looked at me when he shut my door. He actually gave me a real smile.

He throws his backpack in the back seat, leans over and turns on my heated seat and his, then blows on his hands to warm them up. Then he cranks the car on and the *Rocky* soundtrack plays over the speakers. Embarrassed, he grabs his phone to change it from "Eye of the Tiger."

I put my hand out to block him and say, "Don't turn it off. I love that song. We should listen to 'Gonna Fly Now' to celebrate your win. Or I can find classics like 'We are the Champions' and 'Simply the Best.'"

"'Simply the Best'? I don't know that one," he says with a smirk as he puts the car in reverse.

"It's Tina Turner, so you probably wouldn't know it," I add.

Then he hands me his phone and teases, "Let's see how good of taste you have in music."

"You will need to add more of these to your playlist," I tease back.

As I scan his library to see what he likes to listen to, I hear him nonchalantly ask, "So you're friends with Dave's sister, Bree?"

I quickly respond without looking up. "Yes, she's one of my best friends."

I grab the door handle as Charlie turns the wheel sharply to pull out of the parking lot and avoid a car whipping into the middle lane toward us. When we're in the clear, he asks, "So have you seen their basement? They have a basketball court and a huge theater room!"

"No, actually, I have never been to their house. I met her mom for the first time tonight. Bree always comes over to my house for some reason."

His voice drops a little as he asks, "So, you don't know Dave then?"

Where is this coming from? I lean away from the window and tilt my head to the side. "No, I've never met him. I just saw him for the first time tonight. Why do you ask?"

We pull up to a light and Charlie leans onto the steering wheel. He intently watches my expression as he states, "The girls seem to like him."

I don't even think before I respond. "Really? I guess I can see that."

Charlie flinches, then comments, "You were staring at him."

I did look at Dave but only because I was too nervous to look at Charlie, but I'm not about to admit that. I stop myself from smiling about the fact he noticed and eagerly inquire, "Why do you ask?"

Matter of factly, he says, "Just seeing if I have competition."

Competition for what? I let out a little giggle and say what I'm thinking for once. "I doubt you have *any* competition."

Charlie's shoulders seem to relax and a broad smile crosses his face.

Needing to know where this is going, I inquire, "So why would you think I like Dave?"

Charlie plainly answers as he turns onto the main road. "It looked like you were focused on *him* when we first met."

I glance down at my hands. Everyone tells me I never act interested and need to be more direct. This is my chance to change that—to make sure he doesn't get the wrong idea. I muster the courage and say, "Nope. I'm happy to be here with you."

As soon as I utter those words, the butterflies ease and things seem to get lighter in the car. I glance over at him and he's looking right at me with a wickedly, contagious grin. I feel my cheek muscles raise in response.

He mumbles under his breath, "Good," and then adds at a higher decibel, "So, how is Bree doing? I hope she's happier at Smith. The Chase girls in that grade are the meanest in the school, and that's saying something."

Ahhh, that's so sweet of him. I lean in closer with my elbow on the console and relay, "Yeah, I think she's happy. She avoids the drama. She and Chris spend most of their time together when we're not hanging out."

Charlie chuckles and remarks, "Yeah, it looks like you got some aggressive ones at Smith too."

I hesitate before answering, wondering where this is coming from and if he has heard about Ivy or Mare. I casually ask, "Have you met some of the girls in my grade?"

He slides his hands across the wheel again and says, "Yeah, after your Homecoming. We picked Bree up. You weren't there."

I clearly remember that night. Kim was not in any shape to go to the afterparty. "Yeah, I was with a friend. It was a rough night for her."

Charlie says in a low voice, "I heard her dress ripped."

How does he remember that? And I cannot believe someone shared that with him. He must have met Mare or Ivy. It figures they would talk to him.

I lean into the headrest and look out the windshield, then relay what happened that night. "Yes, she was mortified. I can't imagine what I would do if that happened to me. Bree and I shielded her on the dance floor while Chris grabbed a stray jacket. I don't think many people noticed."

Charlie looks at me sideways with one eyebrow raised. It looks like he's about to say something but second-guesses it and changes the subject. "So do you remember the beach trip?"

I tap my lip with my index finger thinking. It was so long ago, but I remember being afraid of getting stung in the water. "A little bit. I remember the sting rays—those slimy things slid right over the tops of our feet as we shuffled through the grit, trying to get to the sand bar."

Charlie hits the steering wheel and exclaims, "THAT'S RIGHT! I remember that. And then we all threw the ball in the pool with Uncle Jim. My sister sat at the edge, kicking water at us."

I giggle and can't help but add, "Yeah, you climbed over me and dunked my head underwater to get the ball. You're still super competitive, I see."

Charlie laughs some more. He has a deep, hearty laugh. "Sorry about that. I guess I'm still the same."

I look out the window at the passing storefronts and softly share, "Yeah, it was so much easier then."

I can't believe I just said that. I steal a look to see if I just blew it again, but Charlie leans in closer with his elbow on my side of the console, looking intrigued. "What do you mean by that, Kelsey?"

I lean back into the heated leather seat, then peer over at him. He has an irresistible, lopsided smile on his face begging for me to continue, and the words just flow out of me. "There wasn't a plan that you were expected to follow. We could just be kids. I'm only fifteen but expected to get perfect grades, to get into the perfect college, then the perfect grad school, and get the perfect job."

I look down at my jeans, embarrassed I just showed a weakness to someone I barely know. Someone who has it all and doesn't need to try. I force myself to look at him under my lashes. He is biting his lower lip, looking out the window. He must think I'm nuts.

I nervously say, "I'm so sorry, I can't believe I just said that. I'm sure it's not the same for you. It looks like everything is easy for you."

Charlie pulls over to the side street and stops. He leans back and looks up through the sunroof. "Actually, it's not, I know how you feel. I think our parents had to work so much harder than everyone else, and they expect us to do the same. No mistakes allowed. We have to be better so we can compete with all these other kids with money and connections."

He taps his fingers on the steering wheel, debating something. Then he gives me an adorable look and asks, "So you want to stop by Starbucks before we go to the party? I need some caffeine."

I breathe a sigh of relief, and am able to formulate the word. "Sure."

Five minutes later, Charlie opens my car door and then the door into Starbucks, being the perfect gentleman. The younger girl behind the register straightens her visor and smooths out her shirt before we walk to the counter. She leans close, eager to take our order or maybe just to get closer to Charlie. I expect to see a heart shape on top of his coffee with her number written on the side.

Totally oblivious to her reaction, Charlie clicks his thumbnail with his ring finger, debating what to order. Could he be nervous or does he do that when he is thinking? He leans over toward me, still evaluating the choices. "What do you want?"

I nudge him in the shoulder. "A tall pumpkin spice latte, of course."

Charlie nudges me back, with a little flirtation in his voice. "That's it?"

The girl behind the counter rolls her eyes and I beam. "Yes."

Charlie shrugs. "That's easy enough."

He turns back and faces the Starbucks girl to order, and she sucks in her stomach. Again, he doesn't seem to notice.

"We would like a tall pumpkin spice latte and a double espresso with bacon and gruyere sous vide bites."

I pull out my credit card, but he lowers my hand, shaking his head no.

I thank him and scan the room for an open seat. I spot a club chair and loveseat toward the front and bolt to grab them before they are taken. The sofa squeaks a bit as I sit down, tilting me toward the middle. I grab the newspaper and skim the New York Times while I wait for Charlie.

A cold gust of air blows into the drafty store. This is why I don't like this Starbucks. The Caribou coffee is much nicer with plenty of seating and a fire. Oh, sitting in front of a warm fire with him right now sounds amazing.

I slide toward the middle of the sofa as someone sits down on the other side. Expecting to see Charlie, I look up and am about to thank him for the drink again, but it's only Tyler, Virginia's boyfriend. He looks rough—really rough. His dark, brown hair is standing up and it seems like he has not showered in a day or two. His green and blue plaid shirt is half-tucked in his jeans.

As I feel something warm slide on my knee, I look down at his slightly trembling hand and back up at him. What is he doing? Then he leans in closer and gruffly slurs, "Kels, I haven't seen you in a while. Not since soccer ended. How've you been?" Oh, he has been drinking whiskey.

I scoot further toward the sofa arm and his hand falls onto the stained pleather. While leaning as far away from him as possible, I answer, "All good. How's Virginia?"

Just then, a pumpkin spice latte with a heart on top slides toward me and an espresso is placed on the coffee table in front of Tyler. I quickly look up and see Charlie standing over Tyler, staring down at him. Could that be jealousy on his face? Or is he just annoyed that this guy is in his seat?

Tyler tenses as I ramble on with the introductions to avoid any confrontations. "Tyler, this is Charlie. He just finished playing a basketball game against my school. He sunk two free throws for the win. Charlie, this is Tyler. He dates Virginia on my soccer team. How long have you guys been going out—a year now?"

Tyler ignores the question. Instead, he makes himself more comfortable by resting his arm behind my shoulders and motions to Charlie to sit in the empty seat next to him. Charlie does not budge from his spot and Tyler does not break eye contact, but he does break the silence. "Have you seen her play yet? I'm one of her biggest fans."

Then Tyler glances over at me and squeezes my tense shoulder. "We should go get some ice cream sometime soon, Kels. It doesn't need to be reserved for only after a game."

My mouth opens slightly, but nothing comes out. I really don't know what has gotten into him. I lean forward to reach for the steaming pumpkin spice latte, take a sip, and then perch myself on the edge of the seat, so his arm is not near me.

Charlie crosses his arms on his chest, staring directly at him. Why isn't Tyler getting the hint he's in Charlie's seat?

Feeling the tension get to a point where there might be a real problem, I lift myself from the squeaky loveseat, careful to not spill my latte, and finish this conversation. "Tyler, I'm moving so Virginia can have my seat when she gets here. Charlie and I are going to sit over at that free table near the counter."

As I stride away, I hear him say, "No, Virginia's not meeting me. We broke up two days ago. I'll see you around, Kels."

So that's why he looks like a train hit him! I look over my shoulder and offer my sympathy. "Sorry to hear that. You guys were cute together."

Charlie follows me to the small bistro table. It's louder over here being so close to the machines but much better than staying put and watching the guys size each other up.

Charlie takes his seat and leans forward so I can hear him. "What was that about?"

I shrug, offering very little. "I have no idea. He's not his usual self and looks awful. He must be devastated Virginia dumped him since they dated so long."

Charlie takes a sip of his espresso and then digs into the sous vide bites, polishing them off in about 15 seconds. "Sorry, I'm starved. Maybe I should have ordered two more of these."

He studies me for a second, his fingers drumming on his thigh. "Not that you would have any trouble finding a date." He points behind him at Tyler. "But I hear you want to go to the Sadie. Want to go with me?"

Now, this is unexpected. I fight the urge to grin and revert back to my normal self-preservation mechanism and deflect. "You're direct. Don't juniors skip the Sadie?"

He leans in so close I can smell the bacon and cheese on his breath. "Yeah, I probably won't know anyone, but I think we could have fun."

He can't seriously want to go to this, so I daringly question him. "Did your parents put you up to this?"

Charlie peers into my downcast eyes, and then slowly moves his hands closer to mine, so our fingers almost touch on the table. "Yeah, but I said I wouldn't mention it if I didn't want to go with you."

Sarcastically I respond, "Oh, I guess I should take that as a compliment?"

He leans back, looking a little put-off. "Yes, you should."

Okay, I need to lay off the sarcasm and not blow this again. I think about it, smile and say, "You're right. It's a compliment, and I would love to go with you if you truly want to go."

Charlie claps his hands together and smiles—a smile so full

that his eyes curve into half-moons. "Then it's set. So do you have plans tomorrow night?"

Did I hear that correctly? He wants to get together tomorrow—the first day of winter break? I pretend to be going over my busy schedule in my head and answer, "Actually I do. Kate, my best friend, is coming back from boarding school."

Charlie tents his fingers together, thinking. "How about I bring a friend, and we all go out? Unless you just want to hang out with Kate and catch up?"

This is perfect. Kate can tell me if he is into me or doing my family a favor. A little too enthusiastically, I accept. "YES, that sounds fun. Her flight gets in around two. We can meet you anytime after four. What are you thinking?"

Charlie leans forward, with a glint in his eye, and gently places his surprisingly soft hand over mine. "I'll come up with something fun for us to do." He flashes another dreamy smile, and I melt.

We continue chatting about random things. Charlie shares some things about his childhood and I do about mine. I hold onto every word, and it seems like he's listening to all of mine. We move from subject to subject with ease, and it doesn't feel like we need to try. It just feels right—almost like we've known each other forever.

As I'm telling him about my last soccer game, Charlie's watch beeps. He looks down and a worried look crosses his face. "What time do you need to be home?"

I look at my watch in disbelief and blurt out, "Midnight!"

Charlie downs his third espresso, then exclaims, "We need to go. I'm going to be late too." He stands up and pulls the table forward so I can easily get out. I bus the table quickly and follow behind him. As we pass the loveseat in the middle, I notice Tyler is gone. I never even saw him leave.

In the parking lot, he opens my door and then moves closer as I hesitate to get in. I feel my breath catch as it looks like he may kiss me, but then he motions for me to get in with his hand and remarks, "We're so late. At least my mom won't be upset this time since we decided to hang out and not go to the party. Please text your mom while I'm driving to let her know we lost track of time and are heading home. Ask her to text my mom too. Otherwise, you may not see me the rest of the holiday for breaking curfew."

Unable to speak with him so close to me, I nod yes and then climb into the passenger seat. I think I would say yes to everything he asks.

NINETEEN

LEXINGTON

As I make my way up the long flagstone path to Kate Lexington's grand Tudor home, the wind whips around the corner and right through the chunky holes of my gray sweater, making me regret my choice of clothes. I kneel down in front of several massive boxwoods and wait for the blistering blast to pass then race to the stoop to ring the antique brass bell.

I stare at the ornate carvings on the front door and then ring the bell again. Remembering that the buzzer wasn't working last summer, I pull the cold iron ring back and let it drop with a thud on the wood. Someone please answer the door!

The door creaks open and Senator Lexington appears. My body freezes but I manage to get the words out. "Hello, Mrs. Lexington.... I didn't think you'd be home."

Instead of asking me to leave, Mrs. Lexington wraps me in a warm embrace like I'm her second daughter. Then holds me at arm's length and says, "Let me look at you. You really have changed in the past few months. You could easily pass for a college girl now."

I sigh in relief and respond, "Thank you, Mrs. Lexington. You look good too. I've missed seeing you."

Noticing my chattering teeth, she whisks me inside. "Come in! Kate's not back yet. Her flight was delayed."

I hesitate under the mirrored glass bell jar and utter, "Oh, I can come back later."

While waving for me to follow her, she says, "Don't be silly. Stay! She should be here shortly. . . . Would you like something to drink? I think I have a can of your favorite flavor of Spindrift. Mr. Lexington has been drinking a lot of the mango ones lately."

I kick off my boots next to her red bottom heels and walk behind her into the cozy gray-green kitchen. She motions for me to sit down at what used to be my normal stool still tucked under the marble island. Mrs. Lexington leans down and grabs a can from the beverage cooler.

She has on a gorgeous black Armani suit with a white silk shirt underneath. Her blonde hair is in a sophisticated bun right above her neck. No wonder all her constituents are enchanted by her.

As I accept the can, I say in a raspy voice, "Thank you. How is your campaign going?"

A triumphant smile crosses her face revealing the faint crow's feet around her crystal blue eyes. "Never a dull moment. My opponent just called to let me know he plans to drop out of the race tomorrow. . . . How is school going?"

I take a sip of the drink and nervously reply, "This year has been an adjustment. It's so weird not having Kate there. I have made some new friends who I spend most of my time with at school. Most of the friend groups have changed."

Senator Lexington picks up on my unease and examines me, "What about Ivy? Do you not hang out with her anymore?"

Before I consider what I'm about to say, I blurt, "NO! After what she did to Kate and how she has treated me. We really don't talk anymore."

Mrs. Lexington slowly picks up the cut-glass tumbler on the counter, swirls the brown liquid, then takes a long pull of her scotch. She lets out a sigh and then lowers her elbows onto the slab, so she is at the same level as me.

She politely asks, "What did she do to Kate?" Even though her voice is as sweet as pie, I can feel she is ready to go full attorney mode on me.

I bite my tongue and try to think about how I can close the can of worms I just opened, but her piercing stare makes me rush, and I say too much again, "Oh, I thought you knew."

She raises herself so her palms are flat on the counter and leans forward in her signature power pose, then inquires, "Know what?" And the cross-examining begins.

I open and close my mouth like a dumb goldfish, and she repeats her question, "Know what, Kelsey? What did she do to my daughter?"

I know I'm no match for her. She was one of the best litigators before she entered politics so I pull out my phone and say, "It may be best just to show you." I hit play on the video and hand my phone to the Senator.

Mrs. Lexington blows the loose strand of hair from in front of her mouth. I nervously smooth my hair and tent my fingers together to prevent myself from picking at my nails. They would certainly bleed with how anxious I am right now.

Her face changes from puzzlement to extreme anger as she glowers at the screen. After watching the video twice, she peers up at me and in a strained voice, one I have never heard from her before, and demands, "How did you get this?"

I look down at my shaking knees and quietly answer, "Your daughter sent it to me. I figured you would have seen this since Smith has a copy."

The Senator slams her palms on the island. Her clear blue eyes are ice. "What? How do you know they have a copy?"

I jump in my seat, hitting my knees on the hard stone and stammer, "Ka-Kate, ughh, Kate told me. The hotel told her Smith had one when she called, asking if there was a video. She is still trying to piece together what happened that night. Since Ivy also spiked one of my drinks at a party this fall, we think Ivy set her up."

Mrs. Lexington smooths her hair and places the loose strand behind her ear. Then she fidgets with her black, high-waisted, wool pencil skirt and purses her lips while interrogating me. "Why would Ivy do that?"

In a very low voice, almost a whimper, I answer, "Because Kate kissed Chris during a dare."

Unsure she heard me correctly, she asks again but in a much higher octave, "She did WHAT?"

At that moment, the front door slams shut, and Kate jovially yells, "I'M HOME!"

Dread sinks in my stomach as Kate bursts into the kitchen looking ready to give her mom a hug but abruptly stops in the doorway sensing something is not right. She looks at her mother and then at me. I mouth, "I am so sorry."

Mrs. Lexington does not move from her spot. Instead, she takes another swig of her scotch and in the dreaded I'm-so-disappointed-in-you tone states, "Kate, Kelsey and I just had an enlightening conversation."

Kate cautiously tilts her head to the left and peers at me while asking her mother, "Yes, and . . ."

Her mother points at the phone and states the reason for her distress. "I just watched a video of you in a very precarious position. Why didn't you show me this video or tell me that Ivy did this to you?"

Kate's lips form an O shape as her shoulders slide back allowing her to inhale more deeply, and then in a surprisingly confident tone that I would have expected from her mother, she justifies her actions, "I just received the video a week ago and planned to show you and Dad when I got home. It doesn't change anything. I'm over it and happy it happened because I got to go to boarding school. I love it there and don't want to leave. Kelsey is not happy at Smith. I don't want to go back to Smith."

Her mother's entire body relaxes as if she drank the entire bottle of scotch. She lets out a sigh and then walks over to give her daughter the long overdue hug that Kate was so excited to receive when she walked in the door. Her mother strokes Kate's long blonde hair and Kate nuzzles into her chest. Mrs. Lexington calmly affirms, "I knew you would love boarding school as much as I did. You are doing so well there. However, I wish you had talked to me about this situation with Ivy prior to your arrival."

Kate stays silent, biting her quivering lower lip, trying not to let her mother see how upset she is about this since she said she was over it. Still, her mother knows better than to believe that. The Senator holds both of Kate's shoulders and looks her square in the eye, then reassures her, "Don't worry. I will handle this. You go spend time with Kelsey. You are lucky to have such a good friend."

Mrs. Lexington turns to me and gives her best campaign smile. "Kelsey, thank you for sharing this with me. You're a true friend to my Kate. Give your mother and father my best."

Kate and I watch her move toward her office, stop at the bar and pour herself another glass of scotch, and then close the door with a sharp snap.

I put my hands over my eyes and apologize to Kate. "I am *so* sorry. I thought she knew. She kept asking me about Ivy."

Kate wraps her arms around me and surprisingly says, "No worries. I know how she is when she wants answers. Besides, you made it easier on me. I don't need to have a long conversation about this. It's over now, and you don't need to worry about Ivy anymore since my mother will take care of her." I can feel her smile on my shoulder and the tension begins to ease.

She quickly pulls away as if nothing is wrong and starts yanking me toward the stairs. "Let's go to my room. I really want to change. A guy spilled his coffee all over me on the flight."

"So that is what I smelled on you. I think there may have been something else in that drink besides coffee," I say as we bolt up a couple stairs.

Kate turns at the landing and bounds the stairs two at a time. "Yep, I think he had a couple whiskeys too. So we have a lot to catch up on. Jack is still wanting to fly in for New Year's, and maybe he will ask you to the spring fling so you can visit me again."

Kate is about to enter her room when I announce, "Well, I might have met someone."

Kate stops dead in her tracks and whips around, almost hitting the door jamb. "What? When? Kels, you have tell me all about him!"

A smile creeps across my face as I say, "Actually, he's a family friend, and we are meeting him in an hour. He's bringing a friend for you. I need for you to tell me if he's going out with me because he is being told to or if you think he likes me."

She claps her hands together and gushes, "Oh, I cannot wait. What are we going to do?"

I jump up and down like a little school girl and say, "We're going ice skating at the St. Regis. May I borrow your lucky pink wool sweater? I'm freezing in this gray one. I wore it because I thought it looked better on me but I may turn blue from being outside."

Kate tilts her head and inquires, "Lucky sweater. Since when do you need any luck?"

"I need all the luck I can get this time. He's a junior."

Kate giggles, then taunts, "You need an older guy to handle you."

"Ha ha."

Smirking at me, she asks, "So how does he compare to Nick or Jack or even Luke?"

This makes me sigh. "Well, they are very different. . . . I want to hear your thoughts before I get my hopes up."

She claps both hands together and exclaims, "This is a first! You didn't give Jack the time of day, and you have never cared about how you looked around Nick."

"I know!" And I feel the burn in my cheeks again.

"Well, tell me everything while we get ready. I want to hear it all!" Kate beams at me and all the tension from her mother's examination disappears.

TWENTY
THIN ICE

The lobby of the St. Regis hotel has been transformed into a winter wonderland. Sparkling garlands in vibrant blues and silvers swoop over the iron railings and cascade down the grand staircase. A life-size gingerbread house is tucked in a corner surrounded by overly excited children eagerly waiting for their turn to enter.

Santa peeks his head out from inside the candy-coated structure, gazes up at the clock, his white mustache curls closer to his red cheeks as he grins, and then he disappears. Mrs. Claus should be joining him shortly; the high tea upstairs ended at 4 o'clock.

Kids dart through the lobby on an obvious sugar high from all the hot cocoa and desserts. Kate dodges one girl as she bolts around us with what looks like an iced brick firmly in her hand. Her mother grabs the velvet bow on the back of her dress, and she jolts backwards. With pure exhaustion in her eyes, she scolds her daughter for ripping off a piece of the gingerbread house.

Kate and I exchange a look. This is utter chaos. We used to come to these teas many years ago. Did we behave this badly? I remember seeing several cocktails in front of the moms instead of cocoa. Hmmm . . . maybe so?

We find the safest place to park ourselves, which happens to be in front of the enormous Christmas tree. Not only does it give us a clear view of the front door, it gives me an excuse to pace. I circle the tree admiring the glittering branches covered in fake snow and Tiffany blue glass ornaments. White feathers flair out the top of the tree, almost tickling the glass chandelier above.

I carefully step around the silver and blue presents so neatly tucked around the bottom and attempt to circle for a second time.

"Kels, stop pacing—you're making me nervous!" Kate says in a serious tone, but from the smirk on her face, I know she's just giving me a hard time.

I scan the room and look toward the door. He's still not here. My heart is fluttering deep in my chest. Or are those butterflies migrating into other parts of my body. I shouldn't be this anxious. Everything felt so natural at Starbucks.

But standing here waiting for him has made me realize how much I really like him, so much more than I thought I would. What if he doesn't feel the same? It would have been so much easier to have not met him than to be rejected at this point.

"Kels, stop overthinking this. It will be fine."

"I didn't say anything!" I softly fire back, feeling exposed.

"You didn't need to say anything. It's written all over your face." She says as nicely as possible.

Do I look that bad? I peer into the glass ball on the tree and see a contorted version of my face. This isn't helpful. I turn toward the bathroom, but Kate grabs my hand.

Now the concern is written all over her face. She whispers loud enough to be heard over the Christmas carols. "Kels, you look fine. Calm down. Everything will be fine. You are worrying for no reason."

It finally sinks in that I'm overreacting once again, and I smile. I turn back toward the door, feeling more confident, and then I see him and catch my breath. He looks even better than yesterday. He is dressed in blue jeans and a fitted puffer coat that accentuates his broad shoulders. The royal blue color of his coat makes his eyes look electric.

While running his fingers through his short blond hair, he yells, "Kels! We made it." It looks like he squeezed in a hair cut.

I wave then feel someone lean in next to me.

"Kels, that's Charlie?" Kate mumbles under her breath. "He's even better looking than Luke!"

I nod and smile, willing the blush in my cheeks to disappear.

"Kels, I'm sorry we're late. There's a traffic pileup out front. We ended up parking in the deck." Charlie seems to have regulated his breathing, but his friend is still puffing away.

Kate speaks first. "You must be Charlie. I'm Kate."

Charlie turns his attention to Kate. "It's nice to meet you Kate. . . . This is Wes." Then he peers back at me and smiles, "Wes, this is Kelsey."

He says it in such a way that it makes me feel like I'm someone he wants to introduce to his friends. Kate notices it too from her pleased expression. We stare at each other for a second or two longer and my cheeks feel hot, not from embarrassment, but more from smiling so brightly.

Kate clears her throat and I look away and peer over at Wes, who is very focused on Kate; his mouth is slightly open, almost like he's in awe. I'm tempted to snap my fingers but opt to not embarrass him. Instead, I try to lighten things up by saying, "Wes, you can call me Kels like all my friends."

Wes nods but stays silent. Kate has really made an impression, but she always has this effect on guys. Luckily, it doesn't seem to be working on Charlie.

Kate flips her hair backwards and puts her hand through

Wes's arm, ushering him forward toward the back elevator. His mouth closes and the goofy grin relaxes at her touch. I shyly smile at Charlie as the two of them walk arm in arm toward the elevator.

Charlie waves his hand across his chest being the perfect gentleman. "After you." His voice is perfectly calm, but his fingers twitch slightly when they stop moving. Maybe he's nervous too? Maybe he does feel the same?

I feel his arm wrap around my waist as he escorts me to the double doors. He whispers in my ear, "You look beautiful," and the butterflies melt away in his warmth.

I rest my head on his shoulder as the packed elevator unloads. When we shuffle inside, Charlie directs me toward the back and away from the rowdy group of college guys. Kate and Wes are sandwiched on the other side. One lanky guy, who smells like a distillery, keeps leering at Kate. She pretends not to notice. Wes does, though.

The elevator jolts to a stop and the doors open. Hardly anyone is around. We walk into the rental room, check out some smelly skates, and head onto the small oval ice rink. As soon as I hit the ice, I instinctively lock my knees, which is the worst thing I can do. I wobble but luckily don't land on my butt. I must look like a giraffe walking for the first time. Charlie notices my unease and slowly slides his arm through mine.

Kate whips right by me and taunts, "Come on, Kels!"

I yell back, "Give me a second to get used to the ice and I'll be ready to race you." But I know she will crush me. Kate's a natural—getting to skate all the time on her school's indoor rink gives her a distinct advantage.

Wes tries to keep up with her, but she's too quick. He seems to love the challenge, though. Charlie stays with me. After one lap, I feel comfortable using the edge of my blades for power and speed. Then after a couple more laps, I'm ready for that race.

Several of the college boys from the elevator, jump on the ice. I watch the distillery guy, feeling brazen, skip across the ice toward Kate. He hip checks her to get her attention then says so loudly that everyone on the rink can hear him, "Want to race. It looks like you can move in those skates."

Kate flips her wrist toward him and firmly responds, "No thanks, I'm here with some friends."

The college guy nudges her again. "I'm sure they won't mind. Just one spin with me."

When Kate doesn't respond, the guy turns in front of her and skates backwards, blocking her from skating without him. Kate rolls her eyes perturbed and explains with much more kindness than he deserves, "I just got in from school and want to spend time with my friends. Maybe another time."

Wes comes up behind Kate and slides his arm through the crook of her elbow, glaring at the college guy. He scoffs at Wes but changes his tune when Charlie and I close in behind them.

The guy grunts, then indignantly speeds off, purposely kicking up wet ice as he pushes off. He circles around by himself, then pulls over to the exit, but doesn't step off the ice. He seems torn between the bar and his friends who are still skating.

I sigh in relief when Kate passes by him, and he ignores her. He doesn't look like the kind of guy who hears the word "no" very often or would listen if someone said it to him. He's a typical Hampton boy with the flipped up collar under a quarter zip pullover sweater.

The rink is tiny so Kate circles around again pretty quickly. This time, the guy madly pushes off the side, cutting us off in the process, and races toward her and Wes. Oh crap! I know something bad is about to happen with how he is pursuing them with such forceful strokes.

I yell out to warn them but am too late. The guy knocks Wes in the shoulder, pitching him forward. Wes stops abruptly as his toe pick hits the ice, and it looks like he's about to faceplant. The guy continues on skating like nothing happened.

Charlie and I are close behind him but not in the right position to grab him. Wes tries to regain his balance by kicking one leg backwards and hits my hand. Boisterous laughter echoes around the rink.

I peer down and see the slice in my glove. There's blood gushing from in between my thumb and pointer finger. Then I feel the pain—a very sharp searing sensation.

I pull off to the side as Wes lands with both hands on the ice. I hear Charlie stop on a dime, then feel him right by my side. I tear off my glove to get a better look but can't see anything. Charlie wraps both hands around my cut and applies pressure as we skate to the exit. People clear out of the way seeing blood dripping on the shaved ice.

Charlie keeps asking, "Are you okay? Can you move your fingers?"

All I can get out is, "I'm fine. It's only a little cut." But I'm not sure if that's the case.

I wiggle my fingers and thumb and luckily, they move easily, but more blood spews out. I cover the cut again and race into the bathroom. From behind I hear him say, "I'll find a medical kit or some bandages."

Kate follows me into the bathroom. I lock my ankles to keep from wobbling and falling forward as I bend over the sink. I muffle the scream as the water hits my hand. There's a long slice in the fleshy part near my thumb, but it doesn't appear to be deep. Kate grabs a stack of towels and blots the wound.

After several minutes, thankfully the blood slows. Maybe I don't need stitches? I snag a couple more clean towels and head out of the bathroom, holding my hand up over my head, eager to forget this and move on with our evening. Charlie is waiting at the entrance with a red bag, trying to calm Wes down to prevent a brouhaha.

Kate immediately takes over with Wes, and Charlie attends to me. Charlie looks at the wound then back up at my face. "How bad is it? I can't see past the blood. Do we need to go to the hospital?"

I shake my head side to side and state, "It looks much worse than it is. Let me go wash it off again."

I disappear into the bathroom and turn on the water. This time, I hold my breath so I don't scream when the water hits the raw tissue. Kate comes in with the medical kit, pulls out the rubbing alcohol and pours it over the cut. OH MY GOD, this hurts!!! I bounce up and down and almost turn my ankle in the clunky skates.

Kate laughs. "If only Charlie could see you now."

HA HA.

Kate wraps the wound while I hold the ball of cotton bandages. After it's snug, we try leaving the bathroom again. Charlie leaps up, voicing his concern. "Kels, how is it?"

I try to act brave and say, "It's much better now. Don't worry. All good. Let's go warm up by the fire."

Charlie seems unsure that this is the right course of action, but he doesn't challenge me. Instead, he offers me an arm and escorts me to the rental area to take off our skates and then to the fireplace at the back of the patio, occasionally studying my hand as we go. Kate and Wes veer to the left toward the bar to order hot cocoa and s'more kits.

As we absorb the heat from the fire, Charlie rubs my good hand and asks, "Are you sure you are okay? I cannot believe that guy tripped Wes to get at Kate."

I move a little closer and respond, "Kate always attracts attention. This is nothing new."

Charlie gives me a funny look and says, "Kels, you really don't see guys looking at you?"

I feel the heat in my cheeks again and look down at my skates, needing a moment to figure out what to say.

I force myself to look at him and timidly answer, "Not really. They always look at Kate or Ivy. I am and prefer to be more . . . invisible."

Charlie's kind, blue eyes widen as he realizes I'm not kidding. He leans in closer and whispers, "You're not invisible. You just don't act interested." Then his face lights up and he adds, "Which is great for me. I don't have to worry about you."

What does that mean? I'm about to ask, but Kate appears with her hands full of goodies. Charlie takes two of the steaming cocoas and hands one to me. I blow on the mug as Kate spreads out the graham crackers, breaks the chocolate into squares, and spears a marshmallow.

Kate raises her stick and asks, "Who wants a s'more?"

Wes puts out a hand and says, "Let me help you with that," and she gladly passes over the stick.

Charlie teases, "I'll make one for the gimp here," then gives me a soft nudge.

I nudge him back and say, "Thanks."

Charlie spears several marshmallows and joins Wes by the fire. Kate and I sit back and watch the guys give each other a hard time about something. I feel her tap my foot and notice her grin.

I mouth, "I know." Never have we been treated like this before. Well, maybe by my dad, but that doesn't count.

Charlie hands me a stick with a slightly charred marshmallow on the end, and Wes gives one to Kate. We both say, "Thanks," in unison. Instead of making one for himself, Charlie takes a seat next to me.

As I squish the marshmallow into the chocolate so it will melt, I ask him, "Aren't you going to have one?"

He shrugs like it isn't that important. "Maybe in a minute."

I take one bite and the marshmallow fluff squirts out the back, landing on the stone floor. Instead of mocking me, Charlie chuckles and offers, "I'll make you another one."

I patiently wait as Kate entertains Wes, thinking that this is going so much better than I imagined. Well, minus the hand injury. But Charlie has been so sweet about it all. Some guys would have bailed or been annoyed they had to deal with something like that and taken me home.

The next marshmallow is perfectly browned at the edges. As I open up the graham cracker sandwich, he places the marshmallow in between. I smash it together as he pulls the stick away. This one I cannot mess up. I take a small bite and luckily, this time everything stays inside the crackers.

Wes and Kate share a look and I know they're making fun of my clumsiness. I'm about to defend myself but notice a commotion at the bar. Management is escorting the college boys out. I peer over at Kate, who has a smirk across her lips. I lean toward her and whisper, "What did you do?"

Kate pops in the rest of her s'more in her mouth, chews for a second, then swallows. "Oh, I may have mentioned something to the bartender that the tall blond guy grabbed my ass, caused the bloody problem on the ice, and that he won't stop harassing me. You know the St. Regis doesn't want a scene. It would make the 10 o'clock news."

Same old, same old. I chuckle and jest, "I should have known you would handle it. You learned from the best."

Wes cocks his head quizzically, then asks, "What do you mean?"

I flatly respond, "Her mother is Senator Lexington."

In unison, they say, "OHHH."

Wes looks at Kate with even more admiration. "That must be hard. My parents are always talking about her—but in a good way. They're huge fans of what she's doing."

Kate is used to these kinds of comments. She has a scripted response, but this time she doesn't give it. "Thanks, she works really hard. Usually, I don't let people know she's my mother and avoid talking about her, but now that I'm at boarding school, it's easier. No one really asks or cares because most of the parents are in politics or on Wall Street. It's nice to be judged for who you are versus who your parents are."

Wow! She has really changed in these few months. Boarding school is really good for her. She hated dealing with the kiss ups here.

Management is rounding everyone up since it's time for the next group of skaters to have the floor. We grab our trash and head for the elevator. As we're waiting, Tyler, Virginia's ex-boyfriend, exits the elevator with some guys.

At first, he doesn't notice me since he's chuckling about something, but then he stops right in front of me and smiles smugly. His eyes begin to meander down my body and pauses at my bandaged hand right below my hip. Then he lunges forward and grabs hold of it as if my hand were about to fall off.

I wince then instinctively pull my hand away while moving closer to Charlie's chest. Tyler's black eyes narrow as he notices Charlie by my side. He forcefully asks, "Are you okay? Did he hurt you?"

I shake my head violently side-to-side and emphatically say, "Tyler, it's just a nick. Not a big deal. Charlie has been a huge help."

Charlie defensively steps in front of me and says, "I got it. She's fine."

Sensing the tension, Kate and Wes bolt into the elevator and hold the button to keep the beeping door open. Charlie pulls me to him with one arm over my shoulder and the other holding my injured hand, almost like he's protecting me. Then, he ushers me into the elevator next to Kate and Wes.

I look through the crack as the doors close, Tyler is still looking at me with low shoulders and a disappointed look on his face. I turn my attention back toward Charlie, who is staring at the closed doors as well. His lips are pursed together and his shoulders are raised and back, almost ready for a fight.

It's obvious that Tyler has really gotten under his skin. I nuzzle in closer and say, "He's usually not like that. He must be having a hard time with the breakup. He's just a friend. . . . Thanks for taking care of me."

Charlie lightly squeezes my waist and lets out a long sigh, then asks, "Who's up for some Velvet Taco?"

"Velvet what?!" Kate questions.

I chuckle at her response—the name is pretty strange. I peer around Charlie and respond, "Velvet Taco—it's a new restaurant next to Whole Foods and Jeni's. They have every sort of taco you can think of."

"Sure, I'm game." Wes shrugs his shoulders, acting like he couldn't care less, but it's obvious he's hoping Kate will say yes.

"I'm game." Kate smirks at Wes.

Charlie sheepishly peers at me and asks, "You game? . . . You can eat tacos one-handed." Then he flashes a fabulously mischievous grin.

I gently nudge him in the hip and reply, "The gimp is game too."

Kate stares up at the "Weekly Taco Feature" board in disbelief. "WTF is right. Have you ever heard of an alligator taco before? That sounds disgusting. Wes, do you have any suggestions?"

Wes brightens as he goes over his favorites.

"Kels, what do you want?" Charlie leans in as he weighs his options.

"I'm thinking the Nashville Hot Tofu and Korean Pork. What about you?"

"Flank and Brisket."

"Those are good. I've had them before."

"Any interest is splitting the tots?"

"Of course. Those are easy to eat one-handed," I banter.

He chuckles and I love it.

We all order and take a seat by the window. Wes is the first to start talking. "So, Kate, how do you like boarding school?"

"I love it. Trying to get Kels to join me next year. We need her on the soccer team."

As she says this, I notice Charlie's hand twitch under the table.

Kate smiles for some reason, then adds, "But Kels's parents would never let her go. Even if it means getting away from Ivy." I wince at her name. Kate really loves to stir up trouble.

"Ivy? Who is Ivy?" Charlie inquires.

"Just a girl in our grade who is causing some trouble. You may have met her at Homecoming?" I answer as nonchalantly as possible.

"Wait . . . wasn't Homecoming back in October? I thought you two just met?" Kate asks as she looks at the both of us.

"Yes, we just met. Charlie's friend's sister, Bree just transferred to Smith. Dave and Charlie picked her up after the dance."

Charlie takes a sip of his drink and then adds, "Kels wasn't there." Then focuses on me with a lopsided grin, "But Dave was looking for *you* after he saw that photo of you and Bree at the dance."

My head whips back, surprised. "Dave was looking for me? Is that why you asked if I knew Dave?"

"Yep." He quickly answers.

All I get is yep? "Why was he looking for me?" I press for more answers.

"He thought you were hot." Charlie smirks as he says it.

I feel the tips of my ears and cheeks turn red. He definitely knows how to push my buttons.

Kate quickly adds to stir the pot, "Why weren't *you* looking for Kels, Charlie?"

Charlie doesn't answer. Instead, he looks toward the pickup area, seeming a little uncomfortable, and Wes is enjoying every minute of it. This is the first time I've seen Charlie flustered.

Our number is called and Charlie quickly scoots out to grab the food, looking a little relieved to get out of this conversation. He wasn't expecting Kate to go there. Wes climbs out to help, leaving Kate and me alone at the table. She points her thumb at Charlie and mumbles, "So that's why you were so nervous? A bit of a step up from Nick and Jack, I have to say."

"Kate, shh, they are coming back," and I take a sip of my drink and pretend like she hasn't said anything.

As we dig into the food, Wes and Charlie tell us about their ski plans over break, and I try to hide my disappointment that he will be gone over New Year's.

Charlie eats the second to last tater tot, motions for me to take the last one, and casually asks Kate, "So Kate, are you going to stay here the entire break or are you going somewhere?"

Kate finishes chewing her last bite and grins at me. "No, I'm going to stay here. I have a friend who may fly in for a couple days and stay through the New Year."

"Oh, is she someone Kels has met too?" Charlie asks flatly.

I sit up straight and try to get Kate's attention to stop her from going there, but she ignores me. Kate quickly corrects Charlie. "Him, and yes, Kels met Jack when she was up visiting this fall."

I squirm in my seat and try to get Kate's attention again, but she's only looking at Charlie.

Wes tries to hide his disappointment as he asks, "So you guys are dating?"

Kate leans back in her seat, giggling and waves off the question as if it's so silly. "No, my guy is in New York. Jack is *not* coming to see me, really." She glances at me to make sure everyone knows her meaning and then looks back at Charlie.

A hush drowns out all the chattering around us. I glare at her but she still is not looking at me. She is intently watching Charlie. I notice his thumb flick his ring finger.

To diffuse the tension, I add, "You know, we should set him up with Kylie. I think she's his type and am sure the Westovers would be fine if Jack and Kylie joined us at the New Year's Eve party. Kate, you can be my date."

Charlie exhales and seems to relax. I think my date comment may have ended it, but Kate presses on. "I don't think *she* is the one he will be looking for at midnight."

What is she doing? I try to prevent this from going any further by adding, "Well, maybe he should go to London with his family then if that's going to be an issue. He should have gotten the hint by now that nothing is going to happen with me."

Kate's eyes finally leave Charlie's face, and I'm surprised when she looks at me with pride. I glare back without the same sentiment. She has some explaining to do on this one when we get back home.

The conversation lightens up after that, even though Wes is still a little pouty. Several times my hand brushes Charlie's under the table, but he never holds on. Maybe he would have if it wasn't bandaged up?

As we bus our table, Wes runs over to talk to some kids from his school. Charlie gives them a quick "hello" and then heads to the bathroom. He doesn't stick around to introduce Kate or me to the crowd. Wes says everyone's names quickly and then talks about something that happened last week. I don't know any of them, and they don't seem to care to get to know us either.

The conversation doesn't last long. Charlie seems to scurry by them and is the first one out the door. He doesn't hold the door open for us like he usually does.

I'm quiet on the car ride home, unsure of what to make of

the date. He seemed so concerned about my hand but then distant around his friends. Maybe he is still upset about the Jack comments?

Kate and Wes do most of the talking in the back seat. Charlie quietly pays attention to the road, following Kate's directions to her house. It's only a short ride from the restaurant.

I look up from staring at my hands when we park in front of Kate's house. Charlie turns to me and says so sweetly, "Kelsey, I'll call you later to check on your hand. . . . Kate, it was nice to meet you. Thanks for keeping Wes—and his temper in check." Charlie seems to lighten up after his jab, but Wes doesn't seem so pleased.

Kate gives Wes a hug, then turns to Charlie and says, "It was nice to meet you. I hope I get to see you both after your ski trip."

I climb out of the car and wave as we reach the front door. Wes runs around the outside like a fire drill to the front passenger seat. As Charlie pulls out of the driveway, Wes punches him in the shoulder, and I turn to hide my laugh.

The door slams behind me and Kate throws off her coat and scarf. I do the same. She moves over to the bench and removes her boots, then motions for me to lift up mine, so she can help the gimp. As I drop my boot on her knee, I ask eagerly, "So what do you think?"

Kate motions for the other boot and takes her time. When the second boot drops to the floor with a thud, she looks up with the biggest smile on her face. She says, "Kels, he's so perfect for you. Confident but not cocky like Jack or Luke. And there's something about him that's so endearing—I can't figure out exactly what it is, but obviously it's a good thing. . . . And, I have never seen you so happy, even with your hand sliced open."

I sigh in relief but still need more confirmation that this is really happening for me. "So, do you think he feels the same?"

She smiles and says, "Uhh, yeah! He couldn't keep his eyes off of you the entire night. . . . I think he would have fed you that s'more if you let him! You should have seen his face when I mentioned you going to boarding school. Pure fear passed over him for a second. But the best indication that he is into you was when I mentioned Jack."

My anger flares. "Is that why you kept bringing up Jack?"

"Yeah, why else? I wanted to see if he was jealous and oh boy, he was. You're not just a family friend to him, Kels."

Still not satisfied, I ask, "Really . . . are you sure? He didn't introduce us to his friends. It seemed like he wanted to get out of there pretty quick."

Kate rolls her eyes and says, "Kels, you read too much into things. He might have just needed to go to the restroom. Relax! Worry when he gives you a reason to worry. Just enjoy the moment! I'm so excited for you!"

"Thanks, I'm excited too. A little too excited."

Kate rolls her eyes again, almost with a full body roll for exaggeration. She's right. I always overthink things, and it never ends well. I told myself after the plane incident, I would change to make things better, and this is my chance to do it. Things are definitely better with him around.

Then the both of us bounce up and down, like one of us just got into our dream college.

"Kate, is that you?" Mrs. Lexington yells.

"Yes, mom."

Mrs. Lexington walks into the room, looking a little happier than before. She hugs her daughter and then glances over at me. "Kelsey, what happened to your hand?"

"Oh, it's nothing," I dismiss the question and try to hide my hand behind my back.

"Let me see that." She gently grabs hold of my wrist and

starts unwrapping the bandage. After she unravels a couple layers, the stain on the gauze turns a brighter shade of red and gets larger. Worried I may get blood on their nice rug, I put pressure on the wound and beeline for the powder room sink.

Mrs. Lexington appears with scissors and cuts the matted layers of cotton. As soon as I pull off the rest, the blood pools around the cut and drips off my thumb. I brace myself against the side of the sink and stick the wound under the running water. Mrs. Lexington sees the long slice of flesh and I hear the dreaded words, "Kelsey, we need to call your mother. You need stitches."

Oh crap!

***

My phone rings and I look at the screen. Oh my God, it's Charlie. I let it ring one more time while practicing my "hello" and answer.

"Kels, I just heard you got stitches! I'm so sorry I didn't take you to the hospital. I just got an earful about—"

"Charlie, it's not your fault. Please don't worry about it. We went over to a friend's house who stitched me up. He's a plastic surgeon and doesn't even think there will be a scar. So it worked out better than us going to the ER. I promise."

I hear a sigh on the other end. "Okay, that makes me feel a little better, but please let me make it up to you?"

"You really don't need to, but sure." I quietly bounce up and down.

"So do you have time tomorrow? I know it's Christmas Eve, but maybe we can go to lunch?"

"Hmmm . . . That should work. My family is not coming over until later that day."

"Great. What sounds good?"

I think for a moment. "How about a ramen noodle bowl or something warm?"

I hear a smile. "That does sound good right now. How about I pick you up at 11 o'clock, and we head down to Krog Street?"

"Perfect . . . this is really sweet of you. Thanks."

"Of course, see you tomorrow."

"See you tomorrow." As soon as I hang up the phone, I dash upstairs to call Kate.

TWENTY-ONE
PRESENTS

THERE'S NOT one spot on my carpet that isn't covered in clothes. I have torn through all my leggings and jeans except for this one last pair. I slip on my light blue cropped ones and they're too tight. AHHHHH—where is my favorite pair of jeans? He's going to be here in fifteen minutes.

I rip off the jeans, throw on a pair of shorts and leap down the stairs. I run past my parents, who are sitting at the island, drinking a cup of coffee together. My mom sighs and shakes her head side to side as I slide in my sports bra, gingerbread socks, and a red and white Christmas fleece flowing over my back like a cape. She's used to my frantic trips to her closet.

I whip through each top, looking for something to go with jeans. Wait, were those jeans really that tight? At this point, I can't remember, and I need a pair of jeans to try on with a top! I race back by my mother and earn another look of disapproval.

What was I thinking waiting this long to get ready? Damn it. There's no time for this! I only have seven minutes—I really hope he's not one of those people who always gets there early. I don't want my mother to answer the door and have to tell him I'm still getting dressed.

As I'm throwing all the clothes left on my shelves onto the floor, my mother appears with my favorite pair of dark blue jeans. YES!

"Thank you, Mom!"

She nods and says, "You're running out of time."

When she looks at my floor, she tries to hide her displeasure, but I know her too well. Somehow she manages to keep her thoughts to herself and offers to help. "Kels, let's go back down to my closet and find you something and fast."

Within seconds, I'm scanning her tops and notice a plastic bag with several hangers inside. I rip off the cover and there's the most gorgeous navy wool sweater I've ever seen. It has fringe on the sleeves that wrap to the chest and angle down into a V shape on the front and back. My mother steps forward to touch the soft wool as I stare. "Kels, I just bought it. . . . It's a Christmas gift. Oh well, try it on. It should look amazing on you."

I throw it over my head, slowly pulling it over my bandaged arm, and look into the mirror. It's perfect! As I twirl, my mother attempts to show me the hidden pockets under the fringe for my phone and money. She flatly states, "This will come in handy since you refuse to wear a coat."

I spin once more to admire the fringe, shifting back and forth as I move. Then my mother appears with a pair of shoes. "You might as well wear my sneakers that match this perfectly." Oh, my! She never lets me wear her Jimmy Choos!

As soon as I slide on the left shoe, I hear a car door slam and the beep of an alarm. I peer into the mirror one last time, smooth my hair, and then holler, "Thank you."

I dash through the hall to grab my phone and money with my mother close behind me. She says with a tender smile, "Have a good time."

I nod, race to the front door, and I swing it open just as he rings the doorbell. Slightly out of breath, I say, "Hey, I tried to beat you to the door."

Charlie steps forward, about to say something, but he's interrupted by my mother. "Hey, Charlie. Tell your parents Merry Christmas for us."

Charlie peers over my shoulder and replies, "I will. Merry Christmas to you all too."

Then he focuses back on me and so sweetly says, "Are you ready to go?"

"Yep." I yell over my shoulder, "Bye Mom," and then shut the door before Gracie escapes out the front.

Charlie gingerly holds my injured hand as we walk down the stairs. "So, how's it feeling?"

"It's a little sore but not that bad."

He winces. "Well, I still feel bad we didn't get that looked at right away."

I put my hand over his and try to ease his concern by saying, "Charlie, it's sweet of you to worry, but really, it all worked out fine!"

He shrugs his shoulders and pulls me close to him. "Okay, let's go find you something to eat where you only need one hand."

In the car, we banter back and forth on which school has the better athletics. Of course, he has to mention our school's notorious recruiting reputation. My only rationale is our size. His school has about double the amount of students than mine, giving them the advantage. But, in his mind, that's still not a good enough reason to justify it. He says the phrase everyone loves to chant, "Built not bought."

So I lay it on thick and comment on how the recruiting did not go in my school's favor this year since he plays for Chase, and surprisingly, he blushes. I even see a tinge of red at the tips of his ears. I watch him open his mouth then close it. After a couple second pause, he casually asks, "So what are your plans for Christmas?"

I place my hand over his. "Well, dinner is at our house tonight with my grandparents, aunt, uncle, and cousins. Those kids will tear apart the house, and we will spend a couple hours cleaning up. While my mom puts out her cookies and carrots for the reindeer, my dad will read me the book *Twas the Night Before Christmas*. Cheesy I know, but it's his thing. His dad read it to him."

"Then, we will hopefully sleep in, open presents, stuff ourselves on my grandmother's famous sticky buns, and relax before heading over to my other grandparents to watch my other cousins rip through their presents. I'm sure that was more info than you needed. . . . What about you?"

"No, that sounds somewhat similar to what we do. Minus my dad reading me a bedtime story." He smirks as I lightly punch his shoulder, and then he grabs hold of my good hand again. "My mom's side of the family will come over tonight and stay for hours. They always cook seven different fish dishes, and we will stuff ourselves. My uncle will look like Santa after eating so much. Then Christmas Day, we get to spend it hanging out in our pajamas. It will be just the four of us. We don't have to drive from house to house opening presents anymore."

"I'm looking forward to when I don't have to go anywhere. My grandparents make us open each present in a circle so they can see everyone's expression. It takes about three hours with the amount of cousins!"

For some reason, Charlie finds this very amusing and can't stop laughing. "What?"

"Your face when you mentioned your cousins was hilarious."

"You mean this face." And I try to recreate the look.

"Nope, that's not it."

I pull down the sun visor and stare into the mirror. I have no idea what look I gave him.

"I don't think you're going to be able to do it again. It was a spur of the moment look."

"Well, at least it was amusing."

He parks the car in the side lot, and we scurry inside the food hall to avoid the cold. The bar at the entrance is packed, and people are hanging out in the main walkway. Charlie makes room for me to pass so no one hits my hand as we maneuver through the crowd. We circle the food hall and decide on Pho Nam.

As we stand in line, I nonchalantly ask, "So when do you head out to Vail?"

He continues to look at the menu as he answers, "The day after Christmas. We're staying at Wes's place until the first. Do you like to travel over the holidays?"

I shake my head even though he isn't looking. "No. My parents prefer to lay low around the holidays, so that's what I'm used to doing. Kate and I will hang out most of the time."

"What about Bree?"

"Next in line," the lady says and beckons us forward.

"Kels, you go first, I'm still deciding."

"Hello, I would like the Beef Pho, please."

Charlie turns to me. "Will you split the Crispy Imperial Rolls with me?"

I nod yes, and he orders, "What she said, one Pho Combo, one Crispy Imperial Roll, and two waters, please."

The lady types in our order, points at the machine to pay, and we scoot out of the way as she yells, "Next." She doesn't seem to be messing around.

Charlie puts his arm around me and we stroll around the loop of restaurants again. "So what about Bree? Will you see her?"

"I think she will be here too. I told her I would introduce her to Kate, but I'm second-guessing that now."

"Why?"

"Bree heard Kate and Chris kissed last summer, and she was not happy about it. She probably thinks Kate still likes Chris, which she doesn't. She never did. It was just a stupid dare."

Instead of asking more about Bree and Chris, he goes right into the subject I'm not prepared to discuss. "So have you kissed someone on a dare?"

I flip my hair over my shoulder and look into the candy shop. "Nope, never have. I try to avoid those kinds of games." Then turn back and look directly at him as I ask, "And you?"

He shakes his head and teases, "Nope, back then I usually had a girlfriend, so I never needed to play."

I'm about to respond but decide to let the whole girlfriend comment go. I really don't want to go there, not yet.

"So do you see Bree much when you are hanging out with Dave at their house?" I ask to change the subject.

He smiles, knowing I'm avoiding his last remark. "Nope, Dave says she's always over at Chris's or your house. Why?"

"Her mother said something to make me think she doesn't want to spend much time at home. It seems like something happened there."

"Yeah, she wasn't so happy at Chase. She had a hard time finding friends, which is understandable. One girl made her life hell because the guy she wanted liked Bree. She tried to make Bree look bad on numerous occasions and Bree fell for it since she has a—let's say—a fiery personality."

I add, "That's an understatement."

He nods and continues. "It's a good thing she left. That girl's family doesn't let things go."

"Well, Bree walked into a similar situation at school, but it sounds like it worked out better for her at Smith than at Chase. Chris is a good guy."

"That's good to hear." Then, he looks at me sideways and says, "Hopefully I can meet him sometime when I get back from skiing."

Blushing slightly, I say, "Yep, we should all get together sometime."

Our number is called and Charlie picks up both trays. I grab the waters and place them under my arm. We find a seat in the far corner, away from the bar area. We both dig right into the rolls and devour four of them in seconds. Charlie offers me the last one, but I break it in half and he gladly accepts his part.

After he wipes the grease off of his fingers, he hands me a spoon for my soup bowl. "So do you have time to walk around afterward?"

"Yep, I don't have to be home until four. What about you?"

"I'm not in any hurry to get back."

I try to remove some fat off the brisket without making a mess but give up and slurp some broth. "Do you mind if we pop into The Merchant to see if I can find a gift for Kate?"

Charlie finishes chewing a meatball, then mischievously smiles and says, "Sure, as long as you agree to a little competition?"

I tilt my head, not following his train of thought.

"Here are the rules: we both have ten minutes to find a gift for one another with a cap of twenty dollars. The store will wrap them for us so you don't have any problems with the one hand, and it will be a surprise." He pats my good hand, and I feel the butterflies again. "We will FaceTime tomorrow so we can open them together. Deal?"

I swallow, trying to calm myself that he wants to exchange presents, then agree, "Deal, but you need to give me some hints on what you like."

He leans forward with the most adorable look and says, "But that will take the fun out of it."

I lean forward and try to mirror his expression. "Okay, you're on!"

Then both of us gobble down the rest of the food, eager to start shopping. Charlie and I set the alarms on our phones for ten minutes, and we scatter. I move to the far end of the store, and he stays around the entrance.

What the hell am I going to find him in here? This store is full of girly stuff like candles, napkins, home accessories, etc. I spot a display of mugs and move that way. Maybe they will have something there? As I scan through them, I see one about skiing with the cheesy saying, *I'd rather be on the slopes.* Not ideal, but it may have to do. I tuck it under my arm and keep moving.

Then, I see it. A mug with a popular phrase, *Keep calm and Pajama On.* Perfect! He spends Christmas in his PJs. I put the other one back and move on to the table with a lot of trinkets and self-help kits. There's even an adorable little sewing kit, but I can't give any of this stuff to Charlie. No—wait. I can work with this.

As I patiently wait in line, I look out of the corner of my eye to see where Charlie is and he's studying something at the far display. It seems like he's checking out the candles. I see him raise his head and I quickly look away.

I hand the gifts to the cashier and ask for a pen and paper to write my note. As she rings me up, I write my message, *For your day in your pajamas and just in case you ever need to stitch me up. Merry Xmas!* How should I sign it? XO. No, it's too early. Just Kels will work.

I stuff the sewing kit in the mug and hand the note to the lady who moves it out of sight just as Charlie peers over my shoulder and whispers, "Find something good?"

I turn and tease, "You'll find out soon enough. Anyways, what are you doing over here? We agreed not to look."

"Yeah, but I saw you looking." He pokes back, keeping his gift hidden behind his back.

"Maybe I peeked over at you, but I didn't see anything. . . . I'll go find Kate's gift and let you check out. . . . I promise not to look." Even though I'm dying to see what he found.

The nice lady hands us our wrapped gifts, and we head back into the building for some dessert, debating who should pay. After much insisting on my part, he reluctantly agrees to let me.

The Jeni's ice cream line stretches around the corner, but for once, I don't mind waiting. Charlie lets me lean up against him and whispers in my ear on how much I'm going to love my gift, and I'm sure I will. All that really matters is he got me something.

After sampling some of our favorites, including Bramble-berry Crisp, Milk Chocolate, and Buckeye State, we decide to order the holiday trio with a scoop of White Chocolate Peppermint, The Matterhorn, and Cognac with Gingerbread. It's an interesting combination, but somehow it works.

We wander through the candy shop and other boutiques grazing on the ice cream. Charlie makes a last-minute decision to buy a bouquet of flowers for his mother and once the lady finishes assembling a truly stunning arrangement, I order one for my mom. My dad always forgets to give her flowers and she needs a centerpiece for the table tonight.

I make my way back to the white peony-like flower the lady called a ranunculus and lean over to smell it, but it has very little scent, unlike the fragrant pink peonies in our backyard. When I leaned in, I must have caught a whiff of the nearby camellias, which have a lemony scent. Charlie appears next to me with an arrangement under each arm and the gift bags from The Merchant looped over his wrist.

"Let me at least grab the bags," I say and he moves his hand out so I can slide it onto my good wrist. We dodge the group of college boys at the long table near the entrance and make it to the car without dropping the arrangements.

As soon as the back door slams shut, he pulls out a single ranunculus inside his coat. I look up at him and then at the flower, transfixed.

"I saw you admiring this and thought you would like one." He has this unsure look on his face as he speaks.

Without thinking, I step forward and kiss him on the cheek. When I pull back, I notice the bemused look on his face. I'm sure he was expecting more than that. I feel him pull me in close, kiss my forehead like my father does and hear him say, "Glad you like it." He pulls away and opens my car door, and I know I just messed up—really messed up.

The car ride home is fine, but it's not the same. He seems a little more reserved like he's debating something. Should I admit I've never kissed someone before or let it go? Maybe he has figured it out.

I don't know what to do now. How do I fix this? Maybe I should kiss him when he drops me off?

As soon as we pull into the driveway, I see him and know my last thought is not a possibility. My father is outside, fiddling with his golf clubs in the back of the car. Charlie parks and walks right up to him, shakes his hand and clearly states, "It's nice to see you, Mr. Grant."

I hand the flowers to my dad and say, "You may want to give these to Mom. She needs a centerpiece and is probably setting up the table *right now*."

But my hint flies right over his head. *So much for being able to fix this!*

He brightly smiles and responds, "Yes, thanks, Kels! She will love these," then carefully places them on the trunk of his car and turns back to Charlie. "So how is school going?"

"Very good. I'm looking forward to the break, though." Charlie keeps eye contact with my dad as he speaks and then looks over at me as if he wants to add something else.

"Yes, I'm sure you are. Any plans?" My father asks casually.

"Yes, we're going skiing until the beginning of the year, and then we will be back. Kels and I plan to get together." He looks over at me, almost like he wants to see how I feel about it.

The peck on the cheek did rattle him, so I quickly respond back, "Yes, Dad. Bree, Chris, Charlie, and I are going to hang out when he gets back."

"Oh, that sounds nice. Well, tell your parents hello and Merry Christmas for me. Kels, can you help me carry some of this stuff in?"

I know exactly what he's doing. He's trying to prevent anything from happening and from the look on Charlie's face, he knows too. As I move to pick up the flowers, Charlie raises his finger. "Kels, let me get your gifts before you go," he quickly mumbles and then dashes to his car.

He returns with the gifts and places them next to the arrangement, then gives me my flower and says, "I will call you tomorrow."

He turns back to my dad and adds, "Merry Christmas, Mr. Grant."

But my father doesn't respond, he's too focused on the large flower in my hand.

As Charlie takes a step toward his car, I say, "Wait, I will walk you to the car."

Charlie walks alongside of me but keeps a respectable distance. When we are somewhat hidden behind the car, I apologize, "Sorry about that. Still a little protective. . . . Thanks for today. I had a lot of fun."

He gives me a quick hug and whispers, "Don't worry about it. I would be protective of you too," and then hops in his car.

I watch him pull out and slowly lumber back to my dad's side. "Really, Dad. Did you have to act like that?"

He acts all innocent and shrugs. "What? I don't know what you are talking about."

I roll my eyes, tuck the flower over my ear to get under his skin, then grab the two boxes off the back of the car and hold them tightly against my chest as I storm inside.

As soon as my phone buzzes the next morning, I race up into my room and shut the door. I take one long breath and hit accept.

Charlie's smiling face appears. His eyes seem to glow like the water in the Blue Grotto as he says, "Merry Christmas, Kels!" The warmth in his voice makes me want to climb through the screen and be with him.

I feel my cheeks raise and respond, "Merry Christmas! How's your day going so far?" Somehow I manage not to giggle like a little girl.

"Good. Real good. We slept in and just finished opening presents. How's yours?"

"Same. I've been setting up my new laptop." I add as if it's not a big deal, but I'm so excited my parents finally replaced my old one that would die in the middle of my reports, causing me to lose my work more times than I could count.

"Cool. Do you have time to open your present now?" He asks eagerly.

"Yep, I got it right here." I playfully lift it in front of my face and put it back down in my lap. "But you go first."

"Okay." He puts the gift close to his ear and shakes it. Then, he slowly pulls off the tape, enjoying my lack of patience. As he reads the note, his eyebrows knit together and he looks up.

"You'll understand in a minute," I claim and shoot him a mischievous grin.

He removes the tissue paper and I hear him chuckle as he lifts the sewing kit out of the mug. "Yes, this may come in handy."

He reads the message on his new mug and says with sincerity, "Thank you, I will use this today. . . . You found the perfect gifts in a chick store. . . . I'm impressed."

I pat my chest and dramatically flutter my eyelashes, which makes him chuckle again.

He places the gifts on his navy blue comforter, then says, "Your turn."

I copy him by shaking it first, then slowly peel each piece of tape off the paper. To tease him even more, I neatly line them up on my desk.

"Oh, come on. You aren't going to reuse the tape," he jests.

I lift the white lid off the bottom and gasp when I see the gorgeous necklace with an engraved K set on the left side of a thin silver bar.

I cover my mouth with both hands. "Charlie, this definitely didn't cost twenty dollars or less."

He waves his hand over his face. "I know, but I couldn't resist. I wanted to get you something nicer than a candle. That's what girls give each other. It's on the same level as a smelly bath bomb."

"So I assume you don't like strong smells." I casually ask but am taking note.

"No, I prefer more subtle, natural."

"Good to know. Charlie, I love it." I hold the silver chain around my neck and angle the phone so he can see it.

"I thought you would," he says triumphantly.

There's a loud noise outside and Charlie whips his head toward the window. He walks over and peers outside. His father is out in his plaid pajama bottoms with some contraption under the goal. Charlie turns back to the screen and says, "So I need to go help my dad put together this basketball rebounder. Will you be around later?"

"Yeah, call me when you have your coffee. Thanks for my gift. I love it. Really love it." I say as my fingers run over the engraving.

"You're welcome. The sewing kit will be in my car in case we need it." Then he winks and says, "Bye."

I hit end, sink into my featherbed and stare up at the fan. He actually got me a necklace!

TWENTY-TWO

NEW YEAR'S EVE

FOR THE PAST SIX DAYS, I've spent practically every minute with Kate. We've visited all our favorite restaurants, have blown through our Christmas money at the mall, and caught up on all the latest shows on Netflix. We've had so much fun that I've been able to keep my mind off of Charlie—well, most of the time.

But tonight, being back here at the St. Regis for the Westover's New Year's Eve party is making me miss him even more. I wish all these parents would stop asking me if I have a boyfriend and why I don't have a date!

During a discussion with one of Mr. Westovers' colleagues, I drifted off thinking about Charlie's New Year's plans, wondering if he will be with someone at midnight, and completely missed the cue that the father wanted to set me up with his son. I ended up being dragged into the middle of the Atlas restaurant and introduced to a tryhard.

After fifteen minutes of listening to this guy drone on and on about being the captain of the lacrosse team and how he just broke the school record in backstroke, I manage to get Kate's attention, who's thoroughly enjoying seeing me stuck.

She and Bree laugh even harder as I motion behind my back for help.

Finally, she finds a stray guy in front of the chocolate fountain and brings him over to listen to this guy's accomplishments, allowing me the opportunity to politely excuse myself without leaving the guy standing by himself again. Instead of joining the others, Kate and I disappear in a plush upholstered bench seat near the kitchen to ensure those guys don't follow us and observe the scene from a far.

Kim is still working the crowd like an expert, entertaining her dad's clients as well as our parents. As if on cue, the crowd laughs at her story about how she was at a fashion show with her mother in Milan when she had to fill in for a model who passed out backstage. As she was prancing down the catwalk during the finale, she twisted an ankle in the five-inch high stilettos and fell on top of the prime minister in the front row. The lady was much more understanding when she found out Kim was only eleven years old and had not yet learned how to walk in heels.

And now she will relay several funny tales about being at boarding school in Brussels. She practiced all of these on us before the parents showed up so I know every story. Brian has stood next to Kim the whole night, holding her hand and keeping an eye out for her parents. They recently found out she has been raiding their bar and threatened to ground her permanently if she has any alcohol tonight.

Several times throughout the evening, Kim's mother has thrown her head forward like she is laughing hysterically at a joke and then discreetly sniffs Kim's drink. It's obvious she's about to do it again and Kim has had enough of it by the disgusted look she's giving Brian.

As her mother leans over, Kim *accidentally* moves her glass up at the same time and spills her Coke all over her mother's gold and red silk dress. Her mother steps back with both hands in the air, sharply inhaling in surprise as the soda seeps into the fabric. Kim snatches several napkins from the passing waiter and immediately starts blotting away as another lady heads to the bar, probably asking for club soda.

Brian suppresses a laugh behind his fist, then pretends to cough as Kim's mother glares at him. He pops a shrimp into his mouth and then grabs his throat, coughing again. Mrs. Westover snickers, thinking he's just trying to be cute, but he's really choking.

The guy next to him gives him the Heimlich. After several sharp heaves under his ribs, we watch a chunk of shrimp fly across the room and land in a woman's drink—a once in a lifetime shot. She gasps as the drink splashes all over her face and poofy, white-blonde hair.

Kim is dragged into the bathroom, looking quite terrified of her mother. She emerges, much more composed, quickly finished her rounds, and motions for us to follow her into the Garden Room. Kate and I slowly slide out of the comfy booth and into the room that looks more like a West Palm Beach greenhouse than a restaurant.

It's enclosed in glass and steel with interior walls covered in ivy. (I'm so glad Ivy couldn't make it tonight!) There are several mature trees with branches lit by glowing twinkle lights and sweet orchids cascading out of concrete urns.

Kim rubs her hand across the enormous wooden horse as she passes, then makes her way to the chairs next to the limestone fireplace. This gives her a view of any parents entering the room. Before she sits down, she hikes up her black sequined dress. Usually, her dresses are on the shorter side, but tonight it's just an inch above her knees to appease her parents.

Mare pulls Nick away from the carving station and joins us by the fire. Bree and Chris follow behind with two overflowing plates. The larger one is full of roast beef, smoked turkey and plenty of rolls. The smaller has a pyramid of chocolate truffles. Bree pops one in her mouth before she sets it in the middle of the table and sinks into the tropical print chair.

Nick collapses into the one next to Bree and Mare plops down on his lap, stroking his dark navy blazer. She actually looks nice tonight. The forest green flare dress (the one she said she was not going to buy when we were dress shopping) really brings out the green flecks in her eyes. She must have gotten her hair done too; it's perfectly smooth, accenting the layers around her face. From the side, she resembles Jennifer Aniston instead of a plain Jane.

I turn my attention to Bree, who is listing off her New Year's resolutions. "This year I'm going to plank every morning for sixty seconds like my brother. I'm going to get an A in French, and I'm going to eat more chocolate, like these," then she grabs another cocoa-dusted truffle.

"So Kelsey, what are *YOUR* New Year's resolutions? Anything you want to share? I noticed a shiny new necklace." Bree turns everyone's attention to my neck, and I know she wants me to mention Charlie, but I'm not ready to say a thing yet.

Picking up on my unease, Kate answers for me. "Kelsey met this guy, Jack, at my boarding school, and he can't stop talking about her. I think he may even muster up enough courage to ask her to our Spring Fling."

Mare stops pawing at Nick and leans forward toward the group. "So wait, a guy you hardly know bought you a necklace?"

I innocently nod, yes.

Mare spins around and hits Nick on the shoulder. "DID YOU HEAR THAT?"

In mid-bite of a truffle, he mumbles, "What?"

Mare spews out, "Kelsey got a necklace for Christmas from a guy she barely knows. What did I get?—I got a candle!"

Nick defiantly defends himself, announcing, "Hey, that candle cost me fifty bucks!"

Then Mare fires back, asking, "And how much do you think that necklace cost?"

But Nick doesn't back down. "Oh, I'm sorry, What did you get me? A picture frame of the two of us! I thought that candle smelled nice, but if you don't want it, go ahead and return it!"

Mare stands up and looks him straight in the eye then interrogates him through a snarl, "So who would you rather have a picture of next to your bed?"

After saying that, Mare turns to look at me. I put both hands up in self-defense and remark, "Whoa, leave me out of this. It's only a necklace."

Mare rolls her eyes and states with venom, "It's only a necklace 'cause you got a necklace!"

Ignoring Mare's temper tantrum, Nick looks around his girlfriend and asks, "Kels, who's the necklace from?"

Mare spins back around and smacks him on the shoulder, looking like a volcano about to explode. "It doesn't matter who, Nick!"

Bree, who never does anything to help Mare, surprisingly says, "Mare, if it makes you feel any better, Chris didn't give me anything for Christmas."

Chris slams down his drink, exasperated. "Oh my God! We said we weren't going to exchange gifts. Stop telling everyone that!"

With her arms firmly crossed over her chest, Bree rolls her eyes and looks the other way, mumbling, "You should know better."

Chris, knowing better this time, only shakes his head.

After several minutes of silence and electricity flowing so freely it could raise the hair on our heads, Kate walks into the center of the group and calmly says, "Okay, I think we are all ready to move on. It's almost midnight."

Mare settles back down in Nick's lap and taunts me in her patronizing voice, "So Kels, who are you going to kiss tonight? That waiter over there can't take his eyes off you."

I follow her hand pointing at the kitchen to the guy who is almost thirty and we make eye contact. Immediately, I turn away and flip my hair to cover my face so the waiter can't see me, then emphatically state, "Mare, I'm good. Don't worry about me."

Just then my phone rings and I gasp—it's CHARLIE!!! Kate giggles then says, "Need to take that, Kels. Mare must have given that waiter over there your number. I'm going to call *my* boyfriend now."

As I get up, Nick's head twists around toward the waiter and then leans forward to stand up, but Mare doesn't get off his lap. I rush to the windows overlooking the fountain and press the FaceTime button and say, "Hello," a little breathlessly and way too enthusiastically.

Charlie has his white collared shirt unbuttoned at the top with a loose blue tie around his neck and a New Year's whistle in his mouth. I can see Dave and Wes in the background on the sofa with some girls all decked out in fancy dresses. They must have gone out somewhere nice tonight. He tells them to be quiet then turns back to me with a smile that meets his brilliant blue eyes.

I feel my smile get bigger and bigger, and fight back the giddiness bubbling inside. After clearing my throat, I ask in my best flirty voice, "How's the skiing?"

"Icy. Wes lost control at the end of the last run. . . . He was bent over so far backwards that he appeared to be parallel with his skis and was flying helplessly down the slope. He took out one slow sign and then another one before he rolled to a stop. Everyone in the gondola pointed. He had too many hot toddies at lunch and is still drinking to ignore the massive bruises on his back and shins as well as his ego. I'm sure it will be on YouTube at some point. It was classic!"

His smile is infectious and I can't stop grinning. All I can manage to get out is, "I'm so glad you called."

Charlie leans forward and says in a soft, silvery whisper, "I know you're at a party with your *friends*, but I wanted to be the first to see you at midnight. When I get back, I want to take you somewhere."

It takes all I have in me not to start bouncing like a 6-year-old eager for her surprise. "Charlie, where?"

Charlie has this look I have not seen before. He must be indulging in the hot toddies too. His ocean blue eyes are bright, calling for me to look deeper. "It's a surprise. You'll see in two days."

My drawl slows trying to persuade him to spill some more clues. "Please, please give me a hint."

He tilts his head and taps his broad chin contemplating how to respond. "Okay, one hint. You need to dress in warm, comfortable clothes since it will be windy. That's all I'm going to say."

I'm about to plead some more but the count down for the ball drop has begun. Charlie and I join in, focusing on one other. "Eight, seven, six, five, four, three, two, one, HAPPY NEW YEAR." Charlie moves his head slightly to blow his whistle, giving me a clear shot of Wes leaning over to kiss a girl. She swiftly moves out of the way and he tumbles forward. There is a loud smack as his head hits and Charlie whips around to see Wes flat on the floor with the girl mocking him, "You idiot! I said you had to wait until midnight!"

The look of shock and concern is all over his face as he turns back toward the camera. "Gotta go. Wes just face planted." I quickly blow him a kiss goodbye and catch a glimpse of a smile before the screen goes black.

I peer into the windows and replay the entire conversation

in my head. He wanted to see me at midnight. He wants to take me somewhere. He—then I feel arms wrap around me and squeeze me from behind. "Happy New Year's, Kels!"

"Happy New Year, Dad!" My jovial father has indulged in one too many bourbons from the silly grin on his face.

"Why aren't you with your friends? Come on, go wish them all Happy New Year," and he drags me across the room, then disappears back into the crowd of adults.

Bree immediately gives me a hug and whispers, "So how's Charlie?"

I blush and respond, "Great, he's with your brother and Wes, who just face planted trying to kiss a girl."

Bree bursts out laughing. "Wes is such a moron!"

"Who's a moron?" Chris comes up from behind and places his chin on Bree's shoulder and his arms cross over her flat stomach.

"You." We answer in unison.

Chris wrinkles his nose but lets it go when Bree kisses him on the cheek.

Mare has her arms wrapped so tightly around Nick that it looks like he may not be able to breathe. When he comes up for air, I mouth, "Happy New Year," and don't bother saying anything to Mare. She ignores me as well.

I collapse into the chair and search for my date. Kate is in the corner yelling into the phone since the noise level has ratcheted up several notches, making it hard for Kate to talk on the phone. I watch her tap the screen in frustration. Within seconds, she has joined me at the table and is inquiring about my call. "So, how's Charlie?"

"He's good. Wes just face planted while trying to kiss a girl, so he's helping him right now."

Kate folds over, laughing. "Oh, I can picture that. He's so—" She can't get the words out, but I know exactly what she is thinking and die laughing too.

237

Nick sinks in the chair next to us and Mare piles on top of him sneering. "What's so funny?"

Kate wipes a tear off her cheek and answers, "Just a guy we know face planted while trying to kiss a girl."

"What an idiot!" Mare isn't too impressed or amused.

Kate and I exchange another look and continue to laugh. Mare is not going to ruin our fun.

Nick leans forward with much difficulty and inquires, "So who's this guy? Is he the one from boarding school?"

This makes us laugh even more. There's no way Jack would fall over while trying to kiss a girl, even while wasted. He would never try without knowing she would say "yes" first.

Nick rolls his eyes and grunts, "What's so funny? You're not actually thinking about going out with a loser like that, are you?"

Kate stiffens. "What's that about Nick? You should be happy for Kels."

Nick shifts under Mare's weight, forcing her to move to his right side, giving him a better view of us. "Happy? Why would I be happy? She'll end up rejecting him. It sucks to be him."

Kate lights up, just like she does every time she is going to egg someone on. "Maybe Kelsey is open to new possibilities. Any guy would be lucky to call her his girlfriend. Just like Mare is lucky to be yours, right?"

Nick rolls his eyes, then brusquely says, "Kate, I haven't missed your inquisitions." When he doesn't elaborate any further, Mare's eyes bug out of her head.

Mare glares at Nick. "You should have said yes. What is wrong with you tonight?"

Kate shifts her body away from Nick in a huff. Nick hasn't made her feel welcome to be back for some reason. Instead of staying around these buzz killers, I stand up, smooth out my dress and face the happy couple. "Guys, you two need to figure out whatever is going on with you. Kate and I will give you some time to work things out!"

Nick opens his mouth, but I don't give him a chance to reply. I pull Kate up from her seat and mumble, "Let's go find some more truffles," and we walk away. We weave through the adults nibbling on decadent treats at the dessert table and around the men sampling bourbon at the curved wooden bar.

As we pass one man at the far end, he enthusiastically sweeps his arm through the air and knocks a gold lamp that looks like a curved gourd or gooseneck off the edge. The waiter moves at lightning speed and catches it before it shatters on the floor like a Christmas ornament.

Kate and I sweep by the rest of the adults and claim two leather armchairs tucked back in the bright green library in front of a massive marble fireplace. Kate sinks into the chair and sighs. "Are they always like that? Nick doesn't seem happy. Neither does she."

I grab two waters on the table behind me as I answer, "Yep, that's pretty normal. I don't really get how they're still together."

She tilts her head, so I know a big question is coming. "So who would you choose? Nick or Charlie? I think you may have your pick."

I swivel the chair toward her and lean in so no one can overhear this conversation. "What are you talking about? Nick, really?"

Kate shrugs and comments, "Just checking. You had a thing for him for so long."

"Nope, that's over. He's not the same guy as before and Charlie . . . well, I don't want to get too excited, but he said he has a surprise for me when he gets back."

Kate swallows the truffle she just popped in her mouth whole. "What! Do you have any idea what it is?"

"All I know is I need to dress warm—but enough about me. How's your guy?"

Kate's frustration returns. "He's at a party with his ex. Let's see how that turns out."

I respond with the same words she said to me the night we went ice skating. "Relax. Don't worry until he gives you a reason to worry."

Kate swivels back and forth then forces a smile. "Thanks, Kels. You're right. I should follow my own advice, but it's so much easier to give it than take it."

TWENTY-THREE

FIRSTS

WE TURN off the main road and onto what appears to be an unmarked, private gravel drive that's hidden under a layer of snow. Massive pines intermixed with bare hardwood trees covered in dripping icicles frame the sides of the narrow road. As we pass an enormous maple, I watch a pair of squirrels skate across the drooping branches, tumble into a snowdrift, then playfully wrestle in a cloud of white dust.

Straight ahead is a picturesque wood cabin. The morning sun is peeking over the shake roof, almost like it's welcoming us. There are no other houses in sight. This place is isolated, remote, quiet—and absolutely amazing.

When I can't imagine anything being more perfect, Charlie pulls beside the house to reveal a spectacular view of a frozen lake. It looks like there's a layer of encrusted diamonds on top. I jump out of the car with both feet, scattering the snow, and shuffle to the crunchy grass patch with the best view of the natural splendor.

Charlie wraps a blue flannel blanket around my shoulders and pulls me close to him. He rests his chin on my shoulder and whispers, "It's beautiful, isn't it?"

"Yes." I reply softly.

We walk up several rickety steps to a covered entry with an oversized bench to rest our bags. Charlie inserts the dull brass key into the lock and opens the door. Instead of a stale empty house smell, I get a whiff of cinnamon and see one of those cinnamon brooms in the corner. Maybe this is why Charlie always has a hint of cinnamon on him?

There's an old, wood burning stove in the corner, an oversized club chair with books laying on the ottoman, and a brown corduroy sofa. A small kitchen is tucked to the left and there is a hall leading to bedrooms on the right. The deck and screened porch are off the back.

Everything is here for comfort and not for show. Charlie drops the small, gray Yeti cooler on the table by the door and turns on the ancient, bronze lamp and several others, making the room glow.

Then, he goes over to the wood burning stove, reaches behind the metal box and turns on the gas. He strikes a long match and throws it in. We both watch the fire lick the bark of the twigs and quartered logs. I move in a little closer, enjoying the warmth on my thin fingers. Charlie steps back to stand next to me but doesn't take his eyes off the flames.

I'm the first one to break the silence. "So, do you come up here a lot with your friends?"

Charlie shrugs as he throws another log onto the fire. "No, I come up here alone. My friends wouldn't like it here."

"Why not?"

Charlie leans forward to turn off the gas now that the fire is roaring and replies, "I've been to their lake and beach houses. This is not their kind of place, and I don't want to hear their snide remarks."

Not sure if I want to know the answer, but I ask anyway, "So, I'm the first person you have taken here?"

Charlie hesitates, then his eyes shift sideways, and he nods.

"Yes, I thought you would like the cabin a little more than my friends would. This is where I go to get away from everything. You know, my grandfather brought me up here before . . ."

And all those memories come flooding back. It was the first day I ever saw my grandmother break down. I instinctively reach for his arm to console him. "I know. . . . I will never forget that day. My grandmother sobbed on the corner of the bed. She could not find the words to tell me your grandfather was killed. My mom told me to give her space, and I left the room. It was the first time I ever saw her cry like that."

Charlie looks down at the rug and his cheeks flush slightly. "I'm ashamed to admit this, but I don't really remember him. Just faint memories of us fishing up here. This place is my connection to him. It grounds me, if that makes any sense?"

Charlie hunches his shoulders looking so much younger as he brings up this sad memory, making me want to wrap my arms around him. I softly say, "Yes, that makes sense. I can see why you love it here. You know, it reminds me of your grand-mother too."

Charlie's voice lowers as he says, "I know. I wish she could come up here now, but her heart has gotten worse."

I should not have mentioned his grandmother either. *What is wrong with me? More positive things, Kels!* Then, it comes to me. "I heard and am sorry. Maybe we can drive our grandmothers up one weekend. I see there's a Big Green Egg and Weber on the deck. We can grill out, let them relax by the fire, and we all can play bridge. My grandmother really wants me to learn."

He smiles and nods in agreement. "Great idea, Kels. You're right, everything revolves around their bridge games."

He gives me a little nudge and then walks toward the bedrooms. I watch him walk, not daring to follow him back there. He returns with some more blankets and opens the back door. I follow him down the mulched path to the newly planked dock surrounded by a sheet of ice. Geese fly above our heads in a V formation, squawking at their leader. Even with their racket, it's so peaceful.

Charlie wipes the cold, white lines of snow off the creaky Adirondack chairs so our blankets don't get soaked. As he shakes his hand, bright red from the cold, I step forward and wrap both hands around his to transfer my warmth. He peers down at our hands and then back up at me. We stand there, staring at one another, and I feel like he may step in, but a wind whips across the water, making us turn our heads away from the blast.

I pull the blanket tighter around my shoulders, lay another blanket on the chair and then make myself comfortable. He settles into the other chair and we silently look out over the icy cove. A six-point buck stands at the top of the hill. Several deer are prancing on the opposite bank. The snow has covered most of the vegetation so they're probably foraging for food, or just trying to stay warm.

Charlie points and quietly says, "See those deer? Sometimes they come up to the house. My grandmother leaves acorns, pecans and hickory nuts out for them under the screened porch so they have food when it snows. We should check before we leave to make sure there's still some left for them."

Of course, she does that. His grandmother is one of the kindest women I've ever met. She can make anyone laugh and has this way about her. I see a lot of her in Charlie.

Charlie slides his hand over mine and I intertwine my fingers in his, enjoying his warmth and touch. When his body shifts further in my direction, I feel my breath catch. *Is this really going to happen? I knew I should've brought gum!*

My stomach tightens in anticipation as I lean toward him. Everything feels like it's moving in slow motion. I can't hear anything but the sound of my heart hammering in my chest.

He moves in so close that I think it's going to happen, but he stops a couple inches from my lips and whispers, "I have wanted to kiss you ever since I dropped you off that first night after Starbucks. You seemed so nervous so I haven't tried. . . . Have you kissed anyone before?"

The word "No" slowly escapes my lips before I even realize it.

Charlie touches my lower lip with his finger and in a low, smoky voice says, "Good. I want to be your first."

Then, his lips press against mine so softly, lingering on my bottom lip. There's no sense of urgency in his kiss. He's letting me get comfortable. I put both of my hands on his defined jaw and press my lips into his. My mouth opens slightly, and he follows my lead. I feel him move closer, his hands firmly on my back. I open my mouth a little wider and his tongue slips into my warm mouth, lighting my whole body on fire. Resisting the urge to climb over the chair into his lap, I lean as far over the armrest as I can. Sensing my urgency, he gives me a slow, slightly parted kiss while smiling, then pulls back to look deeply into my eyes.

I search his eyes and see he is just as into this as I am. He places his hand under my chin and brushes his lips against mine ever so softly, then says, "I would never have thought that was your first kiss."

I peer down at the midnight blue blanket and nervously giggle. "Well, I can tell you have plenty of experience."

Charlie puts his finger under my chin again and raises it, so I am looking directly into his wintery blue eyes. He sweetly whispers, "Yeah, but it's never felt like this."

I blush even more. I don't know the difference, but I certainly felt the electric energy pulse all the way to my toes. It's almost like the way I feel after I run but much more intense and fulfilling.

I pull the corner of the blanket over my legs and ask, "So why did you ask me if I had kissed anyone before?"

Charlie tucks his hands back under his blanket and leans forward in his chair. "Well, when you kissed my cheek at Krog, at first I thought maybe it was a sign you weren't interested, but then I remembered your comment about not ever participating in a dare and thought, well hoped, that maybe the kiss on the cheek was more because of nerves rather than a hint you wanted to be friends."

I nod, then peer off into the distance at the deer, trying to figure out how much I should elaborate on my inexperience, and am about to open up when we are interrupted by Charlie's phone buzzing. He makes an annoyed face, then puts the phone back in his blue puffer coat.

I smooth my dark blonde hair to make sure it's not sticking straight up from all the electricity and suck on my lower lip to savor the taste of his peppermint chapstick.

He looks at me again, but he seems distracted, almost a little bothered, and my nerves get the best of me. So I do what I normally do when I'm uncomfortable, I babble. "So how is school? Anything going on? What's your favorite subject?"

Charlie leans back in the chair and sighs. "Tough. I don't feel like I have enough time to do anything but study and practice. I will be traveling a lot when school starts back. I have a game every weekend."

I sit there listening, wishing he'll invite me to watch him play, but he doesn't, so I hesitantly ask, "Do you mind if I come watch? The ones at home?"

Charlie turns and smiles. "Yes, I was hoping you would come. We may play Smith again in the playoffs."

I heard all about the teams playing again from Nick and Chris as well as the headmistress in assembly. I add, "Yeah, the college scouts should be coming to the playoffs. They've been looking at Clayton. I don't think he looked as good as you during the game though."

Charlie reaches under his seat, grabs a couple acorns and

bounces one across the thin ice. A raccoon must have left a pile of them under the chair. "Thanks for that. He's a beast to guard. Do you know where he's going to school?"

I reach under his seat and grab a handful of acorns too. One of the nuts feels colder than ice and falls like a rock in my lap. I slide one acorn across the frozen lake, thinking about what the boys said at the New Year's Eve party. "Duke, maybe?"

Charlie rubs one of the acorns around in his hand, thinking about something. "That's what I heard too. My parents want me to go to Duke. I've been talking to the coach there, but I doubt there will be two spots for kids from the same town."

Now I get it. He's stressed about college. "Oh, I don't know for certain, but I can find out more when school starts. Do you want to go to Duke and play?"

This time he looks at me and shows a side of him most people probably never see. "I don't know if I want to follow the plan. I may want to go somewhere in the Northeast."

I feel my cheeks raise, surprised and kinda relieved we're on the same page. "Same. I want to get out of the South. When I visited Kate at boarding school, everyone seemed so genuine. No drama, no games."

He leans back in his chair and exhales like a huge weight has been lifted off of him. I don't think he feels like he can talk to anyone about these things.

Charlie turns toward me and adds, "You're exactly right! Everyone is having to one up one another here. That's why I come to the lake. To get away from it all."

Looking around at this perfect getaway, I place my hand on his and state, "I would come up here all the time if I had a place like this."

Charlie kisses me on the lower lip and murmurs, "Well, you can come with me anytime."

I softly kiss him back, not wanting this to end. Now that my nerves have settled, everything just feels right—like this is supposed to happen.

As another blistering gust whips across the cove, making the dock creak and my lips tremble, Charlie chuckles and wraps his blanket around me. We sit there for a moment with our foreheads pressed together and eyes closed. I have never felt so connected to anyone before.

TWENTY-FOUR
A BRIGHT NEW SEMESTER

It's our first day back at school and most of my fellow class-mates seem a little restless. Maybe they're a little on edge since today is the day we receive our exam and semester grades. I really don't know why they make us wait until after our break.

Maybe the school doesn't want to ruin our holiday—or theirs. I'm sure they don't want to field phone calls about grades over their break. Plus, the big donors may not write that fat check at the end of the year if they're not happy with how their kids are doing.

As soon as I climb over the guys at the end of the row and take my seat, Chris leans over and says, "You may not see me for a while when my parents get my French grade. I bombed it."

I pat his knee and try to reassure him. "I'm sure you did better than you think."

He smirks skeptically and says, "We'll see shortly," and then texts Bree, knowing he may lose his phone for the next few weeks. That seems to be the most popular form of punishment with parents.

I look over at Barry and other guys on our row, and they

don't seem to be the least bit bothered. They must know the school will give them a B or C so they can play their sports, or they would be freaking out right now.

I unzip the top pocket of my backpack and pull out the smooth rock I found in the pile of acorns at the lake. Every time I look at it, I think of Charlie. I rest it in the palm of my hand and trace the dark gray veins that run parallel to one another in the middle of the white rock. It reminds me of two people alone in a white forest.

I remember our first kiss, him opening up to me about his future, and the moment when I realized how much I had fallen for him. We spent every minute together during the break, but it wasn't long enough. We only had three days to ourselves before—

Mrs. Williams clears her throat and interrupts my thoughts. "Good morning! I hope everyone had a fabulous break. My girls and I spent time in Aspen skiing with some other Smith families and loved every minute of it. It was such a nice change of pace. Much needed time off so we can gear up for the new year. As you all well know, you will receive your grades today. They will be posted online for your parents to view as well."

Mrs. Williams pauses for effect, grinning like Cruella de Vil. "If you are not pleased with your performance, this is your chance to work hard and start fresh. One of you will earn the prestigious Smith Writing Award in the spring. It is an award colleges want to see on your application. There are also many other awards at Smith. Take advantage of these opportunities. Strive to be better this year. It is never too late to apply yourself. Now, if there is nothing else, you all may be dismissed early."

Chris leans over and whispers in my ear, "Yeah right, like we all have the opportunity to win the writing award. Her daughter received it last year and will get it again this year. It was made for her."

I stifle a laugh knowing he's right; I heard Taylor isn't good at much except for writing.

Chris starts to walk away, then he turns back when he notices I'm not moving. I'm just not motivated to start a new semester here. This one is supposed to be even harder now that they broke us in over the last semester. He has to yank me out of my chair to get me up.

As we walk up the stairs, Nick steps behind us and places one arm over Chris's shoulder and the other arm over mine. As I glance at him in disbelief, Nick jests, "Chris, it was nice seeing you. You will be spending your free time with your French professor. I hear most of the class will be joining you."

Chris sarcastically responds, "Ha-Ha. I'm sure you will join too just to suck up to our teacher."

Nick ignores the snide comment and turns his attention to me. "So Kels, how was your break?"

I shrug. "Good. I enjoyed seeing Kate." Then I peer down at the rock safely in my palm, making me miss Charlie.

Nick curiously looks down at my hand then back up at my face. "So you never told us who called you on New Year's Eve. You disappeared quickly, not letting anyone hear your conversation."

I look ahead toward the glass doors leading to the courtyard and deflect. "Well, it was so loud, and there wasn't a good signal, so I headed to the windows. How was the rest of your break?"

Nick doesn't let it go. Instead, he leans in closer. "So who called? The boarding school guy? What's his name again —Jack?"

I quickly look at Nick, and then back over at Chris, who is also waiting for my answer, and I casually reply, "No, actually a family friend."

From the corner of my eye, I notice Nick's eyebrow raise while Chris looks away bored, searching for someone else, probably Bree.

Nick cross-examines me some more. "Why did he call on New Year's Eve?"

I point at the cut on my hand. "He was checking on me."

Nick looks at my hand and then back at me in mild disbelief. "Well, the conversation didn't last long, so I guess that makes sense. It doesn't explain why he called at midnight, though."

Right as he inquires about midnight, Mare walks in front of the three of us with her hands on her hips, staring directly at Nick, who has his arm around my shoulder. Nick quickly drops it and walks to her side. Mare puts her arm around him, relaxing a little now that he's where he should be—right next to her. She looks at him, then at me, and then at Chris. In a cold, high pitched voice she asks, "What's going on?"

Nick leans away from her and acts like we were talking about the weather. "Nothing, we were just talking."

Mare glares at him and argues, "You were not just talking."

Nick lets out a sigh, then adds, "Yes, we were just asking Kelsey about her New Year's call."

Mare narrows her eyes at him, looking a little miffed he cares about that call. "You should be happy some guy called her on New Year's Eve. It's not like any guys in our class are going to call her, and Kels doesn't have the balls to go out with a junior or senior."

Bree, who snuck up beside Chris, unsuccessfully suppresses her giggle, knowing I did go out with a junior. Chris gives her a funny look and I raise my eyebrows, signaling for her to be quiet. Bree gets the hint and looks away at the girls whispering in the corner.

It takes a lot of strength to not rub Charlie in Mare's face. If I say anything and things don't work out, then I'm going to have to relive this over and over again, and I just don't think I can take it with how I feel about him. So I ignore Mare's slam and walk away from her like she doesn't deserve a response.

TWENTY-FIVE
RISE UP

WE DRIVE by a sea of people outside Mercedes-Benz Stadium and pull right into the entrance for the players and team owners. We slowly climb out of the Lincoln town car and follow Kim into a gold elevator that whisks us to a private floor. The doors open into a wood-paneled lobby that resembles something in a high-end hotel or residence rather than a stadium. There are several doors on the left that lead to the suites. Some are overflowing with guests, others are quiet.

We pass a group of older guys hanging out in a doorway, and Ivy stops to chat. Kim continues on walking to her parent's suite and unlocks the door. The suite is just as nice as the lobby, but with more of a European flair. Her mother must have been involved with the decorating.

Kim drops her bag and goes straight to the marble bar to pull out waters while the guys bolt to the floor to ceiling glass wall. Chris and Nick's heads move in unison, turning a full 180 degrees from one end of the stadium to the other. Their jaws drop almost to the floor.

Nick turns back around and yells, "Guys, the owner of the team, Arthur Blank, is in the box right next to us!"

Chris fist bumps Nick and hollers, "Yeah, this is amazing!"

Kim presses her palms toward the ground, signaling for them to be a little more discreet. As we were getting ready, she told me her parents reluctantly agreed to allow her to bring so many friends into the box. It took a lot of begging. I still can't believe they let us have the whole suite for this game.

Kim pops open her sparkling water and huddles in the corner with Mare and Hope. I grab a water and step through the glass door onto the balcony. Bree has claimed a seat in the front row next to Chris. The rest of the guys are behind them, gawking at the other owner's suite. I sink into the leather seat beside her and watch the fans. Nick settles into the seat next to me.

The hum around us gets louder by the minute. You can feel the energy pulsing in the stadium. I rise to find the restroom and the rest of the girls, but they're not around.

I spot a lady setting out appetizers on the dining table and ask, "Have you seen my friends?"

She responds without looking up, "They left after Ms. Westover asked for me to bring out the food. Maybe ten minutes ago."

"Thanks! Do you happen to know where the restroom is?" I ask, hoping to have some privacy to check for new messages.

She points down the hall and says, "It's on the right," and I follow her instructions. Luckily, the bathroom is empty. The girls must have gone out into the lobby. I check my texts and there's nothing new. *Why hasn't he told me what he's doing tonight?*

As I return to the main room of the suite, my friends are coming back in, giggling like silly school girls about to pull a prank on the playground.

I wait for them to get close and ask, "Where did you all go?"

Mare crosses her arms and snarls as she answers, "Nowhere that pertains to you."

I turn my body away from her and focus on Hope. She's finally speaking to me again. It still feels a little forced, but at least it's not so awkward. "Hope, what are you up to?"

"You'll see soon enough," she says while looking up at the ceiling.

"Fine." I say flatly, feeling somewhat rejected and annoyed with all the secrecy. I return to my seat and watch the crazy mascot wave an enormous flag in the corner of the field. Cheerleaders jump out of the tunnel in two single-file lines, shaking their silver pom poms in the air.

The different branches of the military follow behind them, waving their normal-sized flags. As the flames blow out of various barriers emblazoned with the "Rise Up" slogan, the players launch themselves onto the field. Their hands are high in the air, trying to get the crowd riled up, and it's working.

The Falcons kick off, and the guys are glued to their seats. The girls stay in the main room of the suite while Bree and I talk about school and people watch. As soon as she brings up Charlie, I motion for us to move over to an empty row.

Bree asks about the lake and everything that happened up there. I omit a few things but tell her most of it. I also fill her in on our other dates. He took me on a hike up in the mountains, we explored the Ponce City Market, and walked on the Belt-Line. We spent every day together until school started back, so it's really weird not being able to see him.

Now we only get to text several times a day and talk at night. For some reason, he didn't mention anything about getting together this weekend. He did have an out of town basketball game last night, and he told me all about it this morning. We never got around to talking about tonight, though.

Bree brushes off my concern, saying he's probably with the guys. They were starting to give him a hard time that he has not been around. She doesn't think he needs to mention what he's up to with me, at least not yet. We just started dating, and she's right. I wouldn't want him to check up on me either even though I have nothing to hide.

Bree and I return to our seats so she can talk to Chris during the break. The whistle blows and Nick stands up, announcing, "Halftime," then he asks, "Where's the bathroom?" Typical guy move to not miss a minute of the game.

Mare bolts toward Nick to prevent him from leaving, pleading with her hazel eyes, "Don't leave yet. They're bringing more of those wings you like."

Nick looks over her shoulder and sees wings piled on the platter. Instead of pointing that out and arguing with her, he shrugs and sits back down.

I jump as a loud sound booms around the stadium. An image pops up on the huge screen of Kim, Hope and Mare holding signs saying:

Nick, Go to Sadie with me for the WIN- Love U, Mare

Brian, you and me at the Sadie- Kim

Sam, PLEASE go to the Sadie with me- Hope

Then, the camera crew focuses on the box, and we are live on the Halo screen.

Chris moves out of the shot, and Bree follows. I'm standing next to Nick, looking like I'm the one asking him for a date. I feel an elbow jab into my side as Mare leans over to give him a hug from behind, causing me to fall backwards toward Bree. She stumbles as well, but Chris grabs onto her arm and prevents us from going over the railing. I can't help but wonder if that was done on purpose.

Nick climbs over the chair and gives Mare a kiss. For once, I don't mind their PDA. Sam runs over to Hope, standing next to the food and gives her a hug. Brian lifts Kim into the air and swings her around, then plants one on her lips.

I just stand there in shock next to Chris and Bree. Not once does Chris look over at Ivy, who is intently watching his response and looks completely outraged that he doesn't seem to care that the other guys are being asked to the dance.

One announcer comments, "Luckily, all the guys said yes!"

Another announcer cracks a joke, "I wonder what the fourth guy was thinking—and the girl that got knocked over by the girlfriend?" Then the screen cuts over to advertisements.

Bree looks so relieved in Chris's arms. It would have ruined the rest of the game if Ivy had asked Chris.

All I can say is, "Now that is hard to beat."

This puts Ivy over the edge. She struts over and knocks me out of the way again. She pulls Bree away from Chris and climbs in between the two of them. Then, she gets so close to Chris that her nose is almost touching his. "I can top that. Just wait to see what I have planned" she says, her words dripping with vitriol. Then, Ivy steps over the seat, over all the empty rows, and disappears out the door in a flash.

Chris and Bree look at each other, roll their eyes, and then bust out laughing. Obviously, she can't handle seeing Chris happy with Bree, but her reaction today was much more intense and vicious than usual. She's unraveling.

Our phones start to blow up. So many kids saw the ask at the game. My phone buzzes twice and I look down to see it's from Charlie.

Looks like you made it on the big screen

My heart races as I text back. *Yeah you at the game?*

Charlie texts back immediately. *Yes. How did you get those sweet seats?*

I respond without thinking how this may look. *My friend Kim's parents are part owners*

I see dots.

So you're hanging with Crazy Rich Atlantans?

I stifle a laugh. It would seem that I am. *Ha Ha*

Pausing, I debate if I should ask him into the box. It's a little early to introduce him to everyone, but with all the excitement, no one will really pay much attention. *Want to meet up? You can join us in the box*

Instantly, I regret sending that text. I don't want to look like the clingy girl that needs to see her guy all the time.

No. All good. I'm on the opposite side. Can I see you tomorrow night?

Well, that is better than a no. *Sure! What are we doing?*

I stare at the dots, wishing he would respond faster.

Dinner and then maybe study together?

I can knock out a bunch of things before my game and should be done by 4 o'clock. *That works!*

Charlie responds quickly. *Pick u up at 5?*

I text back feeling a little better. *Can't wait!*

I read the words, *Same,* and smile. I get to see him! But, why didn't he want to come into the box?

I hand my phone to Bree and ask, "What do you think?"

Bree reads the texts, then whispers, "Let me see if my brother posted a photo of the group at the game." Bree looks at Dave's feed and shows me the photo of five guys together up in the nose bleeds and softly explains what is so obvious. "Kels, he's only with the guys. He probably didn't want to bail on them. It's not like you could let all the guys in this box."

Of course, he would not ditch his friends. Not even for a box seat. He just took me to his family cabin. That has to mean something. I need to relax!

TWENTY-SIX
MISSED CALLS

BREE and I walk into the gym a little late. Well, maybe more than a little. I'm not the best with time, and Bree definitely took too long to get ready. We quietly slide into the bleachers behind the Chase bench and away from the girls who are glaring at Bree.

Charlie blocks the bleached blond guy from dunking the ball and gets elbowed in the mouth in the process. Blood flies through the air and onto his gold uniform, but he doesn't seem to notice or care. The other guy is in his face, yelling obscenities.

The assistant ref peels them apart as the main ref blows his whistle to stop the game. He yells to the coach, "Someone needs to wipe the blood off the floor." Then, he points at Charlie and adds, "He's out until all the blood is off his jersey and he's cleaned up!"

Charlie opens his mouth to argue, but Dave grabs him and drags him off the court before he says something that will get him kicked out of the game. One of the trainers examines Charlie's mouth, then hands him a towel filled with ice for him to press on his lip. Dave heads back on the court as Charlie paces back and forth, trying to calm down.

He stops to examine the stains on his jersey. Seeing it will be much easier to run water over his shirt rather than try to wipe it off with the towel, Charlie heads to what must be the locker room. He pulls off the jersey as he opens the door, and the girls above me taunt, "Take it all off, Charlie."

He doesn't turn around to acknowledge the cat-calls. I stare at the locker room door and miss Dave take an elbow in the back. After a few minutes, Charlie strides through the double doors wearing a wrung out jersey and a very swollen bottom lip. He smiles at me to let me know he's fine. I nod and mouth, "Go get him."

As soon as he approaches the bench, his face switches to a determined grimace, letting his coach know he is ready to play. Within seconds his coach puts him in, and it's obvious he's more fired up than before but in more control of his temper.

He steals the ball as it's passed to the top of the key, and throws it down the court for Dave to lay up on the glass. The Chase side explodes, chanting, "Fair and Square!" *When are the other teams going to realize Charlie plays better when they play dirty?*

Chase shuts them down for the next few plays, making it hard for the other team to come back even if our best players are taken out again. The guys seem to relax on the court, resulting in some careless errors. Dave throws the ball to someone who poorly passes it to Charlie, giving the other team the opportunity to take the ball, but Charlie isn't going to have it.

He wrestles the guy to the ground, resulting in the both of them rolling across the floor. The ball bounces down the court, begging for someone else to pick it up, and make a run for the open hoop. The guy who gave Charlie the bloody lip sees the opportunity to get him back. He leaps over Charlie and intentionally kicks him in the head while he's down.

Our side erupts in anger at the blatant foul, but the ref doesn't call it again. He has missed so many of the gabs to the ribs and elbows in the back. Why would we expect him to call this?

By the end of the fourth quarter, Charlie has a very fat lip and is pretty winded. Dave is limping a tad bit. They continue to play as best as they can, and hold the twenty-two point lead. With one minute left, the coach finally puts in the second string, and the other team scores several points very quickly but not enough to even the game. Chase wins 62 to 53.

Bree and I stay in the bleachers until they have emptied out. We make our way to the lobby, chatting about random stuff as we wait for the guys to finish up with the coach. Many other Chase kids are waiting too. Bree nervously keeps looking over at a group near the bathroom doors. She doesn't say anything to them or about them.

As Charlie and Dave push open the doors from the gym, that group of girls rushes over, and circles around them. Dave stays behind, but Charlie politely pushes through and heads straight for me, smiling. I can tell he's drained.

He collapses on the sofa next to me and pops off his shoes to put his sweat pants on before his mother says anything about it. I rub his shoulder and lightly tease, "I think you may be able to compete with Wes with that fat lip. How's it feel?"

He looks up from tying his right shoe with a funny lopsided smile and replies, "Yep, at least it doesn't need stitches. The numbness is wearing off somewhat. I can feel a little now," and he touches his lower lip gently. Then continues on in a somewhat irritated voice, "I can't believe they didn't call that one. He always plays dirty, though. He tried to prove he's as good as their best player who was on the sidelines with an injury tonight. It would have been a much closer game if that guy had played."

I scoot closer to him and needle a little more. "I thought that one guy was going to take you out when you took the jump shot and elbowed him in the neck on your way down."

He lets out a deep chuckle and laments, "Yeah, he got me back when he elbowed me in the ribs a couple plays later. I had a hard time running after that one."

"Hello Charlie, I'm standing here too!" I hear Bree chime in as she stands there patiently waiting for Charlie to address her.

As soon as the words leave her mouth, he pops up, and with both hands, he messes up her hair like a big brother would do. "Hi Bree! Sorry, I should have said something earlier."

She pushes him off and walks toward the window to see her hair. Dave appears out of nowhere and runs both of his hands through her hair as well, making it look like a bird's nest. His laughter booms across the lobby.

Looking really annoyed at being treated like a little kid, Bree sticks out her tongue and smoothes her hair for the second time. She bitterly asks, "Why aren't you messing with Kels? She has more hair than I do."

Dave taunts back, "Because I don't think Charlie would let me touch a hair on her head. Besides, it's so much fun to mess with you." Then, he pretends to reach for Bree again but goes for my hair, and I quickly scoot away, laughing.

Charlie acts all protective by standing in front of me with his hand up, motioning for Dave to stop, but Dave keeps coming at me.

Charlie's dad, who is chatting with his coach, interrupts our fun. "Charlie, come over here for a second."

Charlie warns Dave saying, "Leave them alone. I'll get you back if you don't." Then walks over to his father.

I watch Charlie's shoulders slump lower and lower as the discussion drags on. Bree and Dave disappear to find their parents, and I sit on the sofa, waiting for them to come back, checking my Snaps. Every once in a while, I peer up and catch Charlie mouth, "I'm sorry" and attempt to smile with the slug on his lip.

His mom is the first to step away to say, "Hello," and gives me a big hug. Then, his father strides over with a massive grin on his face and states, "The coach just gave Charlie some exercises to do at home to get back in shape. He should be able to play the entire time and not need a break."

Charlie's mom sighs and exclaims, "I think he played very well considering the beating he was taking out there."

"If he is going to play for Duke, he has to be tougher." Indignantly he fires back, and she wisely lets it go.

I bite my tongue about him possibly going to school up north instead, knowing we will never leave the gym after that has been divulged.

By the time he returns, Charlie's spirits have flipped from playful to worn down, but his father is oblivious and is still going at him. "Did you get everything you needed from the coach, son?"

"Yes, Dad. I can start tomorrow. Kels and I are going to get some protein in us, just like the coach recommended. See you both at midnight, right?"

Sensing her son's defeated morale, his mom places a hand on his shoulder and sweetly says, "You played well. Go treat yourself and Kelsey to something good to eat." She hands him a couple twenties and says, "Here's some money in case you need extra tonight. And yes, curfew is still midnight."

Charlie appreciatively takes the cash and moves closer to me as if he's about to take my hand, but then hesitates. He says, "Thanks, Mom. Bye, Dad. See you at midnight," then motions for me to go first.

As we reach the door, Dave makes a crack about the amount of sprints Charlie will be doing tomorrow morning with his dad and Charlie blows it off, but I can tell it's really bothering him.

The four of us walk in a pack to the car, passing different groups of girls on the way. I notice a petite auburn hair girl stare at us as we get close. She yells, "Hey, see you all at the party? Looks like you will need a cold one on that lip of yours."

Charlie stiffens as he strides past and acts like she wasn't talking to him. Dave veers off toward her and puts an arm around her shoulders, like they are best friends.

Bree scoffs and I hear her say under her breath, "Figures," but she keeps on walking with me and Charlie.

"That's my sister and her friend," carries over the wind, and I deflate as the words sink in. Dave is referring to me as Bree's friend, not Charlie's anything. Maybe Charlie isn't ready to let people know he's dating a freshman? Maybe his friends don't think we're dating?

Charlie is the first one to the car and hops in without opening our doors the way he usually does. I pile into the back seat with Bree. Charlie looks puzzled, and pats the seat next to him. "What are you doing? The front seat is yours."

Bree rolls her eyes as I climb over the console and take my place in the front seat.

Dave's face drops when he sees he has been demoted to the back with his sister, but quickly recovers. As he gets in the car, he enthusiastically relays, "So the party's at Finn's." Then, places his hand on Charlie's shoulder and says, "Let's grab Steak n Shake, then head over."

I pipe in, "Yeah, that sounds good. Bree, what do you think?"

Glancing back, I see she's wringing her hands together, probably wanting to say, "no," but Dave will lay into her for being lame. Charlie peers into the rearview mirror and sees the same thing. He offers another option, "Dave, my parents gave me extra cash for tonight. Let's go somewhere better than a drive-thru and skip the party. I'm not up for it."

Dave mumbles, "Of course you're not," which gets my attention. Maybe he really doesn't want to show up with two freshmen?

Bree lets out a high pitch squeal. I whip my head around and see her rubbing her shoulder with a scowl. She spats at him, "I'm not the only one who doesn't want to go, Dave!"

As I massage the kink in my neck, Charlie leans over the seats with his hand up and curtly says, "Dave, you can go. No one's stopping you. I can take the girls out, and you can hang with everyone else. They're not going to have fun at this party, and you know it."

Charlie's penetrating stare stops Dave for a second, but then he adamantly fires back. "Bree can handle herself. Or are you worried about Kelsey?"

Charlie's eyes flash with anger for a moment, then firmly states, "Kels, can handle herself just fine. It's the others I'm worried about. . . . So which is it? Are you coming with or going to Finn's? Decide!"

Pouting like a little kid, his body slams into the back of the seat, and he stares out the window with his arms crossed. "Go, you know I can't leave Bree."

Bree pushes him in the shoulder; she's furious about how he's treating her. "I don't need a babysitter. You can go. Actually, I think it would be better if you go and see her. Maybe she will focus on *you* for once." Then, Bree quickly slides as far away from him, expecting a retaliating punch. Feistiness must be a family trait.

I've had enough of this and join in beside Charlie. "Okay guys, sibling rivalry hour is over. Dave, you're not going to hurt our feelings if you go. We can drop you off and pick you back up if that will save you from getting into trouble. You decide, but please make a decision before Charlie's stomach eats itself. The growling is getting louder by the minute."

This makes Dave smile and chuckle. "Looks like my sister is not the only one with a little fire in her. Let's go. What are you thinking?"

Charlie holds up the cash. "How about Yeah Burger, then Jeni's?"

As he peers over at me, I nod. Bree does the same. Dave mutters, "Sure, boss," then he reaches into the cup holder, and turns off Charlie's phone that has been buzzing non-stop since we got into the car.

For the next week, Charlie's phone continued to buzz. I see the same frustrated look, and then the swipe to shut it off within fifteen minutes of being with me every night. I so want to ask, but I don't want to be *that* girl. Every time it happens, I repeat in my head, *he's with me and not with whoever's calling.* Still, the doubt has crept in and is getting stronger the longer he avoids this conversation.

By Friday night, I'm ready to see my friends and get away from the buzzing reminder that there's something he's hiding from me. As soon as I can get Bree alone, I'm going to ask her what she knows. Maybe she has some insight into things since she has known him for much longer than I have.

As soon as I step off the escalator, Kim bounces over and throws her arms around my neck. "I'm so glad you made it. We haven't seen you out for weeks. . . . I was starting to wonder if you had mono or something," then leans back to study my face even though she said it like it's a joke.

Mare stifles a laugh then taunts gleefully, "Kelsey—mono. Give me a break. She would actually have to kiss someone.

Unless—did you kiss that boarding school guy? Do we need to worry about you spreading boarding germs to us?"

Nick's eyes narrow as she says this, then inquires, "Yeah, Kels, is there something you need to tell us?"

Bree turns her back so Chris and the others can't see her face. She would never be able to play poker. I turn back to face everyone, and they're waiting for me to answer, making me feel a little trapped. "No, I did *not* hook up with him or anyone at boarding school. And I don't have mono. But thanks for all the concern, guys."

Kim is the first to laugh, followed by Bree, and then everyone else relaxes, except for Nick. "So Kels, where have you been then?"

Before I have a chance to answer, Bree whisks me up the ramp and into the concessions yelling, "I will get the popcorn, you guys find a seat. Chris, you want anything else?"

Chris slides up behind her and kisses her on the cheek. "Junior Mints would be awesome," then disappears down the hall with the rest of the crew.

Bree watches them go, then turns back to me. "So why are you not telling them about Charlie?"

I scan the crowd to ensure no one else I know is in line and whisper, "Because I don't know what we are?"

Bree stiffens. "What do you mean?"

"Well, you heard all the things Dave said in the car. Charlie didn't want to take me to that party, and then his phone has buzzed all week. When he went to the bathroom, I looked and a girl named Brooke keeps trying to reach him. There were eleven missed calls from her!"

Bree peers around the rotund lady ordering enough candy for a Little League baseball team, and then stands back next to me, looking a little shifty. "Well, did you check to see if he has called her back?"

"No, that would have been a good thing to do," I mumble,

looking down at my Uggs, then add, "Do you think he may be seeing her too?"

Bree says a little too loudly, "What? No! You're being paranoid." But from the look on her face, Bree knows something and isn't saying it.

Instead, she pretends to focus on the menu board as she calmly asks, "Have you asked him about her? Brooke Hamilton is his ex and is always at my house with Dave. I thought my brother and her were a thing but every time I walk into the kitchen, Brooke is talking about Charlie this, Charlie that. It annoys my brother, but he still keeps having her over. It's sad, really."

Noticing my finger is bleeding from my picking, I grab a napkin and press it against my cuticle, even more embarrassed than before. "No, I haven't asked him. When I finally broke down and mentioned that his phone keeps buzzing, he acted like it wasn't a big deal and said it was nobody important."

Bree looks up at the menu again, doing everything she can to avoid eye contact. "Then, maybe she isn't? They were a thing for a long time. Her bitch sister was in my class. That family always gets everything they want. Well, except for Charlie now." A smile creeps across her face as she says this.

Knowing this is childish, I ask the question anyway, "If we are a thing, then why hasn't he mentioned me on social media?"

Bree is almost at the register and nonchalantly asks, "Is he active on social media?"

Embarrassed to admit I looked, I nod. "Yes, he posted a picture of the guys traveling to Charlotte today."

Bree twitches her lips, thinking, then cautiously proceeds. "I don't know. Are there any other posts of girls?"

Feeling like a stalker, I pull out my phone and put it out for her to take. "Yeah, from several months ago."

Bree doesn't grab it, instead, she waits for me to continue. "Well, who are the girls?"

"I'm scared to look," I admit.

She rolls her eyes at this and puts out her hand. "Give me your phone."

As she scrolls through his Instagram, she points and gives me the much needed information. "That is Brooke Hamilton."

As I look more closely at the photo, I recognize the voluminous auburn hair that cascades down well below her shoulders. She has natural blonde highlights that frame her thin, heart-shaped face. Piercing dark brown, almost black eyes. Pouty lips that might have been injected at some point. They are colored with a shimmery, bronze pink lipstick. She has a petite, thin nose. The same nose that was high in the air as I passed her at the game last Friday night.

I can see why the boys are attracted to her. She has a presence about her, and she looks like a girl boys would pin up in their rooms, scantily clad in a string bikini.

Bree continues to tap on the photo, and the names Sarah Weston and Amy Little appear. "Those are Brooke's posse." She scrolls some more and sees Brooke plastered to him in a pre-dance photo.

Then, she hands me back my phone, not too concerned. "Well, it looks like he and Brooke are over. He has not posted anything with her in months."

But I cannot let this go, not yet. These questions have been driving me crazy all week. "Then why is she calling him? Why has he not deleted those photos?"

Bree puts her hand up to let the lady know we are next in line while giving me another sideways glance. "Alright, I will tell you what I know, but you cannot freak out."

Then, she orders Junior Mints and popcorn for everyone as promised, making me wait for what seems like an eternity. As we move to the side and away from the crowd, Bree tells me everything, "So Brooke's family expects to get everything they want and will do anything to get it. Her older sister, Lauren is at Yale and still thinks she and her freshman year boyfriend, Davis will get back together. He's been dating another girl for two years now and she still will not let him go.

"I heard from another girl who is friends with the current girlfriend that Mrs. Hamilton flew up to Yale and spoke to an old flame of hers, who happens to be a professor at Yale. Momma Hamilton pleaded with the professor to break them up. She said and I quote, 'Lauren and Davis are meant to be together and this other girl needs to go away.' The professor warned the girlfriend to watch her back."

My hands are over my mouth as she continues on saying, "So Brooke may be the same way. She may not want to let him go. Maybe Charlie knows this so he's keeping you a secret. Protecting you. It's just a thought."

I really do not know what to say. Shocked isn't the right word. Concerned? Scared? I don't know. I give Bree a baffled look and she nods, understanding how upsetting this scenario may be. Before I can ask her to tell me more about Brooke, Kim appears, wrapping her arms around the both of us, saying, "Come on. The movie is starting," and we both jump sky high.

Seeing my twisted expression of shock and surprise, Kim asks, "Are you all right?" I wave her off, rationalizing my behavior, "Sorry, I had too much caffeine and am a little jumpy."

Bree wraps her arm around me to push me along the hall as I process all this new information. I stare at the screen but don't see a thing. I can't even remember what movie we are supposed to be watching. Instead, I just keep replaying one of the craziest things I have ever heard in my head, wondering if Charlie is doing what Bree suggested, and if so, when is he going to fill me in and warn me to watch my back?

· · ·

Sunday, Charlie and I meet up to study and the normal routine returns again. He looks at the phone, then turns it off, so it's not a distraction. I so want to ask about Brooke but refrain. He needs to be the one to bring this up, not me.

After another hour of quietly studying side by side on the breakfast bench, Charlie stops scribbling down French words and takes a long sip of water. He still hasn't showered since basketball practice, but I don't mind. His musky smell is comforting as well as a little distracting, even more so than the constant buzzing of his phone.

I hear the mudroom door open and bags drop. I get up to see if my mother needs any help. Before I'm across the kitchen, my mom walks through the doorway with two Whole Foods bags and drops them on the marble. She waves me off. "I got it honey. There's only a couple more in the hall. How was your day? Are you hungry? I bought your favorite black bean hummus and veggies to dip."

I reach into the bag and pull out the orange tub of hummus from Roots. Charlie appears with the other bags and places them without a thud next to the others. Within seconds, he's by my side, seeing if he can help some more. I hand him the hummus and bag of carrots to place on the table.

Still looking down, my mom says, "Before I forget, I need to give you the cash you asked for last week. How many friends do you need money for again?"

I count all my friends in my head and calculate. "Forty dollars to be on the safe side. I promise to do those errands around the house to pay you back."

While putting the milk in the refrigerator, she asks, "Is it still one dollar a rose?"

I lift one finger, but she doesn't see me, so I confirm out loud, "For the yellow ones, yes. I think the red ones are two dollars now."

Charlie walks back to the counter for the celery sticks and asks, "For what?"

My mom peers into the bag to see if anything is missing at the bottom and reminisces. "They have been doing this fundraiser since I was in high school. Back then, they only had red roses and the boys would buy a rose for the girl they liked and it would be delivered during class, in front of everyone. Some boys would say who the rose was from and some wouldn't. I remember sitting there watching everyone get a rose. My boyfriend, Kel's dad, was at another school so I never got one until we girls started buying them for each other when we were juniors and seniors."

"Dad's still not good about giving you roses," I tease my mom, and she shrugs like it's not a big deal, but I know it bothers her.

I turn back to Charlie and provide him with more details. "Now they have purple roses for secret admirers, red for obvious reasons, and yellow for friends."

My mother goes over to her Chloe purse and counts the bills in her wallet. She proudly announces, "I went to the ATM today so Kelsey can buy a rose for all her friends to make sure none of them feel left out."

Charlie has this look in his eye. Valentine's Day is this weekend and he hasn't mentioned a thing about it. Maybe he forgot? Guys don't seem to like this holiday.

Charlie bites his lower lip contemplating something and all I hear is, "That's nice of you, Kels."

That's not what I was hoping for, so I turn away and look at my mom to hide the disappointment on my face, and change the subject. "Did you see that video that posted today about the phenom runner who trained at Nike when she was seventeen?"

My mom hands me the bills and nods her head, keeping her eyes cast to the floor. "Yes, I cried. It was on a group chat for your ECNL soccer team. Very gut-wrenching to watch."

I continue on saying, "Well, I was thinking. I don't want to buy Nike shoes anymore. The only way for those men to understand what they did was wrong is for them to see it in their sales. Telling her she needs to lose weight to be faster is beyond absurd. She was the fastest woman until she started training with them. She was already slim, but a healthy weight. Like they would pick some magic number like 114 for a man. It would never happen."

Charlie searches on his phone for the video and hits play. We all watch it again. I still tear up. Even Charlie is affected by the video but remains silent. There is not much a guy can say about that except sorry.

I take the opportunity to add, "You know, Ned treats us that way. He cuts us down in front of everyone. He tells some girls they're stupid. Why do we let him get away with it? Some girls have quit playing soccer because of him. So the problem is not just at Nike, it's all over. . . . Can we look into moving to another club? I think a bunch of girls would be up for it. We could start a new team with that female coach Reese is working with on the weekends. She played college ball. . . . What do you think?"

My mom moves her tongue to the side of her mouth, where it bumps out her cheek. "Well, it's an idea. Let me get a pulse from several of the other moms I'm close to and get their thoughts. This video did stir some emotions with the moms."

Charlie pats me on the back and doesn't move his hand this time. It's his way of comforting me. My mom notices and smiles, more of a nostalgic smile. My father does the same thing for her. She politely excuses herself and walks to the master bedroom, probably to drop some hints about flowers to my dad.

TWENTY-SEVEN
ROSES

ROSES ARE EVERYWHERE. They are mostly yellow, but there are some red and violet ones floating down the halls. Girls giggle by their lockers. The guys are aware of the excitement but most of them are keeping their heads down, hoping this day will pass by more quickly.

The heavy classroom door opens and three senior girls enter with roses in their hands. One girl perches herself on the front desk. My history teacher stops, looking slightly annoyed that this student has made herself so comfortable and moves to the side. She tells a joke before handing the floor to the seniors. "How many women received roses from Henry VIII? Not for very long if they did."

The senior waves her off. "Very funny, Ms. Wells." Then she proceeds to read from a list—another stupid list—and I roll my eyes.

"Mare Bradley, a yellow rose. Mare Bradley, another yellow rose. Mare Bradley, a red rose." Mare giggles and raises her hand. A short senior cheerleader bounces over to her and delivers the roses to her friend.

"Jane Windsor, a yellow rose." Jane receives her rose as well as many other girls. I catch myself wondering, how many of them are from me? Maybe I don't need to buy as many next year since so many people are getting multiple roses.

As I enter the cafeteria, I scan the room for my friends. I drop my backpack at the window and notice everyone has at least one yellow rose at my table, but looking around at the others, some girls are not carrying a single one. Yep, I will buy them again next year, but for more girls in my class.

Jane, Hope, and Bree wave the roses for me to smell the sweet clove scent and in unison, say, "Thank you."

Jane adds, "We know you bought these for us," and it makes me smile seeing how happy they are.

Ivy saunters over with purple and red roses draped over her arm, wanting us to see how many she received. She eyes all the yellow roses, leans over so her roses are a couple inches from Bree's face, and taunts, "You know, the boy who gave me the purple rose still has not told me who he is yet, but I think it's Chris. He keeps looking over here. Anyway, I see none of you got a red or purple rose. Not even you, Bree. Chris must have used his money on someone else. Maybe you all should call yourself 'The Yellows.'"

She looks at each one of us, expecting a response, but none of us say a thing. Her opinion doesn't matter anymore. In a huff, she whips around and struts over to her table, trying to act like she won that exchange.

She takes her place next to Mare and continues to brag about her secret admirers. Mare make sure everyone notices the huge pile of roses in front of her. I wonder how many hints she had to drop to get Nick to buy all of those? After her comment about the Christmas candle, I think he felt he needed to go all out.

A crowd has gathered by the front desk, right near the

commons. As I approach, kids part one by one, revealing a gorgeous bouquet of two dozen purple roses. They're an unusual lilac color with tight buds, nothing like the ones in the fundraiser. They look more like the stunning arrangements from florist Michal Evans I see in my mother's office.

As I get closer, I notice one of the girls has removed a stem and is holding it tightly in her hand without wincing. They must not have thorns.

Intrigued, I ask, "Which teacher received these? Didn't Ms. Anderson just get engaged?"

As I get closer, I notice the plastic holder is empty, and Ivy has the envelope crumpled in her palm. She sneers at me then drops the paper on the ground. As it falls right near my feet, I see the bold letters **Kelsey Mercer Grant** staring up at me.

I swoop down to get it and wrestle the note out of the envelope to read the message. *I wish I could see your smile when you receive these flowers.* Oh my God. That is so sweet!

All the girls peer over my shoulder to read the card, frantically asking, "Who are they from?"

I ignore all the probing questions and peer over at Bree, who is looking truly happy for me. She's the only one who knows Charlie stepped up. I give her a look to let her know it's not the right time to mention his name, and she nods in agreement.

Ivy does not handle being one-upped very well and may do something to ruin this for me. Thinking she may throw the vase on the floor—or at me, I move closer to protect it.

The boys grumble all around me. Brian furiously turns to Chris and asks, "Who is the asshole making us all look bad? We are only supposed to give the girls ONE rose!"

Chris doesn't seem as bothered since Bree is not giving him a hard time about it.

Nick stands next to an annoyed Mare. He leans over and whispers something in her ear, but she doesn't respond.

Instead, she flips her hand at him and walks away. He gives me a look, one I haven't seen before, and then he follows her out the door. I watch him go, wondering why he's so upset about this.

Kylie steps in front of everyone and admires the roses. She turns to me and says, "You better take these to a safe place," and hands them to me.

I peer down at the delicate buds and breathe in the sweet yet subtle scent. *He loves subtle. . . .* I lean in and take another deep breath.

Bree steps forward and shows me the photo. She captured a moment florists would kill to advertise. I appear bewitched by the flowers—in a complete state of bliss.

Bree whispers, "Okay if I send this?"

I nod and watch her shoot the photo to Charlie, then post it on her story.

My phone beeps within seconds. It has to be Charlie! I place the flowers on the table, move away from the crowd, and click on the text. Below the photo, he has typed the word *Beautiful*.

I want to FaceTime him but can't in this crowd. Instead, I text back. *Thank you so much! Such an amazing surprise!*

I stare at the screen waiting for a response.

K- I wanted to make sure you had a couple roses too since you bought so many yellow ones for friends.

I hold the phone close to my heart. *OH MY GOSH! So sweet!!!!! Thank you!*

Thoughts for Valentine's Day?

I think for a second and go for it. *Just want to be with you*

And he responds immediately. *Same*

K. Talk tonight? Gotta go to class

K

I sink into the sofa and stare at the flowers a couple seconds longer, then carry them to the front desk in the administration building, knowing they will be safe there. The receptionist, Ursula, beams when she sees them and graciously agrees to watch them for me until after practice.

I spend the last period of the day dodging questions from my class and some upperclassmen. Everyone seems intrigued with me now, wanting to know who my secret admirer is, but I deflect all the questions with the purple comment—purple must mean that the certain someone wants to stay a secret.

I'm just not ready to say anything yet, especially after what Bree told me. Charlie needs to make the first move to announce our relationship to his friends. Maybe these flowers are a sign it's coming.

TWENTY-EIGHT

THORNS

As I walk through campus on this dreary Monday morning, I reminisce about my weekend. It was by far the best one we've spent together. Charlie couldn't have been sweeter.

He made reservations at this charming French bistro, Anis, that had a special menu for Valentine's Day. We stuffed ourselves on *tartare de tomate*, garlicky mussels, and chocolate mousse. Then, we went to a drive-in movie. I didn't even know those existed anymore.

Anyways, while people steamed up their car windows around us, I surprised Charlie with two tickets to the Final Four game, and he went ballistic. He couldn't believe I was able to find tickets. My mom said I needed to do something special for him after seeing the gorgeous roses and called in a favor. I owe her one for that!

All weekend she kept going on and on about the roses. My father froze when he saw them on the kitchen counter and then quickly disappeared into their room—probably to make some calls to get some delivered ASAP.

When my mom realized he forgot about Valentine's Day, she was all passive-aggressive about it. She placed the roses on the breakfast table so they were front and center as a constant reminder of his memory lapse. He will make it up to her somehow. He always does.

As I pause outside the assembly hall, I notice a group of eighth grade girls staring at me. One girl points and announces loud enough that everyone can hear her, "That's the girl who got the two dozen roses on Friday." *Really? People are still talking about this?*

Another girl snorts, freakishly like Mare, and declares in a syrupy Southern accent, "Of course, she got the roses! Look at her! I would kill to have her long thick hair. She looks just like Giselle!"

What is she talking about? I do spend at least 45 minutes blowing out my hair while watching YouTube videos on Geometry and Spanish. I try to mimic Giselle's beachy locks, but her hair is so much more blonde and beautiful. I'm more of a light almond brown with highlights from being out in the sun.

I walk into the bathroom, apply lip gloss to my chapped lips, and stare into the mirror. I do have really long legs, but they're not as lean as hers. My stomach is not soft and sexy; it's more muscle from all the crunches and leg lifts at practice. I'm a solid B—not at all chesty like Victoria Secret models, which is one thing I'm very happy about.

Virginia is a double D. She has to wear two tight sports bras and still complains about the painful bouncing during games and practice. The boys love to watch her play, though. She told her parents that if she's going to play soccer in college, they have to get her a breast reduction. That's not something I ever need to worry about!

I look around and several other girls are standing in the corner, whispering about the roses. God, I did not realize it was such a big deal. They need to move on.

The rest of the day goes on about the same until Carter, one of the sophomore basketball players, gives me a high five and says, "Way to go, Kels! So are you going to say yes now that Nick's taken?"

"What are you talking about?" I fire back at him.

"Oh, come on, Kels. We all knew you had a thing for him last year. It's about time for you to give another guy a chance."

Not sure how to respond to that, I simply say, "Well, you need to wait and see," and then quickly walk away before he says something more embarrassing.

I barely make it to lunch without screaming. Everyone keeps asking who the roses are from. When are they going to drop this? I'm not ready to tell them about Charlie yet.

When I see Bree in the lunchroom, I relax. She and Chris are sandwiched in the middle of the table, along with Kim, Ivy, Mare, Nick, and Brian. Bree scoots over to make room for me.

As I take a bite of my salad, Kim leans over. "So, do you know who the roses are from yet?"

I roll my eyes thinking, *not again*. I exhale and say something so everyone at the table will know to drop the subject, "Well, since they're purple for a secret admirer, he obviously didn't want everyone to know who they're from. Could we please talk about something else? No offense Kim, but I have been bombarded with questions all day. I just want to hang out with my friends."

I jump as Ivy slams her glass on the table and commands the attention back on her. "I agree! I have heard enough of this today. She's not going to say who they are from. Maybe she doesn't know? Maybe she bought them for herself trying to get the attention . . . or they're from one of the guys here at the table so she doesn't want to say?"

Mare glares at her as all the guys look at one another, not wanting anything to do with this conversation. I firmly respond to this insult, "Ivy, that's ridiculous. They are *not* from anyone sitting here."

Ivy mimics my words, "They are not from anyone sitting

here. Well then, let's move on. We have a dance to discuss. Who is sitting with me?" Then she flashes a scathing look at me and says, "Sorry Kels, I heard you are sitting this one out. Hope is taking Sam."

I didn't want anyone to know I was going to the dance, but I can't hold my tongue. "Ivy, actually, I *am* going to the Sadie."

Ivy gives me her infamous death stare and demands to know, "What, with who?"

I suppress a smirk and casually respond back, "Someone you don't know. A family friend."

Ivy laughs. It's more like an evil cackle from a fairy tale witch who's about to steal the beauty from a young child to feed their own vanity. "Of course, it's a family friend. You would never ask anyone you actually like or who liked you."

I glare at her and fire back. "Remember, I *am* the one who received the roses."

All the guys bust out in laughter except Nick, who is staring at me with a strange look on his face. He drops his roll on his tray, well actually he flicks it, then turns away from me.

Bree adds, "Kels, don't you think it's time to tell them?"

Everyone turns to look at me as I glare at Bree, completely caught off guard. Then I sigh, knowing she may be right and say, "Well, he's more than a family friend."

Kim gasps. "What! Why didn't you tell us?"

I knew this was a bad idea. "I—I—"

Bree interjects, "I told her not to say anything," and this gets everyone's attention.

"Why?" Kim looks so confused.

"He has a crazy ex that's not going to be happy about him dating Kels. I know the family well. Her sister was in my class at Chase and she made my life hell. The guy she liked asked me out, and she blamed me. She threw my uniform in the toilet when I was at gym and told everyone I threw hers in the toilet instead. She set up a fake Instagram account in my name and posted some things I don't want to get into now. Her mother told the school and everyone who would listen that I was bullying her. . . ."

Chris places his hand on hers to comfort her, and she keeps on going. "I've been trying to figure out how to shield Kels from that family, but once they show up at the Sadie together, they will know who she is. They already suspect he's been dating someone else since he has been MIA at the parties. He has been spending all his time with Kels."

Everything Bree says sinks in. This weekend will be the first time we show up at a function together. Everyone will know we're dating.

"So how long have you been dating?" Nick asks as his eyes bore into mine.

"Yeah, how long has this been going on? How could you not tell us?" Kim is really upset—more like a little hurt. I owe her an apology since she was so determined to find me a date, and I didn't bother to tell her I had one. But how could I? She will understand once she knows the whole story.

I grab her hand and say, "Kim, I'm sorry. You will be one of the first to meet him this weekend. We can sit at the same table."

Ivy quickly grabs Mare's arm and proclaims, "You and Nick are at my table. Kim, you already said you were sitting with us."

Nick finally stops staring at me and grills someone else. "So Ivy, when are you going to ask Chris?"

Ivy sits up so she is about two inches taller and announces, "I'm not taking Chris. I'm going with a junior—you know Lance, he's on the varsity basketball team."

Nick snaps, "What? You claimed Chris and now he won't be able to go if you don't ask him?"

Ivy picks at her food and then answers honestly for once. "I think he would rather spend the evening with Bree."

We all fall silent, unsure whether this is some sort of trick.

I nudge Bree, and she looks up. "What?"

Nick speaks up. "Did you hear that? Ivy is taking Lance to the Sadie. You guys can go together."

Chris's eyes widen, then he wraps his arms around her and says, "Bree, you don't have to go stag."

Bree doesn't believe it at first. She glances over at Ivy, expecting her to stake her claim, but Ivy doesn't say a thing. She won't even make eye contact. It's obvious this is not easy for her. Bree runs with it and makes it official. "Chris, will you go to the Sadie with me?"

He acts all surprised and then answers, "Yes. Nothing would make me happier." He can't resist rubbing it in Ivy's face.

Bree sinks down next to me and apologizes for lunch. "I'm so sorry. I shouldn't have said anything. . . . I tried to cover for you, but what I said is true. You have to watch your back at the Sadie."

"Did Brooke's sister really do all those things to you?"

Bree lowers her head, almost like she's ashamed. "Yes, it was . . . awful."

I wrap my arms around her, and she doesn't resist being touched for once. "I'm so sorry."

Bree sniffles then says, "Yep, the worst part is my mother believed her over me. Momma Hamilton showed her that Instagram account and said it was mine. She said I did all those things to her daughter, but she did all those things to me."

"I'm so sorry, Bree." Now I know why she and her mother are not close.

"Well, I get to face her this weekend. I've been able to avoid her, but I'm ready to deal with her now. Ironically, Ivy has helped me get ready to stand up to her, but I don't think she will be coming for me. She will be focused on you. She and

Brooke will know all about you the minute you walk in the door with Charlie. Brooke may even crash the dance once she sees a picture of the two of you."

"Well, Charlie still has not said a word about her, so maybe he isn't that worried about it. Maybe it won't be as bad as you think? Maybe Brooke has moved on?"

Bree shakes her head. "No, Charlie told the guys not to tell Brooke about you. Wes and Dave were the only ones who knew about you until one of them grabbed Charlie's phone at lunch last week. He was looking at the photo of you holding the roses and spilled you guys were dating."

"Dave is not happy about this. They have gotten into several fights about it since Dave knows Brooke is going to go ballistic, especially when she finds out he has known about you since Christmas. He doesn't want to blow his shot with her. It's pathetic, really."

"Well, there's not much I can do. Please don't tell anyone else about this and don't tell Ivy or Mare who he is, not yet. Let's see how Charlie handles things at the dance. This is something he needs to address before I can do anything. But I will watch my back. Thank you for—for everything."

Bree recovers. "Sure . . . anything you need. So do you mind if Chris and I go to the dance with you two? We can get ready together."

"Yes, of course, you can go with us to the dance. We can sit together at dinner too! Hope and Sam are at our table. Kim and Brian are stuck with Mare, Nick and Ivy."

"Lucky them." Bree interjects. "Wait! Hope is at your table?"

"I know. She apologized for how she treated me." I try to act like it's not that big of a deal.

"Kels, you are way too forgiving," Bree states.

"I know, but she really is sorry." I firmly reply. I so badly want to tell her that Hope called me after the Falcons' game and confessed why she dropped me. She said Ivy told her that I was the one behind the list, and that I was not the nice girl everyone thinks I am.

Ivy said I was trying to sabotage her chances with Sam, and that I asked someone to put my name next to Sam's so she wouldn't find out. Ivy apologized for being so mean over the summer and said she would stop slamming her now that she wasn't going to be friends with me. Ivy even offered to help her get with Sam and said she would have a better shot without me around.

After Kate told her that I wasn't the one behind the list, she didn't know what to do. She couldn't risk losing Sam and couldn't handle the abuse from Ivy if she started talking to me again. She figured I would be fine since I'm better at dealing with Ivy, but she never thought it would go this far. She owned up to being weak and pleaded for me to forgive her. *What was I supposed to say to that?*

I know Hope and I will never be as close as we were, but we can be friends again. I have known her forever and should at least try. If I could tell Bree all of this, she would understand why I'm acting this way.

Bree interrupts my train of thought. "Kels, sorry. I shouldn't have said anything. You can do what you want."

I nod and move onto the fun details. "Thanks. So you can come over at 2 o'clock. Kim and Hope will be there too. Our hair appointments are at 3 o'clock. Make one around the same time at Drybar. Then, we have a makeup session at Chanel from 4:30 to 6:00. The guys are coming at 7 for photos. . . . I'm so glad you are coming. I thought you would bail out at the end if Chris really did go with Ivy."

"And let her win? No way! I'm done with being pushed around."

"Yep! No more. We won't let the Hamiltons ruin this for us either!"

TWENTY-NINE
READY

KIM STARES into my bathroom mirror, carefully examining her makeup while running her fingers over the line of mascara, lip liner, concealer, and lip gloss on my counter. The lady at the Chanel counter only left us with the task of reapplying our lip gloss, but Kim is still searching for something she can do to make herself look even better. She is very much like her mother in that way—always looking for flaws.

I reapply my lip gloss, pop my lips together to smooth out the lines, and then join Bree, who's anxiously waiting for Kim to wrap it up since the boys are already downstairs. She has her hair up in a beautiful French braid and loose bun to show off her lacy V-neck royal blue dress, one you would find on a runway. Since her mother flew her to New York for a last minute shopping spree, my guess it's from some designer up there.

Hope walks out of my closet, madly fidgeting with the zipper on her dress. Exasperated, she asks, "Can one of you help?" I step over and zip it up, careful not to pull her hair with it.

Usually, Hope goes for the less-is-more classic look, but

tonight she chose a bright red fitted-style, halter dress that flares at the bottom. A dress similar to the ones that were popular in the swing dancing days, but this one is somewhat more racy with a triangle cut out above her chest. She has really come out of her shell being with Sam.

Bree hollers, "Are you ready yet?"

Kim walks out, smacking her bright red lips together. It's the same red as the bottom of her shoes. Without looking, she slips into her 4" high heels and flips her luscious curls to the side, so they sweep across her forehead. She looks into the mirror one last time and says with enthusiasm, "Ready!"

I arch my feet into the 3" high Valentino heels with gold studs that my mother finally agreed to let me borrow and then peer into the mirror for one last look. I push the beach waves off of my forehead and smooth out my silver sequined dress. I decided to wear my hair down so I can cover my face once we walk in the door. There are going to be lots of stares with Charlie on my arm, and I want to be able to hide my cheeks when I blush.

The three of us hold onto the railing as we slowly climb down the stairs since none of us are used to wearing heels this high. Kim's the only one who looks comfortable and glides down as if she's wearing slippers. Her mom made sure she knew how to walk in heels after her catwalk incident.

I'm the last one to descend, so I don't see the guys' reaction but hear the whistle. Chris must have seen Bree. As Charlie comes into view, I see his cerulean eyes widen and mouth open slightly, making me feel like a million bucks. Dave mutters something behind a covered mouth. He waves him off and takes a step toward me to grab my hand.

He pulls me close to him and whispers softly in my ear, "You are so beautiful," and his lips brush my ear lobe. My knees weaken and ankles wobble, but I pull myself back together, knowing everyone is around.

I'm about to compliment him on how amazing he looks in his charcoal gray suit and silver-blue tie, when I hear my father cry out for all to hear, "You should never have let her wear that dress. She looks twenty!"

With the back of her hand, my mom hits him flat on the chest, signaling for him to shut up. My father grunts, then turns and walks into the kitchen, knowing he has already lost this one.

Kim bounces over to Brian and exuberantly asks, "Doesn't Kelsey look so amazing? I picked out that dress for her. Didn't I do a good job?" Brian nods, then very smartly turns to Kim, and says, "You look beautiful too."

"Thank you!" She squeals and latches onto his arm, where she will be planted the rest of the evening.

As Sam quickly compliments Hope, who is nervously standing by his side, I walk over to the antique wood console in the hallway and grab the boutonnière. Looking at what I have in my hands, Charlie banters, "Going old school?"

"Of course, you will be the oldest guy at the dance," I tease while pinning the unique white rose with blue edges to his gray lapel.

Dave mutters under his breath, and I catch something about someone knowing something tonight, which really seems to irritate Charlie. As I open my mouth to ask, he shakes his head like it's nothing, so I let it go, knowing it probably has something to do with Brooke.

My mother breezes into the hall carrying her Canon and suggests, "Let's go outside and get some photos. I promised Charlie's parents I would send them some pictures tonight. They wanted to be here but had a dinner thing. . . ." My mother rambles when she's excited or nervous.

Charlie offers me his arm, and we walk outside into the lovely evening air, filled with the sweet smell of the delicate white flowers. My mother motions for us to gather at the end of the pool. The dogwoods in the distance should be the perfect backdrop for the photos.

Charlie stands behind me and places his warm arms around my waist. The guys follow his lead. They seem a little nervous about their first dance with a date, but Charlie appears to be a pro. He does have at least two more years of experience.

Dave stands behind my mother, mocking us, making Bree turn beet red with all his lovebird comments. She snaps, "Shut it, Dave," but that only encourages him even more.

I feel Charlie's phone vibrate in his pocket. He pulls it out, and then quickly turns it off. Expecting to hear the normal grunt, he only clears his throat, and then says, "Mrs. Grant, sorry to interrupt, but I think we better go. We're all supposed to be seated in forty minutes."

"Oh, you're right. Sorry to keep you guys so long. I think I got a good one to share with everyone's parents," she says while scanning the images on the viewfinder.

Charlie yells over to Dave, "I don't have much room in my car. Can you take everyone?"

Dave looks annoyed and snaps, "Didn't you drive your Land Rover?"

Charlie smirks very mischievously, then replies, "Nope."

Dave grunts, but then agrees, "Fine. That's why I'm here. To tote around all the kiddos."

Charlie looks like he wants to punch him, but Bree beats him to it. She wallops him right in the arm.

Instead of getting angry, Dave gloats. He loves to get under her skin.

Kim and Bree rush upstairs to grab their purses as everyone else shuffles through the house to load up out front. While I wait at the bottom of the stairs for them, my mother cannot stop talking about how Charlie looked at me. She has been so excited about tonight and—

I hear Dave yell, "NO WAY! Your parents let you drive the Carrera!"

I hurry to the front window and peer outside. Charlie is beaming with pride as the guys circle around the car, lightly running their fingers along the sides. He informs them, "They never let me drive this but surprised me today since this is a special occasion."

When he sees me pass over the threshold, he bounces up the steps and wraps his arms around my waist. I give him a quick kiss on the cheek and let him escort me down to the car. He's like a kid in a candy shop.

Sam deftly climbs in the cramped back seat, but Hope is having a hard time getting in without flashing us. Her only option is to sandwich herself between the side of the car and passenger seat, which may not end well. To avoid another mishap, I put my hand out to stop her and say, "Hope, it's not worth it. You might rip your dress."

As soon as the words cross my lips, I know I should not have said that. Kim's face is as bright red as the brakes on the rear wheels. But instead of getting anxious about this dance, she begins to giggle. I'm so glad we can all laugh about it now!

Ready to get the show on the road, Dave motions for everyone to get in his car. After Sam climbs out, Charlie helps lower me into the passenger seat. I feel like I'm riding on the ground being so low.

As we wait for the others to follow behind us, he jests, "I thought your father was going to make you change after that comment."

That was pretty embarrassing and could have turned ugly if he insisted on me changing, but he rarely gets his way. I reply like it wasn't a concern, "Yeah, but my mom knows how to calm him down. They've been together since high school—" I stop mid-sentence and change the subject, "Anyways, he knew I wasn't going to change and to drop it." Then, I lean over to kiss his cheek and give him the compliment I was not able to give in the house. "You look amazing by the way."

He puts his hand on my exposed thigh and says, "You look absolutely stunning in that dress," and kisses me again, more intensely than ever before. My hands move up his chest, over the blue-tipped flower that I pinned over his heart, and feel his heartbeat quickening with mine.

Feeling like we're being watched from behind, I pull away and ask him something that will distract me from wanting to kiss him in front of an audience, "So what did Dave whisper to you? Should I not be wearing sequins this late in the season?"

This makes Charlie snort twice before he answers, "No, guys don't care about those rules! Dave said you looked beautiful, and I was a lucky guy."

"No, he didn't. You're not going to tell me are you?" I tease back.

He smirks ever so slightly and rests his hand on my mid-thigh again, then playfully dismisses the subject saying, "That was the gist of it."

I search through the preselected music channels and find a station playing one of my favorites, "Beautiful People" and I turn it up so loud that we can feel it vibrate all through the car. I open the sunroof and lower my window to let the wind blow through my beach curls, making them a little more wild, but I don't care. The cool spring breeze, Charlie's intoxicating smell, and the blaring music makes me feel so alive and free. Something I haven't felt since our time alone at the lake.

I move to the music with my bare arms above my head, hands out of the sunroof, and head swaying back and forth. I mouth the words, so I don't ruin it for Charlie. I gaze over at him, and he has this expression on his face that I have never seen before. It's almost like he's in a trance.

As "Still Falling For You" comes on, Charlie moves to turn the station, but I take his hand in mine and let him know I want to listen to this one. I lean back in my supple leather seat and gaze at him. He's having a hard time keeping his eyes on the road.

When I hear the words, "Just like that," I lean in and kiss his neck slowly to drive him crazy. He moves his head toward me ever so slightly, so I can reach his ear, and he groans as I lightly nibble on his soft ear lobe.

I feel the car slow. Before we come to a full stop, he turns his head to find my mouth, then kisses me so intensely. I unstrap my seat belt and move farther over the console, avoiding the gear shift so our chests are pressed together, and we get lost in the moment.

HONK. HONK. Dave lays on the horn from behind and we pull away, nervously chuckling. He grabs hold of my hand and punches the gas, leaving Dave in the dust. I fall back into the seat, enjoying the electricity flowing through the car and us.

I feel the need to be close to him—to be alone with him before we walk into this dance. I want this moment to last in case something goes wrong tonight.

Charlie must have picked up on my thoughts because he pulls off the main road. Before he even stops under some tree along a park in the Ansley neighborhood, he kisses me like we don't have anywhere else we need to be.

THIRTY
THE SADIE

As WE PULL into the underground parking deck, a sudden heat wave rushes over me. One the cranked-up air conditioning can't touch. My nerves are getting the better of me, and I can't stop wondering if this is a good idea.

I pull down the sun visor and peer into the mirror to check my makeup one last time and brush my tangled hair. We wind down several floors and find a spot next to Dave, who is enthusiastically yelling at his phone.

Charlie rushes around the outside to help me out of the low riding car, then leans into Dave's 4Runner and smiles. His team is obviously winning.

I move behind Charlie to get a glimpse of the screen but quickly scoot backwards as both yell, "Shoot the ball," then high five each other after the player sinks a three-pointer. I stand there awkwardly as the guys' voices bounce off the concrete walls; they get even more fired up as the other team comes back after several great shots.

When the Geico commercial plays, Charlie searches behind his back for my hand. Dave leans his head out the window, smirking and taunts us, "So you guys finally made it? Found somewhere to continue after the horn interrupted you." Then he guffaws at himself, the only one amused by his humor.

Charlie snorts, ignoring the remark and asks, "Are you going to stay out here or come back later?"

Dave shrugs. "Staying here. Knowing Bree, she's not going to be in there long with her old classmates around. If you get bored with all those freshmen, you can always come watch the game with me."

I feel my shoulders sag as my nagging concern returns about Charlie going to something so juvenile with me, but he eases my mind as he pulls me close to his side and dismisses Dave saying, "All good. See you afterwards."

But Dave isn't done with his snide remarks. Within seconds, he mocks us, "Okay, kids have fun!"

Wow, he's laying it on thick! With the way Charlie is acting, he is not amused. I have never seen his jaw clench like this or witness him flip someone off before. Charlie mumbles, "You're an ass," as we briskly cross the parking lot.

Dave's voice echoes off the walls. "Very grown-up, Charlie. Maybe you will fit right in tonight!" And he laughs hysterically. He must have heard Charlie's ass comment somehow, or he's the type who always has to have the final word, a little like Bree.

Charlie hits the elevator button several times as we wait, looking anxious to get out of the parking deck. When the metal doors clank open, he whisks me in and apologizes, "Sorry about that. I shouldn't have stopped to look at the score. It's your night, and we should already be in there."

I try to act like it isn't a big deal even though it is. "Uh, that's okay—You know, we don't have to go to this freshman dance. You don't need to do this for me."

He pulls away and stares into my eyes with sincere concern. "Kels, I didn't mean it that way. I want to be here with you," and then he kisses me with as much intensity as in the car, removing all the doubt. So engulfed in his warmth and the familiar scent of cinnamon and mint, I'm oblivious to the fact that the elevator door has opened. I jump sky high when someone clears their throat.

We quickly scurry out of the elevator and pass the elderly couple like nothing happened. My head is hung low with my hair in front of my face to hide the redness across my cheeks and neck. A nervous giggle escapes my lips as the doors close. He wraps his arms around me again and chuckles at the fact we just got busted by 70-year-olds.

After a few seconds, he smooths his jacket and adjusts his boutonnière, which got turned sideways. "Okay, we should get in there before we get ourselves kicked out. They have cameras all over the place here."

I accept his arm. We stroll under the stone porte-cochere, up the stairs, and through the double doors. A young gentleman races to grab the door for us while trying to mute the game playing on his phone. When it falls silent, he discreetly slides it into his pocket and motions for us to follow him into the ballroom.

As soon as the doors open, Charlie and I pause to take in the scene. I spot several of my soccer friends from various schools, hanging out in between the columns and twinkling topiary trees. Most of the girls are in groups of five or six while the boys have formed a mass on the dance floor. So, it's true the guys only want a date to get in and will take off as soon as the opportunity arises!

Bree is with a couple girls at the edge of the dance floor with Chris behind her telling a joke to some guys. I feel Charlie's warm hand intertwine in mine and squeeze. I'm not sure if it's for his benefit or mine. This is the first time he will be out with my friends, except for Bree. He motions with his other hand for me to enter, and I take a step forward.

As soon as we pass a group of girls who have overflowed into the table area, I hear the whispers. "Who is this girl with our Homecoming King—Is that Charlie?" His grip tightens as one comment about Blair's sister (the notorious Brooke) floats in the air, but I'm more bothered by the unpleasant looks of deep loathing and hatred being thrown in my direction.

Within seconds, we make it through the gauntlet, and it's time to make some introductions to my friends. But before I have a chance to say anything, Bree announces, "Look who made it! I figured you guys stopped for some alone time before coming here."

She's just like Dave. I glare at her and then blow off her comment. "Hey everyone, I want you to meet Charlie. He goes to Chase and is friends with Bree's brother." Then I point to everyone. "This is Kylie, Robert, Jane, Austin, and you have already met Kim, Brian, and Chris, who is behind Bree." Charlie repeats the names under his breath as I say each one, then gives a long wave after I'm done.

"So, where are you all sitting?" I casually ask.

Bree points at the table across the dance floor. "We saved you both a seat already."

Chris notices us and joins the conversation. "Charlie, I meant to ask you back at Kelsey's house how you guys know each other. Kels said you're family friends."

Charlie tenses at the question, narrows his eyes at me, then answers, "Yep, our mothers are good friends and we met right before New Year's."

An ah-hah look crosses Chris's face. "So *you* called on New Year's to check on Kelsey's hand?"

After a moment, Charlie smiles rather mischievously, then replies, "Yes, but that's not the only reason I called. I didn't want her kissing some other guy at midnight." And he wraps his arms around my waist and gives me a little squeeze.

I see that dangerous glint in Bree's eyes and know it's her turn to torture us. "Smart move, Charlie. That waiter was eyeing her all night. He probably would have lost his job if he approached her, but I think he would have risked it for her!"

I scowl and respond to the jest, "Oh come on, you sound like Mare."

Charlie squeezes my waist again and joins in on the roast. "She really doesn't know what effect she has on people."

I feel the pink rise to my cheeks as Bree gags. Chris has this confused look on his face.

Kim chimes in asking, "So you are the one who sent those gorgeous flowers?" All the boys deflate with this comment.

After appearing to be in shock for the first half of the conversation, Kylie speaks up, "Yeah, did you send them?"

Charlie tilts his head like he is trying to figure out if this is a joke or not, then asks, "Who else would have sent them?"

Chris downs the rest of his Coke and blurts, "We thought it was Henry since he has a thing for Kelsey. We should have figured someone from another school sent them since the girls usually only get one or two roses. Not something like you sent —Ow."

I stifle a laugh as Bree elbows him in the ribs, and then I reply to the Henry comment, "Why do you all keep saying that? I never talk to him. He is into Ivy, not me. And besides, I thought the flowers were absolutely amazing. You guys need to step up next year." And I peer at Charlie, who is not enjoying the banter. He almost looks a little hurt.

Kim nods her head vigorously, then turns to Brian. "Yes, they were some of the prettiest flowers I have even seen."

Jane starts saying, "Kels is always so private. I—," and I'm saved by the bell ringing, signaling we all need to sit down.

Charlie seems a little cold, even distant as we walk to our table. My friends definitely threw me under the bus, and he doesn't know what to make of it. His thumb is moving at light-ning speed over his ring finger.

As Charlie holds the chair for me to sit down, he leans over, and asks in a confused voice, "Have you not told them about me?"

I look down at my hands gripping the linen napkin and whisper back, "Yes, but only recently. I was waiting for you to mention me to your friends due to the Brooke thing. I didn't—"

Charlie's head flips backward and he says a little too loudly, "What Brooke thing?"

Bree, who is sitting down on the other side of Charlie, leans over and explains, "I told her all about the Hamiltons."

Charlie's head whips toward me in complete surprise. "You knew?"

I nod, but don't say a thing. Instead, I let Bree fill him in and as Charlie listens, his face turns a little green, especially when she relays Mrs. Hamilton's scheme with the Yale professor. Then, Bree gives him even worse news. "Brooke's sister, Blair is here and looks really unhappy. She has been craning her neck to look over at our table." Bree tilts her head toward Blair.

Charlie discreetly looks in that direction and sharply exhales. He slumps back in his chair, like he can't take anything more, but then regroups and finally tells me everything I need to know. "Brooke is my ex but still thinks she and I will get back together even though I have made it clear it's NEVER going to happen. Her sister probably thinks we are still together, and if she is anything like Brooke, she will make a scene seeing me here with you."

Charlie turns very serious. "Bree, just warn me if Blair gets close to me or Kelsey. I don't want to leave with food or drink all over Kelsey's gorgeous dress or on my face."

I put my hand on his and answer before Bree can respond, "Don't worry. We know how to deal with her. Blair can't be any worse than our Ivy!" Then Bree and I start laughing.

Charlie is not amused. "It's not funny, she's crazy!"

Thanks to Bree, I am ready for this. I wrap my arms around his neck and stare into his deep blue eyes. With our noses almost touching, I whisper so only he can hear me, "Don't worry. It's just you and me tonight. If she shows up and makes a scene, I'll take her down!"

Charlie kisses me on the lips ever so lightly and then murmurs, "Now that would make this night even better."

When I sit back into my chair, I'm surrounded by shocked looks and flush a crimson red.

"Well, that's a first," Bree announces, and all heads nod in unison.

Trying to lighten the mood, I ask Charlie to tell the table about Wes in Vail, knowing this will make everyone laugh.

As he begins, I rest one elbow on the table and settle in for the story. Even though I've heard it before, I can't wait to hear it again. Charlie goes on about the evening and how Wes tried to kiss a girl but missed and ended up flat on his face.

Blood gushed everywhere. The girls screamed as it got on their dresses. Since he could not walk in a straight line, Dave and Charlie stole a toboggan and dragged Wes over to the Vail Medical center for stitches. Wes had a fat lip that stuck out as far as his nose, which affected his breathing on the slope. Every time he inhaled, the fog would condense on his upper lip leaving small icicles that he would have to snap off since it was so cold in Colorado.

He has a way of telling a story that is just hilarious. Bree adds on some funny things about Wes and by the end of it, tears are running down my cheeks. Hope snorts, and all of us die laughing again, even the other tables turn to see what was so funny.

Kim and Brian are stuck with Ivy, her date Lance, Mare, and Nick. They are at the table to the left of ours. I catch Nick staring at me while I nibble on the salad course since my nerves are still shot from earlier. Ivy is next to Nick and I catch glimpses of her nefarious face throughout the rest of our meal.

Kim occasionally turns around looking concerned, almost like she needs to tell me something, but she's too far away.

After three courses of typical wedding fare, the band walks onto the stage and warms up. Apparently, they are the same band that has played here for thirty years, so I worry there's no way they will play anything we actually want to hear. But the first song out the gate is Ed Sherran's "Thinking Out Loud," and they actually aren't terrible.

Charlie puts his hand out, and I accept it. He zealously leads me to the dance floor with one arm around my waist. We're the only ones out here, but for the first time in my life I don't care.

When I was much younger, my father used to push the furniture out of the way and twirl my mother around. I studied them intently as they glided across the room so I could learn to move like my mother. She competed in some dance competitions before I was born and did pretty well. After giving me some pointers, my dad would give her the last dance. I remember her infectious laugh when he would dip her so low that her hair would skim the floor.

Recalling some of the basics, I place one arm on Charlie's muscular shoulder and the other in his open hand. Instead of keeping it out, I move our clasped hands against his chest and follow his lead. As we glide across the floor, he gently rubs the scar near my thumb, staring only at me.

"Where did you learn to dance?" I ask after he twirls me around.

This makes him grin. He twirls me once more, then tells me, "My parents made me take dance lessons when my sister was becoming a deb. I hated it then, but I'm happy now."

I smile back at him and whisper, "I am too," then rest my head on his shoulder and close my eyes. Through my fingers, I can feel his heartbeat in rhythm with mine. This night has been so much better than I imagined. Just being in his arms makes all the drama leading up to this worth it.

When I open my eyes, I notice other couples have joined us on the floor. Nick is looking at us with narrowed eyes while Mare's head is pinned to the side of his, staring off in the other direction.

They play Michael Buble's "Haven't Met You Yet," which perks everyone up. Charlie twirls me around the dance floor again. I pivot and roll into his body and then spin out, not breaking hand contact. He really has the moves.

When the band changes speed and plays a version of Beyonce's "All The Single Ladies," spasmodic girls stream onto the floor, screaming while their dates sit back and watch. A guy at the table closest to us pours some brown liquid into his coke as he mocks all the girls bouncing around.

When we get pushed into a corner near the stage, Charlie yells over the music, "I'm going to get a drink. Want anything?"

"Water, please. I'll meet you back at the table."

He slides in between the stage and the girls flipping their hands in the air like they are showing off a ring, and I make my way toward the bathroom, which has a line out the door. Bree appears, and I let two girls go ahead of me so we're standing next to each other. A group of chatty girls exit at once, allowing us to go in together. The stalls are open but the counter is packed with girls primping.

I enter a stall to wipe the sweat from under my arms and adjust my strapless bra, then join Bree out in the crowd. Several Chase girls in the back notice us and glare but don't say a thing. Finally, it's our turn in front of the mirror, and I grab a tissue to blot the shine from my nose and my glistening forehead. Then, wave my hands to fan my face. It's even hotter in the bathroom than on the dance floor.

Bree hands me her lip gloss, and I add some shimmer to my lips to match the pinkness in my cheeks. As Bree opens her lipstick, she says into the mirror, "Well, you certainly got all the girls jealous. It was like no one else was there on the dance floor. I would kill to have Chris look at me like that."

As she makes a popping O shape to blot the pinkish red lipstick, I quietly respond, "Thanks, Bree. Charlie seems to be having a good time."

"That's an understatement. I haven't seen him this happy . . . ever." Her tone has a hint of envy so instead of replying, I shrug, and check my teeth for lip gloss. Then, head for the door while sucking on the mint and hold it open for her. "Ready to go?"

Right outside, Nick is pacing back and forth, studying the floor, mumbling something, almost like he's practicing a speech.

"Nick, are you all right?"

His head jolts up, and he steps toward me. "Kelsey, I need to talk to you," he says with serious urgency.

"Okay, what's up?" I ask quietly.

Nick turns to Bree and says firmly, "In private."

Bree shoots me a puzzled look. I shrug my shoulders since I have no clue why he is acting so weird.

Bree scoffs. "Fine," she mutters and then swiftly excuses herself.

Instead of filling me in on what's so important, he rubs his hand through his hair, making the ends stand up in all directions, and scratches the back of his neck, looking everywhere but in my direction. After several girls push open the bathroom door, he grabs my hand and pulls me under the shadow of a tree.

With hunched shoulders, he whispers, "Do you remember when you were upset about the list?"

Not following why this warrants so much secrecy, I nod. "Yes. Why?"

"Well, Mare told me she wanted to make sure I would go with her and that you wanted to take Sam so someone put his name next to yours. She said everyone knew you liked him and that you would never admit it because of Hope."

My mouth falls open. Mare is just as manipulative as Ivy. After a moment, I recover and reply, "And you believed her?"

Nick continues saying, "Yes, but Ivy just told me that you wanted to take me to the dance. Is that true?"

Instinctively, I take a step backwards and feel something poke my scalp. I try to duck, but it makes my hair tangle even more. Nick leans over, chuckling, and removes some of the knots so I'm able to wiggle free from the branches. I pull some leaves from my hair and smooth out the bird nest on the back of my head as best as I can. As soon as I'm finished, Nick steps forward and takes hold of my hand. "Kels, I wanted to go with you."

I stare at my hand between his and then pull it away—it feels so wrong. I reply, "As friends," but Nick takes it as a question and not as a statement, giving him hope.

"No, more than friends. I started dating Mare because I thought you liked Sam."

My hands frantically cross my chest like I'm waving something off and my thoughts flow from my mouth, "No, this isn't happening. Nick, I'm here with Charlie . . . and you're here with your girlfriend."

His whole body stiffens as I say 'girlfriend' and the softness in his eyes disappears. "So who is he to you? A family friend or is he your boyfriend?"

The bite in his tone is unexpected. I take a step to the side, away from him, but he moves toward me again, almost like he is not going to let me leave without an answer. But how do I answer him? I don't want to hurt him, but I don't want to give him the wrong idea. I did want to take him back then.

I peer down at my shoes and see him take another step towards me, so close now that we could be slow dancing. I lift my head and he is staring into my eyes, pleading for me to say something. For so long, I wanted him to look at me like this, but not now. Not anymore.

As I'm about to let him know Charlie is more than a friend, hopefully my boyfriend, I feel Charlie's familiar arms wrap around my waist and chin slide onto my shoulder. Immediately, I lean into him and feel the tension in his shoulders.

His deep voice seems to echo within me as he stiffly asks, "What's going on here?"

Nick steps backwards a few spaces giving me a view of his hands which are now balled into fists. Charlie must see the same thing since his hands are twitching over my stomach and his shoulders have tensed even more. To prevent a fight, I twirl around, grab both of Charlie's knotted hands, and try to block his view of Nick. Then, as sweetly as possibly I say, "Charlie, it's nothing. Let's go dance," and pull on his arm to guide him back to the dance floor.

Charlie doesn't move from his spot. He opens his mouth to say something but then falls silent and glances at me. I can hear Nick stomping off. To get Charlie to focus on me, I press my lips against his and whisper, "It's nothing. I'll tell you later. Come on, let's dance."

Thankfully, his body relaxes as we kiss. Maybe we can get back to having fun again? He accepts my hand and we navigate through a crowd of girls, who seem to have enjoyed the show.

As we pass by a column, Mare jumps toward me like a coiled spring. Her nails scratch down my arm as she snaps angrily, "You told Nick you wanted to take him to the dance!"

I rip her bony fingers from my wrist and square my shoulders. Charlie instinctively steps in front of me, but I step around him and get right in Mare's face. "WHAT?" She already got in between me and Nick; I'm not about to let her do it again.

Mare pushes my shoulders and I fall back into Charlie's

chest. "I saw you two. You are trying to steal *MY* boyfriend. Lucy warned me about you."

After regaining my balance, I fire back. "No, Mare. You are the one who told Nick I wanted to take Sam so you could take him. I'm not trying to steal your boyfriend."

When I turn to walk away with Charlie, I notice the storms brewing in his eyes. "Charlie, I—"

Charlie leans away from me and Mare steps in between us. "I heard you. You didn't deny it when Nick asked you."

Frustrated, I step back so Mare is not right up against me. "Mare, that was last summer. A lot has changed. You are with Nick. And I'm—"

Mare yells, "You're a bitch. You always try to steal other girls' boyfriends. You and Kate—"

Mare's eyes widen and she stops in mid-sentence, finally notices the gathering crowd who's hanging on to our every word. As she backs into the formed semicircle, Charlie twirls me around and holds onto both of my arms. His jaw is clenched, and I can see the muscles bulging in his neck. I have never seen him look so flustered and upset.

"Kels, what's going on?" He says quietly.

I wrap my arms around him, ignoring all the prying eyes, and say, "I have no idea. Nick and I have been friends forever."

Charlie lowers his head so it's resting on my shoulder and sharply exhales. There is much uncertainty and hurt in his voice as he asks, "Is there a reason you didn't tell him about us?"

I tense, and he pulls away from me. I wipe my brow, look at him, and tell him the truth. "I didn't know exactly what I should say. . . . I'm not sure how you feel about me—about us. Brooke was always calling, and you didn't tell me about her until tonight and . . ."

Charlie looks down at the floral carpet when I mention

Brooke; his hands are limp at his sides. "I assumed you knew how I felt. I don't want to see anyone else. I—"

Then, someone pulls us apart and my head almost hits one of those twinkling trees again. I steady myself and see Ivy standing in between Charlie and me with that dangerous spark in her eye, the one she gets when she is ready to tear someone apart. With one hand on her hip and the other pointing at me, she taunts, "Kelsey, it looks like you messed up again. Why can't you leave other girls' boyfriends alone? Hope forgave you. I doubt Mare will."

This is unbelievable. I'm not having the same conversation again! I sweep by her and am about to push through the line of gawkers, but stop when I realize Charlie didn't follow me. He is standing there with his hands out in front of him, looking really uncertain.

Ivy seizes the opportunity and hisses, "Are you going to tell him or am I?"

This gets my attention. I whip around with my fists clenched. "Tell him what?"

Ivy grins maliciously. "That you kissed Nick tonight. Mare saw the whole thing."

Ivy moves next to Charlie, places her hand on his arm and purrs, "It looks like your date would rather be with someone else."

Charlie violently jerks his head at her jab, glares at me with a clenched jaw, and then utters the dreaded words, "I'm leaving!"

He pushes through the crowd and almost knocks over the tree. I see Charlie march toward the front door, but I can't process it—it feels like I'm in a dream. One I'm watching in slow motion like when Sherlock Holmes worked through all the steps on how he would immobilize his opponent. Then, the numbness passes and everything is live. Charlie is almost out the front door and I scream, "Charlie, wait, I didn't kiss him.

She's lying," but he busts through the front door anyways and doesn't look back.

All I see is red. My heart is racing, I feel the droplets of sweat on my palms and the heat rising in my chest. Without thinking, I charge at Ivy, but someone holds me back. Robert. I pull loose and get right in her face. "Ivy, what the hell is wrong with you? You know I didn't kiss Nick. Why would you make something up like that?"

Ivy cooly takes a step back, smoothes her dress and taunts, "I only repeated what I was told!"

I stand there completely still, evaluating her. Her trenchant eyes are in slits. She has been planning this, but my response has her a little worried. Even though my body is rigid, my mind is calm and almost clear. I'm the one in control here.

I face Ivy and say, "I'm sick of your juvenile pranks and abuse. I pity you. You are jealous of everyone and have this deranged feeling you deserve payback for the dare in Paris! You got Kate kicked out of school! You set up Jane and Kylie as well as Hope and me by filling in our dates on that STUPID list, but luckily we all figured it out." I see Hope out of the corner of my eye with her hands covering her mouth.

As Ivy crosses her arms and slowly retreats into the crowd, I move toward her closing the distance between us and continue to broadcast her manipulations, "So did you claim Chris to make sure he couldn't go to the Sadie? It's obvious you had no intention of taking him."

She pulls her neck back and tries to act clueless, almost innocent. "I don't know what you are talking about?"

I continue on with more force. "Now you are starting a rumor about me and Nick. All for a dare! We were just playing a game. Kate took the dare and kissed Chris. So what? You and Chris had broken up. You were done with him until he kissed Kate."

Ivy growls. She looks like she is about to physically attack me, but I don't back down and tear into her some more. "You could never compete with her around and wanted her gone because you know she sees right through you. She would expose all your schemes and you couldn't have that, could you?"

For once, Ivy is speechless. She scans the room looking for backup, but no one is coming to her aid.

Nick pushes to the front. His mouth is wide open, eyes bulging. I point at him and demand, "Tell everyone here that nothing happened with us tonight."

Nick looks completely confused and says nothing.

"Tell everyone that we did *not* kiss!" I snap.

Nick finally speaks up so everyone can hear, "What are you talking about? No, we didn't kiss. I would remember that."

I turn back to face Ivy again. She is cowering in front of the line of onlookers. "I'm beyond done with you. If you hurt my chances with Charlie, I will never, ever forgive you—even after everything we have been through together, our friendship will be over!"

With that, I turn toward the table, push through our audience, and steer toward the front door, not knowing what I will do next. I just need to get out of this room, away from Ivy and Mare.

As I run by the coatroom, I almost take out the young man rounding up the club's security. I step to the side and keep on moving, tears streaming down my cheeks. I bust through the front doors and straight into Charlie's arms.

He's out of breath. As soon as he steadies himself, he pulls me in closer, and I break down on his curved shoulder. Gently rubbing my back and kissing my hair, he guides me away from the passing security guards.

Sobbing, I murmur into his blazer, "Why did you come back?"

Charlie pulls the hair out of my face and holds onto both of my shoulders as I lower my eyes, utterly embarrassed. "Kels, look at me. I saw the whole thing on Dave's phone. Bree live streamed it. I'm so sorry I didn't stay beside you. I should've been there."

I fall back into his chest and continue to shake. Everything I've held inside me this year feels like it may come out, and I don't want to do it here in front of everyone. I whisper, "Can we get out of here?"

Charlie takes off his coat and wraps it around me to keep me from shivering and to hide my face from the kids streaming out the front door. I don't even look up to see who's there. Charlie shields me with his shoulder and supports me all the way to the car.

Dave is thoroughly enjoying whatever he's watching on his phone. "Charlie, Bree and her friends are being escorted out right now!"

Charlie lets out a grunt, then slams the door, and reverses out of the spot. Dave stands behind his car, completely speechless.

I turn on the music to drown out the silence. The song, "Dancing On My Own," vibrates over the surround sound. It's not the more upbeat dance version but the raw one. I curl into my seat watching the cars fly by in a blur, fearing I may be the one in the corner watching Charlie with someone else. That tonight may have been the last time I get to dance with him.

As we stop at a light, I feel Charlie looking at me, pleading for me to look back at him. But I can't. There is no way he is going to see me like this; I'm a snotty mess.

As I stare out the window, I feel his soft hand on mine, reassuring me he's still here. Instinctively, I intertwine my fingers in his, feeling the fast pulse in his palm. Slowly, I exhale with my chin raised to the heavens, relieved I haven't lost him.

The car swerves and jolts to a stop. I glance straight ahead and notice we're in the parking lot of Waffle House. I let out a small chuckle. I should've known.

I move toward the door, but he squeezes my hand tighter, not wanting to let go. Then I hear a faint, "Wait."

I wince, not wanting to talk about this, but I stay in the car. I sink into the seat and steal a glance at Charlie under my lashes. He has one hand on the steering wheel, knuckles turning a pale white, and his head is resting on his clenched fist. As his fingers begin to slowly tap the wheel, he says, "I still don't understand what happened tonight. Why did those girls attack you like that?"

I pull my hand away, place both elbows on my shaking knees, and cover my face. Then, I let it all flood out. I tell him all about Paris, about Kate getting kicked out, Ivy starting a list for the Sadie so Hope wouldn't talk to me and to block Chris from having a date. How Mare hates me because of my friendship with Nick. That someone told Nick I wanted to take him to the dance, which I did before. And how Nick asked me about my feelings for him at the dance.

Sometime during my breakdown, Charlie leans over and gently rubs my back with his right hand, moving closer when I mention Nick. He listens and lets me get it all out.

I still can't look at him with the tears streaming down my cheeks and dripping off my quivering chin. He rummages through the console and pulls out some tissues. I accept them without looking up.

As discreetly as possible, I wipe my dripping nose and hide the disgusting tissue in my fist. With the back of my hand I blot my swollen eyes. I must be covered in red blotches. I rub my knuckle across my lip, expecting to see blood from chewing on the inside of my cheek and bottom lip, but none is transferred to my hand.

Charlie leans back to give me space and to take it all in. His shoulders move up and down as he slows his breathing. After what feels like forever, Charlie whispers, "I wish you had told me."

I bite down on my lower lip and say, "I wish you had told me about Brooke. We both have had our secrets."

Charlie rubs his hands through his hair, leaving it standing up at the ends, and I can't help but chuckle. He turns, and I pull my hair over my face so he can't see me. "Your hair is sticking up like it does after playing basketball."

He looks in the rearview mirror but doesn't do anything to fix his hair. Instead, he reaches for my hand. "Kels, I should have told you about Brooke earlier and let you know why I didn't bring you around my friends. I can't believe you knew about Brooke but didn't say anything."

"Charlie, I didn't want to be that jealous girl. I wanted you to tell me about her first. Bree thought you were over, and you never gave me any reason to think you two were still a thing. I wish you had told me, though, especially after hearing about her mother wanting the professor to get rid of the other girl at Yale."

"Kels, I was afraid Brooke would do something like what these girls pulled tonight. She is crazy, like a little fatal attraction crazy. . . . I didn't want to deal with her or give her an opportunity to scare you off. I've never felt like this before. I didn't want to lose you. I can be myself with you. Comfortable. Happy."

I move my hair out of my face and muster the courage to look him in his eyes. "I feel the same. I didn't want to discuss all the mean girl crap when I could just enjoy being with you. I'm still shocked you chose me."

Charlie sighs. "You really don't know how amazing you are, and that's one of the things I love about you—" He leans in further, and all my vulnerability washes away. I feel warmth flow through me—a kind of lightheaded feeling where everything seems to disappear except for him. *He actually used the word love!*

I hear him say, "You're incredibly funny, you always look for the best in people, you always do things for other people—like you did with the roses. You are the *best* person I know. Anyone would want to be with you. I'm lucky *you* chose me."

Charlie gently lifts my chin and continues on saying, "I'm crazy about you. You're all I think about. I look forward to spending every free moment with you, and I don't want anyone to come between us."

"Neither do I," I murmur and kiss him, showing him I feel the same.

He caresses my cheek and wipes away a stray tear, one full of happiness. He asks sweetly, "Are we okay?"

I nod again and say, "Yes, we're okay."

Our warm foreheads rest on one another. I feel like crying again but am able to hold back the tears. I really don't know what I would have done if he had walked away from me.

"Kels, I know I should have said this earlier, but you're the one I want to be with. After our ice skating date, I have always thought of you as my girlfriend and hope you feel the same."

I feel the smile on my cheeks. "Charlie, of course, I feel the same."

He presses his lips on mine and any fear of losing him is gone.

Charlie opens the car door for me, and I bolt inside to see the damage to my face. As expected, I look a mess. My eyes are blood-shot, my cheeks are bright red. Luckily, no blood is on my lip.

I splash freezing cold water on my face twice, and it removes some of the redness, but the bags under my eyes are atrocious. With my ring fingers, I start on the inner corner of my eyes and press as I move toward my outer corners, then repeat. The fluid does seem to dissipate, and I don't look eighty anymore. I splash some more water around my eyes, which erases most of the spots.

I pinch my cheeks at the fleshy part over the cheekbone as well as my lips, so I'm red in the right places. I pull back my hair and look one more time. It could be worse. At least my navy mascara didn't bleed. It did smear a little, but after running my fingertips under my eye lids, it gives more of the appearance of the smokey eye look women intentionally wear at night.

Before I leave the dingy bathroom, I flip my hair forward and tease it, so I look a little wild and carefree to go with the smokey eye thing. Hopefully, Charlie will be the only one to know I have been crying.

Right after I walk out of the bathroom, I fake a sneeze so people will think I have allergies in case I can't pull off the other look.

Charlie is in the far back booth, giving us some much needed privacy. By the time I sit down, he has already ordered my omelet with hash browns scattered, smothered, diced and covered, and a hot tea. He knows me so well.

I curl into his chest and relax for a moment. He holds me tight, then whispers, "Better?"

I look into his concerned eyes and quietly reply, "Yes."

We just sit there for a while holding each other until our food arrives, and then we dig right in. I didn't realize how all those raw emotions pouring out left me so hollow.

Charlie devours his steak before I even touch my hash browns. He's starving too.

Once he has cleaned his plate and looks content, I dare to ask the question that needs to be brought up so nothing like this happens again. "Any other secrets you want to share? Let's get them all out tonight."

He pauses, wipes his mouth with a thin paper napkin, and taps his bottom lip, thinking. So there is something else, and he's trying to figure out how to say it. I take a deep breath and prepare myself for the worse.

"Well, there is one thing Brooke can say about me that is true." I wait for him to say something that will ruin this moment, and he does. "If she says I was naked in the bathroom with her recently, that is true."

I abruptly move away from him and bite my tongue, so I don't say anything I will regret. We haven't even been close to being naked together. He always stops us before things get too heated.

He places his hand on mine and says, "It's nothing like that. I was in the shower at Dave's after basketball practice. Nobody was home except Dave and me, so I didn't lock the door. I took a hot shower and the bathroom was full of steam. When I walked out of the shower, she was standing there with a weird smirk on her face. Dave was in the other room, laughing. Believe me, I was not amused. She left shortly afterward knowing how unhappy I was with her."

His eyebrows knit together as he speaks, and I notice the dark circles under his eyes. He must have hidden the tears when his head was on the steering wheel.

Instead of being angry about something he had no control over, I curl into his shoulder again, peer up into his brilliant blue eyes and say, "Lucky girl."

He leans over and gives me a soft kiss on the upper lip and whispers, "I'm the lucky one."

THIRTY-ONE
THE AFTERMATH

THERE'S no point in jumping over the puddles and around the ruts on the field. Every inch of my body is covered in thick, slimy mud. My skin and white uniform are probably stained a permanent dark brown. A storm hit in the middle of our game, and the refs refused to call it, even though none of us could see the ball through the torrential downpour. If they had only let the girls play first like usual, then the guys would have been the ones slipping and sliding out there.

My mother and Mrs. Sullivan are waiting by the field, dry as a bone since they were huddled under the awning at the top of the stadium. Nick is still on the bleachers with some of the varsity players, who mocked us during the entire game. Hopefully, I can get out of here before he finds his mom to leave. We haven't spoken since last night, and I really don't know what to say to him. I haven't had a chance to process everything yet; I've been replaying the conversation with Charlie in my head over and over again. We finally made our relationship official!

After unsuccessfully stifling a laugh, my mother greets me. "Kels, you're a sight! Hopefully, I have some spare towels in the trunk for you to sit on. Otherwise, my tan leather will be stained brown with all that mud." She tries to make a joke, but I know she's not kidding. She's a bit of a neat freak.

Mrs. Sullivan smiles at me in her usual, motherly way. "Kels, you played well. That was a tough game, but you all pulled it out in the end. Most of the girls spent more time on the ground than upright. Your strength training certainly paid off today."

AHHH, I would give her a hug right now if I wasn't so disgusting. She has always been so supportive of me. "Thank you so much. How are you doing?

"Fantastic. We are so lucky to be playing here or we would be soaked."

"Yes, I can't believe they didn't call the game," I reply, still pouting. Then, I turn back my attention to my mom and plead, "Hey, do you mind if we get going? I'm supposed to meet Charlie."

My mother completely ignores me; instead, she goes on and on about how she set us up, giving herself a pat on the back.

Mrs. Sullivan seems a little hurt as she says, "Really? Nick never tells me anything anymore. I have to hear all the news from other parents now."

"Mom, Mom." I'm trying to get her attention again, but it's no use. Nick is heading right for us with a very put off look on his face.

He stops next to my mother and completely ignores me, then states, "Mom, I'm soaked and really want to shower. Can we go now?"

Mrs. Sullivan's nose flairs just slightly, looking really peeved about his behavior.

"Well, I was about to tell you how well you played, and that the guy you were up against is a senior and just signed at USC."

Refusing to look in my direction, he responds in a much softer tone, "Thanks, Mom. That's good to know."

Feeling the need to say something, I step forward, splattering some mud onto his socks, and praise him, "Nick, you played so well. That fake and stutter-step you made worked perfectly. You won the game for us with that goal."

Nick stares at me like I didn't say a thing, then looks off toward the car, obviously anxious to get away from me. After a second, I hear him say with very little emotion, "Thanks, Kels."

Feeling both a little disappointed *and* relieved that I don't have to deal with him right now, I turn back toward the moms, careful not to flick any mud on them and say, "I'm ready to go too."

Neither of our moms seem to be in any hurry to leave. Mrs. Sullivan is intensely eyeing her son, somewhat shocked by his coldness. She tries another tactic to get him to engage in the conversation. "Nick, why didn't you tell me Kelsey has a boyfriend? Her mom was just telling me how Kelsey met him when she was ten, and she asked him to the dance because that list left Kelsey without someone to take."

There's another awkward pause and then I hear, "Yeah, Mom. Remember I mentioned that guy at Chase who's a really good basketball player. The one Clayton was worried about. That's him."

Mrs. Sullivan turns to me with a giddy grin. "Ahh, that's your boyfriend. I watched him play. He's very good and easy on the eyes too." She nudges my mom.

Nick growls, "Mooooom!"

Both of our moms chuckle, and my mom adds to the insult. "Kelsey, he *is* really good looking. I knew you guys would make a cute couple. You know—you and Nick can go on a double date now."

Nick grinds his cleat into the concrete, exhales deeply, then announces, "It's not the right time. Mare and I broke up last night."

I hear gasps from the moms. Mrs. Sullivan reaches across the empty space toward Nick, but he steps back, obviously not wanting her pity. "Honey, what happened? Everything seemed fine when you guys left for the Sadie."

"At the dance—we realized we're not a good fit. It's for the best," he states, and then he looks at me like this is all my fault.

Picking up on tension, my mother shifts her gaze between the both of us and I mouth, "I didn't know," as her eyes settle on me.

Nick looks at his mom and utters, "It's getting cold. I'm gonna go to the car to wrap up in a towel. It was nice to see you Mrs. Grant." Then he says, "Bye" to me with a mixture of hatred and sadness in his eyes.

As we watch him walk away with both shoulders hunched forward, my mom gently advises Mrs. Sullivan, "Go check on him. He seems upset. We're going to head home too. I'll call you later."

Without saying goodbye, Mrs. Sullivan follows her son. We slowly trail behind her. Once we get to the car, I shed my jersey top and quickly slip on my sweatshirt, wipe off my brown legs, and then peel off my mud-caked cleats. Luckily, there are some plastic grocery bags scattered in the trunk to stash my cleats in.

I spread the towel over the entire passenger seat and turn on my heated seat to remove the chill in the air, but I still need to deal with the one that's coming from my mom. Her fingernails are tapping away at the steering wheel meaning somehow I'm to blame, and she is not going to let this go.

I start to explain my side of the story, "Sorry Mom, I didn't know they broke up. Charlie and I left after dinner."

"You left! Why?" She asks in that tone of her that lets me know she's really disappointed and can't understand why I do certain things.

I look straight through the windshield and relay, "Mom, Charlie and I got into a fight and needed to leave to figure things out."

"You guys got into a fight? It looked like you were so happy when you left."

"We were happy, and it was the best night ever until Mare and Ivy screwed things up." I add, reminding me that I still haven't figured out how I'm going to deal with them on Monday.

"How did they screw it up, Kels?" She is getting a little more concerned now that Ivy has been mentioned.

"Mare and Ivy accused me of kissing Nick and—."

"They did what? Why would they accuse you of kissing Nick? Did you kiss Nick?—Stop picking your nails."

I drop my hands and flatly respond, somewhat offended, "No! I did not. They made it up. Charlie got upset and left but then came back when he realized I didn't do it."

"But then, why?" She is completely confused.

I tent my fingers together and share some of the things I hoped to avoid discussing. "Because Nick told me he would have rather gone to the dance with me instead of Mare—she eavesdropped on the whole conversation. Mare was hurt and lashed out."

"He said what?" She says in a raised voice.

I rub the back of my neck and answer her, "Yes. I really don't know where that came from or what that was about."

"Oh, Kelsey. This is not good. I was just going on and on about how great Charlie is in front of him, and Nick may like you. Did you know?"

I murmur, "I know. I'm not sure what to do now."

"Kels, you need to talk to Nick. Let him know you care for him as a friend." With a raised eyebrow, she says, "Unless you *do* care for Nick more than a friend?"

'No, Mom. I only like Charlie. I used to like Nick, but now I know it was just a little crush, nothing more. I need to fix this. Nick just recently found out about Charlie."

"You didn't tell Nick? You have been seeing Charlie for over two months. Why have you not told him?" She looks directly at me, perplexed by my behavior, once again.

"Because I didn't want to jinx things with Charlie. This other girl—his ex—wasn't leaving him alone, and I didn't want to say anything if he was still seeing her. Which now I know he wasn't. I didn't want to look like a fool."

"Well, you need to apologize to Nick and relay what you just said to me. You need to make him understand it wasn't that you didn't trust him, you just didn't know what to say yet." She thinks she's just giving advice, but this feels more like a lecture, with her voice becoming more shrill as she speaks.

I feel myself becoming more irritated as she goes on and say, "I know. I know."

When she gets like this, it's just better to agree. But I know I have to fix things with Nick and fast, somehow. He's a good friend, and I don't want to lose him. I don't want things to be like they were with Hope.

This is different, though. He may be hurt, but he won't be afraid to be friends with me like Hope was. Even if she had believed that I didn't have anything to do with the list, she still would've ditched me to avoid Ivy's wrath. She just can't handle the abuse. She would never take Ivy on like I did at the dance.

Mare and Ivy aren't going to let this go. But neither am I.

THIRTY-TWO
MISSING PIECES

Ivy places her tray in front of the empty seat as if nothing has changed. But before she can sit down, Kylie and Jane claim the space. Somewhat stunned to be the one excluded, she moves to the end of the table to sit across from Mare, but the space magically disappears again. Everyone seems to be in agreement that she's not welcome anymore. Well, everyone except Mare, who picks up her food in a huff and follows Ivy to another table, mumbling something about me being a menacing witch.

Ignoring her remark, I whisper to Bree, "What happened after I left the dance?"

Bree howls with laughter, then says, "Oh, you need to see this," making everyone look over at us with curiosity.

Kim scoots closer to get a view of the screen showing Nick standing five feet from Ivy with his finger pointing right at her, yelling, "Ivy, I only put up with you because you were friends with Kels and you dated Chris. I've never liked you. You are toxic to everyone around you!"

Mare steps in between them and snaps, "What about me? I'm friends with Ivy."

Nick waves off Mare, dismissing her like she isn't important at all, and focuses on Ivy, who is trying to break through the line of spectators. He snarls, "Ivy, I knew you were behind Kate getting kicked out. Were you trying to get Kelsey kicked out too? It seems like you've been plotting against her all year."

Lucy appears behind Ivy, pushing her back into the ring, and proclaims, "See, all he thinks about is Kelsey!"

Now there are three girls up against Nick, and he just stands there as red as a tomato.

Ivy barks, "You are such a lost puppy following Kelsey around. Mare deserves so much better!"

Chris joins forces with Nick and lays into Ivy. "You are psycho! I accepted the dare to kiss Kate so you would finally get it through your head that we were over. I would never do that to Bree. This isn't middle school anymore. People don't couple up just to couple up. You have been passed around so much that none of the freshmen want you anymore. Unless they want one thing that you're not even good at."

The boys bust out in laughter. Ivy's date standing behind her says, "This sucks!" and then walks away. Nick takes the opportunity to disappear into the crowd, and it looks like he's heading for the front door.

As Ivy watches her date walk away and takes in all the jeering about her prowess, her confidence seems to shatter, but just for a moment. Somehow she rebounds, raises her chin high in the air, saunters toward Chris like a model in a fashion show, then flicks him on the shoulder, and taunts for all to hear, "You were only a plaything—a toy really. Bree can have you."

Before Chris has time to react, she pushes through the parting crowd, and beelines for the restroom, only to be stopped by Kylie and Jane. I can tell they're yelling but can't hear the words. Kim is there too with her arms crossed over her chest, looking really fired up, and then she joins in.

Somewhat shocked that she would go against Ivy, I pause the video and inquire, "Kim, what are you doing in the middle of that?"

Kim leans in closer and grins. "Well, we need to start with the dinner table conversations. Ivy couldn't believe you were there with Charlie. You know he ignored her at the Homecoming afterparty. Anyways, she kept going on and on about how you weren't even supposed to be at the dance.

"I told her she should be happy for you, but she wouldn't let it go. Then, she told Nick you wanted to take him to the dance, and Mare was beside herself, especially since he could not stop watching you with Charlie. You certainly got everyone's attention when you kissed him at the table. Lucy made things worse by saying to Nick, 'It sucks to be on the other side when the one you like wants someone else.' He turned the brightest red and didn't defend himself, which really made Mare angry—I always thought there was something between the two of you."

I ignore her hint for more information, wanting her to stay on course since she has a habit of getting distracted. She continues on saying, "Anyways, I tried to warn you, but by the time I saw you, you and Ivy were already going at it. You were so awesome, by the way.

"When Jane and Kylie started yelling at Ivy, she denied the whole thing and blamed the list on you, Kels—Ivy was quite convincing. And when it looked like they may believe her, I told them that you are the nicest girl in school and would never do something like that. Then, I confessed I was a part of the list and Ivy wrote the boys' names next to theirs. Ivy would have spit fire at me if she could. When Kylie was about to punch her, the management kicked us all out."

Kim stops as soon as she notices the tears welling in my eyes. "Are you okay?"

I quickly wipe my eyes and reply, "Yes, it just means a lot to hear you say that."

Kim tightly wraps her arm around me and chirps, "That's what best friends do, we stick up for one another."

Bree, who is usually not into sappy stuff, puts her arms around the both of us and confirms, "Yes, that's what we do."

THIRTY-THREE

CHATTANOOGA

I DON'T KNOW what they feed them up here, but whatever is, it must be full of some sort of hormone that works like steroids. These guys are huge and taking our players down at every opportunity. Brian has been flattened several times. The short-range kick to the jaw was the final blow to take him out of the game, and his replacement doesn't look like he will be out there for very long either. Nick is getting knocked around but is able to hold his ground more than the others due to his size.

From the fence, the girls and I watch as the other team blasts the ball into the top right corner, but our goalie, miraculously, is able to get his hands on it and miss the post as he rolls onto the ground. While the other team is clearing the box, our goalie acts like he is going to pass it to the center mid, but instead, he boots the ball to Nick.

Nick settles it with his chest, quickly turns the ball around, dribbles between two defenders, and is about to shoot when he gets checked from the side and goes flying through the air. As soon as he lands, I hear the sickening pop.

Nick doesn't need to utter a word, his actions tell it all. He twists his body back and forth with his wrist tight to his chest.

His face is ghostly white and his jaw is clenched to prevent the screams from escaping. The trainer is on the field in a flash with the coach right behind her.

Flying off the bench, Brian shoves the guy and looks like he is about to pop him in the jaw for Nick's takeout and the kick that has left a massive bruise on the left side of the face, but he refrains at the last minute. The ref steps in between them and flashes a yellow card in the air. It really should be a red.

The boys gather around Nick, so I can't see what is going on. After a few long minutes, Nick slowly emerges from the crowd and walks off the field cradling his wrist. They have wrapped it in a white gauze and blood is leaking through it. The bone must have broken through the skin.

Instead of heading to the bench, they walk toward the exit where Hope and I are standing. Nick is looking at the ground, focused on walking or channeling the pain. As soon as they are close, I get the trainer's attention and ask, "Do you want me to call his parents?" and she nods, looking a little faint.

I quickly dial his mother's cell and she picks up on the second ring. "Mrs. Sullivan, hi, it's Kelsey Grant. Hmmm—Nick hurt his wrist, and we're going to the hospital. Do you want to talk to the trainer?" and I hear a frantic, "YES," on the other end.

The trainer fills Nick's mom in on his current state, then she hands the phone back to me to wrap more gauze around the red-soaked bandage and tie a tourniquet on the upper part of his arm. She wipes the sweat from her brow with the back of her hand and takes hold of Nick's torso. As she guides him, she mumbles, "Kels, she asked for you to come with us to the hospital and call her with updates. She's getting in the car now to meet us there."

We make it to the bus without any incident and get him situated in the front seat next to the window, and I climb in next to him. He shifts over and places his head on my shoulder and whimpers with a brittle voice, "God, this hurts."

I search for his good hand and give him a squeeze. The trainer is scrolling through her phone, searching for the nearest hospital.

"Found it," she yells and slams the bus door closed with the metal lever, then floors it out of the parking lot. As we fly onto the main road, she turns around to check on the patient. He's shaking as if he is stuck in a snowstorm without a coat and pale as the color of ice.

"Nick, we are almost at the Children's Hospital. It's supposed to be a good one." Nick grunts at the children's part but doesn't say anything. Since he's the size of a grown man, I think we would have been fine at a regular hospital, but I don't question her.

We whip into the ER bay and I help Nick out. The receptionist takes one look at him and calls for the nurses to usher him back immediately. I stand there watching him shuffle down the hall with hunched shoulders and head hung low until the heavy metal doors close.

The trainer turns to me in a tizzy. "I have to get back to the team. Another kid is injured. Are you okay here?"

I wave her off, and she bolts out the door. The waiting room is completely empty so I have my pick of seats and choose a cold, orange plastic chair hidden behind an enormous tank with clownfish eating the flakes of food floating at the top. My head is resting in my hands, and I notice my legs are shaking. This is the first time someone I care about has gotten hurt like that, sprained ankles excluded.

My phone beeps loudly in my pocket, causing me to jump and hit my elbow on the armrest, instantly causing a stinging, tingly sensation to radiate through my joint. Why the hell do they call it a funny bone when it hurts so much? After a minute or so, rubbing my elbow, I check my phone for a much-needed distraction.

Instead of texting Charlie back, I call to hear his voice, and he picks up right away. "Hey, how was the game?"

Slumping back into the chair, careful to avoid the arm rest, I sigh and give an overview of the afternoon. "Mine was rough, but it was fine. We won in a penalty kick shootout. Hope scored the winning goal. The boys' game was another story. I'm at the hospital right now."

"Wait, what? Are you okay?" His usual smooth, smoky voice turns a little shaky and gruff.

"I'm fine. Nick is not. He broke his wrist. The bone is poking out. I'm in the waiting room at a hospital. I think they are going to operate tonight. His parents are on their way now."

"Oh, I'm so glad you are okay. Sorry to hear about Nick. Is the whole team waiting with you?" And he seems to calm a little even though his voice is still a little off.

"No, it's just me. Nick's parents asked for me to go so he wouldn't be alone, and I could call with updates," I say, looking up at the white ceiling.

"That's nice of you. I didn't know your families were so close." Again, I can tell he is not too pleased but trying to stay supportive.

"Yes, Nick and I have known each other since kindergarten. We've been friends for a long time and so have our parents. I should be here. No one else is here. The trainer just left." I try to explain, but Charlie butts in, "You are there by yourself! They left you there? I cannot believe that. For a school that recruits, they certainly don't care about their athletes very much!" It's obvious he has given up on trying to hide his thoughts about this.

I chuckle and then tease him to try and lighten the mood somewhat. "Charlie, I thought you had gotten over that...."

He lets out a scoff. "You're right. Sorry."

"No, you're right. They shouldn't have left, but I'm sure someone will be right back. Anyways, the ER is empty. Just me, the fish, and the lady at registration. I'm fine. Don't worry." I attempt to convince him as much as myself. My trainer is a bit clueless and may forget about us all together.

"Well, then stay on the phone with me until someone comes back. Tell me more about the game and how Nick got hurt." He's back to his normal self.

I relay the highlights and listen to his day, which was pretty uneventful. As we chat about nothing at all, I can hear Charlie's voice getting more concerned again. I look at my phone and we have been talking for forty-six minutes. As soon as I start to wonder why no one has come back by now, a nurse enters the drafty waiting room. "Charlie, I'll call you back," I quickly say and hang up as she stops a couple feet in front of me.

The little Southern belle, with smoothed brown hair pulled into a tight low bun, smiles brightly at me, then says, "Are you Kelsey Grant?"

I stand up and nervously fiddle with my sweatshirt. "Yes, I'm Kelsey. How is Nick?"

She pats me on the shoulder, trying to ease my nerves, and calmly says, "He's in surgery. Everything is going well. He should be out in another thirty minutes or so, and then you can see him. Do you mind calling his parents to let them know he's in good hands? The surgeon they were asking about did come in and is in charge of his surgery. Apparently, the doctor is friends with someone they know back home. Anyway, they should be pleased to hear it. If you don't mind letting them know, that would be great. I'm going to get everything ready for Nick when he comes out of surgery."

I nod and thank her for the update, feeling much better about things. I call Mrs. Sullivan to give her the good news. As soon as we hang up, I debate calling my mother, but I don't want to hear it from her just yet, so I curl back into the same chair and call Charlie. He picks up on the first ring and anxiously inquires, "What did they say? Is the school there yet to get you?"

I calmly relay the news, avoiding the fact that I *am* still here all by myself. At this point, I'm getting a little annoyed and hungry and, unfortunately, I don't have any cash on me. Only a phone, and I doubt they accept Apple Pay.

Charlie is not willing to get off the phone with me until someone else is here. I listen to him scribble away and turn the pages of his textbooks while I quietly scroll through my Google docs to see if there's anything I can do on my phone, which is very little. After another thirty long minutes, I can feel myself nodding off and that's the last thing I should do right now. I ask, "Charlie, speak to me in French. I love to hear your accent."

He clears his throat and reads aloud in such a sexy voice that it would put any French man to shame.

"English, please," I tease.

He chuckles then translates, "I would love to go to Paris with you, nibble on warm croissants and sip hot chocolate along the Seine River. Kiss you in the Luxembourg Gardens."

He knows I'm melting from the tone of my voice. "That sounds *perfect* right now. Paris would have been so much better if you were there."

Charlie chuckles then reads more passages from his book, making me wish I was in French rather than Spanish. I'm so focused on him that I don't even notice the double doors open and my soccer coach enter.

When I hear my name, I pop up and silently wave to her so I don't yell in Charlie's ear. As she heads toward me, she rants, "I cannot believe the trainer left you here. She failed to mention you came with her to the hospital. Hope asked about you, and then she told everyone where you were. She's going to be reprimanded for this. Are you okay—how is Nick doing?"

I hear, "Yep, trainer of the year," over my phone and quickly say, "I will call you right back."

"Coach, I'm fine . . . really. Don't worry about me. Nick is still in surgery, and the nurse said he's doing well. He should be ready for visitors shortly."

My coach's shoulders seem to relax as I speak but stiffen again in surprise by something I said. "Are you planning on staying? His parents should be here shortly."

There's no way they are making me leave while Nick is in surgery. I firmly explain why I need to be here, "Nick's parents asked for me to stay so I need to stay. Someone should be here when he gets out of surgery. Don't worry about me. You guys can go ahead if you need to leave."

My coach rests her hand on my shoulder and says in a soft yet serious tone, "That's sweet of you, but I need your parent's permission first."

I bite my lip, and then shuffle back and forth, knowing they're not going to be very happy with me. I mumble, "Okay, I'll call them right now." But before I even dial, my mother's name appears on my screen. She breathlessly lectures me on how she just got off the phone with Nick's mom and heard about his wrist and goes on about how hurt she is that I didn't tell her. My coach patiently waits by my side as I get an earful. When I ask for permission to stay in the hospital alone, she goes off again.

"Alone, what do you mean alone? Someone from the school is not staying there too?" Her voice is getting even more loud and hysterical.

"No, the bus is having issues, and they need to head back. My coach is right here, and you can talk to her," I say and hand her the phone.

Instead of asking for permission for me to stay, my coach apologizes for me being left alone for so long in the waiting room, not knowing my mother had no idea. Her back stiffens as the high-pitched voice on the other end pronounces, "This is inexcusable! That trainer is going to hear from me about this. She should never have left a fifteen-year-old alone in a hospital!"

"Yes . . . Yes, you're right. I have already spoken to her about it. . . . Agreed. . . . Okay. . . . Let me talk to the receptionist to see if there is a better place for Kelsey to wait than in the waiting room," and then she hands me back the phone where my mother proceeds to yell some more.

"Mom, what should I have done? Leave with the trainer while Nick may need my help?"

My mother seems to calm down a bit. "Yes, you should've been there for him, it's just that the school mismanaged this."

My coach puts out her hand so she can talk to my mom again, and I gladly hand it over to her. I hear her say, "Jennifer, the security guard is coming and will stay in the waiting area until Kelsey is called back to be with Nick. He's in recovery right now and should be moved to a room shortly. . . . Yes, agreed. I will talk to Kelsey about it before I leave. . . . Okay, again, I am so sorry about this mishap."

As she hands me the phone, she releases a huge sigh and waits for me to finish my call, which doesn't last more than a minute since my mother has nothing more to say for my behavior.

Then, my coach scolds me like my mother. "Do not leave the waiting area. Do not talk to any strangers. Stay behind the fish tank so nobody will see you when they come in. Okay?"

I nod, feeling like a little kid who can't walk across the street by herself, rather than a high schooler. "Yes, thank you, Coach. I'm fine, really."

She wraps her arms around me with unexpected affection and mumbles, "Kelsey, you are a good friend. See you tomorrow," and she quickly darts out the door.

I collapse into the chair and throw my head back,

exhausted and starved. I haven't eaten anything since the bus ride up, and with how my stomach is eating away at itself, I need to get something fast, or I will be in a hospital bed next to Nick. In the past, I have turned pale and fainted from lack of food. Crap, my backpack is on the bus. I whip around and watch the red lights of the bus turn out of the parking lot, feeling like an idiot.

Hoping they have some fruit or something for people waiting, I peel myself off the chair and head over to the receptionist, who is sitting by the entrance looking bored. "Excuse me, do you happen to have some snacks anywhere? My money is on the bus that just left, and I really need to eat." As the lady rummages through her drawers, Charlie calls.

"Hold on a second," then I listen to the lady tell me she's all out, but I may be able to get something when I go back to see Nick. UHHH.

I thank her and turn back to Charlie. "Hey, the team just left, and I'm about to go back with Nick. My mom just lectured me for being here by myself."

Charlie chuckles, "Well, I heard. My mother just came in and told me to get back on the phone with you. I'm in agreement with your mom on this one. I will feel better when you are in a room with Nick—wait that didn't sound right."

I burst out laughing and hear his laugh on the other end. I turn away from the nice lady, who just answered the phone, and catch the mouth-watering scent of pizza. A lanky guy is walking through the double doors with a red pouch, staring at a piece of paper. "Kelsey Grant? Is there a Kelsey here?"

"Charlie, hold on. A pizza just arrived," I announce and leap over to a guy scanning the empty lobby.

"Are you Kelsey?" he inquires, and I nod as I take the cardboard box out of his hands. I pop open the lid and peer inside to see a pepperoni and cheese pizza with pesto drizzled over the top—my favorite!

I snap it shut to keep the heat in and apologize to the guy for not having a tip. The guy waves me off, letting me know, "The tip was taken care of at the order. You're all good. By the way, I was told to tell you to 'Eat up,'" and he dashes off to make his next delivery.

This has to be from Charlie with that comment! I hit the speaker on my phone and thank him profusely as I make my way to my fish tank corner.

I hear the smile in his voice as he says, "You're welcome. Eat. It may be a long night. I wish I could be more help."

My teeth sink into the warm slice, and then I devour another and another. Charlie continues on with his French, and I listen. As I wipe my greasy fingers with the napkin from the plastic utensil pouch, the nurse appears and sweetly says, "Kelsey, your boyfriend is out of surgery and asking for you. You can go back now."

Charlie heard the entire thing from the grunt and silence on his end. Immediately, I correct her. "Nick and I are just friends." Then put the phone up to my ear and let Charlie know I will call him shortly and thank him again for being such a lifesaver.

I follow the nurse back through several halls until we reach a small room in the corner. Nick is lying on a slightly raised bed with plenty of monitors and an IV drip connected to his left arm. His eyes are barely open, and he seems to be heavily medicated. "Kels, is that you? What is going on? I don't feel so good."

"Nick, you're in a hospital. You broke your wrist and did so well in surgery. You'll be as good as new before you know it." I try to remain as calm as I can, but it's hard to see Nick looking so frail.

Nick rolls his head toward me and reaches for my hand with some uncertainty. "Kels, I—I'm so glad you're here. I had a dream we were fighting. You were with some guy. It was awful."

Yep, he's super-drugged. He can't decipher dreams from reality.

I pat his hand and encourage him to close his eyes. "Nick, sleep. You need your rest. We are all good. I promise you will like Charlie once you get to know him."

Nick's eyes flick open, and then he fades away, saying, "Chaaarrrlieee?"

I let him sleep and call his parents. Due to an accident on the highway, they're still about twenty minutes out and thanked me profusely for staying with him. Then, I call my mother to let her know all is good even though she's usually asleep by now. She said to call her again once we know if we need to stay in the hospital or if we can bring him home. My dad will be up waiting.

Nick stirs, and his eyes flutter open again. "Kels, can you get me some water?"

I pour him some from the side table and he sits up to take a sip.

"How are you feeling?"

He hits the button on his bed to raise the back and mumbles, "Better. I can't really feel anything except a throbbing."

"Yeah, they told me their best surgeon worked on your hand."

"That's good to hear. Can you tell me something so I don't think about how this may change things? Not being able to play basketball and all."

"Sure," and I pause to think of something fun we have done together that made us both laugh. "Nick, do you remember when we learned how to water ski? How you refused to let go of the rope, and my dad dragged you across the water. You body surfed through the waves and ended up with a water burn across your chest!" I laugh out loud at the memory. It's one I will never forget.

Nick smiles slightly. "I may not have gotten up on the first try, but I nailed it on my second. You, on the other hand, kept falling over your skis. It took you three tries to lean back and pop out of the water. . . . I beat you again."

"Nick, it wasn't a contest! And I was not the one that needed oil and aloe applied several times a day to soothe a burn." But his eyes have closed, not ready to banter.

I move back into the seat and pull out my phone to call Charlie when I hear, "Kels, I miss this. . . . I miss you. . . . I love you," and his voice trails off as he lies there still.

THIRTY-FOUR

ASSURANCE

CHARLIE WRAPS his arms around me checking to see if anything has changed on my end. I hold him close, not caring about the dampness on his clothes from baseball practice. While stroking my hair and upper back, he asks, "How are you?"

I raise my heavy head and mumble, "Fine, tired. We checked into a hotel around 1 a.m., and I got very little sleep. We didn't get back until around 3 o'clock today."

"You do look beat," and he stifles a laugh as I pout about hearing how awful I look.

"So, how's Nick? Is he out for the rest of the season?" He winces slightly as he says his name.

"For soccer, yes. But they said he should have a full recovery. He'll be fine to play basketball in the fall," I reply while dragging myself into the kitchen, waving for him to follow.

In one smooth motion, he drops his backpack and wraps his arm around me, probably to make sure I don't stumble, and then asks, "So did he say anything funny while he was drugged?"

Not wanting to have this conversation yet, I look sideways, trying to think of ways to deflect, but he picks up on my unease and leans in closer, searching for my eyes. "Kels, what did he say?"

While grabbing a drink for both of us, I dance around the subject, "Er—something like—so don't freak out. I think it was a joke, or he didn't mean it."

Charlie leans against the island, arms crossed and eyes in slits, waiting for me to elaborate, but I act like I don't notice. Instead, I pour the seltzer into a glass and hand him his drink, hoping he will take a sip and give me more time to think, but he sets it on the island and beckons me to continue with his eyes.

I take a long sip, decide being direct is the best course of action here and tell him, "He said something along the lines of 'I miss you and I love you.'" I say it so quickly that he may miss the last part.

Within seconds, his hands are on both of my arms, and he's staring right into my eyes. "Kelsey, how did you not tell me that?"

Shrugging and avoiding eye contact, I rationalize, "Well, I didn't really know what to say—I don't think he meant it, and he didn't say anything about it today."

He rubs his fingers through his hair and sighs. "Kels, I do think he feels that way. . . . He followed you out of the Sadie, but he then went back inside when he saw me holding you."

"What—really?" I say in complete disbelief.

Charlie leans back, studying me, and then very seriously asks, "Should I be worried here?"

Without thinking, I wrap my arms around him and very clearly state, "You have nothing to worry about. Even if he meant what he said, it doesn't change anything between us. I used to like him until I met you. Now I know it was just a crush. Nothing more. He hasn't met anyone yet to make him understand the difference. But he will. Hopefully, sooner than later because he is a really good friend, and I don't want things to be awkward."

As I hold him, Charlie's knotted muscles in his shoulders and back relax, as do mine, allowing the exhaustion to sink back in. I tossed and turned last night, dwelling on Nick's "I love you" comment and how I was going to address it with him and Charlie. Fortunately, things went better with Charlie than I expected. I doubt the conversation with Nick will go as well, if we ever do talk about it. Maybe he won't remember, which would make things so much easier.

Gracie, who has been patiently waiting for Charlie's attention, jumps up on his leg, begging for a back scratch. Charlie chuckles and gets down on one knee to rub her ears. She's just like me; she cannot get enough of him. With Gracie pressed to his outer thigh, we climb into the tufted breakfast bench, and my head finds his shoulder, and I feel completely wiped out.

Charlie kisses my hair and softly says, "Kels, let's watch a movie. You need to rest . . . you're exhausted." He's right. I can barely keep my eyes open, so I accept his hand to lift me up and drag me to the sofa.

Scrolling through Netflix, he asks, "What do you want to watch? What's your favorite movie?"

"*The Illusionist* but that takes a lot of thinking. How about *The Tourist* since that starts in Paris, and they speak a little French? Or we can go with something you will like—like *Star Wars: The Last Jedi*," I mumble with my head in his lap, enjoying him lightly stroking my hair again. Somehow he never pulls or tangles my hair even when it needs to be brushed, like now.

"Hmmm . . . what is *The Tourist* about?" He searches Netflix trying to find it without any luck.

"Go to Amazon Prime or Apple TV, and look under purchases to find it—so, the British government and a very ruthless, wealthy criminal are searching for a man who disappeared with their money, leaving behind a woman who the government surveils, thinking he'll come back for her. And when she receives a letter with instructions to get on a train and meet a man that could pass for him, they follow her to Venice. The tourist on the train and the woman connect, making her rethink things with the other guy, and she must decide if her previous lover is worth protecting."

While reaching over me for a blanket and tucking it around me, he whispers in that silvery voice I love, "And is he?"

I close my eyes feeling so much better now that he's with me, and before I drift off I hear myself say, "You have to watch. . . ."

THIRTY-FIVE
UNFAIR PUNISHMENT

HEADMISTRESS DANA WILLIAMS walks into the drafty room, removes her overcoat, and then wraps herself in a long cozy sweater, completely missing the fact that Karen Collins is sitting in the chair across from her oak desk. Karen clears her throat, and Dana jumps, knocking her coat off the hanger. She gasps, "Oh my, you scared me half to death—what are you doing here?"

Karen doesn't even attempt to be civil this morning and goes straight to the point. "Dana, Ivy is being bullied. Fix it, or I will find those screenshots of inappropriate photos of your daughter. Since you expelled the Reed boy for sending indecent photos to a girl, the honor council will do the same to Taylor."

Dana stares at her for a moment, completely bewildered by her change of attitude. "Well, good morning to you too, Karen. I'm sorry to hear about your daughter, but what do you want me to do about it? I need details—"

Karen cuts her off. "You do *not* need any details. You just need to know that at the Sadie, several kids attacked Ivy saying some very nasty things about her, and those kids were thrown out of the dance for their behavior. The kids involved are Kelsey Grant, Nick Sullivan, Chris Huntington, Bree Aster, Hope Blakely, Kylie Pruitt, and Jane Windsor."

Dana takes a sip of her coffee, annoyed that she has to deal with something so trivial. "Well, that will be simple enough since they were removed from the dance for defamatory behavior."

Karen rises from the comfy chair looking quite satisfied with herself but then leans over the table and stares down Dana. "Thank you for taking care of this promptly. I'm glad we are in agreement on this," and upon receiving a nod conceding to the plan, Karen marches out of the office.

Dana leans over and hits the button on her phone, "Ursula, I need for you to schedule a meeting with the following students...."

Ursula chirps back, "Certainly, you have time from 2 to 3 o'clock today. I will book them back to back."

Dana rethinks this and responds, "No, let's do it right after the assembly. I can address them as a group. Instead of meeting in my office, I will talk to them in the assembly room. It will be quick and painless this way."

I discreetly text Charlie through the entire assembly. He had a late practice, so we didn't get to see each other yesterday, which is probably a good thing since Brooke showed up at his house demanding that he break up with me. It was so bad that his parents had to ask her to leave. I'm not sure how things would have played out if I was there. Charlie is right about her being crazy.

The bell rings, and I'm about to get up when I hear the dreaded words from our conniving headmistress. "The following students need to stay after assembly: Kelsey Grant,

Nick Sullivan, Chris Huntington, Bree Aster, Hope Blakely, Kylie Pruitt, and Jane Windsor."

Oh crap! Bree whips her head around to look at Chris and me, searching for answers from one of us. Nick is studying his bandaged arm, still highly medicated and unaware of his surroundings. I don't think he even heard his name called.

Hope has her hands over her face. Knowing her, she's more terrified about what her parents are going to say than anything else.

Kim passes by with a puzzled look on her face. Why wasn't she included in this?

Ivy and Mare follow behind her; they both have smirks all over their faces, and it's obvious that they know what's coming.

Some wish us luck as they race out, while others go along as if nothing is happening. The headmistress hangs on stage with one of the guidance counselors, gossiping about something that happened at another school.

When everyone has left the hall, Mrs. Williams clears her throat and begins her lecture, "It has come to my attention that you all were asked to leave the dance this past weekend. This is an embarrassment to the school and will not be tolerated. You all will go to detention during your free periods for the next two weeks and will *not* be eligible to participate in the next three games if you are involved in a sport. The ladies present involved in the play will not be able to perform on opening night. Understood?"

We all look at each other in shock. I am the only one that speaks up to defend myself. "Mrs. Williams, I was not asked to leave the party. Neither were several other people here. This is all a misunderstanding. We—"

"SILENCE—you are not to talk back to your elders, Kelsey Grant."

I sit up straighter in my seat and apologize unnecessarily,

"I'm sorry, but we should have the opportunity to respond to the allegations and set the record straight."

Headmistress Williams completely ignores me and repeats, "Understood."

We all respond like robots, "Understood."

She smiles down at us like she's doing this for our own good, like some sort of righteous, benevolent dictator, but her acerbic tone makes it clear her intentions are not kind.

We wait for her to release us, knowing if we get up without permission, she will add more to the unfair punishment. She looks at each one of us, enjoying the power, and then gleefully says, "You are dismissed."

THIRTY-SIX
THE DEBATE

I YELL, "I GOT IT," as I walk to the front door. Charlie is standing on the stone porch with two bags in his hands. One is from Café Vendôme and the other from Jeni's. With the sweetest smile on his face, he says, "I thought one of these might cheer you up."

I lunge forward and wrap my arms tightly around him. "Awww Charlie, thank you so much! Just seeing you makes me feel better, but these goodies are definitely an added bonus!" I kiss him quickly since my parents are somewhere in the house.

The bags graze my baggy sweat pants and I glance down, embarrassed by what I have on. Usually, I look a little more put together in front of him, but I wasn't expecting him to come over tonight. Charlie dismisses my concern saying, "You look fine. I wish I was in my sweats."

As we walk in the kitchen, I open up the white bag and take in the heavenly smell of the vanilla pastry cream and chocolate chips wrapped in croissant dough. I pull out one of the Brioche Suisse and let Charlie have the first bite. Seeing the look on his face, I hand him the entire thing.

He devours it as I grab the bowls and spoons. I take the

pints out of the bag and notice he brought our favorites: Darkest Chocolate and Brambleberry Crisp. I swipe my finger across the inside of the chocolate lid, and then lick it off. Instead of commenting on my rudeness, he chuckles.

I hold up the ice cream scooper and ask, "Which one do you want?"

Charlie peers over his shoulder into the hall, and then quickly gives me a soft peck and says, "Whatever you want. . . . Now I know why you love this croissant thing so much. What do they call it again? I'll order one when I'm in Paris."

Scooping the slightly melted ice cream into the bowls, I answer, "A Pepito, but in France they're called Brioche Suisse." Picking up on the Paris comment, I look at him and question, "Are you planning some trip I should be aware of? I want to go back."

His eyes don't meet mine as he replies, "Hopefully pretty soon. I've never been and would love to go with you. You need to have some better memories there than the ones from last summer with the Kate stuff."

"Yeah, it would have been so much better if Ivy had not been around, and Kate wasn't in that predicament—speaking of Kate . . . we need to watch the debate tonight. Kate's mom is on, and I told her I would fill her in since she has to miss the beginning. It's starting in five minutes."

Seeing he is off in space somewhere, I nudge his shoulder. "Charlie, did you hear me?"

He shakes his head and says, "What? Uh, yeah. We can watch the debate. I think we need to take a break from school tonight anyways."

I nod in agreement as I hand him his bowl. "Yeah, there's no way I can focus on school right now. Thanks again for getting these. You are so sweet to me."

Charlie takes a seat on the stool at the island and I follow him, eating my Pepito along the way. "So did anything happen at school today? No more Brooke incidents?"

Charlie shrugs, then replies, "Nope, she left me alone today. It was a nice change."

I suck the last bit from my spoon and joke, "Well, maybe your parents scared her off."

Under his breath, he says, "I doubt she cares what anyone thinks."

"Okay, enough about her. Anything happen at practice?"

My phone buzzes, and I ignore it as Charlie says, "No, we got to scrimmage, which was much better than the suicide races yesterday."

When my phone buzzes again, I casually pick it up and see a message from Nick, telling me to open Facebook. Charlie tenses on seeing his name. I scroll through the feed, and there is a photo of Kate drunk in the hall in Paris. Then, another message pops up. Someone has shared the image on Snapchat.

I jump up and knock my stool backwards. "OH MY GOD!" I yell as the seat crashes to the floor.

Charlie jumps up and wallops his knee on the marble. "Ouch! Son of a—I think I may have busted open my scab," he groans and grimaces, then manages to ask, "What is it, Kels? What happened?"

I lean over to check the wound on his knee, and it's not bleeding. He continues to rub it as I show him the photo. Still unsure what is going on, Charlie asks, "Is that Kate? What is she doing?"

I respond while I text Kate, "She's drunk in Paris. Ivy dragged her into the hall."

Charlie reaches for my phone again to examine the photo some more. "This is how Ivy got her kicked out of school?"

I hold my hand out for my phone to check for a response from Kate. "YES! I need to warn Kate. Ivy's mom is running against Kate's mom. The other guy dropped out of the race."

Charlie sits back in his seat, somewhat stunned. "You have got to be kidding me! This debate should be interesting."

"I know. The Collinses must be setting up the Lexingtons. They have to be behind the leak."

Kate isn't answering any of my texts or calls, and I'm panicking. "I can't reach Kate. I need to reach her!"

Charlie quietly gets up from his seat to turn on the television. He finds the station and hollers at me from the doorway, "Kels, the debate has started. Kate isn't going to be able to warn her mother. You can't do anything now."

Dread fills me as I enter the family room and watch the moderator discuss the merits of the debate. Charlie pats the seat next to him, motioning for me to join him. I curl into his shoulder with my feet tucked under my thighs. I point at his feet, letting him know he can put them up and relax. My father does it all the time. Charlie slips his shoes off and hesitantly places his athletic socks on the stitched leather ottoman.

The cameraman focuses on Senator Lexington as she walks onto the stage, looking radiant in her charcoal Armani suit. She has a broad smile across her face. She probably has no idea what's coming. Ivy's mom walks out on the other side, looking a little uncomfortable in the spotlight. They meet in the middle and cordially shake hands.

Charlie jests, "Ivy's mom looks nothing like Ivy. Karen Collins resembles Alicia Florrick from *The Good Wife* in appearance and by the way she holds herself. She seems very reserved and cautious. My mom watches that show over and over again."

I agree with his assessment and hope the audience will too. Well, maybe not—Alicia is somewhat likable and earns respect. Karen Collins is not respectable. She is mean-spirited, manipulative, and calculating, while Katherine Lexington is kind, relaxed, and charming.

The moderator introduces both women and begins with

very generic questions. It appears it will be another boring political debate.

As the debate drones on, I resist the urge to turn it off and watch something else.

I rest my head in Charlie's lap, and he strokes my hair. He comments, "Kels, the Senator and Mrs. Collins agree on most things, surprisingly. I figured they would have very different viewpoints by their demeanor. It appears no one is going to win this debate."

He's right. Neither one has said anything that will impact the voters. The moderator has not baited them into saying something they'll regret. I so wanted to watch the Senator take down Ivy's mom.

As I watch Mrs. Collins put on her act of being honorable, generous, and intelligent, the bile builds up in my throat. I can't stand Ivy or her mother now. Karen Collins spends her days devising ways to manipulate people, but no one would know that by the way she's acting on television.

Ivy is just like her. She lied and got me suspended from the most important game of the season—the one against Chase. It seems I can't win against her, and Senator Lexington can't win this one against Mrs. Collins. This is torture to watch.

The moderator inquires, "Karen Collins, would you support or object to the Heartbeat Law if elected?"

Now, this is a very touchy subject. One that could impact someone I know. There are rumors that my teammate has been throwing up in the bathroom, and it's not from the flu. Charlie and I both lean forward.

Mrs. Collins takes a sip of water, mirroring her opponent. "I am glad you brought this matter up today. I am a supporter of this law. Women have the right to abort an embryo until it becomes a life with a beating heart. Then, it should be in the hands of God, not a doctor. This law ensures we do not have a say in this decision."

The Senator grimaces. This is one bill she does not support and has been lobbying against it. She challenges her opponent, saying, "Karen, this law does not impact those with means, it affects the poor women without fortune. Parents with wealth will drive or fly their daughter to another state for an abortion, leaving behind the girls who do not have the same resources. Since most women have no idea they're pregnant until after six weeks, this bill does not provide the less fortunate with any other option but to have a child they are not prepared to care for and cannot afford to raise. It is not the government's right to force the majority of women into having a child while others more fortunate have the opportunity to decide for themselves."

One point for the Senator. She nailed that question.

Charlie slides back against the softback cushion, nodding his head in agreement. I lean in and nuzzle into his shoulder. "Did you notice what she did there?" I feel him shrug, not getting my meaning.

I quickly explain so we don't miss anything else, "She gave a valid reason why the Heartbeat Law is unfair to the masses. A reason for both sides—the Pro-Life and Pro-Choice—not to support the law since it isn't a solution. At the same time, the Senator didn't tell the audience which side she supports. This is why she is going to win. She is a master at diversion and persuasion."

I turn my head slightly so I can see his face. Charlie's lower lip has dropped as it sinks in. "How did you pick up on that?"

"Many years of watching her respond to things. I practically lived at the Lexington's when my parents were busy building their businesses."

We both turn back to the screen when Karen Collin's clears her throat to get everyone's attention back on her. It's a trait Ivy has learned. Karen's face plainly shows she knows she lost that argument and snickers, "Well, now we know what you would do if your daughter was facing this decision."

The crowd is silent. You could hear a pin drop. The cameraman focuses in on the Senator who is trying to remain calm. She distracts herself by shuffling her papers neatly together to create some sort of order and avoids addressing the rude, intrusive comment.

The moderator clears his throat and asks another question. Charlie says under his breath, "Wow, I know where Ivy gets her vengeful personality."

"Yep, the apple didn't fall far from the tree. But I think the Senator handled it beautifully. She really does remind me of the lady in *Madam Secretary*, now Madam President." I turn down the volume with the remote and ask him. "Do you watch *Madam Secretary*? The Senator and the lady in the show resemble each other."

He shakes his head while still watching the debate.

I turn the volume back up so he can listen to me and the television, then relay one part in a recent episode where she (Madam President) is accused of orchestrating a fake WWIII threat with China to stay in office, and how I wish I had her quick wit. Then add, "You know, the Senator could be president one day; she's a lot scarier than the lady on television." As I say this, the thought crosses my mind that Kate would actually be the better president.

Charlie leans over and kisses my forehead. "I love your wit. You come up with the most unexpected things and have no idea how funny you are." I nuzzle in the crook of his neck, loving how he pays attention to what I have to say and the fact he gets my humor.

The debate continues to drag on, and finally we are at the end. The only thing left are questions from the audience. A lady who looks like she has been through a lot stands up and addresses the two candidates. "This is a question for both women. In light of the photo that surfaced of Senator Lexington's daughter, what is your stance on bullying, especially on social media? You both have daughters in high school, correct?"

Karen is eager to answer this question; it's almost like she was waiting for it. "As parents, we have the responsibility to educate our children and teach them empathy. Kids feel they are invincible and never think something like this will happen to them, let alone be shared for all to see and remember. Parents, counselors, and schools should discuss unfortunate photos like these to show them that accidents happen, and in the world of social media, these incidents are not forgotten and can change a kid's course forever."

As Karen speaks, the Senator looks at her campaign manager and mouths something. The Senator's campaign manager discreetly walks on stage and shows her the photo while Ivy's mom is talking. A frown briefly crosses the Senator's face, and then she composes herself. She whispers something in response, and the manager disappears off stage, allowing the floor to switch to the Senator.

The Senator takes a sip of water and begins with a joke. "I assume the photo you are referring to is of my daughter, who had too much to drink while in Paris on a school trip. At least it's somewhat legal to drink there." She pauses for effect. "That was an unfortunate night for my daughter, one that did result in her going to boarding school. I was quite angry with her until I found out the full story."

She pauses again, glancing at Karen, then articulates her reason for the last comment, "On my daughter's last night in Paris, her roommate brought in a bottle of Champagne to celebrate their trip. My daughter reluctantly agreed, much to my dismay. After drinking, she woke up outside her hotel room to a teacher trying to carry her back into the room. She could not remember much else and did not understand why her roommate was reportedly sober."

The Senator looks at her campaign manager, mouths something, then nods in acknowledgment. She looks directly at Karen Collins and then at the camera. In a sweet monotone, she requests everyone, "Please go to YouTube and search for 'Teen Set Up On School Trip in Paris'. . . . This will clear up what happened that night."

I grab my phone and type in the easy to remember title. A video appears with Ivy dragging Kate into the hallway. Katherine Lexington patiently waits for the chatter to die down before stating, "I think this is a perfect example of bullying and how someone's actions can impact the life of another. Did you notice there were two bottles in the girl's hand who was running down the hall, one champagne and the other a sparkling cider?"

The Senator turns to Karen with one eyebrow raised in a high arc. She calmly says, "Karen, the other girl in the video is your daughter. Did she plan that evening all by herself, or did you help her set up my daughter?"

Karen appears absolutely stunned. Her 'rehearsed' ability to disguise herself as a guardian angel falters under the camera. She stumbles backwards, but quickly recovers, and grips the podium with two hands. She takes a sip of her water, then comments, "I have never seen this video before. Where did you get it?"

The Senator coldly responds, "The hotel. I assume you have seen this since the school, which both of our daughters attended, has a copy of it, too." Katherine pauses again, waiting for Karen to defend her daughter, but nothing crosses Karen Collins' lips. Only fear is present.

In a very serious tone, Senator Lexington continues on with her takedown. "I have known about this video for a while but have not brought it into the campaign since these are young girls who make mistakes, and their actions should not be used as weapons in a campaign. As you all know, I have never targeted the families of my opponents in past campaigns. But Karen, you leaked this photo of my daughter to embarrass her and my family, thinking it would increase your standing in the polls for this election. I am standing here today letting you know IT IS NOT GOING TO WORK."

Karen's confidence continues to wither; she has always been one step ahead, being the perfect chess player, but she has been blindsided. She looks at the moderator and says, "I would like ten minutes to verify the authenticity of this video." Then she scampers off the stage.

The Senator turns to the moderator and requests permission to continue, "I would like to finish answering the question, if I may," and begins speaking in a much softer, yet more authoritative tone before the moderator nods in agreement. "Now, back to your question. Bullying is a serious issue with lasting consequences. After receiving this video, I contacted a company who works with AI to analyze behavior on social media. They can recognize bullying before it escalates.

"I worked with them to create an app. This app will read a person's facial expression and/or language and determine if it may be perceived as negative. Hopefully, this will make the individual think twice before posting the media. If the bully continues to send the negative media, there is a record of it and we can start identifying patterns of negativity before they evolve into something that may become life-changing. Parents with children under the age of 18 years old will be alerted if there is a pattern of abusive media being sent by their child."

She takes another sip of water and states, "The app also alerts the receiver of the negative content so they can decide if they want to open it or not. Parents will be alerted if their child receives three or more negative messages from an individual. This will give parents the opportunity to block further media and appropriately address the behavior with the bully's parents, school, and/or authorities before it escalates. Hopefully, this will limit the amount of bullying on social media as well as identify online predators."

The Senator looks the questioner directly in the eyes and gives a sympathetic smile. "And, I believe your name is Anne, Anne Swift. I am so . . . so sorry about your daughter. I remember her sweet face. She was too young, and the tragedy should never have happened. If you are interested in sharing your experience and valuable insight on bullying, I can arrange a meeting with the company working on this app so we can work together to limit the number of children targeted on social platforms."

Anne chokes out, "I would love to help," then she sits down with her hands covering her face.

The moderator looks around, completely mesmerized by what just transpired, and tries to quiet down the audience. He claps his hands to get everyone's attention, but they ignore him. It doesn't seem like anyone else will have any questions after that.

The moderator shakes his head in frustration, knowing he's lost control. He sits up straight, smiles as he makes an executive decision, and loudly states, "Since it does not appear Mrs. Collins will be returning to the stage, I think we can conclude this debate. Thank you for your time, Senator Lexington. Everyone have a good evening."

Charlie leans back, looking very impressed and lets it be known. "I never want to go against the Senator. I see why you said she's scary."

I burst out laughing, and my body rocks back and forth as I hold my stomach. Tears roll down my cheeks. Charlie is laughing just as hard, only in a much deeper tone.

Karen Collins finally got taken down and for all to witness. Ivy must be seething right now. Kate's family is victorious once again. We continue to relish the moment, making my punishment seem so distant and insignificant now.

As I wipe the tears away, Charlie pulls me back into him and says, "Show me that *Madam Secretary* episode. I want to see what's so similar in the Senator, and how accurately you recalled the one-liner."

I whip my head around, feeling a little stung, but relax as I see the mischievous grin on his face. He leans in and tickles me, making me squirm, but I love every minute of it.

Charlie searches for the *Madam Secretary* episode while I call Kate. It goes straight to voicemail. I'm sure she is on the phone with her mother. She must be mortified that the photo and video were leaked, and everyone saw it during the debate.

I text her hoping for some sort of answer. *Call me when you can. I saw the debate. Your mom did great. Everything will blow over about the photo. It made Ivy look bad. Not you.*

I wait for a minute, not taking my eyes off the stagnant screen, then place my phone in my lap, hoping I'll feel the buzz if she responds. But I know it's unlikely I will hear anything tonight. Her family is in the middle of damage control.

THIRTY-SEVEN
THE BOARD

As several board members walk into the headmistress' office, Dana Williams springs from her chair and greets her board member friends. Clare Stryker, a well respected attorney in town, begins with polite small talk and then deftly rolls right into the question everyone knows the answer to already. "Dana, did you know about that video of Katherine Lexington's daughter in Paris?"

Annoyed that this is coming up again, Dana impatiently slaps her hands on the desk and exclaims, "Clare, you know I handled the situation as quietly as I could. I—"

But she is interrupted by the ditzy debutante, Rachel Bell, who desperately wants to prove her worth. "You are fired, effective immediately. Pack your things in your office and your residence. You have two days to move off this campus."

Headmistress Williams furrows her brow and, with a wave of the hand, dismissing Rachel's feeble attempt to terminate her. She turns to someone she knows has her back, a certain Olivia Bennett, who she recommended to become a board member and socializes with on a regular basis. "Olivia, I'm sure you had no idea that Rachel was going to fly off the handle like this. As you know, I was brought in to raise the funds to modernize this school, and I have done exactly as expected," she says and then sits back in her chair with the utmost confidence that the matter is settled.

She and Olivia have always been on the same page. Just the other day on the flight back in the Bennett family jet, Olivia commented on how impressed she was with the amount of money Dana raised for the building, allowing them to add much needed steam rooms to the locker areas.

Being a powerful lobbyist with the uncanny ability to play both sides without tipping her hand, Olivia Bennett rebukes Dana's plea for her position. "Actually, Dana. We have other plans now, and you *are* dismissed. Clare will serve as acting headmistress until we can find a replacement." As Olivia peers out the window, she offhandedly announces, "The reporters just pulled up. I recommend you walk out through the back door."

Stunned by this turn of events, Dana glares at all three women in front of her, then vehemently argues, "You can't fire me. All the corporate funds for the new Student Center will be pulled with my removal. You need me here to finish the building. We are breaking ground in two months!"

Olivia fires back, "It's done," and turns toward the door to leave the room.

Not accepting what is happening, Dana reaches across the desk for her arm and frantically tries one last thing to change her mind. "I cannot believe you are treating me like this after everything I have done for your children. They—"

Olivia whips back around, infuriated by what is about to exit her mouth, and pries her fingers from her upper arm. She hisses, "We *all* do what is best for our children. *You*, of all people, should understand that."

Seething with anger over the betrayal from her so-called friends, Dana shoves several stacks of papers into the CELINE bucket bag, removing any incriminating documents, and stomps out the door. While dashing by her receptionist, Ursula, the wheels in her head desperately grasp for ways to get the rest of the board in a room together to vote on removing these women and restoring her power. So caught up in her thoughts, Dana misses who is standing right in front of the desk, chatting away with *her* receptionist.

She processes the familiar face and stops short. Her neck rotates like a hawk's, then focuses on her nemesis, who's waving her fingers in the air as if saying goodbye and good riddance. The last conversation between Dana and Katherine was not pleasant. The Senator made it known that she felt her daughter was being mistreated, her family would not contribute any additional funds to make this matter disappear, and they would be rescinding their pledge to donate to the school. As it sinks in that she has been outplayed, her shoulders instinctively slump forward, and she quickens her pace to avoid further humiliation.

While looking back one last time to watch the board members greet the press, she walks right into Ivy Collins and her mother. Ivy falls backwards on the step but quickly regains her balance by grabbing hold of the door handle. Dana pitches forward and drops her bag, dumping all her papers onto the ground. Madly, she pulls all the papers into a stack and jams them back into her bucket bag, without making eye contact with Karen, and scurries down the stone walkway toward her home, adjusting her jacket as she passes by the glass windows of her office.

Karen watches her go, stunned by her frazzled behavior, and asks Olivia and Rachel, "What is that about? I thought we were supposed to meet her here at 9 o'clock."

Olivia waves it off as if it was a personal matter. "Why don't you wait for her in the headmistress' office? She has something she needs to take care of this morning."

Adjusting the collar of her blouse so her diamond necklace is on display, Karen strides into the lobby and notices the gathering crowd. "What is going on in there?" she asks while craning her head into the room.

Again, Olivia waves it off, saying, "Just some school stuff," and points her in the direction of the headmistress' office. As soon as she turns the corner, Karen freezes when she sees the Senator talking to Clare and Ursula.

Clare takes one step in front of Katherine Lexington to block Karen's view, then she puts out her hand, and directs them into the vast office. "Karen, Ivy, thanks for coming in today. Please wait in here, and I will be right in to see you."

Ivy follows the instructions, but Karen is somewhat resistant. She doesn't want to get too close to the Senator, who can't hide the smug expression on her face.

As soon as Karen and Ivy are safely inside the empty office, Clare steps toward the entrance and greets two more reporters, "Hello, thank you for coming today. Please come this way. We will be in the conference room."

As the press takes their seats around the ornately carved table, Clare strides over to the limestone fireplace with a covered easel in front of it and Katherine Lexington takes her place on the other side. "Hello, I am Clare Stryker, the acting headmistress of Smith Academy. As you may have heard, we are expanding our campus in a few months, and I want to present the plans for our new Student Health Center." She motions to the Senator who pulls off the sheet covering the board and reveals THE LEXINGTON STUDENT HEALTH CENTER.

Clare covers the specifics of the building and then turns the presentation over to the Senator to discuss the need for such a place. Her voice brimming with pride, the Senator explains, "In an effort to address bullying, my family has created a safe haven for students, parents, and teachers to discuss their issues with one of the top psychologists in the world, Dr. Sarah Kent. Not only will she be available during the day for appointments and immediate needs, but she will also present a series of lectures open to the surrounding neighborhood and schools so *everyone* can benefit from her twenty-five years of private practice experience. Sarah will be working with Clare Stryker, who is the acting headmistress of Smith Academy. I hope this building will become a model for many more communities. Now I have the pleasure to introduce Dr. Sarah Kent."

As the Senator steps back, Dr. Kent steps forward, relays her vision for the center, then encourages the press to ask questions while enjoying another cup of coffee. The whole press conference doesn't take more than fifteen minutes.

Clare politely excuses herself and finds Karen pacing in the hall, looking very rattled. "Karen, let's go into the office with Ivy. You really should not have left her alone," she says calmly and places her arm around Karen's back to guide her in.

As soon as the door closes, Karen demands, "Where is Dana?"

Clare points at the open seat in front of her desk and says, "Please make yourself comfortable, Karen," and she sinks into the plush swivel chair behind the massive oak desk.

"I prefer to stand, thank you," Karen defiantly states and refuses to move from her spot.

Clare shrugs. "Suit yourself. Now to your question. Dana is no longer employed at Smith. I am the acting head of the school."

Ivy volleys between her mother's terrified face and Clare's, which is void of emotion. Clare steeples her fingers together and addresses a more apprehensive Ivy. "Well, let's get to the reason you both have been called in. I have seen the Paris video. Do you care to explain yourself, Ivy?"

In a very rehearsed manner, Ivy explains her actions, "Kate was drunk. I did not want to get into trouble, so I dragged her into the hall and knocked on the teachers' door so they would find her."

Expecting more, Clare motions with her hands to continue, but Ivy stays silent. Clare asks for more clarification, "So let me get this straight. You left your friend in the middle of the hall in a foreign country where someone could have walked by and grabbed her."

Ivy reluctantly nods.

Clare continues, "Did you not consider that you were putting her in a precarious position?"

Ivy carefully considers this and responds, "No, it was only a minute or so when she was out of my sight."

Clare tilts her head exploring all the possibilities, then comments, "A lot can happen in a minute, especially since you left her in that condition. Which brings me to my next question —why were you carrying two bottles?"

Ivy smiles and explains, "Because I was drinking the cider."

Clare probes further, "Did Kate know you were drinking cider?"

Reluctantly Ivy answers, "No."

"May I ask why?"

Ivy gives a childish explanation. "I didn't want her to make fun of me."

Clare taps her finger on her lips then ponders out loud. "Let me think about this. You were the one who bought the Champagne and cider. Why would she make fun of you?"

Ivy blames Kate. "She asked me to get it."

Clare ticks her finger back and forth as a teacher would do to a kindergartener. "I see a pattern here with you. Did Kelsey Grant ask for you to put alcohol in her Powerade at the Halloween party?"

This throws Ivy totally caught off guard, and she stutters, "I —I don't know what you are talking about."

Clare attempts to be diplomatic, but her irritation is evident in her voice. "I am allowing you to speak candidly about your behavior."

Ivy defers back to the blame game, taking no responsibility for her actions. "She knew it was spiked. She was nervous about going to the party. We all know it's a big deal to get an invite as a freshman."

Clare plays along with this reasoning. "Okay, then why did you send out that video of Kelsey dancing with a boy with the caption LUSH on it?" Then, she pulls out her phone and shows the photo to Ivy and her mom.

Ivy gasps and blurts out, "How did you get that? It was on Snap."

Clare places her phone in the top drawer, smacks the edges of loose papers on her desk to form a neat pile demonstrating she is cleaning house. Then she announces, "Several parents have come forward with grave allegations about you, Ivy. You shared photos of Kim Westover's dress splitting at Homecoming. Then, there were several scenes at the Sadie dance regarding this list. I have been told YOU started the list and filled in several boys' names next to girls' names. Why did you do all these things to your classmates?"

Ivy puts her hands over her eyes to hide her tears. Clare leans forward and hands her a tissue from the box on her desk.

Between sobs, Ivy bellows, "Do you know what happened on that trip to Paris? All those kids dared Chris to kiss Kate. It should have been a quick one but it wasn't. She always gets the boys. I am sick of being second. She—"

"Ivy, do not say another word." Karen interrupts before she incriminates herself even more.

Ignoring her mother's outburst, Clare hands Ivy another tissue. She waits for her to pull herself together, then, in a matter-of-fact tone, says, "Ivy, I am sorry you feel this way, but your actions are inexcusable." Ivy's mouth opens to justify her actions but falls silent when Clare turns her attention to her mother. "Karen, do you have anything to say before I make my decision?"

Astounded, Karen stands up and towers over Clare in an attempt to intimidate her. "Decision! What decision? Ivy was only defending herself against those bullies."

Clare simply responds, "I do not see it that way."

Completely dumbfounded that her family is being treated this way, Karen sinks into a chair and pleads, "You know I cannot make a large donation to the school after all those campaign expenses. With all that I have done for this school, surely you will make an exception."

Clare coldly responds, "Karen, what *exactly* have you done for this school?"

She defends herself by saying, "Well, Clare, you should know exactly all the things I have done for this school. I—"

Smiling, Clare interrupts and goes in for the jugular. "You are head of so many committees here, but I never see you doing any of the work or showing up for the meetings, unless there is time for your grandiloquent speeches to take all the credit. You are a good delegator, not a leader. No wonder things did not work out as planned during your campaign."

Clare leans back in her chair, enjoying Karen's mortified expression as the words sink in. Then she addresses Ivy, "You are no longer welcome at Smith. I recommend you withdraw from the school instead of having an expulsion on your record. Hopefully, you can start over somewhere new and not feel like you are second. Ursula will escort you to your locker. Please pack your things now."

Clare cranes her neck back toward Karen, enjoying the blood draining from her face. "And, Karen, we have determined that your services as head of the PTA and all other social clubs are no longer needed. Mrs. Westover has graciously agreed to take over for you. Please meet with her this week to ensure there is a smooth transition. I'm sure you want the graduation ceremonies and parties to be a success for your son and his classmates."

Karen slams her chair against the wall and launches her weight across the desk. Clare slides back against the wall, stunned by Karen's attempt to assault her, and can see she may not be finished. She is unraveling by the minute after so much loss; her chance to win the Senate race is gone, her daughter is being kicked out of school, and now she has lost all power at Smith.

But somehow, Karen manages to hold back from crawling across the desk and tearing Clare to shreds. She turns her focus to her daughter, who is crying uncontrollably. She lifts her out of the chair, wraps one arm over Ivy's shoulder, and guides her out of the office while saying, "You will regret this!"

We—the ones who were punished for the Sadie—are on the edge of our seats, listening to the lively conversation unfold over the receptionist's phone. As soon as the dismissal seems to wrap up, Ursula turns off the speaker and goes along as if she didn't hear a thing, but we can't hide the smirks on our faces as Ivy and her mother emerge from the office.

Chris taunts with mirth, "Well, no more worries about being second, or third, or fourth. It looks like you have lost, and we won't miss you at all!"

Ivy scans everyone of our faces, shrieks, and runs away, looking absolutely devastated. Bree manages to bite her tongue and so does Hope.

Her mother's dark eyes bore into mine. I lower my gaze, not accepting the hatred deep within them. I'm not to blame for this.

As soon as the back door slams, the laughter roars through the hall. Kylie bends over, holding her stomach, trying to contain the hysterics. Ursula joins in, since she's not been much of a fan of the Collins family either. Hope snorts like a pig, making us all laugh even more.

Hearing the laughter, Mrs. Stryker peaks around the corner, smirking ever so slightly, and then invites us to come in, making all the humor evaporate at once. As we gather in front of her desk, nervous with what may be coming our way, she smiles in such a motherly manner that the air in the room seems to lighten. "Hello, thank you for coming. As you may have heard, I am the interim headmistress until we find a replacement. It has come to my attention that you all have received detention and suspension from sporting events. In light of recent events, your punishment has been rescinded, and I can assure you nothing will be on your record. I apologize for the misunderstanding."

Open mouthed, we all stare at one another and thank her over and over again. With both hands pressing to the floor, Mrs. Stryker, I mean Headmistress Stryker, motions for us to calm down and says, "You are welcome." She doesn't seem to like people gushing around her like this.

Being the first one out the door, I notice Senator Lexington standing in the front lobby with several board members. Her eyes meet mine, and she gives me a wink, making it clear she knows what happened with the new head of the school and then goes back to her conversation.

I should have known—Kate said she would take care of it, but I didn't think she would really do it. I run back to my locker and text Charlie. *I can play in the game today!!!*

Within minutes he responds. *Excellent Time?*

I type, 5

Dots. Then I read, *Be there for the second half after my practice*

Thanks! Jeni's afterwards?

YES!

THIRTY-EIGHT
INTENTIONAL

WHILE SITTING on the hard metal bench on the sidelines, I watch Charlie hug my mother, shake my father's hand, and then take a seat next to Bree. Chris and Nick are on the other side of her. Chris leans forward and waves hello to Charlie while Nick continues to stare at the game. Some girl with bright auburn hair, most likely Brooke, stands up and glares at Charlie, but he pretends not to notice. Can things get any worse?

My coach yells for me to go back in to help the defense. We can't let them score again. I run out on the field and hand the red penny to Megan and then take her spot at midfield. Their defender takes the ball from Jane and passes it down the field toward their quickest striker. I step in front and block her from receiving the ball, and then boot it back down the field to Jane, who loses it.

This happens again and again, so I yell to Hope to get open, but she is double-teamed since Jane is obviously not a threat. She can't keep possession of the ball for more than ten seconds! My other option is for Kylie or Carrie, but they look exhausted from playing the entire game and won't be able to keep the ball.

I boot the ball down the field, and it's intercepted by a Chase midfielder. She deftly dribbles the ball down and crosses it over the middle about fifteen feet in front of me, causing me to sprint toward the striker to prevent an open path to the goal. She traps the ball with her chest, whips around, then fires the ball in my direction at very close range instead of dribbling around me.

I throw my body in the way to block the shot from going into the goal, then twist back around to get ready for another attack, but I'm struck in the stomach by the girl's cleat. I feel the air blow out of me and fly backwards onto my butt and skid toward the goal.

I pull my knees to my chest and lay still, trying to breathe. I hear the whistle and sense the commotion all around me. Hope is by my head asking, "Kels, are you okay?"

I roll onto my back, then answer in between breaths, "Yes. . . . I think so . . . just need a minute."

To my left, Jane is pushing the player who intentionally took me out, and the ref is struggling to pull them apart. I see a red card flash in the air. The girl furiously throws her hands up and walks off the field cussing. She even spits to show her disgust.

Still on the ground, I cross my arms over my stomach, laboring to breathe through the sharp pain in my abdomen, but it isn't working. I need to get up. . . . I need to stretch it out before I cramp even more, so I put my hands up in the air, and Hope lifts me into a standing position. Still not feeling right, I lean over on my knees and exhale, willing the pains to ease.

The girls back away, giving me a view of the sidelines and my parents standing on the bleachers with their mouths covered. Charlie is at the fence, anxiously waiting to see if I will be okay.

I take a couple deep breaths, stand up straight, and give

them a thumbs up. I exaggerate a nod at Charlie so he knows I'm fine, and he seems to relax a little.

My coach is right by my side, asking, "Kelsey, are you okay?"

I nod back even though my stomach feels like it's on fire. "I'm fine."

She slaps me on the back and vehemently says, "You take the PK. I want you to finish this!"

Yep, I'm going to finish this. What a bitchy move! There was no way that was an accident.

As I take my place on the other side of the field waiting for the penalty kick, Charlie's deep voice booms. "You got this, Kels!" This makes me smile, but I don't look at him so he can see. I need to stay focused. I need to relax. I need to score.

I look up at the goalie to see which way her weight is shifted. Yep, she is going to the right. I take two steps, the goalie dives as expected, and I tap it in as planned. The ref blows the whistle, and the game is over.

My teammates race over and circle around me. Everyone is going nuts. This is the first time in a decade Smith has beat Chase.

My parents hug everyone around them. Charlie is in front of them giving Bree a high five. The other Chase kids boo, then stare at Charlie with disgust. Brooke looks horror-stricken. I walk down the line slapping the other girls' hands, saying, "Nice game." The girl who took me out lowers her hand when I pass and calls me a bitch under her breath.

After the game, I notice her standing with Brooke and some other girls gossiping. I was right, it was intentional. Charlie chats with my parents as I wrap things up on the field with my coach.

As I step off the field, my father wraps me in a bear hug and tries to twirl me around like I'm ten, but he has trouble lifting me now. I'm almost his height and about thirty pounds lighter.

Charlie chuckles, enjoying my dad's struggle and the embarrassed expression on my face.

Nick walks by and pats me on the back. "Nice job, Kels. Perfect fake. Just like we practiced at Toca."

I turn and give him a high five. "Thanks, Nick. We practiced that enough times over the years. I'm glad I finally got to use it."

Nick greets both my parents. My mother asks about his mom, feeling a little uncomfortable that Charlie is by my side. Charlie patiently waits for them to finish, and then sticks his left hand out to Nick so he can shake it. Nick's right is still all bandaged up. He politely says, "We have not been formally introduced. I'm Charlie, Kelsey's boyfriend."

Nick shakes his hand and looks him square in the eye. Not in a confrontational way, more out of returned respect. "Nice to finally meet you. I have heard a lot about you, man."

Charlie relaxes with this comment and replies, "I have heard a lot about you, too. How's your wrist?"

Nick looks over at me and says, "Better, Kelsey was a real help that day." Then mumbles as he looks down at his Adidas, "Not sure what I would do without her."

My mother stiffens, and Charlie purses his lips but stays silent.

I immediately change the subject to avoid any more awkwardness, "Mom, Dad, Charlie and I are going to Jeni's. Do you want any ice cream? Nick, we can get you a pint and drop it by your house if you want any."

My dad thinks about it, but my mother taps him in the stomach, signaling he doesn't need it and answers for him, "No, we're good. You two, go have fun."

Nick shifts back and forth, unsure what to say. "No, I'm good. See you all later. It was nice to see you Mr. and Mrs. Grant. Good to finally meet you Charlie."

When Nick walks off, I relax a little, and so does Charlie.

My father missed the whole thing, but my mom picked up on it all, and I know I'll hear all about it later.

I fill Charlie in on everything that happened today with Ivy, her mother and the head of school's dismissal, as well as the stories I heard in the halls about what Mrs. Williams has done in the past. Apparently, her behavior has been the focus of parents for some time, but no one was willing to share their displeasure because they feared retaliation. It even seemed like the teachers were relieved.

I dig into the sundae and notice he has eaten more than half while I went on and on about my day. "Charlie, I'm going to get us another one. Want the same or a different flavor?"

He covers his mouth and says, "You pick."

I stand up and then sit back down as Ivy and Mare walk in. Ivy scans the crowded sitting area like she is looking for someone. Her eyes land on me, they narrow, and then she marches as if she's on a mission. As soon as she is towering over Charlie's head, she yells for everyone in the store to hear, "You got me expelled!"

Charlie whips around as I stand up to challenge her. "No, I didn't. You did that to yourself!"

Ivy puts a hand on her hip and poises like she's in a photo. "How did the new headmistress know about me spiking your Powerade?"

I tilt my head to the side and narrow my eyes. "So you are *finally* admitting it? I have no idea how she heard about that!"

She ignores me and continues on asking, "Did Kate send you the video in Paris?"

After a second I respond, "Yes."

Then in a swift motion, Ivy grabs the half-eaten sundae on the table, and then smashes it in my face. Stunned and shaken, my hands remain by my side with my mouth open wide. The bowl and cold ice cream slide off my nose and cheeks and onto the table. I wipe my eyes and see Ivy walking out of the store, doing her signature "I won" strut, while Mare lowers her phone and smiles with equal parts contempt and pleasure.

Charlie jumps forward, grabs all the napkins on the table, and begins to wipe the chocolate fudge from my forehead. "I was worried about Brooke doing something crazy when she heard about you, but that girl is just the whole package. Utterly psychotic. . . . Kels, I think you may need to get some wet towels for the rest of this."

Without saying a word, I move to the bathroom, which, of course, is occupied. As the door slowly creaks open, I move to the side to let the lady pass, but she freezes after seeing my caramel-covered face. Shocked, she asks, "Are you alright?"

Flatly I respond, "Yes, I just need to wash this off. Do you mind if I step in?" and she quickly moves out of the way.

Pulling stray nuts and a single cherry out of my hair, I fight the urge to cry. I tell myself that there have been too many tears over Ivy and she's not worth it, but seeing myself in the mirror is pretty upsetting. I grab more paper towels and wet them to get all the caramel off my cheeks and the leftover fudge smudges on my forehead. Then splash water on my face and hair, leaving me to look like a drowned rat. I pull my hair into a slicked back ponytail and check the mirror one more time for any spots I may have missed.

As I exit, I feel Charlie's protective arms wrap around me. I stay in his embrace until I feel like I may lose it in the ice cream shop and mumble into his shoulder, "Can we go?" I feel him nod and pull me into his chest and out the door to the car.

We ride home in silence, not really sure what to say about what just happened. Laughing about it would be the best thing to do, but it just doesn't feel right, at least not yet. Maybe one day we will want to share this story at a party.

Charlie starts to open his door to go inside with me, but I say while looking at my lap, "I want to shower and be alone for a while. Can I call you later? . . . Thanks for coming to my game."

I hear him say, "Sure," in a hurt voice as I climb out of the car. I feel his eyes on me as I walk inside with my head slumped forward, feeling so overwhelmed with everything that has happened today. It has been an emotional roller coaster, and I am ready to get off the ride.

As soon as I close the front door, I collapse, not able to hold it in any longer and cry. Really cry . . . my ugly cry.

Hearing the thud, my mother comes around the corner and rushes toward me, asking if I'm okay. When I don't answer, she sinks down next to me while I sob and holds my hand.

Finally, I answer, "Ivy accused me of getting her expelled and then smashed a sundae in my face."

"She did what?" And before I can answer, I feel my phone buzz and see Nick's text telling me to *Check Snap now!*

With our backs to the door and legs stretched in front of us, my mother and I watch an edited video of tonight with me saying, "yes" to getting Ivy expelled and her throwing a sundae in my face. Tears stream down my cheeks as I sit there numb, knowing everyone is watching this right now, thinking I am a narc.

After fifteen minutes of Q and A from my mother and my father trying to listen behind the dining room wall, I stand up to go shower. My phone rings, and it's Kate. I answer, feeling defeated, "Hey, I guess you saw the video too."

"YES! I just saw the video. . . . You got Ivy kicked out of school. Way to go. I didn't think you had it in you."

"Kate, I didn't. Your mother did. I figured you knew. She got Dana Williams fired too."

There is a pause, and then I can hear the smile on the other end. "I knew she was working on something. Several board members have been at the house. I heard many of them were already upset by Headmistress Williams' nepotism. She pushed out the lower and middle school heads to replace them with her own lackeys."

"Yeah, but that's old news. All those parents wrote letters to complain about the changes at the school, and she still kept her job." I remark as I trudge up the stairs to my room.

"Yeah, but the board protected her then. They didn't believe all the other stuff or think it would affect their kids. Those letters revealed some really nasty stuff, though.

"Listen to this! One Harvard alumni wrote that she was at a college event, and it was mentioned that they wanted the Sims' girl to play soccer for them but lost out to Georgetown. This surprised her since she knew Ellie Sims' first choice was Harvard. She didn't think any more about it until she ran into Mrs. Sims at the grocery store and asked why Ellie changed her mind about Harvard.

"Get this—the Sims thought they dodged a bullet. The Smith coach told them that the Harvard coach had a reputation for making promises about scholarships and couldn't keep them. Harvard doesn't give athletic scholarships, you know. He also told the Sims that the coach was *quietly* being investigated for *inappropriate* behavior.

"Ellie's mom was so grateful that Smith had looked out for their daughter when in reality, they were lied to. The coach was not being investigated for anything! The alumni told Harvard what Mrs. Sims said, and the coach flew down to defend his honor. The Smith coach admitted that Headmistress Williams made it clear that if he wanted to keep his job, he had to make sure Ellie went to Georgetown. He apologized and hoped the whole thing would go away by promising to steer another excellent player in Harvard's direction.

"Harvard responded by saying they would not offer another acceptance to a Smith student while Williams was still in charge and the soccer coach was still there. One of the board members made a call and confirmed that what was stated in the letter is true."

"Really? Is that why the coach left mid-year and the assistant coach took his spot?" I stop peeling off my jersey and rest on the side of the tub.

Kate takes a breath and then continues on, "Yep! After what happened to me, I asked several students who graduated, and they told me there were rumors that she coerced the teachers to give her daughters better grades by making it clear they were replaceable. And we all watched her daughters get all those awards, knowing they were not well deserved."

"Yeah, that writing award always manages to go to her daughter Taylor. But why did the board turn on her this time? It doesn't make any sense," I question as I pull another walnut piece out of my hair.

"My guess is when the board heard how she treated one of their friends, they knew even their kids were not safe with her. Kels, I don't think anyone is going to miss Williams. She needed to go. People are celebrating her departure. Now, Ivy getting the boot is just icing on the cake, or should I say the cherry on top. I saw the cherry on your forehead!"

"Ha-ha, Kate. . . . I think seeing Mrs. Collins' face on camera was more amusing. She had no idea your mother had that video. She thought she was going to take your mom down after posting the photo."

And for once, Kate is silent—too silent. "Kate, are you okay? I didn't mean to upset you. Your mother did so well defending you. . . . Mrs. Collins deserved to be taken down. How could she post a photo of someone she's known since kindergarten? That lady is pure evil."

Kate clears her throat and calmly remarks, "Kels, I'm fine, really. My mother asked for permission before she posted the video. I knew it was coming. Mrs. Collins deserved it all, and so does Ivy. They're too predictable and have pissed off way too many people."

"You knew?" And then it hits me—Kate knew about it ahead of time. The Lexingtons set them up. No one would suspect she leaked the photo of her own daughter being drunk in a hall in Paris. The Senator planned this perfectly. The Collins never had a chance against them.

THIRTY-NINE
TEAMS

PACING BACK AND FORTH, looking a lot less comfortable talking in front of a crowd than her predecessor, Headmistress Stryker encourages us to work harder. She presses about how we still have time to improve our grades with all the resources they offer at school, essentially repeating the same old stuff we hear around midterms every year. I focus on every word like it's something new, trying to block out everyone's glares. When she switches gears and announces certain changes will begin effective immediately, she gets everyone else's attention.

The athletes lean in closer as she says, "All practice times have been pushed back to 4 o'clock to make sure every student has access to after school tutorials." When she says, "Any upperclassman who excels in a subject may also tutor for extra credit," she gets a round of applause from the juniors and seniors.

By the end of the assembly, she has changed the entire feel of the school. She has addressed many of the problems that make it difficult to succeed and is *finally* listening to the students' complaints!

I relax knowing this will give the students something else to talk about beside Ivy getting expelled. It may be a better day after all.

As soon as I sit down in my first period, I pull out my phone and see a text from Charlie.

K- Are you ok? Everyone is talking about the video here.

I text back. *Same*

It will blow over. She will start a new school and target some other girl.

I type while biting my lip. *Well I feel sorry for her. This is awful.*

Me too. See you tonight?

Yes! Can't wait!!!

Classes drone on except for English where we got to watch Barry fumble during the presentation, trying to make up things about why Chris in the book *Into the Wild*, was selfish when he took off for Alaska. He even made a joke about him being eaten alive, which didn't happen in the story.

Any time someone asked him about a slide, he would turn to Jane, making it very obvious that she did all the work. In the past, the teacher would pass him for being a star athlete, but we'll see what happens with the new rules. After the speech this morning, I would be pretty worried if I were Barry.

By the time lunch rolls around, I'm ready to go home and debate feigning illness. Nick sees me in the corner alone and walks over, "Want any company?"

I nod and finish chewing my bite of panini.

He climbs into the seat next to me and I notice he has the same fixings on his sandwich. He must have loved my panini on the first day of school. Nick leans over and quietly asks, "How are you doing?"

I shrug my shoulders and look out the window.

He takes a bite and continues as if we are discussing the

weather. "Have you seen the post where people are voting for Team Kelsey or Team Ivy? You are winning, of course. Ivy is not so well-liked at Smith."

I lower my head, embarrassed it's come to this and murmur, "Really? I can't believe this is happening."

Feeling an arm over my shoulder, I curl into him, not thinking how this will look. I close my eyes to fight back the tears. It takes a few moments to gather myself back together. I'm getting used to having these ups and downs.

While wiping my nose, I thank Nick for being here, and he nods. As I raise my heavy head, Mare lowers her phone, and from the grin on her face, I know she got a shot of me and Nick, one that would certainly give people something to talk about—another reason to rip me apart again. She wants payback for my part in her breakup even though I'm really not the one to blame. Another thing that's not my fault and out of my control. I just need to ignore it.

As I slide in between the desks to sit down in the back of the classroom, several girls whip their heads around and scowl. Mare taunts, "Need a shoulder to cry on again, Kels?" and I ignore her and all the jeers.

As soon as I dump my bag on the floor, Bree leans across the row. "What's up with you and Charlie?"

I smile at his name. "Nothing. Why? I'm meeting up with him tonight. He's helping me with my geometry since we have that test tomorrow."

Bree responds, "Maybe not," then discreetly shows me the photo of me and Nick at lunch looking cozy with the words CHEATER at the bottom. Bree switches to the latest general opinion of me and softly lets me know. "You just dropped in the polls. Chase kids are voting against you now."

I look down at my phone, feeling sick, especially after seeing several missed calls from Charlie. Crap, he knows! I desperately text, *Nothing happened with Nick. He is just a friend. I needed a shoulder!*

As the teacher reminds us all phones are required to be in the basket on the desk, Bree puts out her hand to take mine, but I put it back into my pocket and turn on silent mode. I sit there listening to proofs, feeling more and more helpless. I hold onto the smooth rock and pull out my phone every minute, even though I know I could receive a detention for it.

Charlie still has not responded, which is not like him. He must be really mad. The bell rings and I lay my head on the desk letting everyone leave before I get up. Bree and I walk down the stairs toward the fields, saying everything she can think of to cheer me up. "He'll understand. . . . Don't worry. . . . You guys are solid."

As soon as I turn the corner toward the sports complex, Charlie is waiting for me. I drop my bag and run toward him, falling into his arms.

I blurt out, "I am so glad you are here. I was so worried— wait. Don't you have practice?"

Charlie brushes off the last comment. "I skipped. I needed to see you."

I embrace him tighter, not wanting to let him go, afraid he's here to break things off. I start to ramble to delay those words from coming out of his mouth. "And I needed to see you! I can explain everything. Nick was just a shoulder since you weren't here. I only rested my head for a moment before she took that picture. It meant nothing. I really needed you today."

Charlie silently strokes my hair while I rationalize my bad judgement on his shoulder. When I finally come up for air, Charlie holds my cheeks in his palms, and in a soft tone he reassures me we are fine. "It's alright. I understand, but can we get out of here to talk about it without everyone staring at us?"

I look over on the sidewalk, and we have an audience. Several kids are taking photos of us. Who knows what they are saying about us on Snap?

I rush by them to grab my abandoned bag, say goodbye to Bree, who is standing there guarding it, and the both of us head toward the car. Before we pull out, there's a loud commotion outside. Boys are punching each other in the arms like fools. Nick peers into the car as he walks by with them, and Charlie grabs hold of my hand as he passes. I exhale and act like he means nothing to me.

"Where are we going?" I ask.

"Let's go for a hike," is all he says back.

We drive in an eerie silence to a remote spot hidden in a neighborhood with several trails veering off a gravel parking area. I watch his body glide over the rocky terrain as we wander in silence to an overlook.

We climb onto the railing of the newly constructed mini-deck dedicated to a loved one and let our legs dangle over the side. I sit next to him with my hands in my lap, waiting for him to make the first move, gazing at the water rushing around the boulders scattered in the river below. I listen to the hum of the traffic in the distance, searching for the words to begin.

It's like there is a weight between us, and I'm not sure if it's pulling us apart or preventing us from coming together. I close my eyes and try to take in the peacefulness all around me. The light breeze, the birds soaring high around us in the cloudless sky, and the soothing sound of the river. But still, I feel like I'm sinking in the churning waters below, like I'm being tossed around, desperately reaching for a rock, my rock—for Charlie to anchor me again.

I can't take the silence any longer and turn my head upward to peer at Charlie's face, hoping to read his thoughts. His face is blank, unreadable. While giving his side a little squeeze, I say, "I needed this. . . . I needed to be with you. Thank you. . . .

Honestly, I thought you were going to be upset about the picture."

Charlie rubs the back of his neck and continues to look at the water; then, he stares at me with a very serious look on his face. It's one that sends a sudden shiver down my spine as I wait for what he will say next.

His cloudy blue eyes soften as my body tenses. He pulls me closer to him and says, "Yeah, I was not happy when I saw the photo, but I trust you. I do not trust him."

The tiny thing beating so rapidly in my chest starts to slow. I stare back at him and say, "You have nothing to worry about. I would never do anything to ruin this."

I lean in and kiss him softly, hoping I can communicate how deeply I feel about him. As he kisses me with the same sentiment, our irrational fear that one of us may not be as dedicated to this relationship just melts away.

With his arm tucked around my waist and my head nuzzled in the crook of his neck, I take in the simplicity around us and my mind starts to clear. I feel him shift and clear his throat. "So Kels, what are we going to do about Ivy?"

I tense at her name. Honestly, I don't know what to do. She's not at school anymore but has Mare doing her bidding now. Mare is furious about losing Nick, and I relay this to Charlie.

He listens to the situation, trying to think of a solution. Then, he turns to me, slightly annoyed with it all. "Kels, no offense, but you have to stop giving them ammunition. Everyone is watching you and me now, waiting to tear us apart, and you fed them that photo. The guys ripped me a new one since I said you were different. That picture made you look the opposite of different. It looked like you two are much more than friends."

I cringe and peer down at my trembling hands, unable to handle the disappointment and hurt in his eyes. He's right. It did not look good at all. Stammering slightly, I say, "Y-Yes, it looked bad. I frantically tried to reach you once Bree showed me the photo. I am so sorry. I really screwed up. It will never happen again. Please forgive me."

Charlie kisses my hair. "There's nothing to forgive, but please don't do it again. I almost punched my locker when Brooke showed it to me."

The weight returns, knowing not only do I have to deal with Ivy and Mare, but Brooke is also an issue. I mumble, "She is going to make things even worse for you now, isn't she?"

"Kels, she always makes things more difficult, so this isn't anything new. She isn't the problem though, Ivy is. I think you need to share your side of the story. Tell everyone how Ivy set up Kate, how she spiked your drink, about the video. This will all go away. They will see Ivy for who she really is . . . a lying bitch."

I gaze at the water below, needing to clear my head again and think out loud. "By doing that, I expose Kate even more, and that's not an option right now. That's the last resort. I don't want to drag her into this. Plus, she would have to give me permission before I say a thing. . . . As for Ivy spiking my drink, it would put the new headmistress in a precarious position, and some may demand an expulsion to make an example of me because I did take a shot before the Powerade was handed to me. I can't say either of those things. It's too risky."

He leans back and exhales sharply. "You're right, you can't do that. So, what else can we do? Everyone already knows about that list and my school doesn't care about that. They mock the fact your school does it."

I let out one much-needed chuckle about them mocking the list—it should be mocked.

I lean my head in the crook of Charlie's neck again, then pop back up and say, "I'm going to fix this." I check my phone for coverage, all good, and start typing.

To set the record straight, I did NOT get Ivy expelled. She edited the video to make it seem as if I admitted I did have a part in it but that is not the case. It was all her. Her manipulations, lies and actions are the reason she is no longer at Smith. Nick was there for me today like any true friend would be and I want to thank him for it. Charlie and I are grateful for all our friends defending us but there is nothing to defend. We are ignoring the baseless rumors and hope you will too.

Then, I hit send for everyone to see on Snap. Charlie's phone buzzes confirming it's out there. He smiles as he reads my monologue and says, "Perfect."

I stare up into the blue sky and state, "Well, I hope that cleared it up, but if it doesn't I can get Nick to send something out about us being friends too."

Charlie adds, "I don't think you need to do that even if they don't believe what you said. The only thing that matters is we know the truth and are good with it."

He's right, but I still can't stop myself from saying this, "Yeah, but Ivy is not going to let this go. She will not stop until she ruins everything. She wants to ruin us. That's what I am the most afraid of. Both Ivy and Brooke want to break us up."

He gently places his hand on mine, waiting for me to look at him again, and then says, "Well, I'm not going anywhere, and I hope you aren't either."

Without a second thought, I reveal, "Every time I close my eyes, all I see is you. I'll always want to be with you." Even though I'm only fifteen, and he's the only guy I have ever loved, I know those words will always be true.

FORTY

PROWESS

EVEN AFTER MY MESSAGE, several friends who seemed to have been on my side have flipped. They think I'm a cheat as well as a rat. I heard Robert say that I wasn't who he thought I was. That I had fooled everyone into thinking I was the innocent, nice girl, when in reality, I was just a tease, playing all the boys to see how many would fall for me. Then, he joked that my boyfriend must be a real loser to think I can be with only one guy. I had a hard time biting my tongue on that one.

Hearing him make that kind of comment cut like a knife. I doubt I will ever be able to look at him the same way again. As for the others, they are saying such juvenile, ridiculous things that it won't matter in the long run. I can forgive them for it—well, a little later, after all this is over.

As I pull out the books I need for my next few classes and organize the rest of them to kill time before the bell, I hear, "Just ignore them. They are dumb idiots." Then Bree leans against the next locker, looking as bothered as me.

I grab the stray pencils and pens and place them in my canvas pencil pouch and sigh. "Trying, but it's easier said than done. Robert's comment still burns."

Bree tilts her head and stares at me.

"What?" I ask, not sure what I said wrong.

Bree responds, "You know why he said that right?"

Completely puzzled now, I reply, "No, what am I missing?"

"Kels, he's jealous. He's had a thing for you all year. Haven't you noticed he's always close by? He's always looking at you."

"No, really?" She's crazy. There's no way I missed that.

Bree rolls her eyes and scoffs. "Yes, really! Sometimes I wonder about you. . . . So, how are things with Charlie? Nothing to hear here. . . . Keep on moving," she snaps and points at Sarah and Anna, motioning for them to stop eavesdropping.

I squeeze another book into my backpack and slam my locker shut, then lean against it to see if there are any other people around waiting to record whatever I say. "Okay, he trusts me, but he's not happy with my carelessness," I confide in her, and as expected, she doesn't say anything to rub it in, but the look on her face shows she is in agreement with my assessment. She can't hide anything.

While tapping her fingers on the back of her math book, she comments, "Well, that's good he trusts you. You will get through this with him . . . the others are a different story. Ivy is getting a lot more sympathy than I ever thought possible. She has everyone fooled into thinking you set her up."

"Yep, she is good at twisting things and—" I stop suddenly, noticing Bree is biting down on her lower lip, which is a sign she isn't telling me something. "What's up, Bree?"

Bree avoids eye contact, which is another sign she is not telling me something and unconvincingly responds, "All good." Then she changes the subject by asking, "Are you ready for our geometry test?"

I groan, "No, but ready to get it over with so I can focus on getting this target off my back." Then I ask the more pressing question, "So, Bree what are you not telling me? Do I need to be worried?"

Bree hunches her shoulders forward, lowering her head to hide her face in a mass of flowing curls, and a sob escapes. "Chris and I got into a fight."

"What? You guys never fight, only argue from time to time," I say, then wrap my arms around her back to hide her shaking shoulders from the onlookers getting closer. As the phones appear to capture Bree nuzzled against my chest, I turn her away from the crowd. We race up the back stairs and into the nearest bathroom, making it just in time before the flood gates open. I check all the stalls for possible spies while she gets a wad of toilet paper and blows her nose several times.

Through the sniffles, she explains, "I thought about what he said at the dance . . . and even though it was to Ivy . . . he should not have said that. . . . No one, not even Ivy, deserves to be cut down about their sexual prowess—it was a really low blow, and no guy should cut a girl down like that, ever. . . . He thinks I'm being ridiculous and that I'm siding with Ivy of all people."

While holding her tight, I look up at the ceiling, trying to remember what I saw in the video after I left, and it slowly comes back.

Bree pulls away to splash water on her spotty cheeks, trying to get rid of any signs of her crying. As she dries off her face, I respond, "You're right, it's wrong to announce she's not good at certain things, but I see why Chris did it. He hit her where he knew it would hurt to get back at her for all her scheming. I hit my limit with her that night too. Ivy did set herself up though. She brags about hooking up with so many guys at our school and others—she has a reputation and flaunts it on social media. But there's a double standard since the guys are hooking up with her and everyone else they can get their hands on, and nobody is calling them out for it."

Bree listens and then shrugs her shoulders, looking too exhausted to argue, but then she adds, "Yeah, you're right. He still should have said something else."

"Agreed, but he *is* a guy. They are always thinking about those things."

A smirk crosses her face at this, and she relaxes. "You're right. That is all they think about, and it will never change. They don't think about things the way we do." Then, she checks her eyes in the mirror and applies concealer to hide the red marks.

"Speaking of guys not thinking straight. Brooke was over last night with Dave. I could hear her yelling all the way up in my room. She was furious, claiming he didn't defend her at school when Charlie said you were different. She wanted to know what *different* meant and for him to explain how you were better than her—if Dave thought you were better looking than her. He could not get a word in edgewise. . . . Then, she said he owed her and better start defending her. Whatever that means —I feel bad for Dave. Maybe he will realize she is crazy and move on!"

I bust out laughing even though I shouldn't. Brooke is coming for me, it seems. Dave should see all the signs, but he's a guy; they are clueless sometimes.

I joke, "I hope for his sake, he finds someone else and fast. She would not be good for him. Then a horrible thought crosses my mind. "Can you imagine what it would be like if Brooke and Ivy teamed up against me?"

Bree's eyes get huge, and then she points at me laughing. "Yep, you'd be toast, just like us since we're missing our math test right now."

FORTY-ONE
THE FREEZE

AFTER SEVERAL WEEKENDS of Charlie playing back-to-back baseball games, we're finally able to sneak away for a much-needed break. Both of us have kept our heads down and ignored the comments, so things have gotten a little better. Ivy not being at Smith to stir up trouble has made it easier on me, but it has been a little more challenging for Charlie.

She's now at Chase and is fitting in well with that group of Fifteen. Blair has taken her under her wing, and Brooke has been seen whispering with Ivy in the halls, probably searching for dirt on me.

But on the bright side, I've learned who my real friends are and who I want to be around at school. Bree, Kim, and Hope have taken on the full-time job of defending me against the rumors. Chris has had a great time slamming any person who joked about Bree and me being a thing after the photo of me hugging her circulated. Charlie and Dave got a huge kick out of that one too.

But today is our day to relax and get away from it all. We are where Charlie loves to disappear—the lake.

As I navigate down the path toward the dock, I spot Charlie

in the water, doing several laps. I spread out my towel on the Adirondack chair and sink in with my eyes closed and face turned up toward the warm sun. Carpenter bees buzz above my head, trying to find a place to eat a hole in the wooden beams. A frog croaks in the swaying grasses across the cove. A cold breeze whips across the water, giving me a chill, and I wrap the towel around my hunched shoulders, waiting for the sun to warm me up again.

I listen to Charlie gliding through the water and try to clear my head. My thoughts drift to summer and how we can lounge around all day on this dock—maybe take out the canoe and explore the cove. When I feel icy water splash over my leggings and bare feet, I jump back to the present. Charlie's head is resting on his bent arms at the edge of the dock, trying to get my attention, and he has it.

"Charlie, really!" I teasingly reprimand him as I shake my feet and wipe off my leggings, but he ignores my attempt to show my displeasure.

"I thought you were changing. You're still in the same sweatshirt and leggings," he taunts in a raspy voice.

"Yes, I have my suit on, but I'm not sure I want to get in there. You can't stop shaking, and your lips are blue," and I sit back in the chair, feeling quite content here.

"Oh, come on, Kels. Just jump!"

Reluctantly, I place both hands on the wide armrests, pull myself out of my warm spot, and walk to the other end of the dock to ensure he doesn't pull me in with him or splash me at close range. I dip my toe into the water and jerk it right back up as I feel an uncomfortable jolt from the cold. Shaking my head violently side to side, I inform him, "NOPE. NOPE. You are crazy—it's freezing!"

"Come on, it's not that bad. It feels good after a couple minutes," he continues to plead.

"Nope, all good out here. You can join me on the dock."

As I settle back into my chair, I hear a concerning swoosh and slosh and then feel a massive wave of ice-cold water hit me in the chest and face, freezing my reaction for a moment.

Laughter erupts from the water as I squeal, "OHHH—you are going to pay for that," and I race to the edge of the dock to kick water back at him, but he dives under before it reaches him. Fearing he may rise to the surface with an even larger wave pushing off his chest, I grab the towel and move further back on the dock. As anticipated, a rush of water hits my chair, soaking my spot.

He scans the dock and finds me slightly hidden behind one of the massive posts holding up the covered boat slip. He pushes back for a better view treading above the rippling surface and coaxes, "Just jump in! Your body will get used to it. I will keep you warm."

When I don't move a muscle, he gives me that look he knows will tempt me to join him, but I resist. That water is probably 50 degrees so I will freeze in there, and again when I get out. It's only in the low to mid 70s, without the occasional gusts of cold air blowing. No, thank you!

When I don't move any closer, Charlie takes another tactic. He pulls himself up onto the dock and races toward me. Knowing I will never be able to outrun him, I drop the towel and frantically peel off my sweatshirt and leggings. I hear him laugh as I almost stumble when my foot gets stuck.

As his arms wrap around me, I try to wiggle free, but it's no use. He has me firmly in his grasp and is running across the wood planks. He leaps five feet into the air, twists, and lands backwards into the freezing cold water, taking me with him, screaming as we go.

As soon as we break through the surface, the air releases in my chest. Charlie lets go as we tumble into the dark depths of the lake. Every inch of my skin feels like it's burning in the icy cold. When my lungs scream for oxygen, the shock finally wears off, and I shoot to the surface.

I wipe my hands over my eyes and smooth my hair back on my scalp as I hoarsely roar, "Oh my God! It is *so* cold." Hearing him laugh hysterically behind me, I whip around and say, "Charlie, this is not funny," and push off of his chest to head back to the dock, pouting like a 5-year-old.

Before I get too far away, he lunges for me and wraps both arms around me in a tight bear hug. "Where do you think you are going? Come here. I'll keep you warm."

I feign being more upset and squirm but then wrap my trembling thighs around his waist, desperately needing his body heat. As he rubs my upper thigh with his left arm while attempting to tread water with his right arm, he looks at me seriously. "Any better?"

I nod and allow him to kiss me hard, hoping to tame my chattering teeth.

I feel his hands slide up and over my butt and across my back. He tries to tread water with his legs, but I'm too much for him to support, and we sink like an anchor. Coming back up for air, we stay close but with enough room to stay afloat.

As we stare at one another, I can see he wants to say something, but nothing comes out. Instead, he flicks a little water at me and smiles sweetly.

We doggie paddle to another dock about fifty feet away, trying to warm up, but it isn't working. I can't handle the cold like he does. "Charlie, I can't feel my toes and am going in," I state through chattering teeth.

As I frantically dry off my goose-bumped skin, a cool breeze blows and my body shivers like a leaf. Charlie points to the house. "Go hop in the shower and warm up. I will be there shortly. I need to pull up the ladder before I forget."

I yell over my shoulder, "Okay, see you inside," and sprint off the dock and onto the mulch path leading to the cabin. I throw open the screen door and head down the hall, past the bedroom with dark wood bunk beds, and into the hall bath with a small shower where I changed before.

The hot water sizzles and steams as it hits my frozen skin. I arch my head, allowing the water to stream down my neck and back, enjoying the warmth around me.

As I'm rinsing out the shampoo in my hair, I feel the floor in the hall shake a little and pause to listen. He isn't coming in, is he? The footsteps start up again and then fade. When the water pressure changes, I know he's in the other shower and quickly finish up so I don't use all the hot water.

As I step out, I remember my sweatshirt and leggings are still on the dock. What am I going to put on? I wrap myself in a towel and stand in front of the slightly fogged mirror thinking. My bra and underwear are still in my bag at my feet. I can at least put those on so I'm not totally naked in front of him. It will be just like I'm in my bikini, I rationalize.

A door in the hall closes, so I holler, "Charlie, my clothes are still down by the water. Can you grab them?"

There's a light knock, and the door opens slightly. "Here they are," I hear as a reddish hand holding my clothes passes through.

Instead of taking them and shutting the door, I gaze into the mirror and see Charlie's eyes peering sheepishly at me wrapped in a towel with only my bra and underwear underneath. His cheeks glow a bright pink like mine, knowing he got busted. He places my clothes on the counter, and closes the door.

Normally my clothes would be on, and I would be out the door, but I'm not sure if that's what I want. I pull my hair from my face and stare into the mirror. My mind races. . . . Am I ready for this? Do I want this? We are all alone in this cabin, and there may not be a better time. I don't want to lose it in a car. His parents or mine might say we can't come up here alone anymore. . . . We have been together for almost four months now. Isn't it time?

I can feel Charlie right outside, hear him pacing back and forth as I decide how to proceed. Bold—I want to be bold, so I open the door and step out with the towel barely covering my thighs and tucked in right above my breasts. Charlie stops dead in his tracks, speechless. Before I lose my nerve, I quickly pull the corner of the towel and let it fall to the floor, and so does his jaw.

I leap into the air, wrap my legs around his waist, making him fall backwards into the wall. I kiss him like we have just been reunited after several months apart.

Gripping my thighs, he carries me into the guest room and carefully lowers me onto the bottom bunk. Then, he pulls off his thick cotton t-shirt revealing his ripped stomach and defined chest. He slowly lowers himself onto me, tracing a line from my navel up to my neck with his index finger.

As he moves, the heat rushes over me, almost searing my skin. I twist my legs around his hips and pull him close. He nibbles on my neck, then he makes his way back up to my lips and then back down to my neck. I want him, and I can feel he wants me, too.

I flip him over, so I'm on top and slowly slide my bra straps off my shoulders, watching his eyes get bigger by the moment. I reach for the center clasp and am about to pop it open, but he puts his hand over mine and says, "Wait! We can't."

What!?!

Immediately I roll off of him and sit on the side of the bed, bending over so I don't hit my head on the bunk above, trying to process what just happened. Shame and rejection flood through me as I hear the words WE CAN'T repeat in my head.

I feel him lean forward and place his hand on my knee, then whisper, "That didn't come out right."

I look down at my trembling hands and murmur, "How was

that supposed to come out? Don't you want to be with me in that way?"

Instantly, he scoots over, so his chest fits into my curved back and gingerly moves my hair out of my face. He winces when he sees the tears welling in my eyes. "Yes, I do. . . . more than ever—" Then, he runs his hand through his hair and sighs. "You don't know how hard that was to stop you."

I turn to him and question a little too forcefully, "Why did you stop me?"

He flips his legs around, so he is sitting right beside me. With his fingers tightly wound in his lap, he attempts to justify his rejection. "Because we haven't discussed this and we should before things move any further. You haven't been with someone before and deserve for it to be special. My older sister, Ellie, talked to me about this. I don't want you to regret this. I want you to be sure. . . . Kels, please look at me."

I pull my eyes from the pillow on the floor when I feel his hand over mine. His eyes are pleading for me to say something. I grab hold of his cupped hand and confide, "But I do want you."

He sighs and falls back on the bed, barely missing the rail and murmurs, "And I want you. More than you know, but it shouldn't be here in bunk beds," and he punches the wood slats and mattress above him in frustration. "Ouch!"

I laugh as he shakes his hand in an attempt to ease the pain. "Yep, not the most romantic spot."

He raises his head enough to look at me and smiles. "No it isn't," then sinks back into the bed with his elbow covering his eyes. "Do you mind getting dressed? It is so hard sitting next to you almost naked."

Feeling a little better, knowing he is struggling with being next to me in my underwear, I slowly get up and walk into the bathroom to throw on my frumpy clothes. Then I climb back into the bunk bed next to him.

Without thinking, I ask, "How many girls have you been with?"

Charlie looks away, plucking at the plaid comforter and reluctantly answers, "Three—but it didn't mean anything. With you, it will mean everything."

My head jerks back as I process the number three. Three! I figured he had only been with Brooke and asked the question just to confirm they had been together like that. I wasn't expecting him to have been with other girls. Not in that way.

Still, in a bit of shock, I softly repeat the number, "Three."

Charlie pulls me into him and tries to explain while I bury my head in his chest, "Girls are not like you. They don't seem to care about it. They drink and then come on to me at a party. Brooke was ready on our first date. According to my sister, they do care and are desperate for attention. They think that is the only way to get the guy, but you have me. You don't need to feel like you have to do this."

As he explains, I know he's right. I have seen these girls at parties. They chug vodka, disappear in the backyard with a guy for a while, and then show back up to the party, knees dirty and bruised. The boy usually has a smug look on his face, and the girl acts like nothing happened. Usually, the boy does not acknowledge her for the rest of the night, but she keeps looking over at him, pleading for some attention.

Charlie pulls back slightly, and his blue eyes lock onto mine. "Please say something, please."

"You're right. I do want it to be special with you. I feel ready but . . ."

Charlie sighs then turns serious. "You certainly seemed ready, but are you really? Have you thought about this before today?"

Biting my lip, I consider this, and I don't know, but how do you know? So I ask him, "When did you know?"

Charlie chuckles, "Guys are different. We don't need to

know. There's not any emotion in it, well with some exceptions." Then he squeezes my hand and continues. "It is just something we want. I don't know how else to describe it."

I prop my head on my elbow and he does the same, scooting closer to stroke my arm, and he gives me time to think, but my mind is going in so many directions. I can't separate my feelings from thought. Hoping to figure out how I will know, I just start talking. "Well, I have thought about it but probably not as much as you. When I kiss you, I kind of get lost, and it feels like we're moving in that direction, but you always stop us, so I don't know how I will feel once we get to that point. I know I don't want it to happen in a car or at a party or to feel rushed. I want it to be … I don't know what I want it to be. I just know I want it to be with you."

He softly kisses me on the lips and then the nose before saying, "And it will be special. A night that you want to remember, not something you look back on with regret. That is the last thing I want. You mean too much to me."

"Same."

We lay for a couple minutes holding each other until the rumbles in my stomach interrupt the silence. Charlie pops up, barely missing the top bunk, and offers me a hand to get out of bed. "Let's get you some food. I'm hungry, too."

As he dashes out of the room to start an early dinner, I smooth out the covers, place the stray pillow at the head of the bed, then meet him in the kitchen. He already has the frozen burgers on the black granite counter and the orange fire stick in his hand ready to heat up the grill.

While I rinse the plump strawberries in the small metal sink, emotions churn through me. The passion, the hurt and rejection, and then the love behind his words. He stopped because he cared, not because I wasn't the one he wanted.

I pop a strawberry in my mouth and savor the taste of spring, and all the good things that are to come now that we are talking about things that really mean something. I pull out the rest of stuff we brought up in the Yeti and place them on the counter.

As I'm slicing the tomato, I feel his arms are around me again. He kisses my neck so seductively as he moves my wet hair out of the way. I lift up a strawberry, and he takes a bite. I can feel his, "Hmmm," on my shoulder.

"I can get used to this. We need to get away more often," he says, then he gives me a squeeze and lets go to grab something out of the small refrigerator.

Watching him lean over in his white t-shirt and baggy athletic shorts, I ask, "Do you spend a lot of your summer here?"

Charlie responds with his nose still in the refrigerator. "Not as much as I would like."

Rudely inviting myself, I say, "We should come up here after exams. Then the water will be much warmer, and we will want to stay in."

Charlie quietly closes the door with two Fiji waters in his hand, and smirks. "Was it really that bad?"

"Yes, you were blue!" I tease.

"But I would have warmed you up if you stayed in longer," and he demonstrates how he intended to warm me up by kissing me again, and I feel the surging warmth inside every nerve, enticing me to plunge even deeper.

As he pulls away, making me crave the sweet strawberry taste again, I whisper, "Do it again. I'm still numb," and he leans in with so much heat in his eyes. I shut mine, but his lips do not meet mine. Instead, I feel the cold again as he darts to the side and moves toward the screen door.

Black smoke is coming out of the grill behind me. As soon as he raises the lid, the flames flare, and he backs away in a cloud, waving one hand in front of his face and covering his nose with the other. "I think these are toast. Can you grab me two more out of the freezer?"

I reach into the small freezer and find the box of Bubba burgers. After chucking the hockey pucks over the rail for the wildlife to enjoy, he takes two more and places them on the indirect heat and watches them like a hawk.

Spotting a deer on the other side of the cove, I move closer to the railing and lean on both elbows to watch them graze on the budding leaves and grass. Three fawns trail closely behind their mother with their white tails twitching as they move. "Charlie, we need to put out some more feed before we leave."

I hear a quick, "Yep," and a flip of a burger.

After the family disappears in a patch of bushes, I head back inside to set the table, but Charlie reaches for my arm as I pass and asks, "Can you get the cheese out of the fridge? I don't want to leave in case there is another flare up. They're almost ready." He looks up like he forgot something and says, "And don't look under the dome!"

"What? Why?"

"It's for later. You'll see right after dinner. . . . And that reminds me—don't eat too much. . . . I'm going to take you somewhere after we eat and you will need to run up to see it."

"Charlie, you know I hate surprises. Why do you do this to me?" I pretend to be upset, but he knows I love all the thought he puts into things.

"You will like these. I promise."

Charlie pulls the burgers off of the grill, and we dig in, not letting them cool at all. As I squirt ketchup on my burger, I ask the question that has been running through my head, "So did you talk to your sister about us, or was that just general advice?"

He covers his mouth and mumbles, "No, I talked to her about you."

"When?" I try to act like it doesn't matter.

Slowly chewing his last bite, he answers, "A couple weeks ago. Actually the day after the Sadie. When you—"

"Oh! Okay." And I feel my cheeks flush from a pale rose pink to more of a lavender like the roses he sent me for Valentine's Day.

I take another bite of my burger and change the subject. "How does she like Georgetown? She's a sophomore, right?"

Charlie chuckles, knowing what I'm doing. He has gotten pretty good at reading me. "Yes, she loves it there—and she's excited that I finally met someone I care to ask her about. She has always wanted to share the female perspective, but I have not been open to it until now."

"Well, tell her thank you for me. . . . Uh, it will be kind of awkward when I see her this summer, won't it?"

He waves me off. "Not at all, she remembers you and thinks highly of you and your family. She said I would be lucky to end up with a girl like you."

As soon as the words leave his mouth, he shifts in his seat and I do the same. It's too early to be talking about this and we have danced around the idea of us staying together for the long haul twice now. Once about my parents dating in high school and now this comment.

"So, is it time for the later yet?" This makes him laugh again, and he scoots his chair back across the pollen-covered deck and returns with the mysterious, dome covered platter.

With his lips turned upward slightly in a little smirk, he says, "I thought you may like these" and he lifts the dome, revealing four perfectly iced chocolate cupcakes with the letters P - R - O - M.

I feel my hands over my mouth and nose, and my head is bobbing up and down with so much excitement that it makes him laugh out loud.

"I'm relieved to see you so happy—I know it isn't as grand of a proposal like the one at the Falcon's game, but I know you like coming up here and how much you love chocolate—and are you going to leave me hanging?"

My chair teeters as I jump from it and into his arms. "Yes, this is so perfect! I would love to go with you! Wait—are you sure you want to try another dance? The last one was sort of a bust, and Brooke will be at this one. Won't she?"

Charlie rubs my back, trying to slow me down. "Yes. . . . Yes. Let's see how things go and evaluate if it should be a night just for you and me, or if we should attempt another dance together. What do you think?"

I lean in and say, "That sounds like a special plan," and he blushes more than I have ever seen before.

We do a quick pass through the cabin before we go, making sure we didn't leave any evidence that we were in the bedroom, and then drive to my second surprise. All he will say is that we will get a good run in before we head back home.

We drive for about twenty minutes around the lake and I catch glimpses of the sun setting through the trees. Light shades of pinks, oranges, and even purples peak in between the gray-tinted clouds.

As soon as we pull into the parking area, Charlie tells me to hurry so we don't miss it and explains we're running up the mountain and will stop at the fire tower. I'm the one who suggests racing, and he reluctantly agrees, hoping it would get us to the top faster.

It is only a .8 mile trail so I didn't think it would be that challenging, but I'm struggling, forcing myself to raise my knees higher than normal, and lunging for the scattered pine straw patches, so I don't slip on the reddish moss crawling all over the granite face.

Hearing me puffing, a man lifts this toddler off of the trail and gathers onto a rock to let us pass, and I force out a thank you as we sprint by them.

Seeing my opportunity to get in front of Charlie as the trail widens, I veer to the left, over a boulder, and head straight toward the looming tower. He follows my lead, bounding up the rocks, and then slides in right next to me as we approach the summit.

When the pine trees clear, a gust of wind whips me backwards. It doesn't seem to faze Charlie; he effortlessly glides over the cracked surface as I push myself to catch him again.

We both reach for the metal tower. I extend as far as I can, but it's not far enough, and I know he's going to win. But then, he seems to pull back at the last minute, and our hands slap the pipe at the same time.

There's no way we tied. He *so* did it on purpose. I place my hands on my knees and say between breaths, "You won."

Charlie gives me a light punch in the shoulder and teases, "We tied."

I put my arms over my head to get more oxygen and state the obvious, "You won. I know it. You know it." I take another deep breath before I announce, "I'm going to run so many steep trails like this and then we can race again. . . . I'm going to smoke you just like you did to those burgers!"

Charlie leans against the tower, enjoying my feistiness. "Want to bet who will win?"

I peer over at him walking in circles, trying to cool down and smile. "Sure."

He stops moving and grins, giving me the same mischievous grin I love, and taps his finger on his lips while thinking of a wager. "If I win, you'll go on the senior ski trip with me."

Stunned that he would want me to go away with him and his friends, I ask, "Really? Will I be the only sophomore there? Are there any other schools beside Chase going?"

He smirks ever so slightly. "Yep and nope."

Trying to hide my excitement, I casually respond, "Okay, if that's what you want. As long as my parents agree. And if I win?"

He chuckles lightly, seeing right through me again, and says, "If you win, I'll take those dance lessons with you—the ones your mother keeps asking you to do for the Debutante thing." Then, he puts out his hand like he's asking me to dance with him right on top of the mountain with the sun setting in the distance.

I take his hand and he twirls me like a top. Not coming up with something better to wager, I agree, "You're crazy to bet on that, especially since that will not happen until my senior year, making you come back on the weekends from college to live up to your end of the bargain, but it's a deal."

Charlie wraps his arms around my waist and lifts me into the air. As the wind blows, my braided hair whips to the side, and he whispers right in my ear so I can hear over the howling. "I have a feeling, I will be coming back to see you every weekend, even without dance lessons. And, I don't plan on losing the race, but even if I do, I win either way."

He turns me toward the sunset, snuggles up behind me, so his chin is resting on my shoulder, and we gaze into the brilliant reds, oranges, and purples fading over the green pines in the distance. As the sky seems to expand, I realize that it's not a competition, at least not with him. He's right—we both win because we'll be together.

a preview of the

SECOND

BOOK

A Secret or Surprise
PROM
Meet the Ex
A Key
The Man on the Plane

Coming 2021

ACKNOWLEDGMENTS

To a best friend who makes such a difference in this world and will always help someone in need, thank you for taking the time to read the bare bones draft. When we received your approval, we knew this series was worth pursuing. Your advice is worth more than you will ever know.

To our ace who will always be there when needed most and will not shy away when things get tough, thank you for all your suggestions on how to build more muscle and connective tissue to develop the characters and plot. Even though your advice was hard to hear, you were correct. By waiting to formally introduce the malicious ex-girlfriend, we were able to delay the Prom scene in honor of all the students who missed their Prom in 2020 due to the COVID-19.

To an amazing woman who never forgets a birthday and is always there for her family and friends, thank you for carving out the time in your hectic schedule. Your encouragement helped us push through the long nights of editing.

To a dear friend whose creativity and talent brings tears to her clients' eyes, thank you for spending so many long hours perfecting the cover. You created an image that made this book more approachable to all ages. Teens can picture themselves as the girl on the cover. Hopefully this will encourage them to rise above all the mean girl comments and drama.

To a lifelong friend who is always able to find the beauty in everything, thank you for all your support over the years. We have been through a lot together. We hope your prediction that this book will appeal to the *Gossip Girl* generation, as well as the parents who want a glimpse into what is happening in the teenage world these days, proves to be correct. Your "sophisticated Sweet Valley High" comment made us laugh out loud.

To a soccer mom who has raised three amazing kids, thank you for all your suggestions on how to tie up the loose ends and for providing insight on the recruiting process.

To a true friend who makes the best lemon square, thank you for always finding the right balance. You are the kind of friend everyone needs to have in high school and beyond.

To a fabulous writer and editor, thank you for whipping through the novel at lightning speed. We are so grateful we had the opportunity to work with you.

To the individuals who shared their experiences, stories, and urban legends, thank you. Some were so juicy that we had to include them in this novel in one shape or form. Please keep them coming! You never know what will make it into one of the next books.

ABOUT THE AUTHOR

Kelsey Mercer Grant is not only the heroine but also the pen name assumed by the writers. This is our first collaboration together. Initially, we intended to produce a screenplay since this story deserves to be viewed as a major motion picture, but as we got further along, we realized it should be presented as a novel first.

The List was inspired by the unbelievable behavior surrounding a Pre-Debutante Cotillion, a formal dance that has occurred for the past few decades in a well known city in the South. Beginning their freshman year, students from elite private schools are invited to attend, and some conniving girls have learned how to control the narrative and the rules. To make light of the actual list and drama resulting from it, a group of us imagined how much worse it could be, and this book came to life.

We will not make our real names known for many years to come. To the select few who figure out who we are, please do not share our names with anyone. You will understand why we desire to remain anonymous once you read this novel inspired by real-life events.

www.thegrantseries.com

CPSIA information can be obtained
at www.ICGtesting.com
Printed in the USA
BVHW031713161120
593458BV00001B/27

9 781734 767704